DECADENCE FROM DEDALUS

The Second Dedalus Book of Decadence:
The Black Feast

The
SECOND DEDALUS
BOOK OF DECADENCE
the Black Feast

Edited by
Brian Stableford

DEDALUS

Published in the UK by Dedalus Ltd,
Langford Lodge, St Judith's Lane, Sawtry, Cambs, PE17 5XE

ISBN 0 946626 80 4

Distributed in Canada by Marginal Distribution,
Unit 103, 277 George Street, Peterborough, Ontario, KJ9 3G9

First published in 1992
Compilation copyright © Brian Stableford 1992
Introductory essay copyright © Brian Stableford 1992
French translations (unless otherwise stated)
copyright © Francis Amery 1992

Printed in England by Clays Ltd., St. Ives plc

Dedalus would like to express its gratitude to David Blow for his help in originating the
Decadence from Dedalus Series and to Aysha Rafaele for her invaluable assistance in
preparing this title for publication.

Other titles edited by Brian Stableford for Dedalus:

The Dedalus Book of Decadence (Moral Ruins)
The Dedalus Book of British Fantasy: the 19th century
The Dedalus Book of Femmes Fatales
Tales of the Wandering Jew

CONTENTS

INTRODUCTION:
THE PHILOSOPHY OF DECADENCE

The principal inspiration of the French Decadent Movement was Joris-Karl Huysmans' novel *À rebours*, first published in 1884. This was the text which identified a literary tradition of Decadent poetry and prose extending from the work of Baudelaire, and provided that tradition with its wider context. It became the Bible of would-be Decadents of all kinds: those who aspired to artistic Decadence, those who aspired to a Decadent lifestyle, and those who aspired to both. *À rebours* laid out the Decadent doctrine, and instructed the acolytes of the new creed as to what to read, how to appreciate what they read, and how to pass cynical judgment on the affairs of a world which they were fully entitled to despise. It sent people forth on quests for new experience, and offered a philosophical licence to all manner of self-indulgent fetishisms.

Although *À rebours* was not translated into English until 1922 its notoriety in England was assured by the famous passage in Oscar Wilde's novel *The Portrait of Dorian Gray* (1891), which describes its profound effect upon the imagination of the young anti-hero. The book is not named in the passage, but its identity is unmistakable; were anyone in doubt, all possible confusion was cleared away when Wilde was asked to identify it at his trial and did so. The book's potential audience in England was necessarily more select than its potential audience in France, but even those who could not read it for themselves could hear the details of its creed from others, given extra glamour by its esotericism. If we are to understand the philosophy

1

which supported the Decadent Movements in France and England, therefore, we must begin with *À rebours*.

À rebours is a strange and unique book, more a meditation than a novel. It is an elaborate and intense character-study of a minor nobleman named Jean Des Esseintes, and it provides a detailed account of an experiment in lifestyle which he undertakes in the hope of discovering the perfect *modus vivendi*. Des Esseintes is to some extent a caricature—some of his tastes and mannerisms are borrowed, tongue-in-cheek, from the most celebrated of contemporary Parisian men-about-town, Comte Robert de Montesquiou—but he is also to some extent a fantastic self-projection of the author. It should not be forgotten that he is in part a comic figure, but it should not be forgotten either that behind the mask of absurd affectation there is an unmistakable depth of feeling.

The experiment which *À rebours* describes ends—as it is ironically foredoomed to do—in ignominious failure, but the underlying quest which motivates it reflects a genuine yearning. The catalogue of Des Esseintes' follies and affectations is full of flamboyant jokes, but the gloss of humour cannot and does not attempt to conceal the authenticity of his petty hatreds and splenetic rejections of normality.

From the very outset—and there is no hope of understanding the true spirit of the Decadent Movements unless we understand this—*À rebours* accepts that an uncompromisingly Decadent world-view cannot actually *work* as a practical philosophy of life, but it insists that the Decadent's view of life and art is far clearer, aesthetically and morally, than anything which passes for common sense or orthodox faith. Decadent pretensions are, if extrapolated to their logical extreme, admittedly and calculatedly ludicrous; but the distaste and disgust

2

which Decadents feel for those very different aspirations which are tacitly expressed in the state of the world as it is, and as it is in the process of becoming, are perfectly authentic. Self-mockery is an intrinsic element in the pose which Des Esseintes adopts—just as it was in the pose which Oscar Wilde adopted in real life—but the insincerity of his view of himself is merely the velvet glove which overlies the steely sincerity of his mockery of the world.

In spite of the relentless march of technological progress, the world has not changed much since 1884 in any respect to which Decadent criticism has relevance. Decadent lifestyles have nowadays become so commonplace as to seem boring, especially in view of the fact that modern Decadents seem less able than Des Esseintes was to perceive the absurdity of their affectations, but all the things which the Decadents lamented, despised and loathed are still with us; if anything, we have become less able to perceive their stupidity and paradoxicality. For this reason, it is still worth paying attention to Decadent art, and still worth paying heed to Decadent arguments.

The first thing the reader is told about Des Esseintes in *À rebours*, and the key to his entire enterprise, is that he is sick: sick in body, sick in mind and sick at heart. In accordance with the half-baked pseudoscience of the day, Huysmans attributes this sickness to hereditary degeneracy, caused by aristocratic inbreeding and the generations of cosseting which have made each of Des Esseintes' forefathers more effete than his predecessor. This causal explanation of the hero's condition is, in the light of modern knowledge, quite ridiculous, but that does not matter at all; it is the condition itself which is important. It would make no difference whatever to the

3

argument of the book if Des Esseintes' sickness were to be deemed entirely psychosomatic or if—as is certainly more likely and more pertinent—it were attributed by the gradual progression of a syphilitic infection.

It was not actually necessary for a *fin-de-siècle* intellectual to catch syphilis in order to embrace the Decadent philosophy, but it certainly helped. It is not necessary today, either, but the decay of the Decadent philosophy is probably not uncorrelated with the fact that it no longer helps. These days, syphilis can be cured by an injection; it had a very different existential significance in the days when there was no really effective treatment, and the standard prescription involved deliberate mercuric poisoning.

In the 1880s an intimate understanding of the consequences of catching syphilis could not help but alter a man's attitude to the role of sexual passion in human affairs. Syphilis was a powerful antidote to the conventional mythology of love, and its afflictions could hardly help but blight a man's chances of finding contentment and fulfilment in marriage. It was also more difficult for the syphilitic than for the unafflicted man to maintain his faith in the fundamental benevolence of God; prayer and repentance were as unavailing in his case as mercury. The syphilitic of the 1880s was forced by his condition to be an outsider; he was already damned, perhaps to madness and delusion as well as premature death—and he had reason enough to believe that the legacy of his sins might indeed be visited upon his descendants.

Antibiotics have saved modern men from such a plight, at least for a while, but it should not really require the recent advent of AIDS to make us take seriously a world-view which the sick find easier to accept than the healthy; we ought to be able to understand well enough how it might be the case that those who have been forced to stand aside from the common run of human affairs can look at them more objectively, more clinically and with more critical acumen than those who are still enmeshed by the drift-nets of normality.

We must, if we are to fully understand the origins and attractions of the Decadent way of thought, recognise two facts: syphilis, by virtue of its effects on the world-view of its more intellectually-inclined victims, was one of the chief progenitors of the Decadent philosophy; but this does not mean that the Decadent philosophy is mistaken in its claim to offer us a clearer sight of the condition of the world than is contained in the self-satisfied illusions of the healthy man.

By the time the story told in *À rebours* begins, Des Esseintes' debility has already forced him to give up the kinds of activity which most easily qualify as "Decadent" in the vulgar mind. He has finished with all his mistresses, having passed through the various phases of fascination which took him from the stage-door to the gutter in search of deeper depravities. He has concluded his experiments in "unnatural" passion and "perverse" pleasures, and has never been able to get far with his experiments with drugs because they have unfortunately failed to transport him to paradisal dreams, and merely make him vomit. His one desire at the outset of the text is to isolate himself, to seek solace in adequately-furnished privacy.

This is the quest described in the novel: the story it tells is a curious kind of Robinsonade, in which the hero tries with all his might to maroon himself, albeit in luxury. His mission is to surround himself with appropriately delightful artifacts, which must be chosen with the utmost care, so that his relationships with

5

them will not merely replace but vastly improve upon those relationships with actual persons which he has determined to sever.

It is vital to realise that the relationships which Des Esseintes sets out to establish with his surroundings are still, in the most important sense, *human* relationships, even though they are not relationships with persons. He still craves contact with the minds of men, but seeks to refine that contact into a particular kind of perfection by restricting himself to the finest works which the minds of men can produce: their books, their works of art, the incarnations of their occasional genius.

It is no part of Des Esseintes' intention to remove himself from society in search of some mystical communion with God or Nature; he is definitely not that kind of hermit. In fact, Nature is what he loathes more than all else. He recognises and acknowledges the contributions made by the heritage of natural ingenuity to the hothouse flowers and perfumes of which he is a connoisseur, but they are for him primarily and essentially products of culture, crucially remoulded by human artifice. He is in love with the exotic, and for him exoticism is the quintessential manifestation of human imagination and human artistry.

Des Esseintes' antipathy to the natural has as its entirely proper counterpart a similar antipathy to the realistic. He despises works of art which are representative, infinitely preferring those which reach out beyond the actual, seeking to transform and transcend ordinary experience rather than merely recapitulating it. This is one of the reasons why he hopes to find in the company of selected artifacts a sense of being at home which he has despaired of finding in the company of people. People are intrinsically ordinary, and there is something unavoidably tedious about their

6

fleshly presence; it is only in their finest art-work that they really become worthwhile.

Given the nature of Des Esseintes' quest, it is hardly surprising that many of the chapters of *À rebours* are devoted to exhaustive accounts of the choice of colour-schemes for his apartments, and of the authors which he admits to his library, and of the painters whose work he elects to hang on his walls. He occasionally devotes himself to extravagant indulgences of the imagination, especially when he goes out walking, but the only actual orgy described in the text is an olfactory one: a hyperbolically sensual account of an intoxicating riot of perfumes.

In furnishing his rooms, Des Esseintes desires to reconcile two seemingly-contradictory ends: comfort and escape. He desires that his home should become a perfect cocoon, protecting him from all the vicissitudes of life, but he desires also that it should be equipped with magic doorways which will admit him to rich and extraordinary experiences. By means of his collection of fishing-rods, his copy of Poe's *Narrative of Arthur Gordon Pym* and his ability to reproduce all the appropriate odours, he expects to be able to reproduce the sensation of a long sea-voyage without actually needing to abandon his fireside. Only by artifice can the achievement of such a paradoxical miracle be hoped for; in reality, one would have to choose between ease and adventure. Des Esseintes' experiment is a bold attempt to banish reality and obliterate its limitations.

Because of their subservience to this complex ambition, Des Esseintes' tastes in art and literature are inevitably eccentric. Some of his declared passions may seem to the modern reader to be entirely expectable: his love of Moreau's painting and Wagner's music, his

7

adulation of Baudelaire and Mallarmé, and his preference for the later work of Verlaine over the earlier seem nowadays to be matters of course. His choices did not seem so obvious in 1884, and our modern consciousness of Moreau as *the* Decadent painter and of Baudelaire, Verlaine and Mallarmé as the central figures of a particular literary movement owes much to the fact that they were so designated by Des Esseintes. We must not, however, overlook the close attention given by him to other literary works; the word "Decadence" is used in the text not to refer to the intellectual heirs of Baudelaire (although Gautier had long since licensed such a use of the term by posthumously labelling Baudelaire a Decadent) but in a far stricter sense, to the period of Rome's decline. Des Esseintes favours us at an early stage of his narrative with a careful explanation of his preference for the Latin writers of the Decadence—especially Petronius and Lucius Apuleius—over more fashionable writers like Virgil and Horace, and this essay extends to a lengthy account of mostly-forgotten writers of the early Christian era.

At a later point in the text Des Esseintes picks up the thread of this curious literary history again, excusing the fascination with various obscure Catholic apologists which he maintains in parallel with his far more intimate and far more intense relationship with the prose-poetry of Baudelaire and Mallarmé (he considers the prose poem to be the highest form of literary art). He has no affection at all for the mainstream of Christian philosophy and doctrinal elaboration, but there is in early Catholic writers a delicate hint of paganism which he finds attractive, and some later writers in that tradition have cultivated a visionary element which he can admire.

This tradition, as identified and described by Des Esseintes, culminates in the work of Barbey d'Aurevilly, whom Des Esseintes deems to have turned his attention to the Satanic element in the human character—something which appears in its purest state in the fiction and philosophy of the Marquis de Sade. Huysmans was later to carry forward this tradition himself, taking up where Barbey d'Aurevilly had left off in his own fascinated-but-disapproving study of Satanism, *Là-Bas* (1891). By the same token, it is something clearly akin to Des Esseintes' more general fascination with Catholic lore which eventually led Huysmans to the renewal of faith expressed in such works as *En Route* (1895) and *La Cathédrale* (1898).

Barbey d'Aurevilly is still remembered today for his remark that for a man like Baudelaire—who was the best actual role-model for French Decadents, although he fell a little short of the Des Esseintean ideal—the only possible ends were suicide or the foot of the cross, and despite Baudelaire's failure to make that judgment fully prophetic he was probably right (Oscar Wilde's fate might be reckoned a vivid demonstration of that fact). Huysmans' subsequent flirtation with avid faith was not such a terrible betrayal of the ideals of *À rebours* as it may seem at first sight. We must recognise and remember, though, the *exoticism*—both stylistic and thematic—of ideas which appeals to the true Decadent; it is the *escapist* potential of art and religion which he values: their capacity to act as the magical doorway which he so desperately needs.

When he was asked at his trial whether *À rebours* was a moral or an immoral book Oscar Wilde declined to comment, deeming the question impertinent and irrelevant. Elsewhere, of course, he had already expressed the opinion that books could not in any sensible way be classified as moral or immoral, but only as well-written or badly-written. In fact, one of the themes of *À rebours* is the absurdity of certain moral judgments, and Des Esseintes is often at pains to dismiss and ridicule conventional ideas of immorality. This inevitably confuses the question of the morality of the text, and might easily be held to render the question unanswerable, but it is easy enough to see why conventional moralists found certain sections of it very shocking; Huysmans set out to achieve precisely that effect.

In one of the passages best calculated to shock Des Esseintes recalls an earlier experiment of his, in which he took a sixteen-year-old youth to a brothel and then paid in advance for the boy to return for a limited number of fortnightly visits. His motive for doing this, as he recalls explaining to the brothel-keeper, was to turn the boy into a murderer; he reasoned that giving the boy a taste for pleasures he could ill afford would inevitably drive him to robbery, in the course of which career he would ultimately be forced by necessity to turn to violence. His reflection is intensely ironic, because he adds the observation that the boy let him down, never having been featured in the newspapers as the perpetrator of any horrible crime; but the real point of the story is contained in an afterword which construes it as a parable.

What he was doing, Des Esseintes claims, was constructing an allegory of modern education, which takes great care to open the eyes of the poor and underprivileged to that which lies beyond their means, thus sharpening their sense of deprivation. For this reason, he observes, the processes of education which notionally aim at refinement actually have the effect of increasing suffering, envy and hatred.

There is an element of black comedy about all of this, including the interpretation and the conclusion, and the text shows Des Esseintes instantly taking refuge from

10

his bleak observation in an obscure Latin text, but the satirical challenge to our commonplace assumption is by no means ineffectual. A hundred years of universal education have certainly not brought about universal refinement, and one could easily make out a plausible case for their having increased the pain of deprivation—and, in consequence, crime and violence—in exactly the way that Des Esseintes alleges.

At a later point in the text Des Esseintes mourns the apparent decline in the number of brothels in Paris and the corresponding increase in the number of drinking-dens. He argues that there is in fact no difference between whores and barmaids save that a man's relationships with the former are honestly artificial, whereas the latter carry an illusion of spontaneity; in either case the quest for sexual fulfilment has to be paid for, but the indirectness of the exchange which takes place in the tavern allows men to delude themselves that barmaids are conquests honourably won and that their favours are something freely given. His preference, needless to say, is for the honesty of the artifice rather than for the illusion—and in these observations too he finds a kind of allegory and a sign of the unfortunate way the world is going. Again, the passage is ironic, but again there is something in what he says, which still echoes today in a certain kind of feminist rhetoric which claims that the only honest women in the world are prostitutes.

Another homiletic meditation is occasioned by the sight of street-urchins fighting savagely over a shoddy crust daubed with cheese and garlic. This causes Des Esseintes to ask his servant to prepare an equally-disgusting concoction in order that he can throw it into the arena, thus prolonging the fight and increasing its violence. He expresses the hope that this will clearly demonstrate to the boys just what kind of world they are

11

in and how they can expect it to serve them. While waiting for the snack to be prepared, Des Esseintes expresses his disgust at the appalling hypocrisy which suppresses contraception and abortion, and which makes such a virtue out of caring for orphan children, while simultaneously guaranteeing that the lives for which they are saved will be savage and miserable. Again, the passage is essentially black comedy, but the force of its argument can hardly be ignored in a world which has been brought to the brink of ecocatastrophe by overpopulation, and in which those children dutifully "taken into care" in the most highly-developed nations are eventually expelled to live wild in the streets as muggers and rent-boys.

If we are asked, in the light of passages like this, to judge whether *À rebours* is a moral or an immoral book, we can only say that it depends whose morality we are considering, and how effective we deem dark sarcasm to be as a rhetorical strategy. Decadent moralising is characteristically cast in an aggressively challenging mode which holds that nothing is unthinkable, and that much of what is ordinarily taken for granted is sicker than it seems.

The sardonic way of viewing the world which is displayed to such good effect in these little essays in cynical subversion is reflected in all Des Esseintes' evaluative inversions. He is an irredeemably sick man, and so he is ever anxious to find signs of sickness in events and trends which other people consider healthily progressive; by the same token, he is always on the lookout for ways to dignify sickness. He is concerned to point out, for instance, that the hothouse flowers whose beauty he appreciates so keenly are, in fact, frail and sickly by comparison with their natural counterparts and that their lovely delicacy can be regarded as a kind of induced disease. He waxes lyrical, too, on the subject of the way in which their patterns and colours may mimic the pallors and rashes symptomatic of human diseases.

With the aid of such analogies, Des Esseintes is desirous of constructing a new aesthetic philosophy, in which the morbid and the beautiful are categories which will overlap considerably, and perhaps come close to fusion. This is tacitly evident in the early chapter which deals with his taste in visual art, which encompasses not only Moreau's paintings of Salomé but a series of engravings by Jan Luyken depicting the multitudinous tortures inflicted in the cause of religious persecution; it becomes much more explicit in the later chapters which include his appraisals of such modern writers as Villiers de l'Isle Adam, the prolific producer of *contes cruels*, and his beloved Baudelaire.

Baudelaire's great contribution to literature, according to Des Esseintes, had been to break a pattern by which literateurs had devoted their attention to the *ordinary* virtues and vices, which could be expected to be part of the everyday course of human affairs. Earlier writers had, he admitted, sometimes studied conventional monomanias like ambition or avarice, but in general their labours were analogous to those of botanists who restricted their attention to common wild flowers in their ordinary habitats. Baudelaire, by contrast, had dived into the murkiest depths of the soul, to the breeding-grounds of the truly *interesting* intellectual aberrations and moral diseases: to the psychological hothouses where *ennui* and *spleen* brought forth the most gorgeously warped blooms of desire and fascination.

In arguing thus, Huysmans sounded a clarion call for

13

others to do likewise. He laid the ideative groundwork for a new generation of writers who would be unafraid to explore the possible horizons of human derangement. He demanded literary equivalents of the rarest and strangest hybrid flowers, and of the most exotic and intoxicating perfumes. He asked for a literature replete with artificiality, strangeness and delicacy, whose appearances might easily be seen as analogous to the symptoms of disease, in which traditional aesthetic and moral judgments would be casually inverted: a literature of prose poetry and *contes cruels*.

This was what the writers associated with the Decadent Movements in France and England set out to produce.

The last and oddest of all Des Esseintes' inversions of normal expectation is the result of the failure of all previous remedies prescribed by his doctor to halt his decline. The idea itself arises out of a mistake he makes in passing on a prescription written by his doctor to his servant without glancing at it, assuming (wrongly) that it is a recipe for an enema. In fact, the doctor had specified a strength-building diet, but the perverse propriety of taking nourishment into the alimentary canal from the end opposite to that intended by nature is instantly recognised and warmly welcomed by the patient. Having become unable to obtain much nourishment from food or medicine taken by mouth, he derives real as well as aesthetic benefits as soon as he begins to take his sustenance by enema. He rejoices in the fact that although his stomach has always been so unaccommodating that he has never had the chance to become a gourmet, the culinary arts have at last been opened to the expression of his particular genius, and he sets out to plan his menus with enthusiasm.

This new dietary regime is so successful that for a while Des Esseintes believes that he is on the road to recovery, but he is not. At the end of the day, he simply is not fitted for the life he has tried so hard to adopt; like the ill-fated tortoise whose shell he decorates with jewels in an earlier chapter, he cannot stand the aesthetic intensity of his environment, and is doomed to die.

The assumption of the text that Des Esseintes is doomed is not itself objectionable. Any ending in which he were truly saved would be a blatantly dishonest *deus ex machina* (equally dishonest, of course, whether his condition is attributed to hereditary degeneracy or to syphilis). Nor can one really object to the analogy with the tortoise, and the depiction of his plight as that of a man dying of a surfeit of aesthetic riches, which is excusable hyperbole. Alas, such concessions do not save the conclusion of the story from seeming rather silly to the modern reader, who has the benefit of far more sophisticated medical knowledge than was available to Huysmans.

The doctor's final and most brutal prognosis is that Des Esseintes must abandon his experiment and return to the society of his fellow men, or face imminent madness, consumption and death. Des Esseintes—unable to recognise that the doctor is a hopeless quack—is thrown into a quandary, believing the warning but hating the suggested remedy. He is thus presented with an unreasonably sharp dilemma, whose pressure forces him to an unfortunately extreme compromise.

Like the hero of Huysmans' later novels, Durtal—and, for that matter, like Huysmans himself—Des Esseintes finds himself reluctantly drawn to the idea of becoming a monk, and finding seclusion within a community of recluses. He admits that he cannot take the Church entirely seriously, because of the way in which it has devalued itself by cheapening and compromising all its own ideals, most of which were wrong in the first place, but he can see no alternative. Fortunately, there is in the end one thing which can and does serve for him as a perfect justification of religious faith: the sheer impossibility of what that faith requires him to accept!

The modern reader ought not to sympathise with Des Esseintes' absurd dalliance with reinvestment in faith (although the contemporary popularity of ridiculous cults testifies to the fact that such strategies are still popular with the idiotic and the desperate) but it may be worth repeating that it is not as inconsistent with his Decadent ideals as it may seem, and if properly understood might not need to be counted as a betrayal of them.

For the Decadent, who loathes Nature and realism, the fantastic idea of a life beyond death is attractive, because rather than in spite of the fact that he cannot sensibly believe in any such eventuality. It is precisely the fact that the hopeful belief in the immortality of the soul is a frail, sickly thing, easily regarded as a species of insanity, which requires the true Decadent to take it seriously and to hang on to it when all else is gone. After all, what other guiding light can there possibly be for a man who is sick in body, sick in mind and sick at heart, *and for whom all material prescriptions have inevitably failed?*

One hardly needs to add, even as a footnote, that the paradoxical move was a failure. What ultimately became of Des Esseintes we are never told, but Durtal—in *L'Oblat* (1903)—and Huysmans eventually found no solace in the monastic life. They both came to believe that there was no possible escape from life and death, and that suffering simply had to be borne, as the price of one's sins.

Joris-Karl Huysmans died in 1907, at the age of 59, of cancer.

****

It is not until the tenth chapter of *The Picture of Dorian Gray* that the young anti-hero receives from Lord Henry Wootton the "yellow book" which becomes the foundation-stone of his philosophy of life, but much of the groundwork for his conversion has already been laid. It is an earlier monologue of Lord Henry's—a hymn to Beauty—which inspires the fateful wish which allows Dorian to exchange personalities with his portrait, so that the unfading and timeless work of art becomes an actor in the real world while the portrait withers and festers in its frame. In this monologue Lord Henry emphasises the full horror of what time will do to Dorian's awesome beauty, and insists—in the absence of any possible remedy—that it must be exploited to the full while it lasts. He advises the boy not to allow conventional morality to be his guide, but rather to devote himself to the search for new sensations. A new Hedonism, he says, is what the world needs, and he opines that Dorian might, with effort, become its "visible symbol".

That, indeed, is what Dorian — with effort — becomes.

A later passage in the text makes it clear that Lord Henry, like Des Esseintes, is essentially an experimenter; his opposition to all received wisdom is by way of subjecting it to a trial of fire, and his moulding of Dorian's character is supposedly a clinical exploration of possibility—his role is to play Frankenstein to Dorian's Monster rather than Mephistopheles to Dorian's Faust. The precise parallel which Lord Henry draws in comparing himself to a natural scientist is particularly

17

revealing; he represents himself as a *vivisectionist* of human life, and expands his analogy in a fashion which is very similar to the way in which Des Esseintes extrapolates some of his analogies:

> It was true that as one watched life in its curious crucible of pain and pleasure, one could not wear over one's face a mask of glass, nor keep the sulphurous fumes from troubling the brain and making the imagination turbid with monstrous fancies and misshapen dreams. There were poisons so subtle that to know their properties one had to sicken of them. There were maladies so strange that one had to pass through them if one sought to understand their nature. And, yet, what a great reward one received! How wonderful the whole world became to one! To note the curious hard logic of passion, and the emotional coloured life of the intellect—to observe where they met and where they separated, at what point they were in unison, and at what point they were at discord—there was a delight in that! What matter what the cost was? One could never pay too high a price for any sensation.

The next paragraph of this discourse makes art—and especially the art of literature—part and parcel of this curious discipline of experimental human science. A further extrapolation of the argument might represent the arts as instruments of this hypothetical psychological science, just as telescopes and microscopes are instruments of astronomy and anatomy.

If Lord Henry's viewpoint is accepted there can be nothing surprising in his subsequent musings about the total irrelevance of moral considerations to the business of literature and to the experiment of remaking the character of Dorian Gray. Dorian's ill-fated love for the actress Sybil Vane—which briefly threatens him with salvation by convention—is regarded only as an "interesting phenomenon", with no intrinsic value. In this harsh light the reason for the failure of that love becomes highly significant.

Dorian rejects Sybil before he reads the infamous yellow book; it is entirely his own action, and even Lord Henry is surprised and slightly disturbed by it. Dorian falls out of love with Sybil because she loses her ability to act; it makes not the slightest difference to him that the reason that she loses her ability is that her love for him has awakened her to the reality of the world, and forced her to see it clearly, making dissimulation and pretence impossible. This makes it clear that the beauty which Dorian briefly discovered in Sybil was entirely the product of her artifice—he can find nothing to admire in her authenticity, and when she achieves it she becomes worthless to him. This is less surprising when one recalls that he has already traded his own authenticity for the ageless artifice of his portrait.

In view of what Dorian has elected to do to himself and to Sybil, it is entirely to be expected that he should find *À rebours* so absorbing and so appealing, and that he should be so enchanted by its "metaphors as monstrous as orchids, and as subtle in colour". The yellow book is, Wilde's text candidly admits, a "poisonous book", which produces in its reader "a malady of dreaming", but neither "poisonous" nor "malady" can here be construed as a simple insult. Dorian deals with the book as Des Esseintes might have dealt with one of his own favourite texts: he procures nine copies of the first edition printed on especially sumptuous paper, and has them bound in different colours so that they might better suit his various moods. He recognises in the story of Des Esseintes the story of his own life, which he has not yet lived.

There is, of course, one vital difference between Dorian and Des Esseintes: Dorian cannot exhibit the symptoms of sickness; he has delegated that misfortune to his portrait. He and he alone is fitted by his unique artifice successfully to live the Decadent life, untouchable by the ravages of incurable venereal disease. He is, of course, an impossible entity—every bit as impossible as that immortal soul in which Des Esseintes, Huysmans, Wilde and Dorian himself all felt compelled to believe— but that only serves to make him all the more fascinating while he exists.

There is a sense in which the conclusion of *The Picture of Dorian Gray* is every bit as disappointing to the modern reader as the ending of *À rebours*. There is no quack to alarm Dorian with falsely melodramatic prognoses, but it is foolishness nevertheless which drives him unnecessarily on to the sharp horns of his dilemma, determined to take a knife to his syphilitic image lest it should constitute "evidence" against him. His death provides a tidier, and undoubtedly more honest ending than the querulous and paradoxical commitment to faith which ends Des Esseintes' story, but it is by no means obvious that tidiness and honesty are to be reckoned virtuous in a text of this kind. If the conclusion is to be commended at all, better perhaps that it be commended as a casual and thoroughly artificial flourish than a vindication of the vulgar opinion that natural law cannot in the end be cheated.

Oscar Wilde's philosophy of art is more elaborately

laid out in his essay on "The Decay of Lying" than it is in *The Picture of Dorian Gray*, but even cast in non-fictional form it is teasingly removed from direct expression. "The Decay of Lying" is a comic dialogue between two characters called Vivian and Cyril (Wilde's two sons were named Cyril and Vyvyan); Vivian is writing an essay on "The Decay of Lying", from which he quotes liberally and upon which he comments in a fashion so arch that the reader is obliged to suppose that Wilde is making fun of him, even though he must also suspect that there are serious points being made.

Such stylistic contortionism is, of course, entirely in character: Wilde never could decide how seriously he intended his own poses, and he could not in the end refrain from slashing so savagely at his own carefully-crafted self-portrait as to bring destruction upon himself (if each man really is fated to kill the thing he loves, a hopeless libel action is evidently as effective a weapon as any).

The argument which is flippantly displayed in "The Decay of Lying" begins, in true Decadent fashion, with an attack on Nature. Wilde's sarcastic mouthpiece, Vivian, insists that Art has revealed to mankind the deficiencies of Nature: "[her] lack of design, her curious crudities, her extraordinary monotony, her absolutely unfinished condition". Art, he alleges, "is our spirited protest, our gallant attempt to teach nature her proper place." He goes on to stress the uncomfortableness of Nature, and its antipathy towards Mind; thinking, he proposes, can be seen as a kind of unhealthiness, as fatal as any other disease.

When Vivian goes on to reveal the title of the essay he is writing, his commonsensical friend Cyril protests that he sees no reason to think that lying is in decline, and that politicians seem to be keeping the tradition very much alive. Vivian counters with the argument that what politicians, journalists and other everyday deceivers do is better regarded as mere misrepresentation; their efforts lack the magnitude and grandeur desirable in wholehearted lies. Lies, for Vivian, are a species of glorious fantasy which belong to the realm of Art, but for which contemporary artists have, alas, lost their appetite. Too many modern artists, Vivian laments, have fallen into slothful habits of truthfulness; their work has become representative instead of imaginative. Like Des Esseintes, he heaps scorn upon realism, with its tediously detailed studies of everyday vices and its insipid quest to expose "that dreadful universal thing called human nature"—and like Des Esseintes he is not afraid to name names and pulverise reputations.

Vivian continues to argue his case by documenting, in considerable detail, the oft-quoted Wildean claim that "Life imitates art far more than Art imitates life". Cyril challenges him to prove also that Nature imitates Art, and he rises instantly to the challenge, arguing that we must be taught to see such things as "landscapes" and "fogs" by artistic celebrations of the way they play with light and colou.—and though he stops short of stating that our idea of "Nature" is itself a kind of fantasy it is not clear that he needs to.

Having said all this, Vivian returns to his argument that the art of lying is in a state of dereliction. The nineteenth century, he argues, is "the dullest and most prosaic century possible" (he had not experienced the twentieth!) and suggests that even the dreams which afflict the sleep of the middle classes have become tedious. He attacks the Church of England, as Des Esseintes attacks the Church of Rome, for losing sight of the supernatural and the mystical and becoming reasonable.

Some of Vivian's subsequent prescriptions for reviving the art of lying are more tongue-in-cheek than his destructive arguments, commending the good work which is done at dinner-parties and in the ordinary processes of education, but insisting that there remains much room for further improvement. He is more serious, however, when he claims that it is in the Arts where the true Renaissance can and must be sought. On this subject Vivian waxes lyrical. He looks forward eagerly to the day when the commonplaceness of modern fiction has finally bored everyone to distraction, so that imagination will once again be compelled to take wing;

> And when that day dawns, or sunset reddens, how joyous we shall all be! Facts will be regarded as discreditable, Truth will be found mourning over her fetters, and Romance, with her temper of wonder, will return to the land. The very aspect of the world will change to our startled eyes. Out of the sea will rise Behemoth and Leviathan, and sail around the high-pooped galleys, as they do on the delightful maps of those ages when books on geography were actually readable. Dragons will wander about the waste places, and the phoenix will soar from her nest of fire into the air. We shall lay our hands upon the basilisk, and see the jewel in the toad's head. Champing his gilded oats, the Hippogriff will stand in our stalls, and over our heads will float the Blue Bird singing of beautiful and impossible things, of things that are lovely and that never happen, of things that are not and that should be.

Hard on the heels of this flight of fancy Vivian lays down, by way of summary, a series of formal doctrines for his new (or renewed) aesthetics. The first is that Art never expresses anything but itself: that it is not a reflective product of its age but something which evolves and moves according to its own innate whims. The second is that all bad art is inspired by attempts to make art more representative, and that any attempt by an artist to be true to Life or Nature is a mistake. The third restates the dictum that Life (and Nature) imitate Art rather than *vice versa*. The fourth, the *quod erat demonstradum* of the exercise, is that Lying—"the telling of beautiful untrue things"—is the proper aim of Art.

These claims are, of course, much more modest than those made by Lord Henry Wooton or Des Esseintes—who, being Lies themselves, were fully entitled to be more extravagant than the artists who created them. It might be noted, however, that Oscar Wilde made a more strenuous effort to live by his philosophy than Joris-Karl Huysmans ever did; and that his determination to live as a work of art, unfettered by realism of outlook or any particular respect for the dictates of nature, cut tragically short his dazzlingly brilliant career as a Liar *par excellence*, and landed him in Reading Gaol.

A few brief addenda to Wilde's views on art—which may be taken to reflect his final recorded thoughts upon the matter—can be found in Laurence Housman's book *Echo de Paris* (1923), which recalls a conversation between Wilde, Housman and two other friends which took place in Paris in the autumn of 1899. Here we find Wilde advising one of his acolytes to learn life only by inexperience, so that it will always be unexpected and delightful; "never realise" is, he suggests, the ideal dictum. We also find him ready to associate the beauty of failure and the nobility of exile, on the grounds that only by tasting utter failure, with or without a leavening of intermediate success, can an artist perceive his own soul—and, within his own soul, the world entire.

These comments are easily read in isolation as a melancholy but superficial comedy, which attempts to make a virtue of disaster by the same strategy of casual inversion which marked all Wilde's most famous epigrams, and which matches his temperament so closely to that of Des Esseintes. The notion of the artist perceiving his own soul is, however, twice elaborated and re-emphasised later in the conversation. The first time the issue is raised again is to clear up a misconception. Wilde finds it necessary to insist that he spoke of perception and not of knowledge, and to state frankly that understanding of oneself, or the world, is impossible: that the soul is always a stranger, and a hostile one. He had said much the same thing in what is perhaps the best of his many fantasies, "The Fisherman and his Soul", and he reiterates it yet again here in the second of two brief tales which he volunteers to tell his hearers (because he knows that he will never write them down). This allegorical prose poem explains how a man sells his burdensome soul for its proper price—thirty pieces of silver—but becomes miserable because he is no longer capable of sin; after searching the world in the hope of finding and regaining his soul he finally buys it back at what is now its proper price—his body—but finds it unutterably foul.

This allegory serves to remind us that Vivian's flight of fancy regarding the rewards of a renaissance of Lying is deliberately optimistic. The power of the imagination does not merely reveal wonders, but also horrors. That clear sight which penetrates the sham of realism finds *all* manner of chimerical monsters. The true Decadent knows this, and never forgets it.

If we combine Wilde's fragmentary prescriptions with Huysmans'—or rather, because it is not *quite* the same thing, with Des Esseintes'—we can obtain a reasonably complete manifesto for Decadent literature.

It is, first and foremost, a literature which is not representative; it does not desire to be true to commonplace conceptions of "Life" or to "Nature", both of which it despises and makes every attempt to de-mythologise. Decadent literature points instead the way to an opposite ideal, wherein life and nature would become entirely subject to every kind of clever artifice. Because this ideal is incapable of attainment in practice, Decadent literature is essentially pessimistic, and sometimes brutally horrific, but this makes it all the more ruthless in demolishing the pretensions of rival philosophies, which it mocks mercilessly, taking delight in turning everything which is ordinarily taken for granted topsy-turvy.

Decadent literature is rich in fantasies, and sympathetic to everything which encourages the cultivation of fantasy; it is for this reason (and this reason only) that it is generally in favour of opium, hashish and other psychotropics, even though it recognises quite clearly that such substances are ultimately mind-rotting and life-consuming. It applauds those who have sufficient power of imagination not to require artificial aids, but is prepared to take an intense clinical interest even in the most hazardous derangements of the senses—for instance, those induced by ether or by tertiary syphilis. Decadent literature is ever eager to make its fantasies as gorgeous as possible, but its exponents know well enough that those who

26

undertake Odysseys in Exotica will encounter all manner of chimeras.

The true Decadent, knowing the futility of taking refuge in the commonplace, desires to confront all these chimeras, to see them clearly even though no understanding of them or reconciliation with them is possible. He desires this, in part, because he has an avid hunger for sensation, which can sometimes override the oversimple distinctions which are normally drawn between the pleasant and the unpleasant; he knows that horror is a stimulant. But he desires it for another reason too, which is that he feels that there is some essential truth in horror: that the world is sick at heart, and that acceptance of that truth demands that even the most obvious of evils—pain, death, and disease—may require aesthetic re-evaluation, and at the very least deserve to be more thoroughly and conscientiously explored.

We should not ask whether Decadent literature is moral or immoral; that is a question fit only for lawyers to raise. It is, intrinsically and proudly, a literature of moral challenge; it is sceptical, cynical and satirical. It recognises that everyday morality does not work either in practical or in psychological terms, and is therefore a sham, but that ideal morality is—perhaps, but not necessarily, unfortunately—unattainable. The moral of a Decadent prose poem or *conte cruel*, if it has a moral at all, is likely to recommend that we should make the best compromises we can, recognise that they are compromises, and refuse to be ashamed of them. Decadent literature is, however, a literature dedicated to the smashing of icons and idols, and it is always ready to attack stern moralists of every stripe; it is fiercely intolerant of intolerance and revels in the paradoxicality of such a stance.

27

For some time now it has been difficult to take the Decadent pose entirely seriously. Antibiotics have dramatically reduced the horrors of venereal disease, and in so doing have devastated the pattern of symbols, metaphors and analogies that lies at the heart of *À rebours*. HIV viruses are now beginning to take up some of the imaginative slack left behind by the once-dreaded spirochaetes, but the modern medical context forbids any simple regeneration of the outmoded tropes. Diseases do not threaten us the way they used to, and in becoming less mysterious have become less fascinating. The same sort of thing has happened to perfumery and flower-breeding; they have been reduced from the arcane mysteries they once were to mere matters of industrial chemistry. We know now that the world is not as magical as it once seemed; even religious men now find it far more difficult than they did before to believe six impossible things before breakfast, and those who can still do it run a far greater risk of being called crackpots.

Despite Vivian's charmingly vivid hopes, the realistic novel has so far kept the perceived hegemony in the literary world which it won in the late nineteenth century. Romance flourishes alongside it, but its quality is often compromised and undermined by its sheer quantity; the contemporary glut of genre fantasy serves mainly to demonstrate that even the most exotic products of the mythopoeic imagination can be regulated by convention in such a way as to become every bit as tedious, repetitive, colourless and moralistically simple-minded as the dullest products of representative art. For this reason, the hopes of the Decadents have become as much of a mockery as their fears.

Time and progress have not eroded everything which

the Decadents aspired to do; their black humour remains as clever and mordant as ever, but far too many modern commentators on the Decadent Movements are prone to forget that their leading figures were, after all, comedians. There are as many people today who make the mistake of thinking that Huysmans meant exactly what he wrote as make the same mistake (with slightly more excuse) in respect of Jane Austen; sarcasm is unfortunately invisible to those who have fully realised the importance of being earnest.

In view of the unfortunate dereliction into which Decadent ideals have fallen, it may be worth restating those Decadent ideas which can bear restating, and which may need restating now more than they needed to be stated then.

Firstly, there is not the slightest reason why art should be restricted and contained by narrow realism, or why realistic representation should be considered one whit more worthy than the wildest fantasy. Magic is useless to engineers but it is invaluable to dreamers, and no man was ever born who was not a dreamer as well as an engineer. Authentically imaginative artists are among the most valuable men alive, and their products should be treasured.

Secondly, it is absurd and stupid to admire and idolise "Nature" when anyone with an atom of intelligence can see that what we carelessly call "human nature" is all artifice. Nature is neither balanced nor bountiful, despite what certain myths ask us to believe; it is cruel and chaotic. The wise man is one who can recognise artifice for what it is, and put a proper value upon it.

Thirdly, we desperately need and ought most ardently to desire a literature of moral challenge, which will fiercely oppose, stoutly defy and hopefully cure the disease of moral absolutism in whatever form it manifests itself. The greatest tragedy in human history—which is still ongoing—has been the hijacking of moral philosophy by religious dogma, and if there is one thing that everyone in the world ought to pray for it is the annihilation of religion.

Fourthly, we should be prepared to perceive and confront the horrors which lurk inside us, even though we may not ever understand or overcome them. They are, after all, ourselves.

****

1.

"AN INVITATION TO THE VOYAGE"
by Charles Baudelaire

There is a wonderful country, the so-called land of Cockayne, which I dreamed of visiting in the company of an old friend: a strange land, lost in the mists of our North; one might deem it the Orient of the Occident, the European China, so heated and capricious is the fancy which has free rein there, so enduring and obstinate is the wise and delicate greenery which decorates it....

A true land of Cockayne, where all is beautiful, lush, tranquil, authentic; where the luxury of pleasure is reflected in nature; where life is full and every breath is sweet; where disorder, turbulence and the unforeseen are excluded; where happiness is wedded to silence; where the cuisine is poetic, rich and flavoursome all at the same time; where everything reminds me of you, my dearest angel.

You know that feverish malady which takes possession of us in our chilly miseries, that nostalgia for lands unknown, that anguish of curiosity? There is a country made in your image, where all is beautiful, lush, tranquil and authentic, where fancy has built and furnished a western China, where life is full and every breath is sweet, where happiness is wedded to silence. It is there that we must live, it is there that we must go to die!

Yes, it is there that we must go to breathe, to dream and to overfill the hours with an infinity of sensations. A musician has penned an "Invitation to the Waltz"; who will likewise compose an "Invitation to the Voyage" which one might offer to the woman one loves, to the bosom companion one chooses?

Yes, it is in that atmosphere that one must seek the good life—out there, where the leisurely hours have room for more thoughts, where the clocks sound their good humour with a more profound and more significant solemnity.

On illuminated panels, or on gilt-edged leather of a sombre sumptuousness, complacent pictures live discreetly, calm and profound as the souls of the artists who created them. The light of the sunsets, which so richly colours the dining-room or the salon, is filtered by beautiful curtains or by tall leaded windows with many panes. The furniture is heavy, curiously-wrought and fantastically-formed, guarding with locks the secrets of delicate souls. Mirrors, metallic surfaces, drapes, gold jewellery and porcelain perform a visual symphony, silent and mysterious; and every object, every nook and cranny, including the cracks of the drawers and the pleats of the curtains, breathes out an exotic perfume, a Sumatran forget-me-not, as if it were the very soul of the place.

A true land of Cockayne, I tell you, where all is as rich, tidy and bright as a clear conscience, as a well-stocked kitchen, as a gorgeous golden necklace, as a gaudy display of precious stones! All the treasures of the world are accumulated there, as if it were the house of a man of achievement, to whom the world owes everything. Strange land, as far superior to all others as Art is to mere Nature—which is here remade as a dream: corrected, ornamented, transfigured.

Let them search, let them search still more, let them unceasingly push back the horizons of their happiness, these alchemical gardeners! Let them offer rewards—sixty or a hundred thousand florins—to the man who can achieve their problematic goals! For myself, I have already found my black tulip and my blue dahlia....

Incomparable flower—rediscovered tulip, allegorical dahlia!—it is there, is it not, in that beautiful land which is so calm and so dreamlike, that you live and flourish? Would you not find a perfect frame in your own analogue; would you not be mirrored there, as the mystics would have it, by your archetypal counterpart?

Dreams...always dreams! The more adventurous and sensitive the soul is, the further dreams transport it from the possible. Every man carries within himself an appropriate measure of natural opium, incessantly secreted and replenished...and yet, between birth and death, how many hours can we count to the credit of positive pleasure, or of actions planned and carried out? Shall we ever dwell within—shall we ever even enter— the scene which my imagination has designed....the world made in your image?

All this treasure—these furnishings, this luxury, this perfect order, these perfumes, these miraculous flowers—it is you. More than that—you are the great flowing rivers and the tranquil canals; the huge ships which ply them, laden with riches, whose sailors work to the monotonous rhythms of their chants, are the thoughts stirred in my head as it rests on your rising and falling breast. You lead them gently towards that sea which is the Infinite, mirroring meanwhile the profundity of the sky in the clarity of your beautiful soul....and when, wearied by the swell and heavy with the produce of the Orient, they return to their port of origin, they are still my thoughts, immeasurably enriched, returning from the Infinite to you....

****

2.

THE DISCIPLE
by Oscar Wilde

When Narcissus died, the pool of his pleasure changed from a cup of sweet waters into a cup of salt tears, and the Oreads came weeping through the woodland that they might sing to the pool and give it comfort.

And when they saw that the pool had changed from a cup of sweet waters into a cup of salt tears, they loosened the green tresses of their hair and cried to the pool and said, "We do not wonder that you should mourn in this manner for Narcissus, so beautiful was he."

"But was Narcissus beautiful?" said the pool.

"Who should know that better than you?" answered the Oreads. "Us did he ever pass by, but you he sought for, and would lie on your banks and look down at you, and in the mirror of your waters he would mirror his own beauty."

And the pool answered, "But I loved Narcissus because, as he lay on my banks and looked down at me, in the mirror of his eyes I saw ever my own beauty mirrored."

****

3.

DES ESSEINTES' DREAM
from À REBOURS
by Joris-Karl Huysmans

Des Esseintes had always been infatuated with flowers, but this passion—which, during his sojourn at Jutigny, had extended to all flowers, no matter what species or genus they belonged to—had eventually been purified and narrowly focused on a single kind.

For a long time now he had despised the commonplace plants which bloomed in Parisian markets in moistened pots, beneath green awnings or red parasols. While devoting time to the refinement of his literary tastes and his aesthetic preferences, preserving his affection for no works save those finely sifted and distilled by subtle and tormented minds, and while simultaneously hardening his distaste for widely-held notions, his love of flowers had also been purged of its dregs and superfluities; it had, as it were, been clarified and rectified.

He was fond of comparing the stock of a horticulturalist to a microcosm in which all the social classes were represented. There was wretched floral riff-raff—mere weeds like the wallflowers, whose true milieu was the window-box, their roots crammed into milk-cans or old earthenware pots. There were also pretentious, conventional and stupid flowers, like roses, whose place was to be bedded down in porcelain pots painted by young ladies. Lastly, there were flowers of noble descent such as orchids, charming and delicate, thrilling and sensitive—exotic flowers which, in Paris, must be exiled to the warmth of glass palaces. These

35

were the princesses of the vegetable realm, living apart, having nothing at all in common with the plants of the street or the bourgeois blooms.

Although Des Esseintes could not help experiencing a certain interest, born of pity, in the flowers of the lowest class as they wilted in the exhalations of the sewers and sinks of the slums, he loathed utterly the bouquets which matched the cream and gilt of the new houses; the delight of his eyes was entirely reserved for the rare and distinguished plants brought from afar, maintained by careful artistry in tropical conditions faked by the controlled breath of stoves.

Once his definitive choice had settled on hothouse flowers, it had to be further modified by the influence of his general philosophy of life and the specific conclusions at which he had now arrived; previously, in Paris, his natural penchant for the artificial had led him to forsake the real flower for its image, faithfully reproduced by virtue of the miracles of rubber and wire, cotton and taffeta, paper and velvet. Consequently, he possessed a marvellous collection of tropical plants fashioned by the hands of true artists, who had followed Nature step by step while creating anew. They had taken each bloom from the time of its birth to the fullness of its maturity, even simulating its withering, making note of its subtlest nuances, the most transient aspects of its wakefulness or repose. They had observed the tenor of its petals when ruffled by the wind or crumpled by the rain, sprinkling its unfolding corolla with drops of dew or glue, presenting it in full flower when the branches are bowed by the weight of sap, and with a withered stem and shrivelled head to reflect the time of discarded petals and falling leaves. This admirable art-work had long held him in thrall, but now he dreamed of another kind of floral display; having had his fill of artificial flowers aping real

36

ones he wanted natural flowers which would imitate fakes.

He brought his intelligence to bear on this problem; he did not have to search for long or go very far, because his house was situated in the very heart of the horticulturalists' territory. He took himself off directly to visit the greenhouses of the Avenue de Chatillon and the vale of Aunay, returning exhausted and broke, wonderstruck by the vegetal extravagance which he had witnessed, unable to think of anything except the species which he had acquired and the haunting memories of bizarre and magnificent blossoms.

Two days later, the carriers arrived. With his list in his hand Des Esseintes went forth to confirm his purchases, one by one.

The gardeners brought down from their wagons a collection of various species of the genus Caladium, which bore upon their turgid and hairy stems enormous heart-shaped leaves; although they maintained a general appearance of kinship no two of them were exactly alike. There were extraordinary specimens among them. Some, including the "Virginale", were roseate, and looked as if they had been cut out of oilcloth or English sticking-plaster: others, such as the "Albane", looked as if they had been fabricated from the pleural membrane of an ox or the diaphanous bladder of a pig. Others, especially the "Madame Mame", had the appearance of zinc, parodying bits of stamped metal tinted with imperial green, splashed with paint and streaked with red and white lead. There were those, like the "Bosphorus", which produced the illusion of starched calico flecked with crimson and myrtle green; while there were others, like the "Aurora Borealis", which displayed leaves the colour of raw meat, purple-streaked along the sides, with violet fibrils and tumescent leaves sweating blue

37

wine and blood.

The Albane and the Aurora presented the two extremes of temperament to be found in this kind of plant: chlorosis and apoplexy.

The gardeners brought in more new varieties. These affected the appearance of simulated hide criss-crossed by counterfeit veins. Most of them bore livid fleshy patches mottled with pink spots and flakes of scurf, as if they were being eaten away by syphilis or leprosy. Others had a vivid pink hue like scars on the mend, or the brown tint of coalescing scabs; others were blistered as though they had been cauterised by burning irons; yet others displayed hairy teguments pitted with ulcers and embellished with cankers; finally, some appeared to be covered with dressings—plastered with black mercurial lard or green unguents of belladonna, dusted with the powdered yellow mica of iodoform.

Riotously reunited with one another before Des Esseintes, these flowers—more monstrous now than when they had first surprised him—were mingled with others as though they were patients in a hospital, behind the glass walls of their hothouses.

"Sapristi!" he exclaimed, enthusiastically.

A new variety related in its general appearance to the Caladiums, Alocasia metallica, excited even greater admiration. This one was endowed with a ground-colour of greenish bronze glittering with flecks of silver; it was a masterpiece of artifice—one might easily take it for a length of stove-pipe made into a spearhead by some practical joker.

Next, the men unloaded bunches of bottle-green lozenge-shaped leaves. From the midst of each one rose a sturdy stem at the tip of which quivered a huge ace of hearts as polished as a pepper. As if to defy the norms of plant life, from the middle of the bright vermilion hearts there jutted fleshy and fleecy tails, white and yellow in colour, some of which were straight, others spiralling forth like pigs' tails. This was Anthurium, an araceous plant recently imported into France from Colombia; it had been assigned to the same family as Amorphopallus, a plant from Cochin-China with leaves shaped like fish-slices and long black stems as chequered with scars as the maltreated limbs of a Negro slave.

Des Esseintes was exultant.

Fresh batches of monstrosities continued to descend from the carts. There was Echinopsis, thrusting from beds of cotton-wool wadding pink flowers like the stumps of amputated limbs. There was Nidularium, opening its sword-like petals to reveal a chasm of flayed flesh. There was Tillandsia Lindeni, trailing its broken ploughshares the colour of unfermented wine. There was also Cypripedium, whose complex, incoherent colours might have been devised by some demented inventor; it resembled a shoe or a pin-tray, on top of which a human tongue curled back tautly, exactly as depicted in medical works dealing with diseases of the throat and mouth. Two little wings as red as a jujube, which might have been borrowed from a toy windmill, completed the baroque assembly: a combination of the underside of a tongue, the colour of wine-dregs and slate, and a glossy wallet whose lining secreted viscous glue. Des Esseintes could not take his eyes off this unbelievable Indian orchid; the gardeners, impatient with his slowness, began loudly to read out the labels stuck in the pots which they were bringing in.

Des Esseintes watched, somewhat startled, savouring the sound of the forbidding names of the verdant plants. Encephelatos horridus was a gigantic iron artichoke painted with rust, like those put on the gates of grand houses to keep trespassers at bay. Cocos micania was a kind of palm, slender and toothed, completely surrounded by a crown of leaves which looked like paddles and oars. Zamia Lehmanni was a huge pineapple, a monumental Cheshire cheese planted in a bed of heather, bristling at the top with barbed spears and primitive arrows. Cibotium spectabile, the most highly-prized of its genus by virtue of the craziness of its structure, outdid the wildest products of the imagination by projecting from its palmate foliage the enormous tail of an orang-utan, hairy and brown and contorted at the tip like a bishop's crozier. But he scarcely paused to contemplate these items, awaiting with impatience the group of plants which he found most fascinating of all: the ghouls of the vegetable world, the carnivores. The Antillean fly-trap with the furry stem secreted a digestive fluid, and had curved spines upon its leaves which folded over, interlocking to form a cage around the insects which it caught. Drosera, from the peat-bogs, was garnished with glandulous hairs. Sarracena and Cephalotus opened voracious maws capable of dissolving and absorbing whole pieces of meat.

Nepenthes, last but not least among these, was a fantasia surpassing the familiar limits of formal eccentricity. He could never tire of turning back and forth in his hands the pot in which this floral extravaganza was arrayed. It resembled a rubber-plant in that it had elongated leaves of dark metallic green, but from the tip of each leaf there extended a green thread, a dangling umbilical cord supporting a greenish urn dappled with purple, like some sort of German porcelain pipe, or a singular bird's-nest swinging gently to and fro, displaying an interior carpeted with hairs.

"This one is truly extraordinary," murmured Des Esseintes.

He had to interrupt his voluptuous indulgence because

the gardeners, in a hurry to depart, were emptying their carts as fast as they could, scattering tuberous Begonias, and black Crotons like sheet-metal spotted with red lead.

Then he noticed that there was still one name on his list: the Cattleya from New Granada. His attention was drawn to a winged bell-flower, of a lilac hue so delicate as to be almost mauve; he took it up and held it to his nose, but quickly recoiled; it had an odour like varnished wood, like a toy-box which he had once owned, and gave him the horrors. He decided that he must take care to avoid it, and almost came to regret having admitted to the midst of so many odourless plants one which evoked such disagreeable memories.

Alone once more, he surveyed the tidal wave of vegetation which flooded his hallway; the species were all mingled together, crossing swords, spears and curved daggers with one another in a massive display of green weapons, above which floated, like barbarian battle-standards, harsh and dazzling flowers of every colour.

The atmosphere of the room was becoming rarified; soon, in a shadowed corner, at floor-level, a light shone, whitely and softly. He was drawn to the spot, where he found that it came from certain Rhizomorphs which sparkled like night-lights as they breathed.

"These plants are utterly amazing," he said to himself, as he stepped back again to take in the entire assembly at a glance. His objective was achieved; not one of them looked real. Cloth, paper, porcelain and metal had seemingly been lent by Man to Nature in order to permit her to create these monstrosities. When she had not been able to imitate the work of human hands she had been reduced to copying the internal organs of animals, or borrowing the vivid hues of their putrescent flesh and the hideous splendours of gangrene.

41

"It is, after all, only syphilis," thought Des Esseintes, as his gaze was drawn and held by the horrible stripes of the Caladiums, caressed by a ray of sunlight.

He had a sudden vision, then, of humankind in its entirety, ceaselessly tormented since time immemorial by that contagion. From the beginning of the world, all living creatures had handed down from father to son the everlasting heritage: the eternal malady which had ravaged the ancestors of man, whose disfigurations could be seen on the recently-exhumed bones of the most ancient fossils! Without ever weakening in its destructive power it had descended through the centuries to the present day, cunningly concealing itself in all manner of painful disguises, in migraines and brochial infections, hysterias and gouts. From time to time it clambered to the surface, preferentially assaulting those who were badly cared for and malnourished, exploding in lesions like nuggets of gold, ironically crowning the poor devils in its grip with diamond-studded head-dresses, compounding their misery by imprinting upon their skin the image of wealth and well-being.

And here it was, brought forth once again in all its unparalleled splendour, upon the coloured foliage of plants!

"It is true," mused Des Esseintes, returning to the starting-point of his argument. "It is true that for the most part Nature, on her own, is incapable of producing species as depraved and perverse as these; she simply supplies the raw materials, the seed and the soil, the nourishing matrix and the elements of the plant, which man then raises up, shapes, paints and sculpts to suit himself.

"As stubborn, confused and narrow-minded as she is, she is in the end submissive, and her master has succeeded in changing the components of the soil by means of chemical reactions, in developing hardier subspecies and carefully contrived hybrids, in skilfully and methodically taking cuttings and grafting stocks so that nowadays the same branch may put forth blooms of different colour, and in devising new shades and modifying structures as he wishes. He chisels her blocks of stone, finishes off her sketches, puts his own stamp upon them, and imprints them with his hallmark."

It went without saying, he realised, as he continued his reflections, that Man could achieve within a few years a process of selection which sluggish Nature could not contrive even over centuries. Decidedly, as time went by, the world's horticulturalists were becoming the truest artists of all.

He was a little tired, and he felt stifled by the atmosphere of the hothouse; the excursions he had undertaken during these last few days had exhausted him; the transition between the sedentary life of a recluse and the activity of liberated existence had been too sudden. He left the hallway and went to lie down on his bed.

Absorbed as he was, however, by his unique fascination, he was wound up like a coiled spring. He carried into his sleep a train of thought which soon rolled on into the dark madness of a nightmare.

He found himself upon a path which led through the depths of a twilit forest; he was walking beside a woman he had never met, nor seen, before. She was lanky, with stringy hair and a bulldog face, with freckles on her cheeks and irregular teeth jutting out beneath a snub nose. She was wearing a white apron like a maid's, and a long scarlet sash was draped across her breast; she had calf-length boots like a Prussian soldier's and a black bonnet with a plaited frill and a ribbon rosette. She had the manner of a foreigner and the appearance of a fairground hawker.

He asked himself who this woman was, feeling that he had known her for a long time and that she was somehow intimately involved with his life; he sought in vain among his memories for her origin, her name, her occupation, her relevance to him; he could not remember anything at all about his inexplicable yet undeniable association with her.

He was still searching his memory when, all of a sudden, a strange mounted figure appeared before them, trotting ahead for a few minutes before turning round in the saddle.

His blood ran cold, and he stood as if rooted to the spot by horror. The ambiguous and sexless rider was green of face, and it opened its purple eyelids to reveal eyes of a terrible, luminous cold blue; its mouth was surrounded by pustules; its extraordinarily emaciated arms, like the arms of a skeleton, bare to the elbows and shivering with fever, projected from ragged sleeves; and its fleshless thighs shuddered in their over-large riding-boots.

Its frightful and penetrating gaze was fixed on Des Esseintes, chilling him to the marrow; the woman with the bulldog face, even more terrified than he, held fast to him and howled loudly enough to wake the dead, with her head thrown back and her neck taut.

He was immediately able to interpret the meaning of the terrifying vision. He had before his eyes the incarnation of the Great Plague.

Spurred on by terror to remove himself he ran along a narrow side-path until he came to a pavilion surrounded by laburnums; he went inside and flung himself down into a chair in a corridor.

After a few seconds, when he was beginning to get his breath back, the sound of sobbing made him raise his head; the bulldog-faced woman was before him.

44

Grotesque and lamentable, she wept hot tears, wailing that she had lost her teeth while she fled. She began taking clay pipes from the pocket of her apron, breaking them up and embedding the white pieces of the stems in the gaps in her gums.

"All well and good," said Des Esseintes to himself, "but she is very silly—those stems cannot possibly take hold." Indeed, they all dropped out of her jaw, one after another.

At that moment, the sound of a galloping horse became audible. An awful terror seized Des Esseintes. His legs turned to jelly as the sound of hoofbeats grew louder, but desperation brought him to his feet nevertheless, like the crack of a whip. He threw himself upon the woman who was by now stamping her feet on the bowls of the pipes, pleading with her to be quiet, and not to betray them by the sound of her boots. She fought against him, and he dragged her to the end of the corridor, strangling her cries in her throat. He suddenly perceived a tap-room door, with green-painted shutters; it was unlocked and he pushed it, prepared to leap through—and abruptly caught himself up.

Before him, in the middle of a vast moonlit clearing, gigantic white clowns were hopping about like rabbits.

Tears of discouragement welled up in his eyes; never, never could he bring himself to cross that threshold. "I would be flattened," he thought—and as if to justify his anxieties the number of gigantic clowns was multiplied; their somersaults now filled up the entire horizon and the entire sky, which they bumped continually with their heads and their feet, turning and turning about.

Then the sound of the horse's hooves stopped. It was there in the corridor, behind a round window. More dead than alive, Des Esseintes turned round, and through the circular aperture he saw two pointed ears, an array of yellow teeth, and two nostrils breathing vaporous jets which reeked of phenol.

He sank to the ground, abandoning all thought of fight or flight. He shut his eyes so that he would not meet the frightful gaze of Syphilis, which stared at him from behind the wall. It penetrated his closed eyelids anyhow, and he felt it slide down his clammy back, while all the hairs on his body stood on end in pools of cold sweat. He was ready for anything, even hopeful that it might be ended by some coup de grâce; a century—which doubtless lasted less than a minute—went by, and then, all a-quiver, he re-opened his eyes.

It had all vanished without trace; as though there had been an abrupt change of scenery wrought by theatrical trickery, a desolate stony landscape now extended into the remote distance: pallid, empty, split by ravines, utterly lifeless. This desolate place was illumined by a soft white light, reminiscent of the glow of phosphorus immersed in oil.

On the ground something moved; it became a woman, very pale, naked save for her legs, which were clad in green silk stockings.

He looked at her curiously. Her hair was curled with split ends, as though it had been crimped by irons that were too hot. Two urns like those of Nepenthes hung from her ears. Her half-flared nostrils displayed the colour of boiled veal. Her eyes were enraptured. She called to him in a low voice.

He had no time to respond, for the woman was already changing; flamboyant colours lit up her eyes and her lips took on the vivid red of Anthuriums; the nipples of her breasts flared up, as glossily varnished as two red peppers.

A sudden intuition came to him. "This is the Flower," he told himself. His obsessive reasoning persisted even

46

in his nightmare, drawing an analogy between vegetation and infection just as it had done during the day.

Then he observed the frightful irritation of the breasts and the mouth, and discovered that all the skin of her body was stained with sepia and copper. He recoiled in horror, but the woman's eyes fascinated him and he advanced slowly towards her. He tried to dig his heels into the ground to stop himself, and fell to the ground, only to rise up again and continue to move towards her.

He was close enough to reach out and touch her when black Amorphophalli sprang up all around them, stabbing at the belly which rose up and fell again like the swell of the sea. He thrust them aside and pushed them away, utterly disgusted to see these warm, firm stems swarming between his fingers. Then, suddenly, the odious plants had disappeared and two arms were trying to wind themselves around him. A frightful anguish set his heart pounding—for the eyes, the frightful eyes, of the woman had become blue, bright, cold and terrible.

He made a superhuman effort to free himself from her embrace, but with an irresistible grip she seized and held him. Haggard and horrified, he saw between her uplifted thighs the blossoming of a cruel Nidularium, which opened wide its bloody maw, surrounded by sword-blades.

His body brushed the edge of that hideous wound, he felt death come to claim him—and awoke with a start, choking, ice-cold, mad with fear, sighing: "Ah! Thank God! It is naught but a dream!"

****

4.

FAUSTINE
by Algernon Charles Swinburne

Ave Faustina Imperatrix, morituri te salutant.

Lean back, and get some minutes' peace ;
Let your head lean
Back to the shoulder with its fleece
Of locks, Faustine.

The shapely silver shoulder stoops,
Weighed over clean
With state of splendid hair that droops
Each side, Faustine.

Let me go over your good gifts
That crown you queen ;
A queen whose kingdom ebbs and shifts
Each week, Faustine.

Bright heavy brows well gathered up :
White gloss and sheen ;
Carved lips that make my lips a cup
To drink, Faustine,

Wine and rank poison, milk and blood,
Being mixed therein
Since first the devil threw dice with God
For you, Faustine.

Your naked new-born soul, their stake,
Stood blind between ;
God said " let him that wins her take
And keep Faustine."

But this time Satan throve, no doubt ;
Long since, I ween,
God's part in you was battered out ;
Long since, Faustine.

The die rang sideways as it fell,
Rang cracked and thin,
Like a man's laughter heard in hell
Far down, Faustine,

A shadow of laughter like a sigh,
Dead sorrow's kin ;
So rang, thrown down, the devil's die
That won Faustine.

A suckling of his breed you were,
One hard to wean ;
But God, who lost you, left you fair,
We see, Faustine.

You have the face that suits a woman
For her soul's screen—
The sort of beauty that's called human
In hell, Faustine.

You could do all things but be good
Or chaste of mien ;
And that you would not if you could,
We know, Faustine.

Even he who cast seven devils out
Of Magdalene
Could hardly do as much, I doubt,
For you, Faustine.

Did Satan make you to spite God?
Or did God mean
To scourge with scorpions for a rod
Our sins, Faustine?

I know what queen at first you were,
As though I had seen
Red gold and black imperious hair
Twice crown Faustine.

As if your fed sarcophagus
Spared flesh and skin,
You come back face to face with us,
The same Faustine.

She loved the games men played with death,
Where death must win ;
As though the slain man's blood and breath
Revived Faustine.

Nets caught the pike, pikes tore the net ;
Lithe limbs and lean
From drained-out pores dripped thick red sweat
To soothe Faustine.

She drank the steaming drift and dust
Blown off the scene ;
Blood could not ease the bitter lust
That galled Faustine.

All round the foul fat furrows reeked,
Where blood sank in ;
The circus splashed and seethed and shrieked
All round Faustine.

But these are gone now : years entomb
The dust and din ;
Yea, even the bath's fierce reek and fume
That slew Faustine.

Was life worth living then ? and now
Is life worth sin ?
Where are the imperial years ? and how
Are you Faustine ?

Your soul forgot her joys, forgot
Her times of teen ;
Yea, this life likewise will you not
Forget, Faustine ?

For in the time we know not of
Did fate begin
Weaving the web of days that wove
Your doom, Faustine.

The threads were wet with wine, and all
Were smooth to spin ;
They wove you like a Bacchanal,
The first Faustine.

And Bacchus cast your mates and you
Wild grapes to glean ;
Your flower-like lips were dashed with dew
From his, Faustine.

Your drenched loose hands were stretched to hold
The vine's wet green,
Long ere they coined in Roman gold
Your face, Faustine.

Then after change of soaring feather
And winnowing fin,
You woke in weeks of feverish weather,
A new Faustine.

A star upon your birthday burned,
Whose fierce serene
Red pulseless planet never yearned
In heaven, Faustine.

Stray breaths of Sapphic song that blew
Through Mitylene
Shook the fierce quivering blood in you
By night, Faustine.

The shameless nameless love that makes
Hell's iron gin
Shut on you like a trap that breaks
The soul, Faustine.

And when your veins were void and dead,
What ghosts unclean
Swarmed round the straitened barren bed
That hid Faustine.

What sterile growths of sexless root
Or epicene ?
What flower of kisses without fruit
Of love, Faustine ?

What adders came to shed their coats ?
What coiled obscene
Small serpents with soft stretching throats
Caressed Faustine ?

But the time came of famished hours,
Maimed loves and mean,
This ghastly thin-faced time of ours,
To spoil Faustine.

You seem a thing that hinges hold,
A love-machine
With clockwork joints of supple gold—
No more, Faustine.

Not godless, for you serve one God,
The Lampsacene,
Who metes the gardens with his rod ;
Your lord, Faustine.

If one should love you with real love
(Such things have been,
Things your fair face knows nothing of,
It seems, Faustine) ;

That clear hair heavily bound back,
The lights wherein
Shift from dead blue to burnt-up black ;
Your throat, Faustine.

Strong, heavy, throwing out the face
And hard bright chin
And shameful scornful lips that grace
Their shame, Faustine,

Curled lips, long since half kissed away,
Still sweet and keen ;
You'd give him—poison shall we say ?
Or what, Faustine ?

5.

Verses from
THE SONGS OF MALDOROR
by the Comte de Lautréamont

Perhaps, dear reader, it is repugnance that you want me to invoke in you as I begin this enterprise! How can you tell that you will not rather snort it up, with your nostrils arrogantly flared, bathing in infinite voluptuousness, extended to the limit of your desire, rolling over on your belly like a shark, slow and majestic in the beautiful black air, glowing redly, as if you understood the importance of this performance and the equal importance of the appetite to which you are fully entitled? I assure you that the uncertain holes of your ugly snout will be stimulated, if you will only make a preparatory effort to inhale three thousand times the accursed consciousness of the Eternal! Your nostrils, extraordinarily dilated by the unimaginable contentment of static ecstasy, can ask nothing more of infinity than to be filled with the fragrance of perfumes and incense, for they will be utterly possessed by a surfeit of happiness, as the angels are who dwell in the peace and splendour of the pastures of Heaven.

****

I will establish, briefly, the fact that Maldoror fared well during the earliest years of his life, when his life was happy; it is done. He perceived as time went by, however, that he had been born evil: an extraordinary accident of fate! He concealed his nature as best he could for many years, but in the end—because such mental effort did not come naturally to him—every passing day brought the blood rushing to his head, rendering him powerless to support such an existence any longer, and he launched himself resolutely upon his evil career....what a blessed relief it was! Who would have thought it? Whenever he embraced a rosy-cheeked little child he wanted to rip its cheeks apart with a razor, and would frequently have done it, save that Justice, with all its punishments in train, stopped him every time. He was not a liar; he accepted the truth and avowed that he was cruel. Do you hear me, humanity? He dares to repeat it with this quivering pen. Thus it proves itself more powerful than mere will...an irresistible curse! Might a stone withdraw its consent from the law of gravity? Impossible. Impossible, likewise, for evil to ally itself with good. This I have demonstrated, here above.

****

There are those who write in the hope of winning the applause of men, by means of the noble sentiments which they may have, or which they invent by imagination. As for me, I dedicate my genius to the depiction of the delights of cruelty! Such delights are not transitory or artificial; they were born with humankind and will end with humankind. Might genius not be allied with cruelty according to the secret dispensations of Providence? In any case, must one be forbidden genius, simply because one is cruel? The point is clearly proven by my words; no more is required of you than your attention, if you will grant it....I beg your pardon, but it seemed just then that all my hairs stood on end— but it is nothing, for it was easy enough to smooth them down again with my hand. This singer does not pretend that his melodies are entirely original; on the contrary, he has the satisfaction of knowing that his hero's arrogant and wicked thoughts are echoed in the minds of all men.

****

All my life, without a single exception, I have seen men with cramped shoulders carrying out stupid acts by the score, brutalizing their fellow men and perverting their souls by any available means. They name the inspiration of their actions: fame. While watching these exhibitions I wanted to laugh like all the others, but I found the strange expression impossible to reproduce. I took a sharp-bladed knife and slit the flesh at the sides of my mouth where the lips meet. For a moment I believed that my purpose was achieved. I looked in a mirror at the mouth which I had mutilated by an act of will. It was a mistake! The blood which flowed abundantly from the two wounds prevented me at first from distinguishing whether it was really the same kind of laugh that other men produced. But after spending a few minutes comparing them, I saw all too clearly that my laugh did not resemble that of men at all, and that it might be said that I was not actually laughing at all.

I have seen men with ugly faces and terrible eyes deep-set in shadowed sockets, whose hardness surpasses that of rock, their rigidity that of steel, their cruelty that of sharks, their insolence that of youth, their insensate fury that of criminals, their perfidy that of hypocrites— most extraordinary performers with the strength of character of priests, the most secretive beings on earth, colder than anything else in the universe—who exhaust the moralists that seek to understand their hearts and who bring down on themselves the implacable wrath of the heavens. I have seen them all, at one and the same time; now the strongest fist is raised towards heaven, like that of an infant who has learned to disobey his mother, probably inspired by some hellish spirit, while eyes full of bitter remorse and hatred suffer in glacial silence, without the courage to voice the profound and ungrateful thoughts which they nurse in their breasts, replete with injustice and horror, grief-stricken by the compassion of the merciful God; again, every minute of the day, from the beginning of infancy until the end of decrepitude, they pour out incredible curses, utterly lacking in common sense, against everything which breathes, against themselves and against Providence, prostituting women and children, dishonouring thereby those parts of the body consecrated to decency. Then, the waters of the ocean rise up, dragging ships down in to their abyssal depths; hurricanes and earthquakes topple houses; plague and various other diseases decimate families at prayer. But men never perceive all this. I have seen them blushing too, or turning pale with shame on account of their conduct on this earth—but rarely.

Tempests, sisters of the hurricanes; blue firmament, whose beauty I will not admit; treacherous sea, image of my heart; earth, full of mysteries; inhabitants of the heavenly spheres; Universe entire; God, who created it magnificently, it is you that I invoke: show me a man who is good!...But, by your favour, grant me a tenfold increase in my natural strength; because, were I confronted by such a monster I might die of astonishment—men have died of lesser causes.

****

I sought a soul resembling mine, but could not find it. I scoured every corner of the earth; my perseverance was unrewarded. Nevertheless, I could not be content with

58

my isolation. There had to be someone who could sanction my conduct; there had to be someone whose ideas were similar to mine.

It was morning; the sun rose above the horizon in all its splendour, and before my eyes there arose also a young man, whose presence brought forth flowers wherever he went. He came towards me and held out his hand, saying: "I have come to you, you who have sought me. Blessed be the happy day!" But I answered: "Go away; I have not summoned you; I have no need of your friendship..."

It was evening; the night had begun to extend its dark veil over everything. A beautiful woman, whose form I could not quite make out, also cast her spell upon me, and looked at me compassionately; however, she did not dare to speak to me. I said: "Come towards me, so that I can see the contours of your face more clearly, for the light of the stars is not strong enough to display them at this distance." Then, in a modest manner, with her eyes lowered, she set her foot upon the grassy lawn and came to my side. As soon as I could see her plainly I said: "I see that goodness and justice have taken up residence in your heart: we could never live together. For the moment, you admire my beauty, which has turned more than one head; but sooner or later you would regret having given your love to me, for you do not know my soul. Not that I would ever be unfaithful: to her who surrenders herself to me with total abandon and trust I similarly surrender myself; but get this into your head and never forget it: wolves and lambs do not look upon one another with kindly eyes."

What was it that I required for myself, having rejected with such disgust the loveliest that humanity had to offer? I could not say what it was that I needed. I was not yet accustomed to keeping a strict account of the

59

phenomena of my mind according to the methods recommended by philosophy.

I sat down upon a rock, beside the sea. A ship had just hoisted full sail in order to depart that shore. An almost imperceptible break in the horizon was just becoming manifest; it approached gradually, driven by the wind, rapidly increasing in size. A storm was about to unleash its fury; already the sky was darkening, becoming as black and hideous as the hearts of men. The ship, which was a huge man-o'-war, began to drop its anchors so that it would not be swept on to the coastal reef. Gusts of wind whistled furiously from every point of the compass, ripping the sails to shreds. Claps of thunder burst forth amid flashes of lightning, but could not drown out the cries of lamentation which emerged from that house without foundations, that mobile sepulchre. The massive waves had not yet broken the anchor-chains, but their impacts had opened up the ship's side, letting in water...

The breach is enormous; the pumps are impotent to stem the foaming flood of salt water which beats mountainously down upon the bridge. The distressed ship fires its cannon to sound the alarm, but it founders slowly and majestically...

He who has not seen a ship foundering in a hurricane, by the intermittent light of lightning-flashes in the deepest gloom, while those it contains are overwhelmed by the despair that you know so well, knows nothing about the hazards of life. At the end, a single great cry of immense suffering is let loose from the decks of the vessel, while the sea redoubles the force of its irresistible attack; it is the cry of those who have been pushed to the limits of human endurance. Each one wraps the cloak of resignation about himself, and consigns his fate to the hands of God. They huddle together like a flock of sheep. The distressed ship fires its cannon to sound the alarm, but it founders slowly and majestically...

They have plied the pumps all day, but their efforts are all in vain. Night has come, deep and implacable, to bring the gracious spectacle to its climax. Each one says secretly to himself that once he is in the water, he will not be able to breathe, for as far as he can contrive to recall there is not a single fish to be numbered among his ancestors, but he resolves to hold his breath for as long as possible, in order to prolong his life by two or three more seconds; this is the vengeful irony with which he wishes to confront death.... The distressed ship fires its cannon to sound the alarm, but it founders slowly and majestically.... He does not know that as a ship sinks it creates a powerful vortex around itself; that silt sucked up from below into the hectic water, a counterpart of the tempest which rages on high, stamps its own imprint on the spasmodic and virile movement of the element. Thus, despite the composure which he stores up for the future, one doomed to drown should be happy enough, upon adequate reflection, to extend his life within the turbulence of the abyss by even as much as half a normal breath. It will be impossible for him to defy death, though that is his greatest wish.

The distressed ship fires its cannon to sound the alarm, but it founders slowly and majestically....

Something is wrong! It is no longer firing its cannon; it is no longer wallowing. The petty cockleshell is completely engulfed. O Heaven! how can one live, after having experienced such sensations? It was granted to me to be a witness to the death-agonies of a number of my fellow men. Minute by minute I followed the uncertain course of their agonies. At one moment, the bellowing of some old woman, driven mad by fear, was foremost in that commerce. At another, only the screaming of a child at its mother's breast drowned out the orders directed at

61

the helm. The vessel was too far away to allow me to make out the groaning-sounds carried by the wind, but I exerted the power of my will to bring it closer, until the optical illusion was complete.

After a quarter of an hour, when a gust of wind stronger than the rest broke the back of the ship, drowning the cries of the petrels with its mournful howling and augmenting the pleas of those about to be offered up as human sacrifices, I pricked my cheek with a dagger and thought to myself: "Their suffering is greater still!" I had, by this means, some standard of comparison. From the shore I addressed them, hurling threats and imprecations at them. It seemed to me that they should heed me! It seemed to me that my hatred and my speech, regardless of the distance, were annihilating the laws of sound and making themselves clearly evident to those ears which had been deafened by the roaring of the wrathful waves! It seemed to me that they ought to be aware of me, and expend their resentment in impotent rage!

From time to time I raised my eyes towards the cities slumbering on firm ground; and, seeing that no one there suspected that a vessel had foundered some miles from the shore, and that I had a bird of prey for a crown and empty-bellied leviathans of the deep for a platform, I recovered my courage and my hope: I was so sure of their destruction! They could not possibly escape! As a further precaution, I had been to fetch my double-barrelled shotgun, so that if some survivor attempted to swim towards the rocks in order to escape imminent death a bullet in the shoulder would fracture his arm, to prevent him from carrying out his plan.

At the furious height of the storm I saw a man in the water, his hair standing on end, making desperate efforts to stay afloat. He had taken in a great deal of water, and was being tossed about like a cork before being dragged down into the depths. Soon, however, he reappeared, his hair in disarray, and, fixing his eyes upon the shore, he seemed to be about to defy death. His composure was admirable. A huge and bloody wound, caused by the jagged edge of a hidden shoal, was slashed across his brave and noble face. He could not have been more than sixteen years of age, because the flashes of lightning illuminated, for bare fractions of a second, the peach-like fuzz on his upper lip. Now he was no more than two hundred metres from the cliff, and I could see him quite clearly. What courage! What indomitable spirit! How the insistent thrust of his head seemed to defy destiny as he fought his way through the waves, which did not part easily before him. I had already made up my mind. I owed it to myself to keep my promise: the final hour had tolled for all and none must escape. Such was my resolution; nothing could change it...

A sharp sound was heard, and the head immediately sank from sight, never to reappear.

I did not take as much pleasure in the murder as one might expect; this was, I suppose, because I had had my fill of the unending slaughter. I was simply acting out of habit, unable to let the opportunity pass; but it afforded me no more than a slight thrill. My senses are blunted and hardened. What pleasure could be induced by the death of this human being, when there were more than a hundred whose last struggles against the waves would provide me with such a spectacle as the ship went down? I had not even the allure of danger to add spice to this death, for human justice, shaken by the violence of the frightful night, was asleep indoors some distance away.

Now that the years bear down upon me, I can sincerely affirm this supreme and solemn truth: I was not quite as cruel as I was said to be by other men—while, all the time, their own wickedness caused untold misery year after year. Then, my fury knew no bounds; I was seized by fits of cruelty, and I became terrible to behold for anyone who came within range of my wild eyes, if he was one of my own kind. If it was a horse or a dog, I let it pass: have you noted what I have just said? Unhappily, on the night of that storm, I was the victim of one such fit; my reason had taken flight (ordinarily my cruelty was moderated by caution) and everything which fell into my hands that night was doomed to perish. I do not pretend that this excuses my sins. The fault is not entirely with my fellow men. My sole concern is to establish the facts while awaiting the Day of Judgment, anticipation of which makes me scratch the nape of my neck....but what does Judgment Day matter to me?

My reason never takes flight, as I have just said in order to mislead you. When I commit a crime, I know what I am doing; I did not want to do otherwise! Standing on the rock, while the hurricane lashed my hair and my cloak, I was ecstatic as I watched the force of the storm beating down on the ship beneath the starless sky. I was triumphant as I followed the shifting fortunes of the drama, from the moment the vessel dropped its anchors until the moment when it was engulfed: a deadly garment which dragged to the bottom of the sea all those who had adopted it as a cloak.

But the moment approached when I myself was to be cast as an actor into that scene of disordered nature. When the place where the vessel had been involved in its combat clearly showed that it had gone to spend the rest of its days on the sea-bed, some of those carried off by the waves began to reappear on the surface. They clung to one another, arms about waists, in twos and threes, and by that means they failed to save their lives, for their movements were hindered and they went down like leaky pots....

What is this army of sea-monsters which forges through the waves so speedily? There are six; their fins are powerful, carving a way through the swell.

From the human beings who are thrashing their limbs in the unsupportive continent, the sharks soon make an omelette without eggs, which is shared out according to the law of the strongest. Blood is mixed with water, and water is mixed with blood. The scene of carnage is adequately illuminated by their ferocious eyes.... But what is this further agitation of the waters, out there upon the horizon? One might take it for an approaching waterspout! What strokes! I see what it is: an enormous female shark coming to claim her share of the duck's liver paté and the meal of cold beef. She is furious, for she arrives starving. A struggle commences between her and the other sharks, to decide which of them will have the few quivering limbs which float here and there, mutely, on the surface of the red cream. To the right and to the left she directs her bites, causing fatal wounds. But three living sharks are still about her, and she is obliged to turn hither and yon in order to avoid their manoeuvres.

With a previously unknown emotion growing within him, the spectator on the shore follows the course of this new kind of naval battle. He fixes his eyes upon that courageous female shark whose teeth are so powerful. He hesitates no longer, but brings his rifle up to his shoulder, and with practised skill he puts his second bullet into the gills of one of the sharks, during the brief moment when it looms up from the waves.

Two sharks remain, which surge forward all the more strongly in consequence. From the top of the rock the man with the taste of brine in his mouth hurls himself into the sea and swims towards the prettily-coloured carpet, holding in his hand the steel dagger which he is never without. Henceforth, each shark has one enemy to deal with. He advances upon his weary adversary and, taking his time, stabs it in the belly with his sharp blade. The mobile fortress easily disposes of the last adversary...

Finding themselves thrown together, the swimmer and the female shark he has saved look into one another's eyes for a few minutes, each one astonished to find such ferocity in the other's expression. They swim around in circles, never losing sight of one another, saying to themselves: "I have deceived myself; now, here is one more evil than myself." Then, by common consent, they glide through the water towards one another with mutual admiration, the female shark cutting through the water with its fins, Maldoror beating the waves with his arms; and they hold their breath in profound admiration, each one desirous of contemplating, for the first time, a living reflection. Coming to within three metres of one another they fall abruptly and effortlessly upon one another, like two lovers, embracing with dignity and recognition as tenderly as brother and sister.

This demonstration of amity is followed by carnal desire. Two wiry thighs press tightly against the thick skin of the monster, like two leeches; arms and fins are simultaneously entwined about the body of the beloved objects which they surround with love, while the throats and breasts of the couple are soon formed into a single glaucous mass, as if they were some exhalation of the seaweed.

In the midst of the storm which continued to rage about them, lit by flashing lightning, borne away upon a marriage-bed of foaming waves by an undersea current, as though in a cradle, tumbling over one another as they fell into the abyssal depths, they joined together in a

66

long, pure and horrid copulation!
At last I had managed to find someone like me!
Henceforth, I was no longer alone in the world!
She had the same ideas as I!
I was face to face with my first love!

****

6.

VIOL D'AMOR
by Count Stanislaus Eric Stenbock

One time there was much in vogue a peculiarly sweet-toned kind of violin, or rather, to be accurate, something between a viola and a violoncello. Now they are no longer made. This is the history of the last one that was ever made, I think. This somewhat singular story might in some way explain why they are made no longer. But though I am a poetess, and consequently inclined to believe in the unlikely, this I do not suppose was the history of Viol d'Amors in general. I may add, by way of prefix, that its peculiar sweetness of tone was produced by the duplicated reverberation of strings below, with yet another reverberation within the sounding-board. But to my story.

I was once in Freiburg—Freiburg in Baden, I mean. I went one Sunday to High Mass at the Cathedral. Beethoven's glorious Mass in C was magnificently rendered by a string quartette. I was specially impressed by the first violin, a   dignified, middle-aged man, with a singularly handsome face, reminding one of the portraits of Leonardo da Vinci. He was dressed in a mediaeval-looking black robe ; and he played with an inspiration such as I have seldom, if ever, heard. There was likewise a most beautiful boy's treble. Boys' voices, lovely in their 'timbre' as nothing else, are generally somewhat wanting in their expression. I was going to stay in Freiburg some time, as I knew people there. The first violinist had aroused my curiosity. I learnt that he was an Italian, a Florentine, of the ancient noble family

68

of da Ripoli. But he was now a maker of musical instruments, not very well off–who nevertheless played at the Cathedral for love, not money ; also that the beautiful treble was his youngest son, and he was a widower with five children. As he interested me, I sought to procure an introduction, which I succeeded in getting without difficulty.

He lived in one of those beautiful old houses which linger still in towns like Freiburg. He seemed somewhat surprised that an Englishwoman should go out of her way to visit him. Fortunately I was familiar with Italian, being myself an Italian on the mother's side, and was at that time on my way to Italy. He received me with much affability. I was ushered into a long Gothic room, done in black oak : there was a very beautiful Gothic window, which was open. It was spring-time, and the most delightful weather. There was a strong scent of May about the room, emanating from a hawthorn-tree immediately opposite the window, which had the extraordinary peculiarity of bearing red and white blossoms at the same time. The room was full of all sorts of odds and ends of things–caskets, vessels, embroideries– all exquisitely artistic. He told me these were executed by a son and daughter of his. We began to interest one another, and had a long talk. As we were talking, in walked a tall, grave-looking young man. He was of the pure Etruscan type–dark, and indeed somewhat sombre.

With a perturbed air, not noticing me, he suddenly made this singular remark, 'Saturn is in conjunction with the moon : I fear that ill may betide Guido.'

'This is my son Andrea,' his father explained, 'my eldest son ; he goes in much for astronomy, and indeed also for astrology, in which you probably do not believe.'

At that moment in walked another young man. This was the second son, Giovanni. He was also dark, like his brother, and tall, but had a very pleasing smile. He reminded me rather of the portrait of Andrea del Sarto. It was he who manufactured—to use the word in its proper sense—these beautiful objects which were lying about the table. After him came in two sisters : the elder, whose name was Anastasia, was a tall, stately girl, with dark hair and grey eyes, but pale face : very much like the type we are familiar with from the pictures of Dante Gabriel Rossetti. The younger sister was quite different: she was fair, but fair in the Italian manner : that glorious, ivory-white complexion so different from the pink and white of the North. Her hair was of that glorious red-gold colour which we see in Titian's pictures, but her eyes were dark. Her name was Liperata. It appears Anastasia was the eldest of the family, then came Andrea and Giovanni, then Liperata, and lastly,Guido, whom I had not seen as yet.

I omitted to mention, though it does not seem here of any significance at all, that Anastasia wore a blue gown of somewhat stiff mediaeval cut, but very graceful all the same. I learnt afterwards it was both designed and made by herself.

Presently there entered the room a boy of about fourteen. This was Guido. He was fairer than his brothers, though also somewhat of the Etruscan type, and was not so tall for his age. He looked singularly fragile and delicate. His complexion was more delicate than a rose-petal : he had those long, supple, sensitive hands which indicate the born musician. His somewhat long hair, of a shade of brown, had a shadow of gold on it, as if it had been gold once. But in his strange-coloured eyes, which were grey-blue, streaked with yellow bars, there was a far-off look, like a light not of this world, shining on a slowly-rippling river of music. He went straight to the window,also not noticing there was a stranger in the room, and said, 'Ah, how beautiful the May-tree is! I shall only see it bloom once more.' He seemed indeed to be looking through the blooming hawthorn at that pale planet Saturn, which then was, for *it*, singularly large and brilliant. Andrea shuddered, but Giovanni bent down and kissed him, and said, 'What, Guido, another fit of melancholia?'

As you may imagine, I was interested in this singular family, and soon our acquaintance ripened into intimacy. It was to Anastasia that I was specially drawn, and she to me. Anastasia inherited the musical tastes of her father, and was herself no mean executant on the violin.

Andrea was not only occupied with astronomy and astrology, but even with alchemy and such like things, and occult sciences generally.

The whole family was very superstitious. They seemed to take astrology and magic as matters of course. But Andrea was by far the most superstitious of them all. It was Giovanni who was the breadwinner of the family, together with his special sister, Liperata, who assisted him in his work, and herself did the most charming embroideries. The only thing was that their materials were too costly, and required a large outlay to be made before they could sell anything.

For though the musical instruments the father produced were super-excellent of their kind, and fetched large prices, he took so much care about his work that he was sometimes years in producing one violin. He was then absorbed in one idea, in producing a Viol d'Amor, an instrument which he said was the most beautiful in all the world, and which had unjustly fallen into disuse. And *his* Viol d'Amor was to excel all others that had ever been made. He had left Florence, he said, because he could not stand this great Republic (for though of one of the most ancient noble families, he was an ardent

Republican) being converted into the capital of a tenth-rate monarchy. 'They will be taking Rome next,' he said. And he did not know that what he was saying was soon to come true.

They were not well off, certainly, but it was Anastasia who managed the household and cared for everyone. And she was the most excellent of manageresses. And so their life was very simple, but nevertheless was elegant and refined.

I very often enjoyed their simple, truly Italian hospitality, recompensing them by purchasing some specimens of Giovanni's excellent workmanship, and a violin from the old Signor da Ripoli, which I have still, and would not part with for the world. Though, alas! I myself cannot play upon it. To cut a long story short, I had to go on with my journey, but I did not wholly lose sight of them, so to speak, and I corresponded frequently with Anastasia.

———————————

One day, just about a year afterwards, I received the following letter from Anastasia :–

'DEAR CECILIA,– A great calamity has fallen upon us. It is so out of the common that you would hardly believe it. Of course you know how my father is devoted to his Viol d'Amor. You also know that we are all rather superstitious, but none to the same degree as Andrea. It appears that one day Andrea was poring into some old book, which was in that mongrel tongue, half Latin and half Italian, before the days of Dante, when he came across a passage (you know, I know nothing about the manufacture of musical instruments ; but it appears that leather thongs are necessary to procure the complete vibration of the Viol d'Amor). In this passage it said that preternatural sweetness of tone could be procured if the thongs were made of the skin of those who loved the maker most.–[I had heard of this superstition before : I think there is some story in connection with Paganini of a similar nature, but nevertheless quite different. For as the legend goes about Paganini, the strings of a violin were made of the entrails of a person, which necessitated their murder ; but here it would appear from the rest of the letter it did not do so, and was a freewill offering.]– Andrea conceived the fantastic idea of cutting off part of his own skin and having it tanned unbeknown to our father, telling him he had got it from the Clinic, because he had heard human leather was the best. To effect this he had to invoke the assistance of Giovanni, who, as you know, is so skilful with all instruments, and is also, as perhaps you do *not* know, a most skilful surgeon.

'Giovanni, not to be outdone by his brother, performed the same operation on himself. They were obliged to confide in me, and, as you know, I am very good as a nurse, and clever at bandages and such like. So I managed, with a little bandaging, and nursing, and sewing up the scars, to get them quite well again in a very short time. Of course no word of this was ever said to Liperata or Guido. And now comes the dreadful part of my story. How Guido could have divined anything I cannot understand. The only explanation I can offer is this. He is a very studious boy, and very fond of poring into the old books in Andrea's library. He might have seen the same passage, and with his extraordinary quick intuition have guessed. Anyhow he appears to have gone to some quack Jew doctor, and had a portion of his skin cut off in the same manner, and brought the skin to his brothers to be dealt with in the same way, which it *was*. The operation had been performed badly, and, as you know, the child is very delicate, and it has

73

had the most disastrous results. He is hopelessly ill, and we do not know what to do. Of course we cannot tell our father. It is equally impossible to tell a doctor. Fortunately our father does not believe in doctors and trusts in *us*. It is a good thing all three of us know something of medical science : I think things are getting a little better. He rallied a little yesterday, and asked to be taken from his bed to the sofa in the long room. At his own request he was placed just opposite the May-tree, with the window open. This seemed to revive him. He became, comparatively speaking, quite animated, especially when a slight wind blew some of the red and white blossoms on to his coverlet. Giovanni and I have some hope, but Andrea has not. Liperata of course does not understand what it all means. Nor does our father, who is intensely anxious about Guido, whom he loves best of all.– Ever affectionately,

'ANASTASIA.'

'P.S.– Good news at last! the Viol d'Amor is completed. Father came down and played it to us. Oh! what a divine tone it has! Guido first burst into tears, and then seemed to grow quite well again for some time afterwards. Father left the Viol d'Amor with me, that I should play to Guido whenever he wished it. Yes, there *is* hope after all, whatever Andrea may say.'

Not long afterwards I received another letter from Anastasia in deep mourning. It ran thus :–

'The worst has happened. Last Friday, after having been for several days considerably better, Guido seemed almost himself again. I was alone with him in the long room. (One thinks of trivialities in great grief ; I was wearing that same blue dress I had on when I first saw you.) There was a wind, also rain, which pattered against the window-pane, and the wind blew the blossoms of the May-tree like red-white snow to the ground. This seemed to depress Guido. He begged me to sing to him, and accompany myself on the Viol d'Amor. "It is so sweet of tone," he said, with a sweet, sad smile. "I am rather tired, though I do not feel much pain now. I shall not see the hawthorn bloom again."

'I began to sing an old Etruscan ballad–one of those songs that linger about the country parts of Tuscany, of a very simple, plaintive cadence, accompanied softly on the Viol d'Amor. It would be soothing, I thought, at any rate. And it was. Guido laid his head back and closed his eyes. Gradually the rain ceased and the wind stilled. Guido looked up. "That is better," he said, "I was afraid of the wind and the rain ; and *you* stopped them with the Viol d'Amor! Look! the moon is beginning to shine again." It was a full moon, and it shone through the hawthorn-tree, making strange shadows on the window, and one ray shot direct on Guido's pale face. "Go on singing," he said faintly. So I sang on, and played on the Viol d'Amor. I felt some dreadful presentiment. I dared not stop singing and playing. It seemed that a shadow literally crept through the doorway, and came up to the bed, and bent over it. Then suddenly all the strings of the Viol d'Amor snapped! A strange wail seemed to come out of the sounding-board. I dropped it, and looked! Then I saw it was too late.

. . . .

'Father took the Viol d'Amor and broke it in pieces, and cast it into the fire. His silent agony is too terrible to describe. I cannot tell you any more now.'

I was in Freiburg once again, and of course the first thing I did was to go and see my old friends. The Signor da Ripoli was very much aged. He still plays in the Cathedral. Did he, or did he not, ever know what had happened? Anyhow, he has made no further attempt to construct a Viol d'Amor ; nor may the word even be mentioned in his presence.

Giovanni and Liperata have gone back to Italy, where they have set up a workshop for themselves. It is rumoured that Liperata is shortly to be married. But Anastasia remains with her father. I do not think that she will ever marry. Andrea has become a victim to settled melancholy. He lives quite by himself in a lonely tower. It was he who had the following inscription put on Guido's tomb :—

'La musica e l'Amor che mouve
il Sole e l'altre Stelle.'

7.

PÉHOR*
by Remy de Gourmont

Sensitive though poor, imaginative though forever hungry, Douceline learned early in life to delight in caresses and embraces. She loved to pass her hands across the cheeks of little boys, and to put her arms around the necks of little girls, stroking them as she might have stroked a cat. She loved to kiss the knitted fingers of her mother's hands, and whenever she was banished to the corner to do penance for her petty sins she would occupy herself in kissing her own palms and her own arms, and the bare knees which she would raise up to her lips one by one.

Such was her curiosity in respect of her sensations that she was quite untroubled by modesty or shame. If she was scolded, roughly or ironically, for her narcissistic amorousness she would firmly deny that there was anything excessive in her tenderness, while hiding her eyes behind her hands. In secret, however, she maintained the habit of caressing herself, never admitting that it might qualify as a vice. She became so adept in concealing her predilection, even from herself,

*Translator's note: Péhor was a god of the Midianites, one of the many rival tribal deities demonized by the Children of Israel at the behest of their own jealous God; the name is rendered Baal-peor ("master of the opening") in the Authorised Version of the Old Testament. *Numbers* 25 describes how Phineas, the son of Eleazer, obeys Moses' command to punish those Israelites who have "committed whoredom" with Midianite women by killing Zambri (Zimri in the A.V.), son of Salu, and Cozbi, daughter of Sur (Zur in the A.V.). Phineas slew them both with a single blow of his spear, presumably while they were copulating.

that she reserved her most intimate attentions to times
when she was safely asleep.

****

When the time came for her first communion
Douceline was enthralled by all the solemn preparations
which had to be made. She was thrilled to be given a few
sous in order to buy a holy picture of the kind which all
the females of the region mounted upon their walls.

The images of the Holy Virgin did not attract her;
Douceline preferred the portraits of Jesus, especially
those which displayed his most gentle expressions—the
ones which tinted his cheeks with rouge, which painted
his beard with flames, which set his blue eyes alight
with the reflected glow of a diffuse aureole. One picture
of Jesus which she saw had a visitant nun at his feet,
bathing in the glow of his redly shining heart and
declaring: *My saviour is everything to me and I am
everything to him.* In another he looked down, tenderly
and a little ambiguously, at a worshipper who proclaimed:
The sight of his eyes has blessed my heart.

One image, in which the Sacred Heart was pierced by
a dagger, dripping blood the colour of red ink, carried a
legend which debased one of the most beautiful
metaphors of mystical theology: *The Lord's gift to his
most favoured children is the wine which intoxicates the
souls of the innocents.* The Jesus from whose breast that
jet of carmine sprayed had an infinitely loving and
reassuring face, a blue robe decorated with little golden
flowers, and delicate—almost translucent—hands where
two tiny stars were made captive. Douceline adored this
image absolutely, and when it became hers she made a
vow, writing on the back of the picture: *I give myself to
the Sacred Heart of Jesus, because it is given to me.*

Frequently thereafter, when she looked up from her

half-open missal, Douceline would lose herself in contemplation of that loving and reassuring face, murmuring without opening her mouth: "To you! To you!"

As far as the mystery of the Eucharist was concerned, Douceline understood nothing of its intended significance. At communion she received the host without emotion, without any remorse for her incomplete and insincere confessions, without any experience of holy affection. Her heart was entirely reserved for the loving and reassuring face.

****

Douceline finally succeeded, by the force of dogged perseverance, in memorising the catechism. She noted therefrom the preference which Jesus had for beautiful souls and his corollary disdain for beautiful faces, and afterwards spent hours looking at herself in a mirror, utterly dismayed to find herself so pretty. Chagrined by this discovery, she prayed so fervently to become plainer that she gave herself a fever, awakening one morning with pustules all over her face.

In the delirium which attended her illness she proffered grateful words of love; when she had recovered she thanked Jesus effusively for the white pockmarks which now marked her forehead and cheeks. She offered up these thankful prayers while kneeling on a hard stone floor, and when her grazed knees bled she kissed the wounds and sucked up the blood, saying to herself: "This is the blood of Jesus, because he has given me his own heart".

During the weeks which passed while she was weakened by the anaemia which followed her fever her secret habit was once again revealed to her conscious mind. She would occasionally wake to discover herself engaged in her caresses, but would quickly abandon them and return to sleep. One night, though, she woke to find her fingers sticky with blood. She was very frightened, and quickly got up to wash herself, but the blood had stained her nightgown too, and seemed to be everywhere.

Her mother was fast asleep. Fearfully, Douceline snatched up the consecrated picture from the shelf where she had placed it, and turned it around so that she might hide herself from the face of Jesus. She took off her nightgown and got dressed, all a-tremble; then she took the picture out into the fields, and buried it.

She returned, weeping and nearly fainting, to the house. Her mother had awakened by that time, and took care to explain to her what had occurred. Douceline accepted the explanation, as she was bound to do. Nevertheless, she could not believe that what had happened was entirely natural. She felt bitterly resentful of the fact that her own Jesus, whom she had felt compelled to suffocate beneath the soil, had borne silent witness to her sin and degradation. That Jesus now seemed to her to be dead.

When her mother went back to bed, though, Douceline tried to calm herelf by recalling to mind the stories she had been told of the lives of the saints. As she drifted back to sleep herself, all the strange names which she had stored up in her head while listening to sermons and legends seemed to echo in her ears like the sound of bells. She continued to hear them tolling, louder than the peals which called the faithful to mass on Sundays, as she slipped into a dream; but one name gradually separated itself from all the rest, sounding and resounding within the imaginary chimes:

Pé-hor—Pé-hor—Pé-hor—Pé-hor.

Demons are like obedient dogs; they come when they

are called. Péhor loves the daughters of men, and still remembers fondly the days when he excited the passions of Cozbi, daughter of that Sur who was prince of the Midianites. Péhor came in response to Douceline's call; he was drawn to her by the combined attraction of her freshly-attained puberty and her earlier self-pollution; he took up his chosen lodging in the inn of her vice, where he consented to be caressed, relishing the carnal attentions of her feverish hands, without any fear that he might suffer here the kind of blow with which, in olden times, Phineas had simultaneously cut short the delights of Cozbi and the pleasures of Zambri, while the son of Salu was entered in the body of the daughter of Sur.

Although it was the middle of the night, the room was illuminated by the demon's presence. All the objects in it were haloed with light, as though they had become luminous themselves and had acquired the power to radiate warmth.

All was calm, and a ruddy shadow seemed to descend upon Douceline, closing all the doors of her perception. Then, ecstasy came.

Douceline savoured the moment of pleasure's arrival, and all the thrilling frissons which travelled the length and breadth of her body before eventually becoming localised. The red shadow which lay upon her was interrupted and traversed by messenger lights which insinuated themselves into every fibre of her being, dancing to a rapid rhythm. In the end, there was an explosive sensation like the bursting of a skyrocket: an exquisite *crack* which flashed within her brain and down her spine, through the marrow of her bones and into all her mucous membranes, hardening the nipples of her breasts. All the silken hairs which dressed her skin were elevated; stirred up as grass might be stirred

81

when lightly brushed by a skimming breeze.

After the last quiver of her startled flesh, the valves of her heart seemed to open wide, and the filtered pleasure coursed through her veins to touch every cell in her body.

Péhor, at that moment, rose up out of his hiding-place and magnified himself, growing swiftly into the image of a beautiful young man. Douceline, who was by now beyond the reach of astonishment, admired and loved him upon the instant. She laid her head upon his shoulder, and fell contentedly asleep, conscious of nothing save for the fact that she was gladly held in the embrace of Péhor.

****

From that night on, Douceline's life continued in a similar fashion. By day she delighted herself with the memory of her nights, recapitulating her delectation by dwelling luxuriously upon the impudicity of her encounters, upon the acuity of the caresses and the crushing pressure of the kisses of the invisible and intangible Péhor. She gloried in the languorous pleasures which continued to surge within her, almost magically, after that first sweetly-perfumed eruption of joy.

What a being Péhor was! She never wondered, though, what *manner* of being he might be; she was heedless of everything save for the enjoyment. The multiplicity of the spasms which overcame her reduced her to an animal level of consciousness, and she lived in a carnal dream.

In constantly renewing her solitary debauchery, she played the part of the virginal Psyché, abandoning herself to whatever dark angel cared to claim her. She had not the strength of will or the reticence to resist; she did not care whether her visitant came clad in rust-red

82

shadows or fulgurant with cerebral light.

Douceline had reached the age of fifteen when, in the shed where her family's milch-cow was kept, an itinerant peddler of religious tracts took advantage of her enervated state of mind to press his attentions upon her. She let him do what he wanted, and did not suffer any pain or indignity at all while he did it, having already been amply deflowered by the demon of her audacious imagination. The man's lewd grunts and grimaces made him altogether ridiculous in her eyes, and when he looked at her—having straightened his clothing again—with an amorously fond expression she rose promptly to her feet and burst out laughing. Then she shrugged her shoulders and went away.

But she was punished for what she had allowed to be done to her: after that, Péhor came to her no more.

In the weeks that followed, she no longer dreamed about Péhor when she tended the cow in the shed; instead, she could not help but remember the peddler, and not altogether without shame. The incident had left its legacy, and she became afraid. She had seen pregnant women in church, lighting candles to the Holy Virgin and praying that they might safely be delivered of their burdens, and she in her turn lit a large candle and placed it on its spike, praying that her own belly might not swell up.

She recognised the fact that her demon had been exorcised, and took the opportunity to devote herself once again to her prayers. She began to avoid the cowshed, preferring to be on her knees on the paving stones of a small chapel where an image of Jesus was lodged. Here she took herself to look up into the loving and reassuring face, as she had so loved to do in earlier times.

Even without the interventions of Péhor, however,

she continued to indulge her secret vice. But now it seemed that she had begun to be corroded by its effects: her cheeks became hollow, and she was continually seized by fits of coughing. She was so tormented in her sleep that she felt as if she might as well have spent her nights in the stinking straw of the cowshed, trampled by the hooves of the cow.

****

A morning eventually came when Douceline trembled so violently that she could not put on her stockings. She had to lie down again, and terrible pains began to afflict her belly. Her inflamed ovaries throbbed as though they were constantly being pricked by bundles of needles. From that morning on, she was unable to get up.

During the days which followed, as she lay in agony upon her desolate bed, she was frequently visited by fanciful dreams of an unexpected naïvety, which recalled to her mind the icons of her lost innocence. Her rapturous delusions showed her, in succession, God the Father, all clad in white like a priest she had once seen celebrating mass during Lent; St. John playing in the celestial groves with curly-fleeced and beribboned lambs; Our Lord, dressed all in gold with a long red beard; and the face of the Holy Virgin, smiling from a blue-tinted cloud.

In later days, however, these consoling apparitions abandoned her. It was as though the sky itelf had darkened above her, to reflect her more recent complicity with the demon. The hypocrisy of her child-like visions could not be sustained, and the impenitent sinner yielded herself again to the memory of the horrible infamies which she had celebrated with he whom she had chosen to be her eternal master. Péhor returned to lodge once again in the secret residence where she had consented to become impure.

Douceline felt herself ravaged afresh by the demon's caresses, which were now excruciating instead of tender. It was as though her flesh were being teased by stinging nettles or bitten by a great host of ants. Her ripened private parts were all engorged, opened up like a split fig, and they seemed almost to be rotting while she still lived.

While she endured the hours of unremitting agony the laughter of Péhor resounded in her belly like the changes rung on Maundy Thursday, which seemed to emerge from all the graves and tombs of humankind.

Péhor abandoned himself entirely to the hilarity of his demonic satisfaction, and to amuse himself further he puffed himself up with rude vapours, which he let out loudly in gusts of noisome wind. Then he subjected her, as he had so often done before, to his amorous kisses—save that now he substituted mordant bites for ecstatic spasms. Douceline screamed in pain, but it seemed to her that Péhor cried out more strongly than she did, filling up her abdomen with the shrill stridency of his voice, and making it vibrate with resonance.

It seemed, as the end approached, that there began a great stir and bustle in the filthy haven where the demon had found asylum, which gradually spread through the pit of her stomach a terrible sensation of squeezing and choking.

Péhor was at last taking leave of his residence.

As he broke out of his hiding-place, Péhor drove his talons into Douceline's breast; he tore at her heart, and rent the soft spongy tissue of her lungs. Then her throat dilated, like the swollen neck of a serpent regurgitating the sticky remains of its digested prey, and a great gout of blood spurted from her mouth, ignominiously expelled as though by a drunken hiccup.

She was able to take one last breath, although she

was very near to losing consciousness. Her eyes were closed, and her hands were cast wide; she floated upon the soft waves of the tide which fate sends to carry the damned away, like wrecked ships, to the abysmal depths of Hell.

She felt a single kiss applied very precisely to her lips: a kiss excrementally and purulently rank. Thus the soul of Douceline quitted the world: sucked in and swallowed up by the demon Péhor, and securely ensconced within his entrails.

****

8.

ROXANA RUNS LUNATICK
by R. Murray Gilchrist

Amongst the May poetry in the ninety-first volume of the *British Review* is the following composition by Lady Penwhile, whose Roxana had shaken the town for a whole season. 'Placed in the hand of the Satyr who guards the Puzzle-Pegs at N____, with a tress of hair for Hyperion.'

If so be that Hyperion visit thy stately lawn on the anniversary of our parting, O Satyr, wilt thou tell him that R____ hath oft sigh'd for him there, and that, tho' she has worn green Hellebore, such as he gave her a year agone– when he vow'd an early return– her hopes grow ever fainter and fainter. Say to him that she is bound in golden chains, but that her heart sings when she thinks of him–(ay, her heart is ever singing)– whisper that she loves him more as every moment passes. And when thou hast done all this, bid Pan trill from his pipes, whilst thou chantest this ditty.

Five halting verses follow, wherein 'tis told that the lovers had parted, that Roxana had wedded an old man, that she felt incapable of expressing in words the vehemency of her passion. But dear, pleasing ghosts haunted her chambers day and night.

My lord's cast-off doxy sent the journal, with a venomous letter bidding him rub his forehead, for fear of the cuckoo. So he pondered in his book-room, his half-blinded eyes fixed upon the logs ; and, after many struggles with his better nature, he devised a plot worthy of Satan himself.

For Roxana was a prize worth keeping. She was pale, exquisitely pale. One forgot her eyes, but remembered that somewhere in her face was seen the sudden starting of a timid woman's soul....Hast ever watched the heart of a palm-catkin when a wanton hand has fired it ? Lurking under the outer blackness are red and yellow intermixed. Such was the colour of her hair that fell from nape to heel. Hands that alone might have quenched lawless desires : of a subtle pink, like the ivory that comes from Africk.

Few women could have given such devotion as she gave my lord. By some stratagem, some wild persuasion in her moment of wavering, he had gained possession. Compassion weakens distaste, and he had posed long as one broken-hearted. How daintily did she acknowledge his requirements, how sweet her service had become! When he had decided concerning Hyperion, his punctilio was greater than ever : the house rang with shrill commands for madam's comfort, and he sat hour after hour listening to her tenderest songs. She was a lutanist too, and great in the Italian masters.

On Oak Day, when men and maids bore the garland through the park, a country fellow came to mistress and delivered her a note. My lord was not present, but she grew faint and chill, and had much ado to applaud the pageant. With unseemly haste she withdrew to her chamber and read there—

'Many days have passed ere I could summon courage. At twilight to-morrow we will meet ; I have discovered the place. What manner of love was mine erstwhile that thou wert false?'

In her cabinet were many choice silks. She made a bag of the richest, and put the folded sheet inside, and spread ambergris upon it, then hung it between her breasts. That night as she slept her fingers relaxed, and my lord took thence the token, and read it, gnashing his teeth. He put it back : so that in the morning flush, when her hand sought the thing, it seemed untouched.

That day passed so wearily! In her spouse's company she was gay and brilliant ; all her paleness had disappeared, and a feverish red pulsed in her cheeks. And he was brimful of paradox and of jesting, but sometimes she trembled because of the fearsome coldness of his looks. Once, when she fawned upon him he put her away, not untenderly.

'Sweetheart,' he said towards sunset, 'an' if thou wert false!'

'Ay, me,' she faltered, for the repetition of Hyperion's words struck her with terror. 'False! false!'

It was growing dusk ; he peered close to the clock-face. 'More than two months have passed since we came here,' he noted, breaking the ominous silence. 'And yet this place is strange to you. Let us visit the old house— see, here are the keys! Dearest, lean on my arm.'

They passed through the garden to the porch and so to the mildewed avenues of the pre-Elizabethan part where all the lumber was stored. My lord saw Roxana's bodice swell as if the threads would burst. Soon they reached a great hall lighted with green windows, whose dimness scarce revealed the many sacks of too long-garnered grain, where the mice ran in and out. There, near the foot of a staircase that led to the gallery, he left her, and she heard the clicking of a lock.

My lord went to an upper chamber whence he could see the outlet of the maze. The belling of his red-eyed dogs as they strutted in their leash tickled his ears : he laughed and rubbed his forehead. The moon rose, and he could hear Roxana clamouring in the hall. After a while he descended by another way, and took out his deathhounds, and went towards the trysting-place.

Roxana could not know what happened in the darkness. The agony of the man whose every vestige of clothes was torn away, and whose white flesh gaped bloodily, was hidden from her by the seven feet of masonry that parted them as he leaped madly into the courtyard. Nor could she hear his worn, querulous cry—such a cry as the peewit makes before dawn. Yet, withal, her hands began to drum in her lap.

When the darkness was intense my lord came back. He felt for Roxana in the place where he had left her. She was not there : an hour before she had climbed to the gallery. He groped painfully round the walls.

In one corner soft delicious things like nets of gossamer fell on his fingers. He stooped to the floor, and touched more of them. Above was a sound of tearing, but no panting nor indrawing of breath. Another web fluttered past his face ; his lips began to quiver. It was Roxana's hair.

9.

Passages from
A SEASON IN HELL
by Arthur Rimbaud

At one time, if I remember correctly, my life was a feast at which all hearts were opened and all wines flowed.

One evening, I sat Beauty on my knees. I found her bitter, and I abused her.

I have taken up arms against justice.

I have run away. O witches, O misery, O hatred, it is to you that my treasure has been entrusted!

I contrived to erase from my mind all human hope. Upon every joy, to strangle it, I pounced as noiselessly as a wild beast.

I have summoned executioners so that, in perishing, I might bite the butts of their rifles. I have called up plagues, in order to suffocate myself with blood and sand. Misfortune has become my god. I have stretched myself out in the mire. I have desiccated myself with the appearance of crime. And I have sported cleverly with madness.

Spring has brought me the frightful laugh of the idiot.

But lately, having found myself at the point of uttering the last *croak*, I am minded to go forth in search of the key to that ancient feast, where I might perhaps recover my appetite for life.

That key is charity—this inspiration proves that I have been dreaming!

"You will remain a hyena, and all the rest..." exclaims

the demon who crowned me with such agreeable poppies. "Attain death with all your appetites, your egotism and all the deadly sins."

Ah! I have taken up too many of them. But my dear Satan, I beseech you to look upon me with a less irritated eye. While you await the few petty infractions which are still owing—you, who admire in a writer the lack of descriptive and instructive abilities—I, the damned, offer you these few horrid pages torn from my notebook.

Bad Blood

I have, by virtue of my Gaulish ancestry, pale blue eyes, a narrow skull and a lack of skill in the arts of strife. I suppose that my mode of dress is as barbarous as theirs; but I do not butter my hair.

The Gauls were the most inept flayers of cattle and burners of grass of their era.

From them, I have: idolatry and a love of sacrilege— oh, every possible vice: wrath, love of luxury (how magnificent is luxury!) and, above all, mendacity and sloth.

I have a horror of all trades. Masters and servants, all peasants, unspeakable! The hand which guides the pen is no better than the hand which guides the plough— what an age of hands this is! I shall never be handy. After all, domesticity requires too much control. The honesty of living as a beggar is heart-breaking. Criminals are as disgusting as eunuchs; for myself, I am intact, and it's all the same to me.

But who has made my tongue so perfidious that it has so far been able to guide and protect my slothfulness? Wherever I have dwelt I have been idler than a toad, never using my body to make a living. There is not a family in Europe that I do not know—I mean families like my own, who hold to the declaration of the Rights of Man—I have known every son of such families!

If only I had antecedents at some point or other in the history of France!

But no—nothing.

It is quite evident to me that mine has always been inferior stock. I cannot comprehend revolution. My race never rose up except to pillage, like wolves worrying a beast they have not killed.

I recollect the history of France, eldest daughter of the Church. As a liegeman, I would have made the journey to the Holy Land; I have in my head the roads which cross the Swabian plains, views of Byzantium and the ramparts of Suleiman; the cult of the Virgin Mary and pity for the crucified awaken in me in the midst of a thousand profane enchantments...leprous, I am sitting on broken pots and nettles, at the foot of a wall corroded by the sun... Much later, as a mercenary, I would have camped out beneath the night-skies of Germany.

Ah, again! I dance at the witches' sabbat in a red clearing, with old women and children.

I do not remember anything more distant than this land and Christianity. There is no end to these meetings with my past selves, but I am always alone, without family; I do not even know what language I spoke. I never see myself among Christ's disciples, nor in the council-chambers of the Nobles who are Christ's representatives.

What was I in the last century? I can only rediscover my present self. More vagabonds, more indistinct wars. Inferior stock is everywhere: the people, so to speak, reason; the nation has science.

Oh, science! Everything is improved. For the body and the soul—our provisions for life's journey—there are medicine and philosophy: old wives' remedies and new arrangements of popular songs. And the diversions of princes and the games which they forbade: geography, cosmology, mechanics, chemistry....!

Science, the new nobility! Progress. The world is on the march! Why does it not turn around?

This is the fantasy of numbers. We advance in the *Spirit*; this is absolutely certain, I speak with the voice of the oracle. I understand, but not knowing how to explain myself without heathen words, I would rather be quiet.

Heathen blood comes back! The Spirit is close at hand; why does Christ not help me by giving my soul nobility and liberty? Alas, the Gospel has gone! The Gospel! The Gospel!

I await God avidly. I am of inferior stock, since time immemorial.

Here I am on the shore of Brittany. How the towns light up in the evening. My day is done; I am quitting Europe. The marine air will scorch my lungs, ruinous climates will tan my skin. To swim, to trample the grass, to hunt, especially to smoke; to drink liqueurs as strong as molten metal...as my cherished ancestors did, gathered around their fires.

I shall return with limbs of iron and darkened skin, wild-eyed; from my features I shall be judged to belong to a mighty race. I shall have gold; I shall be lazy and coarse. Women are attentive to those fierce invalids who return from hot lands. I shall dabble in politics. Saved!

In the meantime, I am accursed, I loathe my fatherland. Best to have a good long drunken sleep on the beach.

There is no escape. Let us take to these roads again,

replete with my vice: the vice which has thrust its roots of suffering into my side since I attained the age of reason, which climbs into the sky, beats me, knocks me down, drags me along.

The end of innocence and timidity. It is resolved: not to carry through life my disgust and my treason.

Go on! The march, the burden, the desert, ennui and anger.

To whom shall I hire myself? Which beast must be adored, which holy image assaulted? Which hearts shall I break? What lie must I uphold? In whose blood should I wade?

Instead, protect oneself from justice—life simply goes on, brutishly—to lift up, with a withered fist, the lid of one's coffin, to lie in it, to suffocate. Thus to avoid old age and danger: terror is so un-French!

Ah, I am so utterly forlorn that I could dedicate my impulses towards perfection to any divine image at all.

Oh what abnegation, what marvellous charity is mine, even while I am down here!

De profundis Domine, how stupid I am!

When I was very much a child I admired the intractable convict upon whom the prison gates close and close again forever; I visited inns and hotels which might have been blessed by his presence; I saw *with his mind* the blue sky and the flourishing labour of the countryside; I sniffed out his destiny in the towns. He had more strength than a saint, more common sense than a traveller, and himself—himself alone!—to bear witness to his fame and reason.

On the roads, during the winter nights—without shelter, without clothing, without bread—a voice would grip my icy heart: "Weakness or strength: look at you, this is strength. You know not where you are going, nor

95

why you go; go everywhere, respond to everything. You cannot be killed again, if you are already a cadaver." In the morning I would have such a forlorn expression and such a mortified countenance that those I encountered *probably did not even see me.*

In the towns the mud would suddenly seem to me to be red and black, like a mirror when a lamp swings back and forth in a neighbouring room, like a treasure in the forest! Good luck, I would cry, and I would see a sea of flame and smoke in the sky—and, to the left and right of me, all the wealth of the world ablaze like a million thunderbolts.

But orgiastic indulgence and the amity of women were forbidden me. Not even a companion. I could see myself before an exasperated crowd, facing a firing-squad, weeping with a misery which they could not have understood, and *forgiving!* Like Joan of Arc! "Priests, professors, masters, you are making a mistake in delivering me up to justice. I have never been one of these people here; I have never been a Christian; I am of the kind which sang under torture; I do not understand laws; I have no moral sensibility; I am a brute beast; you are making a mistake..."

Yes, I have eyes which are closed against your light. I am an animal, a negro. But I might be saved. You are negroes in disguise, you maniacs, predators, misers. Merchant, you are a negro; magistrate, you are a negro; general, you are a negro; emperor, restless dotard, you are a negro: you have drunk duty-free liquor distilled by Satan. The nation is inspired by fever and cancer. Invalids and the aged are so respectable that they demand to be boiled alive. The shrewdest thing is to quit the continent where madness is on the prowl, seeking to take these wretches hostage. I am going to the true realm of the children of Ham.

Do I understand nature now? Do I understand myself? *No more words.* I entomb the dead in my guts. Cries, drumbeats, dance, dance, dance, *dance*! I cannot even see the hour when, as the white men disembark, I shall fall into oblivion.

Hunger, thirst, cries, dance, dance, dance, *dance!*

The white men are disembarking. The cannon! We must submit to baptism, wearing clothes, and work.

I have received in my heart the *coup de grâce*. Ah, I had not foreseen this!

I have done no evil. The days will pass me by lightly, repentance will be set aside for me. I shall not have undergone the torments of a soul nearly dead to goodness, where stern light flares up like funerary candles. The lot of a son of good family, an early grave flooded with limpid tears. Doubtless debauchery is stupid, vice is stupid, corruption must be cast aside. But the time has not yet come when the clock will strike nothing but the hour of unmitigated woe! Am I to be lifted up like an infant, to play in paradise forgetful of all misery!

Quickly! Are there other lives? To sleep amid riches is impossible. Wealth has always been so public. Divine love alone concedes the keys of wisdom. I see that nature is nothing but a display of benevolence. Farewell chimeras, ideals, errors...

The rational song of the angels rises from the vessel of salvation; it is divine love—two loves! I may die of earthly love or die of devotion. I have left souls whose pain will be aggravated by my departure! Among the shipwrecked, you have chosen me; those who remain, are they not my friends?

Save them!

Rationality is born in me. The world is good. I shall bless life. I shall love my brothers. These are no longer childish promises, nor the hope of evading old age and death. God is my strength, and I praise God.

Ennui is no longer my lover. Rages, debaucheries, madness, whose elations and disasters I know—my entire burden is laid down. Let us look down, without dizziness, into the depths of my innocence.

I will no longer be capable of asking for the refreshment of the bastinado. I do not believe that I have set forth on my honeymoon with Jesus Christ as a father-in-law.

I am not a prisoner of my rationality. I have said: God. I desire freedom in salvation: how is that end to be pursued? Frivolous inclinations have deserted me. No more need of devotion to duty nor of divine love. I do not regret the passing of the age of tenderheartedness. Everyone has his reason, scorn and charity; I retain my place at the summit of this angelic ladder of common sense.

As for conventional happiness, domestic or not...no, I cannot. I am too dissipated, too feeble. Life flourishes in labour, an ancient truism; as for me, my life is not heavy enough, it flies away and hovers on high, far above the activity which is the focal point of worldly existence.

What an old woman I am becoming, bereft of the courage to love death!

If only God would grant me celestial calm, on high, the prayer—like the saints of old—saints! strong men! anchorites, artists of a kind no longer necessary!

An unending farce! My innocence would make me weep. Life is the farce acted out by everyone.

Enough! Here is the punishment. *Get going!*

Ah, my lungs are scorched, my head is throbbing! Night rolls in my eyes by virtue of this sunlight! My heart...my limbs...

Where are we going? Into combat? I am weak! The others advance. My equipment, my weapons...the weather!....

Fire! Fire at me! Here! Or I surrender. Cowards! I shall kill myself! I shall hurl myself under the horses' feet!

Ah!....

I will get used to it.

That would be the French way, the path of honour!

Night in Hell

I have swallowed a prodigious draught of poison—thrice blessed be the counsel which has come to me!—my guts are afire. The violence of the venom torments my limbs, deforms me, casts me down. I am dying of thirst, suffocating, unable to cry out. This is Hell, eternal suffering! See how the flames leap up! I burn, as one must. Ho, demon!

I have caught a glimpse of that conversion which leads to goodness and happiness. Let me describe the vision; the atmosphere of hell cannot tolerate hymns! It was of millions of charming creatures, a sweet spiritual harmony, strength and peace, noble ambitions and I know not what.

Noble ambitions!

And yet this is life—if damnation is eternal! A man who wishes to mutilate himself is certainly damned, is he not? I believe that I am in Hell, therefore I *am* in Hell. That is the fulfilment of the catechism. I am the slave of my baptism. Parents, you have secured my misery and your own. Poor innocent! Hell has no power over pagans— I am still alive! Much later, the delights of damnation will become more profound. A crime, quickly, that I might fall into oblivion at the behest of man-made law.

Shut up, shut up! This is shame, and reproach: Satan himself says that fire is ignoble, that my anger is utterly foolish—enough! Errors have been whispered to me, magic spells, false perfumes, puerile music—and to think that I grasp the truth, that I see justice: my judgment is sane and settled, I am ready for perfection....Pride. My scalp is dry. Pity! Lord, I am afraid. I am thirsty, so thirsty! Ah, childhood, grass, rain, rocks in a pool, *moonlight as the clock struck twelve*...the devil is in the belfry at such an hour. Mary! Holy Virgin!....the horror of my stupidity.

Down there, are they not honest souls, who wish me well? Come...I have a pillow over my mouth, they cannot hear me, they are phantoms. Anyway, no one ever thinks about anyone else. Let no one approach. I smell something burning, to be sure.

The hallucinations are innumerable. That is surely what has always afflicted me: lack of faith in history, obliviousness of principles. I shall keep quiet about it: poets and visionaries would be jealous. I am a thousand times richer than they, let us be as mean as the sea.

Ah, look there! The clock of life has suddenly stopped. I am no longer in the world. Theology is to be taken seriously; hell is certainly *below*—and Heaven on high. Ecstasy and nightmare slumber in a nest of flame.

What mischief is performed while one waits in the countryside...Satan, Ferdinand, runs riot with the wild seeds...Jesus walks on the purplish brambles without trampling them down...Jesus once walked on troubled waters. The lantern showed him to us standing up, white-skinned and brown-haired, flanked by an emerald wave....

I will unveil all mysteries: mysteries religious or natural, death, birth, the future, the past, cosmogony, the void. I am a master of phantasmagoria.

Listen!....

I have all the talents! There is no one here and there is someone: I do not wish to spread my treasure far and wide. Do they want negro songs or belly-dancing? Do they want me to disappear, or to immerse myself in the quest for the *ring*? What do they want? I will make gold, or sovereign remedies.

Have faith in me, then; faith is a solace, a guide, a healing. All of you, come—even the little children—that I may console you, that one might pour out his heart to you...the marvellous heart! Poor men, labourers! I do not ask for prayers; with your confidence alone I shall be happy.

And let us think about me. I have scant regret on behalf of the world. I am lucky that I no longer suffer. My life, regrettably, was naught but tender folly.

Bah! Let us make all the faces we can.

Decidedly, we are outside the world. There is no longer any sound. My sense of touch is gone. Ah, my château, my Saxony, my wood of willows! Evening, mornings, nights, days....How tired I am!

I ought to have a Hell of my own for wrath, a Hell of my own for pride, and a Hell to cherish; a concert of Hells.

I am dying of lassitude. This is the tomb; I am going to be with the worms, horror of horrors! Satan, joker, you wish to melt me with your charms. I protest. I protest! One prick of the fork, one gush of flame.

Ah, to climb again to life! To stare upon our deformities. And that poison, that kiss a thousand times accursed! My weakness, the cruelty of the world! My God, have pity, hide me, I am still too bad! I am hidden and I am not.

It is the fire which rises up again with its damned soul.

101

Delirium I
The Foolish Virgin
The Infernal Spouse

Let us hear the confession of one of the company of Hell:

"O divine Spouse, my Lord, refuse not the confession of the saddest of your servants. I am lost. I am drunk. I am impure. What a life!

"Forgive me, divine Lord, forgive! Ah, forgive! How many tears! How many more tears in time to come, I hope!

"In time, I will understand the divine Spouse! I was born to submit myself to Him—the other can beat me for now!

"At present I am at the bottom of the world! Oh my friends!...no, not my friends...Never was there such delirium, such torture...how stupid it is!

"Ah, I am suffering, I cry out! Truly I suffer. And yet all is permitted to me, burdened with the scorn of the most scornful hearts.

"Anyhow, let us make this confession, only to repeat it twenty times more—every bit as mournful, every bit as insignificant!

"I am the slave of that infernal Spouse which spoiled the foolish virgins. It is definitely the same demon. It is not a ghost, it is not a phantom. But I who have lost my virtue, who am damned and dead to the world—no one will kill me!—how can I describe him to you? I can no longer even speak. I am in mourning, I weep, I am afraid. A breath of fresh air, Lord, if you will grant it...if you will only grant it!

"I am a widow...I was a widow...but yes, I was perfectly respectable once, and I was not born to become a skeleton! He was little more than a child...his mysterious delicacy had seduced me. I had abandoned all my responsibilities in order to follow him. What a life! Real life is somewhere else. We are not in the world. I go where he goes, as necessity dictates. He often loses his temper with me—*with me, poor soul,* the Devil! He is a Devil, you know, *he is not a man.*

"He says: 'I don't like women. Love is in need of reinvention, that's certain. They are capable of no more than desiring a secure position. Once that is gained, feelings and beauty are set aside; there remains only cold disdain, the common fodder of marriage nowadays. Or else I see women showing signs of goodwill, with whom I myself might have become good friends, devoured from the beginning by brutes as sensitive as blocks of wood....'

"I listen to him glorifying infamy, turning cruelty into charm. 'I am of distant race; my forefathers were Scandinavian; they pierced their sides and drank their own blood. I will lacerate every part of my body, I will tattoo myself, I want to become as ugly as a Mongol; you will see, I will howl in the streets. I want to become utterly mad with rage. Never show me jewellery; I would grovel and writhe on the carpet. The wealth which I desire is to be stained all over with blood. Never shall I work....' On many a night his demon seized me, and we rolled over and over as I wrestled with him! Often, at night, drunk, he lies in wait in the street or in the house, in order to frighten me to death. 'My throat will certainly be cut; it will be *disgusting*'. Oh, those days when he wants to go out walking with criminal intent!

"Sometimes he spoke, in an oddly compassionate manner, about the dying who are brought to repentance, about the unfortunates who most certainly exist, about painful labour, about heart-breaking departures. In the dens where we got drunk he would weep on behalf of the

103

throng which surrounded us, the livestock of misery. He would help drunkards to their feet in the dark streets. He had the pity which a bad mother reserves for little children. He would go forth with the affectations of a little girl learning the catechism. He pretended to be enlightened on every subject: commerce, art, medicine. I followed him, as necessity dictated.

"I saw all the decor with which, in the imagination, he surrounded himself: clothes, fabrics, furniture; I lent him weapons, another form. I saw everything which touched him, as he would have wished to create it for himself. When he seemed to me to be in low spirits, I set myself to follow him in strange and complicated acts, going all the way whether they were good or evil: I was certain that I could never enter into his world. How many hours have I spent at night, sitting up beside his dear sleeping body, trying to find out why he wished so fervently to avoid reality. There was never another man with such a vocation. I realised—without fearing for him—that he could pose a serious danger to society. Perhaps he has the secret of *changing life*? No, he is merely in search of it, I would tell myself. At the end of the day, his charity is bewitched, and I am its prisoner. No other soul could have had the strength—the strength of desperation!—to bear it, to be protected and loved by him. Besides, I did not imagine that it could happen to another: one sees one's own Angel, never the Angel of another, that's what I think. I was inside his soul as though I were inside a palace which has been emptied so that no one will look upon a person as lacking in nobility as you, that's all. Alas! I was so dependent on him. But what did he want with my lifeless and cowardly existence? He wasn't making me any better, though he wasn't killing me! Sadly vexed, I would sometimes say to him: 'I understand you.' He would shrug his shoulders.

"So, as my grief was unendingly renewed, and I became more wretched in my own eyes—as I would have in all eyes which cared to fix their stare upon me, were I not condemned to be forever forgotten by everyone—I was more and more starved of his benevolence. With his kisses and his loving embraces, it was a kind heaven, albeit a gloomy one, which I entered, and in which I would have wished to be left: poor, deaf, dumb and blind. I was already accustomed to it. I saw us as two good children, free to wander in the Paradise of sorrow. We were well suited. Deeply moved, we worked together. But after a penetrating caress he would say: 'How peculiar all these things you have experienced will seem to you, when I am no longer here. When you no longer have my arms beneath your neck, nor my breast to rest yourself upon, nor this mouth upon your eyes. Because it will be necessary for me to go away, far away, one day. Then it will be necessary that I help others; it is my duty, though it is one I can scarcely relish...dear heart...' Immediately I saw myself, after his departure, prey to giddiness, precipitated into the most frightful darkness: death. I made him promise that he would never desert me. He made that lover's promise twenty times. It was just as meaningless as my saying: 'I understand you.'

"Oh, I have never been jealous of him. He won't leave me, I suppose. What would he become? He has no skill; he will never work. He wishes to live as a sleepwalker. Would his goodness and kindness, on their own, give him rights in the real world? For a few moments, I forget the pitiable state into which I have fallen; he will make me strong, we shall travel, we shall hunt in the desert, sleep on the pavements of unknown towns, without cares, without troubles. Or else I shall wake up, and find that laws and customs have changed—thanks to his magical power—the world, in remaining the same, will leave me to my desires, my pleasures, my nonchalance. Oh, to have that adventurous life which exists in children's books for my recompense—I have suffered so much, will you give it to me? He cannot. I know nothing of *his* ideal. He has told me that he has regrets, and hopes; but they can take no account of me. Does he speak to God? I am in the profoundest depths of the abyss, and I no longer know how to pray.

"If he explained his sorrows to me, could I comprehend them any better than his mockeries? He attacks me, he spends hours making me ashamed of everything that ever had the power to affect me, and becomes impatient if I weep.

"—'You see that elegant young man going into that fine and placid house? His name is Duval, Dufour, Armand, Maurice, isn't it? A woman devoted herself to loving that stupid miscreant; she is dead, most certainly a saint in Heaven by now. You will destroy me as he has destroyed that woman. That is our destiny, we who have charitable hearts...' Alas! He had days when all men bestirring themselves seemed mere playthings of bizarre delirium; he would laugh dreadfully, excessively—then he would resume his mimicry of a young mother, a beloved sister. If he were less wild, we might be saved! But his gentleness too is deadly. I am in his power—oh, I am mad!

"One day, perhaps he will disappear as if by magic; but it is necessary for me to know, if he is taken up to heaven, so that I may see something of the assumption of my little friend."

An odd couple!

****

10.

THE VIRGIN OF THE SEVEN DAGGERS
by Vernon Lee

I

In a grass-grown square of the city of Grenada, with
the snows of the Sierra staring down on it all winter, and
the sunshine glaring on its coloured tiles all summer,
stands the yellow free-stone Church of Our Lady of the
Seven Daggers. Huge garlands of pears and melons
hang, carved in stone, about the cupolas and windows;
and monstrous heads with laurel wreaths and epaulets
burst forth from all the arches. The roof shines
barbarically, green, white, and brown, above the tawny
stone; and on each of the two balconied and staircased
belfries, pricked up like ears above the building's
monstrous front, there sways a weather-vane, figuring
a heart transfixed with seven long-hilted daggers. Inside,
the church presents a superb example of the pompous,
pedantic, and contorted Spanish architecture of the
reign of Philip IV.

On colonnade is hoisted colonnade, pilasters climb
upon pilasters, bases and capitals jut out, double and
threefold, from the ground, in mid-air and near the
ceiling; jagged lines everywhere as of spikes for exhibiting
the heads of traitors; dizzy ledges as of mountain
precipices for dashing to bits Morisco rebels; line warring
with line and curve with curve; a place in which the mind
staggers bruised and half stunned. But the grandeur of
the church is not merely terrific – it is also gallant and
ceremonious: everything on which labour can be wasted
is laboured, everything on which gold can be lavished is
gilded; columns and architraves curl like the curls of a

107

peruke; walls and vaultings are flowered with precious marbles and fretted with carving and gilding like a gala dress; stone and wood are woven like lace; stucco is whipped and clotted like pastry-cook's cream and crust; everything is crammed with flourishes like a tirade by Calderon, or a sonnet by Gongora. A golden retable closes the church at the end; a black and white rood screen, of jasper and alabaster, fences it in the middle; while along each aisle hang chandeliers as for a ball; and paper flowers are stacked on every altar.

Amidst all this gloomy yet festive magnificence, and surrounded, in each minor chapel, by a train of waxen Christs with bloody wounds and spangled loin-cloths, and madonnas of lesser fame weeping beady tears and carrying be-wigged infants, thrones the great Madonna of the Seven Daggers.

Is she seated or standing? 'Tis impossible to decide. She seems, beneath the gilded canopy and between the twisted columns of jasper, to be slowly rising, or slowly sinking, in a solemn court curtsy, buoyed up by her vast farthingale. Her skirts bulge out in melon-shaped folds, all damasked with minute heart's-ease, and brocaded with silver roses; the reddish shimmer of the gold wire, the bluish shimmer of the silver floss, blending into a strange melancholy hue without a definite name. Her body is cased like a knife in its sheath, the mysterious russet and violet of the silk made less definable still by the network of seed pearl, and the veils of delicate lace which fall from head to waist. Her face, surmounting rows upon rows of pearls, is made of wax, white with black glass eyes and a tiny coral mouth; she stares steadfastly forth with a sad and ceremonious smile. Her head is crowned with a great jewelled crown; her slippered feet rest on a crescent moon, and in her right hand she holds a lace pocket handkerchief. In her bodice, a little clearing is made among the brocade and the seed pearl, and into this are stuck seven gold-hilted knives.

Such is Our Lady of the Seven Daggers; and such her church.

One winter afternoon, more than two hundred years ago, Charles the Melancholy being King of Spain and the New World, there chanced to be kneeling in that church, already empty and dim save for the votive lamps, and more precisely on the steps before the Virgin of the Seven Daggers, a cavalier of very great birth, fortune, magnificence, and wickedness, Don Juan Gusman del Pulgar, Count of Miramor. "O Great Madonna, O Snow Peak untrodden of the Sierras, O Sea unnavigated of the tropics, O Gold Ore unhandled by the Spaniard, O New Minted Doubloon unpocketed by the Jew" – thus prayed that devout man of quality – "look down benignly on thy knight and servant, accounted judiciously one of the greatest men of this kingdom, in wealth and honours, fearing neither the vengeance of foes, nor the rigour of laws, yet content to stand foremost among thy slaves. Consider that I have committed every crime without faltering, both murder, perjury, blasphemy, and sacrilege, yet have I always respected thy name, nor suffered any man to give greater praise to other Madonnas, neither her of Good Counsel, nor her of Swift Help, nor our Lady of Mount Carmel, nor our Lady of St. Luke of Bologna in Italy, nor our Lady of the Slipper of Famagosta in Cyprus, nor our Lady of the Pillar of Saragossa, great Madonnas every one, and revered throughout the world for their powers, and by most men preferred to thee; yet has thy servant, Don Juan Gusman del Pulgar, ever asserted, with words and blows, their infinite inferiority to thee.

"Give me, therefore, O Great Madonna of the Seven Daggers, O Snow Peak untrodden of the Sierras, O Sea unnavigated of the tropics, O Gold Ore unhandled by the Spaniard, O New Minted Doubloon unpocketed by the Jew, I pray thee, the promise that thou wilt save me ever from the clutches of Satan, as thou hast wrested me ever on earth from the King's Alguazils and the Holy Officer's delators, and let me never burn in eternal fire in punishment of my sins. Neither think that I ask too much, for I swear to be provided always with absolution in all rules, whether by employing my own private chaplain or using violence thereunto to any monk, priest, canon, dean, bishop, cardinal, or even the Holy Father himself.

"Grant me this boon, O Burning Water and Cooling Fire, O Sun that shineth at midnight, and Galaxy that resplendeth at noon – grant me this boon, and I will assert always with my tongue and my sword, in the face of His Majesty and at the feet of my latest love, that although I have been beloved of all the fairest women of the world, high and low, both Spanish, Italian, German, French, Dutch, Flemish, Jewish, Saracen, and Gypsy, to the number of many hundreds, and by seven ladies, Dolores, Fatma, Catalina, Elvira, Violante, Azahar, and Sister Seraphita, for each of whom I broke a commandment and took several lives (the last, moreover, being a cloistered nun, and therefore a case of inexpiable sacrilege), despite all this I will maintain before all men and all the Gods of Olympus that no lady was ever so fair as our Lady of the Seven Daggers of Grenada."

The church was filled with ineffable fragrance; exquisite music, among which Don Juan seemed to recognize the voice of Syphax, His Majesty's own soprano singer, murmured amongst the cupolas, and the Virgin of the Seven Daggers, slowly dipped in her lace and silver brocade hoop, rising as slowly again to her full height, and inclined her white face imperceptibly towards her jewelled bosom.

The Count of Miramor clasped his hands in ecstasy to his breast; then he rose, walked quickly down the aisle, dipped his fingers in the black marble holy water stoop, threw a sequin to the beggar who pushed open the leathern curtain, put his black hat covered with black feathers on his head, dismissed a company of bravos and guitar players who awaited him in the square, and, gathering his black cloak about him, went forth, his sword tucked under his arm, in search of Baruch, the converted Jew of the Albaycin.

Don Juan Gusman del Pulgar, Count of Miramor, Grandee of the First Class, Knight of Calatrava, and of the Golden Fleece, and Prince of the Holy Roman Empire, was thirty-two and a great sinner. This cavalier was tall, of large bone, his forehead low and cheek-bones high, chin somewhat receding, aquiline nose, white complexion, and black hair; he wore no beard, but a moustache cut short over the lip and curled upwards at the corners leaving the mouth bare; and his hair flat, parted through the middle and falling nearly to his shoulders. His clothes, when bent on business or pleasure, were most often of black satin, slashed with black. His portrait has been painted by Domingo Zurbaran of Seville.

II

All the steeples of Grenada seemed agog with bell-ringing; the big bell on the tower of the Sail clanging irregularly into the more professional tinklings and roarings, under the vigorous but flurried pulls of the damsels, duly accompanied by their well-ruffed duennas, who were ringing themselves a husband for the newly begun year, according to the traditions of the city. Green garlands decorated the white glazed balconies, and

111

banners with the arms of Castile and Aragon, and the pomegranate of Grenada, waved or drooped alongside the hallowed palm branches over the carved escutcheons on the doors. From the barracks arose a practising of fifes and bugles; and from the little wine shops on the outskirts of the town a sound of guitar strumming and castanets. The coming day was a very solemn feast for the city, being the anniversary of its liberation from the rule of the Infidels.

But although all Grenada felt festive, in anticipation of the grand bullfight of the morrow, and the grand burning of heretics and relapses in the square of Bibrambla, Don Juan Gusman del Pulgar, Count of Miramor, was fevered with intolerable impatience, not for the following day but for the coming and tediously lagging night.

Not, however, for the reason which had made him a thousand times before upbraid the Sun God, in true poetic style, for showing so little of the proper anxiety to hasten the happiness of one of the greatest cavaliers of Spain. The delicious heart-beating with which he had waited, sword under his cloak, for the desired rope to be lowered from a mysterious window, or the muffled figure to loom from round a corner; the fierce joy of awaiting, with a band of gallant murderers, some inconvenient father, or brother, or husband on his evening stroll; the rapture even, spiced with awful sacrilege, of stealing in amongst the lemon trees of that cloistered court, after throwing the Sister Portress to tell-tale in the convent well – all, and even this, seemed to him trumpery and mawkish.

Don Juan sprang from the great bed, covered and curtained with dull, blood-coloured damask, on which he had been lying dressed, vainly courting sleep, beneath a painted hermit, black and white in his lanternjawedness, fondling a handsome skull. He went to the balcony, and looked out of one of its glazed windows. Below a marble goddess shimmered among the myrtle hedges and the cypresses of the tiled garden, and the pet dwarf of the house played at cards with the chaplain, the chief bravo, and a threadbare poet who was kept to make the odes and sonnets required in the course of his master's daily courtships.

"Get out of my sight, you lazy scoundrels, all of you!" cried Don Juan, with a threat and an oath alike terrible to repeat, which sent the party, bowing and scraping as they went, scattering their cards, and pursued by his lordship's jack-boots, guitar, and missal.

Don Juan stood at the window rapt in contemplation of the towers of the Alhambra, their tips still reddened by the departing sun, their bases already lost in the encroaching mists, on the hill yon side of the river.

He could just barely see it, that Tower of the Cypresses, where the magic hand held the key engraven on the doorway, about which, as a child, his nurse from the Morisco village of Andarax had told such marvellous stories of hidden treasures and slumbering infantas. He stood long at the window, his lean, white hands clasped on the rail as on the handle of his sword, gazing out with knit brows and clenched teeth, and that look which made men hug the wall and drop aside on his path.

Ah, how different from any of his other loves! The only one, decidedly, at all worthy of lineage as great as his, and a character as magnanimous. Catalina, indeed, had been exquisite when she danced, and Elvira was magnificent at a banquet, and each had long possessed his heart, and had cost him, one many thousands of doubloons for a husband, and the other the death of a favourite fencing master, killed in a fray with her relations. Violante had been a Venetian worthy of Titian,

113

for whose sake he had been imprisoned beneath the ducal palace, escaping only by the massacre of three jailers; for Fatma, the Sultana of the King of Fez, he had well-nigh been impaled, and for shooting the husband of Dolores he had very nearly been broken on the wheel; Azahar, who was called so because of her cheeks like white jasmin, he had carried off at a church door, out of the arms of her bridegroom – without counting that he had cut down her old father, a Grandee of the First Class; and as to Sister Seraphita – ah! she had seemed worthy of him, and Seraphita had nearly come up to his idea of an angel.

But oh, what had any of these ladies cost him compared with what he was about to risk tonight? Letting alone the chance of being roasted by the Holy Office (after all, he had already run that, and the risk of more serious burning hereafter also, in the case of Sister Seraphita), what if the business proved a swindle of that Jewish hound, Baruch? – Don Juan put his hand on his dagger and his black moustache bristled up at the bare thought – letting alone the possibility of imposture (though who could be so bold as to venture to impose upon him?) the adventure was full of dreadful things. It was terrible, after all, to have to blaspheme the Holy Catholic Apostolic Church, and all her saints, and inconceivably odious to have to be civil to that dog of a Mahomet of theirs; also, he had not much enjoyed a previous experience of calling up devils, who had smelled most vilely of brimstone and assafœtida, besides using most impolite language; and he really could not stomach that Jew Baruch, whose trade among others consisted in procuring for the archbishop a batch of renegade Moors, who were solemnly dressed in white and baptized afresh every year. It was odious that this fellow should even dream of obtaining the treasure buried under the Tower of the Cypresses.

114

Then there were the traditions of his family, descended in direct line from the Cid, and from that Fernan del Pulgar who had nailed the Ave Maria to the Mosque; and half his other ancestors were painted with their foot on a Moor's decollated head, much resembling a hairdresser's block, and their very title, Miramor, was derived from a castle which had been built in full Moorish territory to stare the Moor out of countenance.

But, after all, this only made it more magnificent, more delicious, more worthy of so magnanimous and high-born a cavalier...."Ah, princess...more exquisite than Venus, more noble than Juno, and infinitely more agreeable than Minerva"...sighed Don Juan at his window. The sun had long since set, making a trail of blood along the distant river reach, among the sere spider-like poplars, turning the snows of Mulhacen a livid, bluish blood-red, and leaving all along the lower slopes of the Sierra wicked russet stains, as of the rust of blood upon marble. Darkness had come over the world, save where some illuminated courtyard or window suggested preparations for next day's revelry; the air was piercingly cold, as if filled with minute snowflakes from the mountains. The joyful singing had ceased; and from a neighbouring church there came only a casual death toll, executed on a cracked and lugubrious bell. A shudder ran through Don Juan. "Holy Virgin of the Seven Daggers, take me under thy benign protection," he murmured mechanically.

A discreet knock aroused him.

"The Jew Baruch – I mean his worship, Senor Don Bonaventura," announced the page.

III

The Tower of the Cypresses, destroyed in our times by the explosion of a powder magazine, formed part of

115

the inner defences of the Alhambra. In the middle of its horseshoe arch was engraved a huge hand holding a flag-shaped key, which was said to be that of the subterranean and enchanted palace; and the two great cypress trees, uniting their shadows into one tapering cone of black, were said to point, under a given position of the moon, to the exact spot where the wise King Yahya, of Cordova, had judiciously buried his jewels, his plate, and his favourite daughter many hundred years ago.

At the foot of this tower, and in the shade of the cypresses, Don Juan ordered his companion to spread out his magic paraphernalia. From a neatly packed basket, beneath which he had staggered up the steep hillside in the moonlight, the learned Jew produced a book, a variety of lamps, some packets of frankincense, a pound of dead man's fat, the bones of a stillborn child who had been boiled by witches, a live cock that had never crowed, a very ancient toad, and sundry other rarities, all of which he proceeded to dispose in the latest necromantic fashion, while the Count of Miramor mounted guard, sword in hand. But when the fire was laid, the lamps lit, and the first layer of ingredients had already been placed in the cauldron; nay, when he had even borrowed Don Juan's embroidered pocket handkerchief to envelop the cock that had never crowed, Baruch the Jew suddenly flung himself down before his patron and implored him to desist from the terrible enterprise for which they had come.

"I have come hither," wailed the Jew, "lest your lordship should possibly entertain doubts of my obligingness. I have run the risk of being burned alive in the Square of Bibrambla tomorrow morning before the bullfight; I have imperilled my eternal soul and laid out large sums of money in the purchase of the necessary

116

ingredients, all of which are abomination in the eyes of a true Jew – I mean of a good Christian; but now I implore your lordship to desist. You will see things so terrible that to mention them is impossible; you will be suffocated by the vilest stenches, and shaken by earthquakes and whirlwinds, besides having to listen to imprecations of the most horrid sort; you will have to blaspheme our Holy Mother Church and invoke Mahomet – may he roast everlastingly in hell; you will infallibly go to hell yourself in due course; and all this for the sake of a paltry treasure of which it will be most difficult to dispose to the pawnbrokers; and of a lady, about whom, thanks to my former medical position in the harem of the Emperor of Tetuan, I may assert with confidence that she is fat, ill-favoured, stained with henna, and most disagreeably redolent of camphor...."

"Peace, villain!" cried Don Juan, snatching him by the throat and pulling him violently on to his feet. "Prepare thy messes and thy stinks, begin thy antics, and never dream of offering advice to a cavalier like me. And remember, one other word against her Royal Highness, my bride, against the Princess whom her own father has been keeping three hundred years for my benefit, and by the Virgin of the Seven Daggers, thou shalt be hurled into yonder precipice; which, by the way, will be a very good move, in any case, when thy services are no longer required." So saying, he snatched from Baruch's hand the paper of responses, which the necromancer had copied out from his book of magic; and began to study it by the light of a supernumerary lamp.

"Begin!" he cried. "I am ready, and thou, great Virgin of the Seven Daggers, guard me!"

"Jab, jab, jam – Credo in Grilgroth, Astaroth et Rappatun; trish, trash, trum," began Baruch in faltering tones as he poked a flame-tipped reed under the cauldron.

"Patapol, Valde Patapol," answered Don Juan from his paper of responses.

The flame of the cauldron leaped up with a tremendous smell of brimstone. The moon was veiled, the place was lit up crimson, and a legion of devils with the bodies of apes, the talons of eagles, and the snouts of pigs suddenly appeared in the battlements all round.

"Credo," again began Baruch; but the blasphemies he gabbled out, and which Don Juan indignantly echoed, were such as cannot possibly be recorded. A hot wind rose, whirling a desertful of burning sand which stung like gnats; the bushes were on fire, each flame turned into a demon like a huge locust or scorpion, who uttered piercing shrieks and vanished, leaving a choking atmosphere of melted tallow.

"Fal lal Polychronicon Nebuzaradon," continued Baruch.

"Leviathan! Esto nobis!" answered Don Juan.

The earth shook, the sound of millions of gongs filled the air, and a snowstorm enveloped everything like a shuddering cloud. A legion of demons, in the shape of white elephants, but with snakes for their trunks and tails, and the bosoms of fair women, executed a frantic dance round the cauldron, and, holding hands, balanced on their hind legs.

At this moment the Jew uncovered the Black Cock who had never crowed before.

"Osiris! Apollo! Balshazar!" he cried, and flung the cock with superb aim into the boiling cauldron. The cock disappeared; then rose again, shaking his wings, and clawing the air, and giving a fearful piercing crow.

"O Sultan Yahya, Sultan Yahya," answered a terrible voice from the bowels of the earth.

Again the earth shook; streams of lava bubbled from beneath the cauldron, and a flame, like a sheet of green lightning, leaped up from the fire.

As it did so a colossal shadow appeared on the high palace wall, and the great hand, shaped like a glover's sign, engraven on the outer arch of the tower gateway, extended its candle-shaped fingers, projected a wrist, an arm to the elbow, and turned slowly in a secret lock the flag-shaped key engraven on the inside vault of the portal.

The two necromancers fell on their faces, utterly stunned.

The first to revive was Don Juan, who roughly brought the Jew back to his senses. The moon made serener daylight. There was no trace of earthquake, volcano, or simoom; and the devils had disappeared without traces; only the circle of lamps was broken through, and the cauldron upset among the embers. But the great horseshoe portals of the tower stood open; and, at the bottom of a dark corridor, there shone a speck of dim light.

"My lord," cried Baruch, suddenly grown bold, and plucking Don Juan by the cloak, "we must now, if you please, settle a trifling business matter. Remember that the treasure was to be mine provided the Infanta were yours. Remember also, that the smallest indiscretion on your part, such as may happen to a gay young cavalier, will result in our being burned, with the batch of heretics and relapses, in Bibrambla tomorrow, immediately after high mass and just before people go to early dinner, on account of the bullfight."

"Business! Discretion! Bibrambla! Early dinner!" exclaimed the Count of Miramor. "Thinkest thou I shall ever go back to Grenada and its frumpish women once I am married to my Infanta, or let thee handle my late father-in-law, King Yahya's treasure? Execrable renegade, take the reward of thy blasphemies." And

119

having rapidly run him through the body, he pushed Baruch into the precipice hard by. Then, covering his left arm with his cloak and swinging his bare sword horizontally in his right hand, he advanced into the darkness of the tower.

IV

Don Juan Gusman del Pulgar plunged down a narrow corridor, as black as the shaft of a mine, following the little speck of reddish light which seemed to advance before him. The air was icy damp and heavy with a vague choking mustiness, which Don Juan imagined to be a smell of dead bats. Hundreds of these creatures fluttered all round; and hundreds more, apparently hanging head downwards from the low roof, grazed his face with their claws, their damp furry coats, and clammy leathern wings. Underfoot, the ground was slippery with innumerable little snakes, who, instead of being crushed, just wriggled under the tread. The corridor was rendered even more gruesome by the fact that it was a strongly inclined plane, and that one seemed to be walking straight into a pit.

Suddenly a sound mingled itself with that of his footsteps, and of the drip-drop of water from the roof, or, rather, detached itself as a whisper from it.

"Don Juan, Don Juan," it murmured.

"Don Juan, Don Juan," murmured the walls and roof a few yards farther – a different voice this time.

"Don Juan Gusman del Pulgar!" a third voice took up, clearer and more plaintive than the others.

The magnanimous cavalier's blood began to run cold, and icy perspiration to clot his hair. He walked on nevertheless.

"Don Juan," repeated a fourth voice, a little buzz close to his ear.

But the bats set up a dreadful shrieking which drowned it.

He shivered as he went; it seemed to him he had recognized the voice of the jasmin-cheeked Azahar, as she called on him from her deathbed.

The reddish speck had meanwhile grown large at the bottom of the shaft, and he had understood that it was not a flame but the light of some place beyond. Might it be hell? he thought. But he strode on nevertheless, grasping his sword and brushing away the bats with his cloak.

"Don Juan! Don Juan!" cried the voices issuing faintly from the darkness. He began to understand that they tried to detain him; and he thought he recognized the voices of Dolores and Fatma, his dead mistresses.

"Silence, you sluts!" he cried. But his knees were shaking, and great drops of sweat fell from his hair on to his cheek.

The speck of light had now become quite large, and turned from red to white. He understood that it represented the exit from the gallery. But he could not understand why, as he advanced, the light, instead of being brighter, seemed filmed over and fainter.

"Juan, Juan," wailed a new voice at his ear. He stood still half a second; a sudden faintness came over him.

"Seraphita," he murmured – "it is my little nun Seraphita." But he felt that she was trying to call him back.

"Abominable witch!" he cried. "Avaunt!"

The passage had grown narrower and narrower; so narrow that now he could barely squeeze along beneath the clammy walls, and had to bend his head lest he should hit the ceiling with its stalactites of bats.

Suddenly there was a great rustle of wings, and a long shriek. A night bird had been startled by his tread and had whirled on before him, tearing through the veil of vagueness that dimmed the outer light. As the bird tore open its way, a stream of dazzling light entered the corridor: it was as if a curtain had suddenly been drawn.

"Too-hoo! Too-hoo!" shrieked the bird; and Don Juan, following its flight, brushed his way through the cobwebs of four centuries and issued, blind and dizzy, into the outer world.

V

For a long while the Count of Miramor stood dazed and dazzled, unable to see anything save the whirling flight of the owl, which circled in what seemed a field of waving, burning red. He closed his eyes; but through the singed lids he still saw that waving red atmosphere, and the black creature whirling about him.

Then, gradually, he began to perceive and comprehend: lines and curves arose shadowy before him, and the faint splash of waters cooled his ringing ears.

He found that he was standing in a lofty colonnade, with a deep tank at his feet surrounded by high hedges of flowering myrtles, whose jade-coloured water held the reflection of Moorish porticoes, shining orange in the sunlight, of high walls covered with shimmering blue and green tiles, and of a great red tower, raising its battlements into the cloudless blue. From the tower waved two flags, a white one and one of purple with a gold pomegranate. As he stood there, a sudden breath of air shuddered through the myrtles, wafting their fragrance towards him; a fountain began to bubble; and the reflection of the porticoes and hedges and tower to vacillate in the jade-green water, furling and unfurling like the pieces of a fan; and, above, the two banners unfolded themselves slowly, and little by little began to stream in the wind.

Don Juan advanced. At the further end of the tank a peacock was standing by the myrtle hedge, immovable as if made of precious enamels; but as Don Juan went by the short blue-green feathers of his neck began to ruffle; he moved his tail, and, swelling himself out, he slowly unfolded it in a dazzling wheel. As he did so, some blackbirds and thrushes in gilt cages hanging within an archway, began to twitter and to sing.

From the court of the tank, Don Juan entered another and smaller court, passing through a narrow archway. On its marble steps lay three warriors, clad in long embroidered surcoats of silk, beneath which gleamed their armour, and wearing on their heads strange helmets of steel mail, which hung loose on to their gorgets and were surmounted by gilded caps; beneath them – for they had seemingly leaned on them in their slumbers – lay round targes or shields, and battle-axes of Damascus work. As he passed they began to stir and breathe heavily. He strode quickly by, and at the entrance of the smaller court, from which issued a delicious scent of full-blown Persian roses, another sentinel was leaning against a column, his hands clasped round his lance, his head bent on his breast. As Don Juan passed he slowly raised his head, and opened one eye, then the other. Don Juan rushed past, a cold sweat on his brow.

Low beams of sunlight lay upon the little inner court, in whose midst, surrounded by rose hedges, stood a great basin of alabaster, borne on four thick-set pillars; a skin, as of ice, filmed over the basin; but, as if someone should have thrown a stone on to a frozen surface, the water began to move and to trickle slowly into the other basin below.

"The waters are flowing, the nightingales singing," murmured a figure which lay by the fountain, grasping,

123

like one just awakened, a lute that lay by his side. From the little court Don Juan entered a series of arched and domed chambers, whose roofs were hung as with icicles of gold and silver, or encrusted with mother-of-pearl constellations that twinkled in the darkness, while the walls shone with patterns that seemed carved of ivory and pearl and beryl and amethyst where the sunbeams grazed them, or imitated some strange sea caves, filled with flitting colours, where the shadow rose fuller and higher. In these chambers Don Juan found a number of sleepers, soldiers and slaves, black and white, all of whom sprang to their feet and rubbed their eyes and made obeisance as he went. Then he entered a long passage, lined on either side by a row of sleeping eunuchs, dressed in robes of honour, each leaning, sword in hand, against the wall, and of slave girls with stuff of striped silver about their loins, and sequins at the end of their long hair, and drums and timbrels in their hands.

At regular intervals stood great golden cressets, in which burned sweet-smelling wood, casting a reddish light over the sleeping faces. But as Don Juan approached the slaves inclined their bodies to the ground, touching it with their turbans, and the girls thumped on their drums and jingled the brass bells of their timbrels. Thus he passed on from chamber to chamber till he came to a great door formed of stars of cedar and ivory studded with gold nails, and bolted by a huge gold bolt, on which ran mystic inscriptions. Don Juan stopped. But, as he did so, the bolt slowly moved in its socket, retreating gradually, and the immense portals swung slowly back, each into its carved hinge column.

Behind them was disclosed a vast circular hall, so vast that you could not possibly see where it ended, and filled with a profusion of lights, wax candles held by rows and rows of white maidens, and torches held by rows and rows of white-robed eunuchs, and cressets burning upon lofty stands, and lamps dangling from the distant vault, through which here and there entered, blending strangely with the rest, great beams of white daylight. Don Juan stopped short, blinded by this magnificence, and as he did so the fountain in the midst of the hall arose and shivered its cypress-like crest against the topmost vault, and innumerable voices of exquisite sweetness burst forth in strange, wistful chants, and instruments of all kinds, both such as are blown and such as are twanged and rubbed with a bow, and such as are shaken and thumped, united with the voices and filled the hall with sound, as it was already filled with light.

Don Juan grasped his sword and advanced. At the extremity of the hall a flight of alabaster steps led up to a dais or raised recess, overhung by an archway whose stalactites shone like beaten gold, and whose tiled walls glistened like precious stones. And on the dais, on a throne of sandal-wood and ivory, encrusted with gems and carpeted with the product of the Chinese loom, sat the Moorish Infanta, fast asleep.

To the right and the left, but on a step beneath the princess, stood her two most intimate attendants, the Chief Duenna and the Chief Eunuch, to whom the prudent King Yahya had entrusted his only child during her sleep of four hundred years. The Chief Duenna was habited in a suit of sad-coloured violet weeds, with many modest swathings of white muslin round her yellow and wrinkled countenance. The Chief Eunuch was a portly negro, of a fine purple hue, with cheeks like an allegorical wind, and a complexion as shiny as a well-worn door-knocker: he was enveloped from top to toe in marigold-coloured robes, and on his head he wore a towering turban of embroidered cashmere. Both these great personages held, beside their especial insignia of office, namely, a Mecca rosary in the hand of the Duenna, and a silver wand in the hand of the Eunuch, great fans of white peacock's tails wherewith to chase away from their royal charge any ill-advised fly. But at this moment all the flies in the place were fast asleep, and the Duenna and the Eunuch also. And between them, canopied by a parasol of white silk on which were embroidered, in figures which moved like those in dreams, the histories of Jusuf and Zuleika, of Solomon and the Queen of Sheba, and of many other famous lovers, sat the Infanta, erect, but veiled in gold-starred gauzes, as an unfinished statue is veiled in the roughness of the marble.

Don Juan walked quickly between the rows of prostrate slaves, and the singing dancing girls, and those holding tapers and torches; and stopped only at the very foot of the throne steps.

"Awake!" he cried. "My princess, my bride, awake!"

A faint stir arose in the veils of the muffled form; and Don Juan felt his temples throb, and, at the same time, a deathly coldness steal over him.

"Awake!" he repeated boldly. But instead of the Infanta, it was the venerable Duenna who raised her withered countenance and looked round with a startled jerk, awakened not so much by the voices and instruments as by the tread of a masculine boot. The Chief Eunuch also awoke suddenly; but with the grace of one grown old in the ante-chamber of kings he quickly suppressed a yawn, and, laying his hand on his embroidered vest, made a profound obeisance.

"Verily," he remarked, "Allah (who alone possesses the secrets of the universe) is remarkably great, since he not only –"

"Awake, awake, princess!" interrupted Don Juan ardently, his foot on the lowest step of the throne.

But the Chief Eunuch waved him back with his wand, continuing his speech – "since he not only gave unto his servant King Yahya (may his shadow never be less!) power and riches far exceeding that of any of the kings of the earth or even of Solomon the son of David –"

"Cease, fellow!" cried Don Juan, and pushing aside the wand and the negro's dimpled chocolate hand, he rushed up the steps and flung himself at the foot of the veiled Infanta, his rapier clanging strangely as he did so.

"Unveil, my beloved, more beautiful than Oriana, for whom Amadis wept in the Black Mountain, than Gradasilia whom Felixmarte sought on the winged dragon, than Helen of Sparta who fired the towers of Troy, than Calixto whom Jove was obliged to change into a female bear, than Venus herself on whom Paris bestowed the fatal apple. Unveil and arise, like the rosy Aurora from old Tithonus' couch, and welcome the knight who has confronted every peril for thee, Juan Gusman del Pulgar, Count of Miramor, who is ready, for thee, to confront every other peril of the world or of hell; and to fix upon thee alone his affections, more roving hitherto than those of Prince Galaor or of the many-shaped god Proteus!"

A shiver ran through the veiled princess. The Chief Eunuch gave a significant nod, and waved his white wand thrice. Immediately a concert of voices and instruments, as numerous as those of the forces of the air when mustered before King Solomon, filled the vast hall. The dancing girls raised their tambourines over their heads and poised themselves on tiptoe. A wave of fragrant essences passed through the air filled with the spray of innumerable fountains. And the Duenna, slowly advancing to the side of the throne, took in her withered fingers the topmost fold of shimmering gauze, and, slowly gathering it backwards, displayed the Infanta unveiled before Don Juan's gaze.

The breast of the princess heaved deeply; her lips opened with a little sigh, and she languidly raised her long-fringed lids; then cast down her eyes on the ground and resumed the rigidity of a statue. She was most marvellously fair. She sat on the cushions of the throne with modestly crossed legs; her hands, with nails tinged violet with henna, demurely folded in her lap. Through the thinness of her embroidered muslins shone the magnificence of purple and orange vests, stiff with gold and gems, and all subdued into a wondrous opalescent radiance. From her head there descended on either side of her person a diaphanous veil of shimmering colours, powdered over with minute glittering spangles. Her breast was covered with rows and rows of the largest pearls, a perfect network reaching from her slender throat to her waist among which flashed diamonds embroidered in her vest. Her face was oval, with the silver pallor of the young moon; her mouth, most subtly carmined, looked like a pomegranate flower among tuberoses, for her cheeks were painted white, and the orbits of her great long-fringed eyes were stained violet. In the middle of each cheek, however, was a delicate spot of pink, in which an exquisite art had painted a small pattern of pyramid shape, so naturally that you might have thought that a real piece of embroidered stuff was decorating the maiden's countenance. On her head she wore a high tiara of jewels, the ransom of many kings, which sparkled and blazed like a lit-up altar. The eyes of the princess were decorously fixed on the ground.

Don Juan stood silent in ravishment.

"Princess!" he at length began.

But the Chief Eunuch laid his wand gently on his shoulder.

"My Lord," he whispered, "it is not etiquette that

128

your Magnificence should address her Highness in any direct fashion; let alone the fact that her Highness does not understand the Castilian tongue, nor your Magnificence the Arabic. But through the mediumship of this most respectable lady, her Discretion the Principal Duenna, and my unworthy self, a conversation can be carried on equally delicious and instructive to both parties."

"A plague upon the old brute!" thought Don Juan; but he reflected upon what had never struck him before, that they had indeed been conversing, or attempting to converse, in Spanish, and that the Castilian spoken by the Chief Eunuch was, although correct, quite obsolete, being that of the sainted King Ferdinand. There was a whispered consultation between the two great dignitaries; and the Duenna approached her lips to the Infanta's ear. The princess moved her pomegranate lips in a faint smile, but without raising her eyelids, and murmured something which the ancient lady whispered to the Chief Eunuch, who bowed thrice in answer. Then turning to Don Juan with most mellifluous tones, "Her Highness the Princess," he said, bowing thrice as he mentioned her name, "is, like all princesses, but to an even more remarkable extent, endowed with the most exquisite modesty. She is curious, therefore, despite the superiority of her charms – so conspicuous even to those born blind – to know whether your Magnificence does not consider her the most beautiful thing you have ever beheld."

Don Juan laid his hand upon his heart with an affirmative gesture more eloquent than any words.

Again an almost invisible smile hovered about the pomegranate mouth, and there was a murmur and a whispering consultation.

"Her Highness," pursued the Chief Eunuch blandly,

"has been informed by the judicious instructors of her tender youth, that cavaliers are frequently fickle, and that your Lordship in particular has assured many ladies in succession that each was the most beautiful creature you had ever beheld. Without admitting for an instant the possibility of a parallel, she begs your Magnificence to satisfy her curiosity on the point. Does your Lordship consider her as infinitely more beautiful than the Lady Catalina?"

Now Catalina was one of the famous seven for whom Don Juan had committed a deadly crime.

He was taken aback by the exactness of the Infanta's information; he was rather sorry they should have told her about Catalina.

"Of course," he answered hastily; "pray do not mention such a name in her Highness's presence."

The princess bowed imperceptibly.

"Her Highness," pursued the Chief Eunuch, "still actuated by the curiosity due to her high birth and tender youth, is desirous of knowing whether your Lordship considers her far more beautiful than the Lady Violante?"

Don Juan made an impatient gesture. "Slave! Never speak of Violante in my princess's presence!" he exclaimed, fixing his eyes upon the tuberose cheeks and the pomegranate mouth which bloomed among that shimmer of precious stones.

"Good. And may the same be said to apply to the ladies Dolores and Elvira?"

"Dolores and Elvira and Fatma and Azahar," answered Don Juan, greatly provoked at the Chief Eunuch's want of tact, "and all the rest of womankind."

"And shall we add also, than Sister Seraphita of the Convent of Santa Isabel la Real?"

"Yes," cried Don Juan, "than Sister Seraphita, for

130

whom I committed the greatest sin which can be committed by living man."

As he said these words, Don Juan was about to fling his arms about the princess and cut short this rather too elaborate courtship.

But again he was waved back by the white wand.

"One question more, only one, my dear Lord," whispered the Chief Eunuch. "I am most concerned at your impatience, but the laws of etiquette and the caprices of young princesses *must* go before everything, as you will readily admit. Stand back, I pray you."

Don Juan felt sorely inclined to thrust his sword through the yellow bolster of the great personage's vest; but he choked his rage, and stood quietly on the throne steps, one hand on his heart, the other on his sword-hilt, the boldest cavalier in all the kingdom of Spain.

"Speak, speak!" he begged.

The princess, without moving a muscle of her exquisite face, or unclosing her flower-like mouth, murmured some words to the Duenna, who whispered them mysteriously to the Chief Eunuch.

At this moment also the Infanta raised her heavy eye-lids, stained violet with henna, and fixed upon the cavalier a glance long, dark, and deep, like that of the wild antelope.

"Her Highness," resumed the Chief Eunuch, with a sweet smile, "is extremely gratified with your Lordship's answers, although, of course, they could not possibly have been at all different. But there remains yet another lady –"

Don Juan shook his head impatiently.

"Another lady concerning whom the Infanta desires some information. Does your Lordship consider her more beautiful also than the Virgin of the Seven Daggers?"

The place seemed to swim about Don Juan. Before his eyes rose the throne, all vacillating in its splendour, and on the throne the Moorish Infanta with the triangular patterns painted on her tuberose cheeks, and the long look in her henna'd eyes; and the image of her was blurred, and imperceptibly it seemed to turn into the effigy, black and white in her stiff puce frock and seed-pearl stomacher, of the Virgin of the Seven Daggers staring blankly into space.

"My Lord," remarked the Chief Eunuch, "methinks that love has made you somewhat inattentive, a great blemish in a cavalier, when answering the questions of a lovely princess. I therefore venture to repeat: do you consider her more beautiful than the Virgin of the Seven Daggers?"

"Do you consider her more beautiful than the Virgin of the Seven Daggers?" repeated the Duenna, glaring at Don Juan.

"Do you consider me more beautiful than the Virgin of the Seven Daggers?" asked the princess, speaking suddenly in Spanish, or, at least, in language perfectly intelligible to Don Juan. And, as she spoke the words, all the slave-girls and eunuchs and singers and players, the whole vast hall full, seemed to echo the same question.

The Count of Miramor stood silent for an instant; then raising his hand and looking around him with quiet decision, he answered in a loud voice:

"No!"

"In that case," said the Chief Eunuch, with the politeness of a man desirous of cutting short an embarrassing silence, "in that case I am very sorry it should be my painful duty to intimate to your Lordship that you must undergo the punishment usually allotted to cavaliers who are disobliging to young and tender princesses."

So saying, he clapped his black hands, and, as if by magic, there arose at the foot of the steps a gigantic Berber of the Rif, his brawny sunburned limbs left bare by a scanty striped shirt fastened round his waist by a wisp of rope, his head shaven blue except in the middle where, encircled by a coronet of worsted rag, there flamed a topknot of dreadful orange hair.

"Decapitate that gentleman," ordered the Chief Eunuch in his most obliging tones. Don Juan felt himself collared, dragged down the steps, and forced into a kneeling posture on the lowest landing, all in the twinkling of an eye.

From beneath the bronzed left arm of the ruffian he could see the milk-white of the alabaster steps, the gleam of an immense scimitar, the mingled blue and yellow of the cressets and tapers, the daylight filtering through the constellations in the dark cedar vault, the glitter of the Infanta's diamonds, and, of a sudden, the twinkle of the Chief Eunuch's eye.

Then all was black, and Don Juan felt himself, that is to say, his own head, rebound three times like a ball upon the alabaster steps.

VI

It had evidently all been a dream – perhaps a delusion induced by the vile fumigations of that filthy ruffian of a renegade Jew. The infidel dogs had certain abominable drugs which gave them visions of paradise and hell when smoked or chewed – nasty brutes that they were – and this was some of their devilry. But he should pay for it, the cursed old grey-beard, the Holy Office should keep him warm, or a Miramor was not a Miramor. For Don Juan forgot, or disbelieved, not only that he himself had been beheaded by a Rif Berber the evening before, but that he had previously run poor Baruch through the

133

body and hurled him down the rocks near the Tower of the Cypresses.

This confusion of mind was excusable on the part of the cavalier. For, on opening his eyes, he had found himself lying in a most unlikely resting-place, considering the time and season, namely, a heap of old bricks and rubbish, half-hidden in withered reeds and sprouting weeds, on a ledge of the precipitous hillside that descends into the River Darro. Above him rose the dizzy red-brick straightness of the tallest tower of the Alhambra, pierced at its very top by an arched and pillared window, and scantily overgrown with the roots of a dead ivy tree. Below, at the bottom of the precipice, dashed the little Darro, brown and swollen with melted snows, between its rows of leafless poplars; beyond it, the roofs and balconies and orange trees of the older part of Grenada; and above that, with the morning sunshine and mists fighting among its hovels, its square belfries and great masses of prickly pear and aloe, the Albaycin, whose highest convent tower stood out already against a sky of winter blue. The Albaycin – that was the quarter of that villain Baruch, who dared to play practical jokes on grandees of Spain of the very first class.

This thought caused Don Juan to spring up, and, grasping his sword, to scramble through the sprouting elder bushes and the heaps of broken masonry, down to the bridge over the river.

It was a beautiful winter morning, sunny, blue, and crisp through the white mists; and Don Juan sped along as with wings to his feet, for having remembered that it was the anniversary of the Liberation and that he, as descendant of Fernan Perez del Pulgar, would be expected to carry the banner of the city at High Mass in the cathedral, he had determined that his absence from the ceremony should raise no suspicions of his ridiculous adventure. For ridiculous it had been – and the sense of its being ridiculous filled the generous breast of the Count of Miramor with a longing to murder every man, woman, or child he encountered as he sped through the streets. "Look at his Excellency the Count of Miramor; look at Don Juan Gusman del Pulgar! He's been made a fool of by old Baruch the renegade Jew!" he imagined everybody to be thinking.

But, on the contrary, no one took the smallest notice of him. The muleteers driving along their beasts laden with heather and myrtle for the bakehouse ovens, allowed their loads to brush him as if he had been the merest errand-boy; the stout black housewives, going to market with their brass braziers tucked under their cloaks, never once turned round as he pushed them rudely on the cobbles; nay, the very beggars, armless and legless and shameless, who were alighting from their go-carts and taking up their station at the church doors, did not even extend a hand towards the passing cavalier. Before a popular barber's some citizens were waiting to have their topknots plaited into tidy tails, discussing the while the olive harvest, the price of spart-grass and the chances of the bull-ring. This, Don Juan expected, would be a fatal spot, for from the barber's shop the news must go about that Don Juan del Pulgar, hatless and covered with mud, was hurrying home with a discomfited countenance, ill-befitting the hero of so many nocturnal adventures. But, although Don Juan had to make his way right in front of the barber's, not one of the clients did so much as turn his head, perhaps out of fear of displeasing so great a cavalier. Suddenly, as Don Juan hurried along, he noticed for the first time, among the cobbles and the dry mud of the street, large drops of blood, growing larger as they went, becoming an almost uninterrupted line, then, in the puddles, a little red stream. Such were by no means uncommon vestiges in those days of duels and town broils; besides, some butcher or early sportsman, a wild boar on his horse, might have been passing.

But somehow or other this track of blood exerted an odd attraction over Don Juan; and unconsciously to himself, instead of taking the short cut to his palace, he followed it along some of the chief streets of Grenada. The bloodstains, as was natural, led in the direction of the great hospital, founded by St. John of God, to which it was customary to carry the victims of accidents and street fights. Before the monumental gateway, where St. John of God knelt in effigy before the Madonna, a large crowd was collected, above whose heads oscillated the black and white banners of a mortuary confraternity, and the flame and smoke of their torches. The street was blocked with carts, and with riders rising in their stirrups to look over the crowd, and even by gaily trapped mules and gilded coaches, in which veiled ladies were anxiously questioning their lackeys and outriders. The throng of idle and curious citizens, of monks and brothers of mercy, reached up the steps and right into the cloistered court of the hospital.

"Who is it?" asked Don Juan, with his usual masterful manner, pushing his way into the crowd. The man whom he addressed, a stalwart peasant with a long tail pinned under his hat, turned round vaguely, but did not answer.

"Who is it?" repeated Don Juan louder.

But no one answered, although he accompanied the question with a good push, and even a thrust with his sheathed sword.

"Cursed idiots! Are you all deaf and dumb that you cannot answer a cavalier?" he cried angrily, and taking a portly priest by the collar he shook him roughly.

"Jesus Maria Joseph!" exclaimed the priest; but

turning round he took no notice of Don Juan, and merely rubbed his collar, muttering, "Well, if the demons are to be allowed to take respectable canons by the collar, it *is* time that we should have a good witch-burning."

Don Juan took no heed of his words, but thrust onward, upsetting, as he did so, a young woman who was lifting her child to let it see the show. The crowd parted as the woman fell, and people ran to pick her up, but no one took any notice of Don Juan. Indeed, he himself was struck by the way in which he passed through its midst, encountering no opposition from the phalanx of robust shoulders and hips.

"Who is it?" asked Don Juan again.

He had got into a clearing of the crowd. On the lowest step of the hospital gate stood a little knot of black penitents, their black linen cowls flung back on their shoulders, and of priests and monks muttering together. Some of them were beating back the crowd, others snuffing their torches against the paving-stones, and letting the wax drip off their tapers. In the midst of them, with a standard of the Virgin at its head, was a light wooden bier, set down by its bearers. It was covered with coarse black serge, on which were embroidered in yellow braid a skull and crossbones, and the monogram I.H.S. Under the bier was a little red pool.

"Who is it?" asked Don Juan one last time; but instead of waiting for an answer, he stepped forward, sword in hand, and rudely pulled aside the rusty black pall.

On the bier was stretched a corpse dressed in black velvet, with lace cuffs and collar, loose boots, buff gloves, and a blood-clotted dark matted head, lying loose half an inch above the mangled throat.

Don Juan Gusman del Pulgar stared fixedly.

It was himself.

The church into which Don Juan had fled was that of

137

the Virgin of the Seven Daggers. It was deserted, as usual, and filled with chill morning light, in which glittered the gilded cornices and altars, and gleamed, like pools of water, the many precious marbles. A sort of mist seemed to hang about it all and dim the splendour of the high altar.

Don Juan del Pulgar sank down in the midst of the nave; not on his knees for (O horror!) he felt that he had no longer any knees, nor indeed any back, any arms, or limbs of any kind, and he dared not ask himself whether he was still in possession of a head: his only sensations were such as might be experienced by a slowly trickling pool, or a snow-wreath in process of melting, or a cloud fitting itself on to a flat surface of rock.

He was disembodied. He now understood why no one had noticed him in the crowd, why he had been able to penetrate through its thickness, and why, when he struck people and pulled them by the collar and knocked them down they had taken no more notice of him than of a blast of wind. He was a ghost. He was dead. This was the after life; and he was infallibly within a few minutes of hell.

"O Virgin, Virgin of the Seven Daggers," he cried with hopeless bitterness, "is this the way you recompense my faithfulness? I have died unshriven, in the midst of mortal sin, merely because I would not say you were less beautiful than the Moorish Infanta; and is this all my reward?"

But even as he spoke these words an extraordinary miracle took place. The white winter light broke into wondrous iridescences; the white mist collected into shoals of dim palm-bearing angels; the cloud of stale incense, still hanging over the high altar, gathered into fleecy balls, which became the heads and backs of well-to-do-cherubs; and Don Juan, reeling and fainting, felt himself rise, higher and higher, as if borne up on clusters

138

of soap bubbles. The cupola began to rise and expand; the painted clouds to move and blush a deeper pink; the painted sky to recede and turn into deep holes of real blue. As he was borne upwards, the allegorical virtues in the lunettes began to move and brandish their attributes; the colossal stucco angels on the cornices to pelt him with flowers no longer of plaster of Paris; the place was filled with delicious fragrance of incense, and with sounds of exquisitely played lutes and viols, and of voices, among which he distinctly recognized Syphax, his Majesty's chief soprano. And, as Don Juan floated upwards through the cupola of the church, his heart suddenly filled with a consciousness of extraordinary virtue; the gold transparency at the top of the dome expanded; its rays grew redder and more golden, and there burst from it at last a golden moon crescent, on which stood, in her farthingale of puce and her stomacher of seed-pearl, her big black eyes fixed mildly upon him, the Virgin of the Seven Daggers.

"Your story of the late noble Count of Miramor, Don Juan Gusman del Pulgar," wrote Don Pedro Calderon de la Barca, in March 1666, to his friend, the Archpriest Morales, at Grenada, "so veraciously revealed in a vision to the holy prior of St. Nicholas, is indeed such as must touch the heart of the most stubborn. Were it presented in the shape of a play, adorned with graces of style and with flowers of rhetoric, it would be indeed (with the blessing of heaven) well calculated to spread the glory of our holy church. But alas, my dear friend, the snows of age are as thick on my head as the snows of winter upon your Mulhacen; and who knows whether I shall ever be able to write again?"

The forecast of the illustrious dramatic poet proved, indeed, too true; and hence it is that unworthy modern hands have sought to frame the veracious and moral history of Don Juan and the Virgin of the Seven Daggers.

11.

THE FUTURE PHENOMENON
by Stéphane Mallarmé

A pale sky above the world at the end of its decrepitude might disappear with the clouds: the threadbare purple tatters of sunsets fade into the dormant river at the horizon, drowned by rays of light and water. The trees languish in *ennui*, and beneath their blanched foliage (blanched by the dust of the ages rather than that of the roads) the Showman of Past Things has erected his tent: many streetlamps await the dusk, retouching the faces of a miserable crowd of men, conquered by the undying malady and sin of centuries, beside their puny accomplices pregnant with the wretched fruits with which the earth shall perish.

Into the unquiet silence of all the eyes, imploring the descending sun which slides into the water with a despairing cry, the Showman's patter spills: "The spectacle inside has no signboard to advertise it, for there is nowadays no painter capable of displaying a pale shadow of it. I bring with me, alive—preserved over the years by superscientific means—a Woman of the olden days. Some novel and naïve madness, an ecstasy of gold or I know not what, which she called her *hair*, is draped with silken grace about a face illuminated by the blood-tinted bareness of her lips. Instead of the conceit of clothing she has a body; and even her eyes, which have the semblance of exotic stones, cannot surpass the glare emitted by her blissful flesh: from the breasts uplifted as though they were replete with eternal milk, nipples towards the sky, to the lithe legs which guard the

140

salinity of the primal sea."

Mindful of their paltry spouses—bald, ghastly and full of horror—the husbands press forward; their wives too, moved by melancholy curiosity, desire to see.

When all have contemplated the noble creature, relic of some earlier accursed age—some indifferently, for they will not have the power of understanding, but others heart-broken, their eyelids moist with resigned tears—they will look at one another; then the poets of those times, sensible of the rekindling of their extinguished eyes, will make their way towards their lightsource, their brains intoxicated for a moment by an ambiguous glory, haunted by Rhythm, forgetful of the fact that they exist in an era which has outlived beauty.

****

12.

THE TEACHER OF WISDOM
by Oscar Wilde

From his childhood he had been as one filled with the perfect knowledge of God, and even while he was yet but a lad many of the saints, as well as holy women who dwelt in the free city of his birth, had been stirred to much wonder by the grave wisdom of his answers.

And when his parents had given him the robe and the ring of manhood he kissed them, and left them and went out into the world, that he might speak to the world about God. For there were at that time many in the world who either knew not God at all, or had but an incomplete knowledge of Him, or worshipped the false gods who dwell in groves and have no care of their worshippers.

And he set his face to the sun and journeyed, walking without sandals, as he had seen the saints walk, and carrying at his girdle a leathern wallet and a little water-bottle of burnt clay.

And as he walked along the highway he was full of the joy that comes from the perfect knowledge of God, and he sang praises unto God without ceasing; and after a time he reached a strange land in which there were many cities.

And he passed through eleven cities. And some of these cities were in valleys, and others were by the banks of great rivers, and others were set on hills. And in each city he found a disciple who loved him and followed him, and a great multitude also of people followed him from each city, and the knowledge of God spread in the whole land, and many of the rulers were converted, and the priests of the temples in which there were idols found that half of their gain was gone, and when they beat upon their drums at noon none, or but a few, came with peacocks and with offerings of flesh as had been the custom of the land before his coming.

Yet the more the people followed him, and the greater the number of his disciples, the greater became his sorrow. And he knew not why his sorrow was so great. For he spake ever about God, and out of the fulness of that perfect knowledge of God which God had himself given to him.

And one evening he passed out of the eleventh city, which was a city of Armenia, and his disciples and a great crowd of people followed after him ; and he went up on to a mountain and sat down on a rock that was on the mountain, and his disciples stood round him, and the multitude knelt in the valley.

And he bowed his head on his hands and wept, and said to his Soul, "Why is it that I am full of sorrow and fear, and that each of my disciples is as an enemy that walks in the noonday?"

And his Soul answered him and said, "God filled thee with the perfect knowledge of Himself, and thou hast given this knowledge away to others. The pearl of great price thou hast divided, and the vesture without seam thou hast parted asunder. He who giveth away wisdom robbeth himself. He is as one who giveth his treasure to a robber. Is not God wiser than thou art? Who art thou to give away the secret that God hath told thee? I was rich once, and thou hast made me poor. Once I saw God, and now thou hast hidden Him from me."

And he wept again, for he knew that his Soul spake truth to him, and that he had given to others the perfect knowledge of God, and that he was as one clinging to the

143

skirts of God, and that his faith was leaving him by reason of the number of those who believed in him.

And he said to himself, "I will talk no more about God. He who giveth away wisdom robbeth himself."

And after the space of some hours his disciples came near him and bowed themselves to the ground and said, "Master, talk to us about God, for thou hast the perfect knowledge of God, and no man save thee hath this knowledge."

And he answered them and said, "I will talk to you about all other things that are in heaven and on earth, but about God I will not talk to you. Neither now, nor at any time, will I talk to you about God."

And they were wroth with him and said to him, "Thou hast led us into the desert that we might hearken to thee. Wilt thou send us away hungry, and the great multitude that thou hast made to follow thee?"

And he answered them and said, "I will not talk to you about God."

And the multitude murmured against him and said to him, "Thou hast led us into the desert, and hast given us no food to eat. Talk to us about God and it will suffice us."

But he answered them not a word. For he knew that if he spake to them about God he would give away his treasure.

And his disciples went away sadly, and the multitude of people returned to their own homes. And many died on the way.

And when he was alone he rose up and set his face to the moon, and journeyed for seven moons, speaking to no man nor making any answer. And when the seventh moon had waned he reached that desert which is the desert of the Great River. And having found a cavern in which a Centaur had once dwelt, he took it for his place

144

of dwelling, and made himself a mat of reeds on which to lie, and became a hermit. And every hour the Hermit praised God that He had suffered him to keep some knowledge of Him and of His wonderful greatness.

Now, one evening, as the Hermit was seated before the cavern in which he had made his place of dwelling, he beheld a young man of evil and beautiful face who passed by in mean apparel and with empty hands. Every evening with empty hands the young man passed by, and every morning he returned with his hands full of purple and pearls. For he was a Robber and robbed the caravans of the merchants.

And the Hermit looked at him and pitied him. But he spake not a word. For he knew that he who speaks a word loses his faith.

And one morning, as the young man returned with his hands full of purple and pearls, he stopped and frowned and stamped his foot upon the sand, and said to the Hermit : " Why do you look at me ever in this manner as I pass by ? What is it that I see in your eyes ? For no man has looked at me before in this manner. And the thing is a thorn and a trouble to me."

And the Hermit answered him and said, " What you see in my eyes is pity. Pity is what looks out at you from my eyes."

And the young man laughed with scorn, and cried to the Hermit in a bitter voice, and said to him, "I have purple and pearls in my hands, and you have but a mat of reeds on which to lie. What pity should you have for me ? And for what reason have you this pity ?"

"I have pity for you," said the Hermit, " because you have no knowledge of God."

" Is this knowledge of God a precious thing ?" asked the young man, and he came close to the mouth of the cavern.

145

"It is more precious than all the purple and the pearls of the world," answered the Hermit.

" And have you got it ?" said the young Robber, and he came closer still.

" Once, indeed," answered the Hermit, " I possessed the perfect knowledge of God. But in my foolishness I parted with it, and divided it amongst others. Yet even now is such knowledge as remains to me more precious than purple and pearls."

And when the young Robber heard this he threw away the purple and the pearls that he was bearing in his hands, and drawing a sharp sword of curved steel he said to the Hermit, " Give me, forthwith, this knowledge of God that you possess, or I will surely slay you. Wherefore should I not slay him who has a treasure greater than my treasure ?"

And the Hermit spread out his arms and said, " Were it not better for me to go unto the outermost courts of God and praise Him, than to live in the world and have no knowledge of Him ? Slay me if that be your desire. But I will not give away my knowledge of God."

And the young Robber knelt down and besought him, but the Hermit would not talk to him about God, nor give him his Treasure, and the young robber rose up and said to the Hermit, " Be it as you will. As for myself, I will go to the City of the Seven Sins, that is but three days' journey from this place, and for my purple they will give me pleasure, and for my pearls they will sell me joy." And he took up the purple and the pearls and went swiftly away.

And the Hermit cried out and followed him and besought him. For the space of three days he followed the young Robber on the road and entreated him to return, not to enter into the City of the Seven Sins.

And ever and anon the young Robber looked back at

the Hermit and called to him, and said, " Will you give me this knowledge of God which is more precious than purple and pearls ? If you will give me that, I will not enter the city."

And ever did the Hermit answer, "All things that I have I will give thee, save that one thing only. For that thing it is not lawful for me to give away."

And in the twilight of the third day they came nigh to the great scarlet gates of the City of the Seven Sins. And from the city there came the sound of much laughter.

And the young Robber laughed in answer, and sought to knock at the gate. And as he did so the Hermit ran forward and caught him by the skirts of his raiment, and said to him : " Stretch forth your hands, and set your arms around my neck, and put your ear close to my lips, and I will give you what remains to me of the knowledge of God." And the young Robber stopped.

And when the Hermit had given away his knowledge of God, he fell upon the ground and wept, and a great darkness hid from him the city and the young Robber, so that he saw them no more.

And as he lay there weeping he was aware of One who was standing beside him; and He who was standing beside him had feet of brass and hair like fine wool. And He raised the Hermit up, and said to him : " Before this time thou had'st the perfect knowledge of God. Now thou shalt have the perfect love of God. Wherefore art thou weeping ?" And He kissed him.

13.

FUNERAL ORATION
by Jean Lorrain

I have just buried my friend Jacques. We were friends as children and as adults; we were still as close at thirty-four years of age as we had been in the little coastal village where we grew up together, scarcely touched by the somnolence and deadening calm of the province, with our eyes and our dreams eternally reaching out for the shifting horizons of the unquiet sea.

Even here, in Paris, I am still haunted by the vision of that interment in the country cemetery, its desolation increased by the calm white winter landscape; the memory pursues me like some obsessive nightmare.

Here, as down there, huge and heavy snowflakes fall from a blank leaden sky, continually impressing upon me the knowledge that there is nothing more tedious and oppressive than a graveyard clad in white, as though sheltering beneath a swansdown coverlet...

In my vision, I am very much aware of the delicacy of the gates before each tomb, and the dark leaves of the evergreen bushes, each sharply emphasized by a fine edging of rime. The town is close by but there is no evident sign of its nearness, no noise of workshops or factory bells; all its various cries and murmurs are stifled by the thick snow, extinguished by its slow and gentle fall. It is like an autumnal fall of huge petals, immaculately white against the ink-black backcloth of the sea which shows between the high cliffs, immaculately white against the profundity of the sad grey sky.

148

The ceremony is already over; there is a confusion of great winter overcoats, which are powdered with hoarfrost as their wearers hasten across the cemetery. At the entrance the members of the family are arranged in their proper hierarchy, all dressed in black, bare-headed, shivering while they shake the proffered hands of all the guests, swamped by condolences and steeped in solemnity.

Jacques' brother has a sickly pallor, which becomes sicklier still beneath the sombre sky; some such pallor must have descended upon Napoleon's frozen troops as they suffered atrociously during the retreat from Moscow.

An expensive silk hat, gleaming among the shaggy head-dresses of the locals, attracts my attention; it signals the presence of a Parisian, who seems out of place at this pauper's funeral. I recognise de Saunis, a member at Jacques' club, whose path I have already crossed as we arrived at the railway station.

I go up to him, and we shake hands.

"Have you come from Paris for the sole purpose of attending the ceremony?" I ask.

"Yes I have," he replied, lightly, from the depths of his furs. "I would never take the trouble for a wedding, but for a funeral, always." Then, after a pause, he continued, "Poor Armenjean was only thirty-three, wasn't he? Too soon for a man to be cashing in his chips. What did he die of—anaemia, is that what they said? Worn out by life, more like—first by riotous living and then by ether....that dreadful ether! A nice habit which he picked up from that Suzanne!"

So saying, the swaggering oaf takes a side path, slipping away, bowing his head beneath the falling snow, seemingly quite delighted to have spoiled the kindly impulse which brought him here by spreading a little stupid gossip; but there are others within earshot, and I suppose he must put on an exhibition for the provincials, sustaining his reputation as a Parisian of the fin de siècle by making an Entertainment out of speaking ill of the dead, pursuing his stupid trade as a commercial traveller to the grave.

At the cemetery gateway, another surprise awaits. The door of a coupé is thrown back and Madame ***, a relative of Jacques'—a handsome woman in her thirties who has been, I believe, more or less his mistress—falls into my arms, stifling her sobs theatrically. No one could be better suited by the combination of healthy complexion, blonde hair and mourning-dress.

"What a tragedy this is, my friend!" (She calls me her friend, although she has only seen me twice in all her life, and conducts herself as if it were the end of the world!) "I knew he was ill, of course, but how could I foresee this? I have come from Rouen this very morning—I did not receive the telegram until yesterday and I had twenty-five people coming to dinner in the evening....impossible to put them all off—an official dinner! After the soirée I quite lost my head...I felt like an actress who has just lost her mother."

I look into her eyes, which are dark blue and very beautiful, and all awash with pearly tears; she is more of an actress than she cares to admit, this handsome relative, for she did not allow her bereavement to cause her to miss one of the few balls of the winter. Rouen is thirty leagues away from this provincial hole, and her black dress fits her very well, as if it had come from a fashion-house.

But Madame has pulled me up into her coupé, and all the while she dabs at her eyelids with a fine lace handkerchief. "He loved the girl so much that he couldn't live without her, that he had to die for her as she died." She clasped her arms nervously about me, saying

150

meanwhile in the unmistakable fashion of a jealous woman: "Was she at least pretty, this Suzanne...brunette or blonde...because, you know, he has died as she died, an etheromaniac...poisoned...."

While I gave her the information she requested, there emerged and was displayed before me a hidden drama of Jacques' last years, which I had somehow contrived not to notice. From the few words I had earlier exchanged with de Saunis and the conversation I was now having with Madame ****, a pattern emerged, clearly revealed to my eyes at last. I beheld the alarming silhouette of poor Suzanne Evrard, as I behold it now: as some kind of ghoul or vampire. That phantasmal and tragic being was once a pretty girl, perhaps a little too tall and a little too broad, but with such a supple figure that she seemed like a huge, heavy, weary flower; but I recall now as if in a sinister dream the flashing glimmer of her great black eyes—the feverish eyes of an etheromaniac, flaring amid the dull pallor of her complexion.

Two particular scenes emerge from the mists of memory to parade themselves before me, synthesizing for me the image—which I have until now refused to recognise—of a deadly evil spirit.

The first occasion was two years ago, on the night of the Opera Ball, when Jacques, Suzanne, myself and the rest of our motley crew of male and female merrymakers were stranded at the Maison d'Or, until three in the morning...

I see it very clearly, like a memory recovered under hypnosis: the remains of the supper, half-consumed desserts still scattered about the stained tablecloth, the marquise's crystal champagne-glasses still half-full, the women standing before the mirrors in order to readjust their masks and to arrange the cowls of their dominoes upon their foreheads.

Jacques, having had his fill and then some, had crossed his arms before him on the table, rested his head upon them, and gone to sleep. He was very pale, poor chap, but nevertheless appeared very handsome by the light of the low-burning candles, which were on the point of splitting on the candlesticks: his pallor was like the pallor of a corpse, but his handsomeness was the handsomeness of one sunk in depravity, worn out by living to the utmost. His thin red moustache was curled up at the ends, and he had the impertinent profile of a swashbuckling pirate.

Suzanne rose from her seat and stood behind him, her great satin domino billowing around her and making her even larger than she was. She put her gloved hand on the shoulder of the sleeper in order to awaken him and tell him that it was time to go.

"He's as tight as a tick," sneered one of the others—and, indeed, Jacques was so stupefied by drink that he simply sank further forward on the table, and made no move to get up.

Suzanne took off her gloves then, and laid her bare fingers gently on the nape of his neck, at first stroking him teasingly and amorously, then scratching him with the tip of a fingernail while she imitated the purr of a cat. Jacques still did not stir. Evidently being of the opinion that serious illnesses require drastic remedies, the girl in the domino brought forth from the folds of her costume a gilded bottle, removed the stopper and tilted it over a champagne-glass. She brought the glass to the lips of the sleeper, and I saw Jacques start, suddenly awakened. Suzanne, smiling as ever, put the glass into his hand—and he, surprisingly sober all of a sudden—drained it. He got up, staggering more than a little, slipped on his fur-lined cloak, and begged our pardon. Then we left.

The restorative which Suzanne had poured into him was simply ether, that ether which never lets go, and which, six months later—by which time she fully deserved the name of etheromaniac—had put an end to her life. Now I can see her, standing there enfolded by her black domino, pouring poison into her lover, the act making a tragic and horrific mockery of the gesture which she made with the other hand, readjusting her mask of green satin. But at the time, I did not see her thus: Suzanne seemed then to be a fantasy of a different kind, the creation of that mask of pale green satin, which matched the delicate shade of her sleeves and the ribbons of her domino.

The second memory is more recent. Suzanne was already dead, and had been for at least ten months. I was with a party of night-prowling friends, run to ground at Les Halles, at the Soulas or some similar all-night restaurant.

Clustered about the counter were market-gardeners in smocks, silken kerchiefs wrapped around their heads, drinking punch or hot toddy, conversing in rusty and raucous voices, harsh with catarrh. From a spiral staircase draped with green serge there came the sound of a waltz picked out by the finger of a drunken man.

In the next room, which was separated from the counter by a partition, an amusing scene was being enacted. A furious customer, assisted by a policeman and the proprietor of the establishment, had caught hold of the silken sleeves of a young woman.

This creature, a habitual haunter of the all-night restaurant, had approached the customer in the booth where he had eaten his meal. In order to get rid of the drink-cadger the man—a merchant from the provinces— had rummaged in his breast-pocket and given her twenty sous. Then, when the time came to pay his bill, the out-of-towner could not settle up; suddenly sobering up, he realised that twenty francs had gone missing, and jumped to the conclusion that instead of giving her a franc he must have given her a louis.

In a towering rage the man had immediately rushed down to the room below, where the girl was still to be found, stretched out on a bench, dead to the world. Now, while she loudly and stubbornly denied the charge brought against her, lashing out all the while at the proprietor and laughing at the policeman, she was gradually being stripped of her clothing as they rummaged about in search of the missing coin.

I can still see the great body of the woman lying on the bench, with her bare legs dangling out of her faded dress, her bonnet over her ear, and her happy, dazedly besotted smile, while careful inspection proved that there was nothing hidden in her black stockings. I can still see the drunken victim of the supposed theft, with his fixed stare and ruffled hair, strands of which hung limply down over his forehead. I remember his manner, despairing but determined, his murderous countenance. I remember the shrug of the shoulders with which the proprietor resigned the hope that he might collect what was due to him, and the way that the policeman, ambling back to his beat, paused at the corner to make the same gesture, tiredly and uncaringly.

But that which I remember most clearly of all is the glimpse which I caught of a person esconced in a corner of the dive. He wore an elegant black suit and a white cravat, and the buttonhole of his cape was decorated with a sprig of heather. He huddled over a flask of whisky, which he was mixing with ether.

He drank a large dose of the ether—a dose which would have scorched the stomach and entrails of someone like you or me. That etheromaniac—that exhausted

154

night-prowler, that gallivanting party-goer, that neurotic who never went to his bed before eight o'clock in the morning and never got up until seven in the evening when the city lights were burning again—that was him: Jacques, my childhood friend, the recently deceased! In the space of four years, one of the favoured sons of our fatherland had graduated from being a mere tippler of wine to become the victim of a terrible craving. What can one say? He sought to forget, and he forgot....

I see again the prematurely aged face and the sickly complexion of that man who was twenty-nine-years old but looked as if he were fifty: dismal, mute and taciturn as he lurked in that shadowed corner of Les Halles. Ether had claimed him, in the same way that morphine had claimed so many others: Jacques, the lover of that poor Suzanne. Jacques—my friend Jacques—had become in the ten months following her death one of the oh-so-charming sots of the fin de siécle.

I saw that I had wrought a kind of legend out of Jacques' death, which I wanted to believe: that he had taken to the drug in order to poison the memory of an adored mistress, who had died while their affair was still in the full flush of its honeymoon, fervent with new-born love and sensual intoxication. But it was all a lie.

Now, I perceived the truth of the matter—the sinister and terrifying truth. Suzanne was an ether-addict, and she had made an addict of him, too. The woman had been slain by her vice, but her influence extended beyond the tomb; she had left her lover a fatal bequest. Jacques had outlived her, but he had become an accessory to her crime, and in due course the dead had claimed the living.

They are together now, forever.

I have just buried my friend Jacques. We were friends as children and as adults; we were still as close at thirty-four years of age as we had been in the little

155

coastal village where we grew up together, scarcely touched by the somnolence and deadening calm of the province, with our eyes and our dreams eternally reaching out for the shifting horizons of the unquiet sea.

****

14.

AMOR PROFANUS
by Ernest Dowson

Beyond the pale of memory,
In some mysterious dusky grove;
A place of shadows utterly,
Where never coos the turtle-dove,
A world forgotten of the sun:
I dreamed we met when day was done,
And marvelled at our ancient love.

Met there by chance, long kept apart,
We wandered, through the darkling glades;
And that old language of the heart
We sought to speak: alas! poor shades!
Over our pallid lips had run
The waters of oblivion,
Which crown all loves of men or maids.

In vain we stammered: from afar
Our old desire shone cold and dead:
That time was distant as a star,
When eyes were bright and lips were red.
And still we went with downcast eye
And no delight in being nigh,
Poor shadows most uncomforted.

Ah, Lalage! while life is ours,
Hoard not thy beauty rose and white,
But pluck the pretty, fleeting flowers
That deck our little path of light:
For all too soon we twain shall tread
The bitter pastures of the dead:
Estranged, sad spectres of the night.

15.

THE PORTALS OF OPIUM
by Marcel Schwob

I had always made every effort to avoid living a
regulated life after the fashion of other men. The endless
monotony of repeated and habitual actions exasperated
me. My father having left an enormous fortune at my
disposal, I had no desire but to live life to the full, but
neither sumptuous houses nor *de luxe* carriages attracted
me. The frenzy of hunts and the indolence of spas were
equally unappealing to my restless mind: it was all *too
little*. Men live nowadays in extraordinary times, when
the novelists have shown us all the facets of human life
and have revealed the underside of every thought. How
can one help but be utterly tired of commonplace
sentiments and experiences? Is it any wonder that many
of us allow ourselves to be attracted towards the gulf
where shadows mysterious and unknown remain? Is it
any wonder that some are possessed by a passion for the
exotic and the sublime research of new sensations, or
that others are eventually overcome by a broad
compassion which extends itself over all possibilities?

My various pursuits had created in me an extravagant
curiosity regarding human life. I felt a painful desire to
be alienated from my own existence, so that I might
sometimes be a soldier or a merchant—or the woman
that I saw passing by, shaking her skirts—or that
lightly veiled young girl who just now entered a tea-
room and half-lifted up her veil to bite into a cake, before
pouring water into a glass and relaxing, with her head
bowed.

Given all this, it is easy enough to understand how I

came to be haunted by curiosity as to what lay behind one particular portal.

There was in a remote district a high grey wall, pierced only by railed openings set at a great height, with false windows palely drawn upon its implacable surface; and set in the base of that wall on the uneven ground, devoid of any peepholes through which one could obtain a glimpse of what lay within, was a low door set in an arch. It was sealed by an iron lock in the form of coiled serpents; and crossed with green bars. The lock and the hinges were rusted. In the long-deserted street the nettles and thistles had sprouted in clusters about the threshold, and the door was mottled by whitish flakes like those on the skin of a leper.

From time to time, my dull walks brought me to that silent street, and I addressed the question of the puzzling door. Were there living beings behind that mysterious portal? What extraordinary existence might be led by those who passed their days in the shadow of the great grey wall, cloistered from the world by the little low door which one never saw standing open?

One evening, while I was wandering among the crowds, looking for curious individuals, I remarked a little old man with an odd limping gait. He had a red handkerchief dangling from his pocket, and he continually struck the pavement with a twisted cane, as though with derision. Under the gaslights this figure seemed perpetually striped by shadow, and his eyes sparkled so greenly that I was irresistibly reminded of *the image of the door*: I became instantly certain that he had some connection with it and that he had been through it.

I followed that man. I could not know for certain that he had anything to do with my puzzle, but it was impossible for me to act otherwise—and when he reached the end of the deserted street where the door was, I was illuminated by one of those sudden presentiments that sometimes take hold of us, and I felt that I had a perfectly clear idea of what would happen.

He knocked twice, or perhaps three times, on the door. It turned on its rusty hinges, without grating.

I did not hesitate: I sprang forward. I stumbled over the legs of a beggar who was sprawled out along the wall, but whom I had not seen. On his knees he had an earthenware bowl, and there was a tin spoon in his hand. He lifted his stick and cursed me in a raucous voice, but I paid no heed. The door was silently closed again, behind me.

I found myself in an immense gloomy garden, where the weeds and brambles sprouted to knee-height. The ground was soaked, as though by continual rain; it seemed to be soft clay, to judge by the way it clung to my boots at each step. I groped my way forward through the gloom, towards the muffled noises which the old man made as he went on ahead of me. I soon saw a crack of light; there were trees in the distance upon whose branches paper lanterns were hanging, giving out a faint and diffuse reddish light. The silence was less profound now, for the wind seemed to breathe slowly in the branches.

On approaching closer, I saw that the lanterns were painted with oriental flowers and that they described in the air the words:

HOUSE OF OPIUM

Rising up before me was a white house, square in shape, with long narrow windows. Drifting from within came the sound of slow discordant music, whose rhythm was beaten out by drums, and overlaid by the chanting of dreamy voices. The old man paused at the threshold and turned towards me, gracefully shaking his red handkerchief, and I accepted his gestured invitation to enter.

In the corridor beyond I met a thin yellow creature, clad in a loose robe; she too was old, with a shaky head and a toothless mouth. She ushered me into a rectangular room, with white silk stretched over its walls. The hangings were decorated with vertical black stripes, rising as far as the ceiling.

I saw before me a carefully-organised assembly of lacquered tables. A thin flame smouldered in a lamp of red copper; there was a porcelain pot full of a greyish paste, a number of pins, and three or four pipes with bamboo stems and silver bowls. The old oriental woman rolled some paste into a pellet, mounted it on a pin and melted it in the flame. Then, placing it carefully in the bowl of the pipe, she tamped it down and sealed it with a plug.

Without pausing for reflection, I took the pipe and lit up, and I took two puffs of an acrid and poisonous smoke, which instantly stupefied me.

Although there was no sense whatsoever of any transition, I saw passing before my eyes the image of the door, and the bizarre figures of the old man with the red handkerchief, the beggar with the bowl and the old woman in the yellow robe. The black stripes upon the wall seemed to become magnified in width as they approached the ceiling, and to diminish nearer to the floor, in a kind of chromatic scale of dimension—which, it seemed to me could be heard resonating in my ears. I seemed to hear the sound of the sea—of waves which broke in rocky grottoes, explosively driving out the air with their mute blows. The room seemed to have turned topsy-turvy, although I had had no impression of movement; it appeared to me that my feet had taken the

161

place of my head and that I was lodged upon the ceiling. Eventually, I suffered a complete annihilation of my activity; I desired only to remain eternally where I was, and to continue that experience.

It was then that a panel slid aside somewhere in the chamber, through which there entered a young girl like none I had ever seen before. She had a body powdered with saffron and eyes upraised towards her temples; her eyelashes were decorated with gilt, and the shells of her ears were delicately limned in pink. Her teeth, which were as black as ebony, were spangled with constellations of tiny fulgurant diamonds, and her lips were painted blue. Thus decorated, with her skin spiced and painted, she had the aspect and the scent of those Chinese ivory statues which are curiously pitted and enhanced with gaudy colours. She was naked to the waist; her breasts hung down like two pears, and a brown skirt chequered with gold floated above her feet.

The desire for strange experience which had taken hold of me became so violent at that moment that I hurled myself towards that painted woman, grovelling before her. Each of the colours of her costume and her skin seemed to the hyperaesthesia of my senses to be a delicious sound in that harmony which enveloped me; each of the gestures and the poses of her hands was like some rhythmic element of a dance, infinitely varied, of which my intuition somehow understood the whole.

I said to her, pleadingly: "Daughter of Lebanon, if you have come to me from the mysterious depths of opium, stay, stay....my heart desires you. Until the end of my days I will nourish myself on that unparalleled drug which makes you appear before my eyes. Opium is more powerful than ambrosia, because it bestows the immortality of the dream, rather than the miserable eternity of life; more subtle than nectar, because it creates beings so strangely brilliant; more just than all the gods, because it reunites those who are made to love one another!

"But if you are a woman born of human flesh, you are mine—forever—because I would give everything that I have to possess you...."

She fixed upon me those eyes which glistened between her golden eyelashes, came slowly closer, and sat down in a casual manner which made my heart beat faster.

"Is it true?" she whispered in my ear. "Would you give your fortune to possess me?" She shook her head incredulously.

I can assure you that madness had me completely in its grip. I snatched my cheque-book from my pocket. I signed a blank cheque and threw it across the room; it fell upon the parquet.

"Ah!" she said. "But would you have the courage to become a beggar in order to be with me? It seems to me that I would like you better then. Tell me—do you want that?"

She began to undress me deftly. Then the old oriental woman led in the beggar who had been beside the door when I entered; he came in hastily and when he had put on my discarded vestments he took himself off again. As for me, I put on his patched cloak and his underclothes full of holes, and took up his stick, his spoon and his begging-bowl.

When I was thus clad, she said: "Go!" And she clapped her hands.

The lamps went out, the panel fell back into place. The girl summoned by the opium vanished. Amid the vivid confusion of the walls I saw the old man with the red handkerchief, the old woman in the yellow robe, and the hideous beggar dressed in my clothes, who threw themselves upon me and pushed me into the mouth of a dark corridor. I passed through it, and was drawn on through a maze of sticky tunnels, with viscous walls to either side of me. An inestimable time flowed by; I lost track of the hours—I seemed to be dragged along interminably.

Then, all at once, white light flooded over me. My eyes quivered in their orbits; my eyelids were screwed up against the sun.

I found myself sprawled before a little low door set in an arch, sealed by an iron lock wrought in the form of coiled serpents and crossed with green stripes: a door identical in every way to the mysterious door through which I had passed before, but set in an immense whitewashed wall. An empty and desolate country extended before me; the grass was parched, the sky was deep blue and cloudless. Everything was unfamiliar to me, including the heap of dung which lay beside me.

I was lost—as wretched as Job and as naked as Job—in that place behind the second door. I pounded on it, I shook it, but it is as firmly closed now as it ever was. My tin spoon rattles against my empty begging bowl, hollowly.

Oh yes, opium is more powerful than ambrosia, bestowing upon life the eternity of misery; it is more subtle than nectar, corroding the heart with such vitriolic cruelty; it is more just than all the gods, punishing the curious who have desired to violate the secrets of the beyond.

Oh, exceedingly just, subtle and powerful opium!

Alas, alas, my fortune is laid waste—alas, alas, my wealth is lost!

****

164

16.

THE SPHINX
by Oscar Wilde

In a dim corner of my room for longer than my fancy
thinks
A beautiful and silent Sphinx has watched me through
the shifting gloom.

Inviolate and immobile she does not rise she does not
stir
For silver moons are naught to her and naught to her the
suns that reel.

Red follows grey across the air, the waves of moonlight
ebb and flow
But with the Dawn she does not go and in the night-time
she is there.

Dawn follows Dawn and Nights grow old and all the
while this curious cat
Lies couching on the Chinese mat with eyes of satin
rimmed with gold.

Upon the mat she lies and leers and on the tawny throat
of her
Flutters the soft and silky fur or ripples to her pointed
ears.

Come forth, my lovely seneschal! so somnolent, so
statuesque!
Come forth you exquisite grotesque! half woman and
half animal!

Come forth my lovely languorous Sphinx! and put your
    head upon my knee!
And let me stroke your throat and see your body spotted
    like the Lynx!

And let me touch those curving claws of yellow ivory and
    grasp
The tail that like a monstrous Asp coils round your
    heavy velvet paws!

A THOUSAND weary centuries are thine while I have
    hardly seen
Some twenty summers cast their green for Autumn's
    gaudy liveries.

But you can read the Hieroglyphs on the great sand-
    stone obelisks,
And you have talked with Basilisks, and you have looked
    on Hippogriffs.

O tell me, were you standing by when Isis to Osiris
    knelt?
And did you watch the Egyptian melt her union for
    Antony

And drink the jewel-drunken wine and bend her head in
    mimic awe
To see the huge proconsul draw the salted tunny from
    the brine?

And did you mark the Cyprian kiss white Adon on his
    catafalque?
And did you follow Amenalk, the God of Heliopolis?

166

And did you talk with Thoth, and did you hear the moon-
    horned Io weep?
And know the painted kings who sleep beneath the
    wedge-shaped Pyramid?

LIFT up your large black satin eyes which are like
    cushions where one sinks!
Fawn at my feet, fantastic Sphinx! and sing me all your
    memories!

Sing to me of the Jewish maid who wandered with the
    Holy Child,
And how you led them through the wild, and how they
    slept beneath your shade.

Sing to me of that odorous green eve when crouching by
    the marge
You heard from Adrian's gilded barge the laughter of
    Antinous

And lapped the stream and fed your drouth and watched
    with hot and hungry stare
The ivory body of that rare young slave with his
    pomegranate mouth!

Sing to me of the Labyrinth in which the two-formed bull
    was stalled!
Sing to me of the night you crawled across the temple's
    granite plinth

When through the purple corridors the screaming scarlet
    Ibis flew
In terror, and a horrid dew dripped from the moaning
    Mandragores,

And the great torpid crocodile within the tank shed
　　slimy tears,
And tare the jewels from his ears and staggered back
　　into the Nile,

And the priests cursed you with shrill psalms as in your
　　claws you seized their snake
And crept away with it to slake your passion by the
　　shuddering palms.

WHO were your lovers? who were they who wrestled
　　for you in the dust?
Which was the vessel of your Lust? What Leman had
　　you, every day?

Did giant Lizards come and crouch before you on the
　　reedy banks?
Did Gryphons with great metal flanks leap on you in
　　your trampled couch?

Did monstrous hippopotami come sidling toward you in
　　the mist?
Did gilt-scaled dragons writhe and twist with passion as
　　you passed them by?

And from the brick-built Lycian tomb what horrible
　　Chimera came
With fearful heads and fearful flame to breed new
　　wonders from your womb?

OR had you shameful secret quests and did you harry
　　to your home
Some Nereid coiled in amber foam with curious rock
　　crystal breasts?　　　168

Or did you treading through the froth call to the brown
  Sidonian
For tidings of Leviathan, Leviathan or Behemoth?

Or did you when the sun was set climb up the cactus-
  covered slope
To meet your swarthy Ethiop whose body was of polished
  jet?

Or did you while the earthen skiffs dropped down the
  grey Nilotic flats
At twilight and the flickering bats flew round the
  temple's triple glyphs

Steal to the border of the bar and swim across the silent
  lake
And slink into the vault and make the Pyramid your
  lupanar

Till from each black sarcophagus rose up the painted
  swathèd dead?
Or did you lure unto your bed the ivory-horned
  Tragelaphos?

Or did you love the god of flies who plagued the Hebrew
  and was splashed
With wine unto the waist? or Pasht, who had green
  beryls for her eyes?

Or that young god, the Tyrian, who was more amorous
  than the dove
Of Ashtaroth? or did you love the god of the Assyrian

Whose wings, like strange transparent talc, rose high

above his hawk-faced head,
Painted with silver and with red and ribbed with rods of
Oreichalch?

Or did huge Apis from his car leap down and lay before
your feet
Big blossoms of the honey-sweet and honey-coloured
nenuphar?

HOW subtle-secret is your smile! Did you love none
then? Nay, I know
Great Ammon was your bedfellow! He lay with you
beside the Nile!

The river-horses in the slime trumpeted when they saw
him come
Odorous with Syrian galbanum and smeared with
spikenard and with thyme.

He came along the river bank like some tall galley
argent-sailed,
He strode across the waters, mailed in beauty, and the
waters sank.

He strode across the desert sand: he reached the valley
where you lay:
He waited till the dawn of day: then touched your black
breasts with his hand.

You kissed his mouth with mouths of flame: you made
the hornèd god your own:
You stood behind him on his throne: you called him by
his secret name.

You whispered monstrous oracles into the caverns of his
ears:
With blood of goats and blood of steers you taught him
monstrous miracles.

White Ammon was your bedfellow! Your chamber was
the steaming Nile!
And with your curved archaic smile you watched his
passion come and go.

WITH Syrian oils his brows were bright: and wide-
spread as a tent at noon
His marble limbs made pale the moon and lent the day
a larger light.

His long hair was nine cubits' span and coloured like
that yellow gem
Which hidden in their garment's hem the merchants
bring from Kurdistan.

His face was as the must that lies upon a vat of new-
made wine:
The seas could not insapphirine the perfect azure of his
eyes.

His thick soft throat was white as milk and threaded
with thin veins of blue:
And curious pearls like frozen dew were broidered on his
flowing silk.

ON pearl and porphyry pedestalled he was too bright
to look upon:
For on his ivory breast there shone the wondrous ocean-

emerald,

That mystic moonlit jewel which some diver of the
    Colchian caves
Had found beneath the blackening waves and carried to
    the Colchian witch.

Before his gilded galiot ran naked vine-wreathed
    corybants,
And lines of swaying elephants knelt down to draw his
    chariot.

And lines of swarthy Nubians bare up his litter as he
    rode
Down the great granite-paven road between the nodding
    peacock fans.

The merchants brought him steatite from Sidon in their
    painted ships:
The meanest cup that touched his lips was fashioned
    from a chrysolite.

The merchants brought him cedar chests of rich apparel
    bound with cords:
His train was borne by Memphian lords: young kings
    were glad to be his guests.

Ten hundred shaven priests did bow to Ammon's altar
    day and night,
Ten hundred lamps did wave their light through
    Ammon's carven house – and now

Foul snake and speckled adder with their young ones
    crawl from stone to stone
For ruined is the house and prone the great rose-marble

monolith!

Wild ass or trotting jackal comes and couches in the
    mouldering gates:
Wild satyrs call unto their mates across the fallen fluted
    drums.

And on the summit of the pile the blue-faced ape of
    Horus sits
And gibbers while the fig-tree splits the pillars of the
    peristyle

THE god is scattered here and there: deep hidden in the
    windy sand
I saw his giant granite hand still clenched in impotent
    despair.

And many a wandering caravan of stately negroes
    silken-shawled,
Crossing the desert halts appalled before the neck that
    none can span.

And many a bearded Bedouin draws back his yellow-
    striped burnous
To gaze upon the Titan thews of him who was thy
    paladin.

GO, seek his fragments on the moor and wash them in
    the evening dew,
And from their pieces make anew thy mutilated
    paramour!

Go, seek them where they lie alone and from their
   broken pieces make
Thy bruisèd bedfellow! And wake mad passions in the
   senseless stone!

Charm his dull ear with Syrian hymns! he loved your
   body! oh, be kind,
Pour spikenard on his hair, and wind soft rolls of linen
   round his limbs!

Wind round his head the figured coins! stain with red
   fruits those pallid lips!
Weave purple for his shrunken hips! and purple for his
   barren loins!

AWAY to Egypt! Have no fear. Only one God has ever
   died.
Only one God has let His side be wounded by a soldier's
   spear.

But these, thy lovers, are not dead. Still by the hundred-
   cubit gate
Dog-faced Anubis sits in state with lotus-lilies for thy
   head.

Still from his chair of porphyry gaunt Memnon strains
   his lidless eyes
Across the empty land, and cries each yellow morning
   unto thee.

And Nilus with his broken horn lies in his black and oozy
   bed
And till thy coming will not spread his waters on the
   withering corn.

Your lovers are not dead, I know. They will rise up and
   hear your voice
And clash their cymbals and rejoice and run to kiss your
   mouth! And so,

Set wings upon your argosies! Set horses to your ebon
   car!
Back to your Nile! Or if you are grown sick of dead
   divinities

Follow some roving lion's spoor across the copper-coloured
   plain,
Reach out and hale him by the mane and bid him be your
   paramour!

Couch by his side upon the grass and set your white
   teeth in his throat
And when you hear his dying note lash your long flanks
   of polished brass

And take a tiger for your mate, whose amber sides are
   flecked with black,
And ride upon his gilded back in triumph through the
   Theban gate,

And toy with him in amorous jests, and when he turns,
   and snarls, and gnaws,
O smite him with your jasper claws! and bruise him with
   your agate breasts!

WHY are you tarrying? Get hence! I weary of your
   sullen ways,
I weary of your steadfast gaze, your somnolent
   magnificence.

Your horrible and heavy breath makes the light flicker
in the lamp,
And on my brow I feel the damp and dreadful dews of
night and death.

Your eyes are like fantastic moons that shiver in some
stagnant lake,
Your tongue is like a scarlet snake that dances to
fantastic tunes,

Your pulse makes poisonous melodies, and your black
throat is like the hole
Left by some torch or burning coal on Saracenic
tapestries.

Away! The sulphur-coloured stars are hurrying through
the Western gate!
Away! Or it may be too late to climb their silent silver
cars!

See, the dawn shivers round the grey gilt-dialled towers,
and the rain
Streams down each diamonded pane and blurs with
tears the wannish day.

What snake-tressed fury fresh from Hell, with uncouth
gestures and unclean,
Stole from the poppy-drowsy queen and led you to a
student's cell?

WHAT songless tongueless ghost of sin crept through
the curtains of the night,
And saw my taper turning bright, and knocked, and
bade you enter in?

Are there not others more accursed, whiter with leprosies
   than I?
Are Abana and Pharphar dry that you come here to
   slake your thirst?

Get hence, you loathsome mystery! Hideous animal, get
   hence!
You wake in me each bestial sense, you make me what
   I would not be.

You make my creed a barren sham, you wake foul
   dreams of sensual life,
And Atys with his blood-stained knife were better than
   the thing I am.

False Sphinx! False Sphinx! By reedy Styx old Charon,
   leaning on his oar,
Waits for my coin. Go thou before, and leave me to my
   crucifix,

Whose pallid burden, sick with pain, watches the world
   with wearied eyes,
And weeps for every soul that dies, and weeps for every
   soul in vain.

17.

SAINT SATYR
by Anatole France

Consors paterni luminis,
Lux ipse lucis et dies,
Noctem canendo rumpimus:
Assiste postulantibus.

Aufer tenibras mentium;
Fuga catervas daemonum;
Expelle somnolentiam,
*Ne pigritantes obruat.**
>   *(Breviarum Romanum.*
>   Third Day of the Week: at matins.)

Fra Mino had elevated himself above his brothers by means of his humility; although he was still young he governed the monastery of Santa-Fiora wisely. He was devout. He took pleasure in prolonging his meditations and his prayers; sometimes he had ecstatic visions. After the fashion of St. Francis, his spiritual father, he composed songs in the language of the common people to celebrate that perfect love which is the love of God. These works were without any fault of metre or meaning, for he had studied the seven liberal arts at the University

* Consort of the Father's light, Light of light and day, We interrupt the evening with prayers: Help us, Thy suppliants. Remove darkness from our minds; Scatter the demon hosts; Expel somnolence, Lest we weaken in our duty to Thee.

of Bologna.

One evening, while Fra Mino was walking beneath the arches of the cloister, he felt his heart fill up with confusion and sadness, inspired by the memory of a Florentine lady whom he had once loved, in the first flower of his youth, before the habit of St. Francis had extended its protection to his flesh. He prayed to God, asking that this image might be banished, but the sorrow remained in his heart.

"The bells," he thought, "say as the angels do: *Ave Maria*; but their voice fades away in the mists of the heavens. On the wall of this cloister, the master honoured by Perouse has painted a marvellous picture of the Marys contemplating the body of the Saviour with inexpressible love—but darkness has veiled the tears in their eyes and the mute sobbing of their mouths, and I cannot weep with them. That well in the middle of the courtyard was covered just now with doves which had come to drink from it, but they have flown away, having found no water in the hollow of the curb-stone. Witness, Lord, that my soul is hushed like the bells, cloaked by darkness like the Marys, dried up like the well. Why, Divine Jesus, is my heart arid, dark and mute, when you are its dawning light, its birdsong and its nourishing stream?"

He could not bear the prospect of returning to his cell, and so—thinking that prayer would dissipate his sorrow and calm his anxiety—he went through the low door which led from the cloister to the church. The building, which had been erected more than a hundred and fifty years earlier on the site of a Roman temple by the Margaritone, was full of silent shadows. He crossed the nave and went to kneel down in the chapel behind an altar dedicated to St. Michael, whose legend was depicted in the frescos on the wall—though the dim light of the lamp suspended from the vault was insufficient to allow him to make out the figure of the archangel, fighting demons and weighing souls. The moon, however, sent through the window a silvery ray which fell upon the tomb of Saint Satyr, which was placed in an arcade to the right of the altar. This tomb, shaped like a wine-vat, was far older than the church, and closely resembled a pagan sarcophagus save for the fact that the sign of the Cross was inscribed in triplicate on its marble walls.

Fra Mino remained prostrate before the altar for some considerable time, but it proved impossible for him to pray, and as midnight approached he felt that he was weighed down by the same torpor that had overwhelmed Christ's disciples in the Garden of Gethsemane. Then, while he spread himself out upon the floor, devoid of courage and discretion, he saw something like a white cloud rising up above the tomb of Saint Satyr. He soon realised that this cloud was made up of a multitude of clouds, each one of which was a woman. They floated upon the dark air, and their lithe limbs shone through their flimsy costumes. And Fra Mino saw that within this company young men with the feet of goats could be discerned, giving chase to the women. Their nudity left no room for doubt as to the frightful ardour of their desires; nevertheless, the nymphs fled from them, and wherever their swift feet fell there sprang forth flowers and streams. Each time a goat-foot extended his hand towards one of them, believing that he could seize her, a willow-tree would suddenly shoot up to hide the nymph within its cavernous hollow trunk, and its pale foliage would quiver with the light murmurs of mocking laughter.

When all the women had contrived to hide themselves in the willows, the goat-foots, couched by the grass of the newborn meadows, played their reed pipes, drawing from them such sounds as might trouble every living creature. The enraptured nymphs peeped out from the branches, and little by little they came forth from their shady retreats, drawn forward by the irresistible fluting. Then the goat-men threw themselves upon their prey with demonic fury. In the arms of their insolent captors, the nymphs did their utmost to maintain their banter and mockery, but they soon laughed no more. With their heads thrown back and their eyes blurred with joy and horror, they called upon their mother, or cried out: "I will kill myself!", or maintained a coy silence.

Fra Mino wanted to turn his head away, but he could not do it, and his eyes remained open in spite of his best efforts.

Meanwhile, the nymphs, while winding their arms about the loins of the goat-men, teasingly nipped and caressed their hairy lovers. Entwined about the goat-men, the nymphs enfolded them and bathed them with their own undulating flesh, livelier than the water in the streams which ran nearby beneath the willows.

Confronted with this vision, Fra Mino fell into sin in both spirit and intention. He longed to be one of those demons, half men and half beasts, and to hug to his bosom after their fashion the Florentine lady whom he had loved in the days of his youth, but who was now dead.

But already the goat-men were dispersing. Some were collecting honey from the trunks of oak-trees, others were making pipes out of reeds, others were bounding towards one another and clashing their horned heads together. The still bodies of the enchanting nymphs, exhausted by their love-making, were strewn about the meadow. Fra Mino groaned as he lay upon the stone floor, for the desire to sin had been so fervent within him that he was burning with shame from top to toe.

Suddenly, one of the recumbent nymphs, happening by chance to catch sight of him, cried out: "A man! A man!"

She pointed her finger at him, and said to her companions: "Look there, my sisters—that is no goatherd! No reed-pipe is to be seen beside him. Nor could he be taken for the master of one of those farms on the hillside whose little vineyards are guarded by images of Priapus carved from beech-wood. What is he doing in our company, if he is neither goatherd, nor cowherd, nor vine-grower? His expression is gloomy and severe, and in his eyes I can detect no love for the gods and goddesses which inhabit the heavens, the woods and the mountains. He is dressed in a barbaric fashion. Perhaps he is a Scythian. Let us approach this stranger, my sisters, and make certain that he has not come in enmity to foul our fountains, fell our trees, tear open our mountain-sides and betray the mysteries of our happy haunts to savages. Come with me, Mnaïs; come, Aegle, Naere and Melibea."

"We're coming!" replied Mnaïs. "We're coming, arms at the ready!"

"We're coming!" they all cried together.

Fra Mino saw that as they raised themselves up, they gathered roses by the handful, and they advanced towards him in single file, armed with roses and thorns. But the distance which separated him from them— which had at first seemed short, for he thought that he could almost touch them, and felt their breath upon his flesh, suddenly seemed to increase, and he saw them coming as if from a distant forest. Impatient to reach him, they broke into a run, menacing him with their thorny flowers. Threats spilled from their own flowery lips. But as they came closer, a change came over them; with every step they took they lost something of their

182

grace and brilliance. The gloss of their youth faded while the bouquets of roses withered in their hands. To begin with, their eyes became hollow and their mouths subsided. Their necks, so recently pure and white, became deeply creased; locks of grey hair trailed over their wrinkled foreheads. As they came further, their eyes became bloodshot, their lips drew back to their toothless gums. They came further still, carrying dried-out roses in their black and twisted arms, which were like the old vines which the peasants of Chianti feed to their fires in the winter nights. And still they came on, nodding their heads and all a-tremble on their spindly legs.

When they had reached the place where Fra Mino was pinned down by fright they were no more than horrid witches, bald and bearded, with great hooked noses and flabby, pendulous breasts. They crowded around him:

"Oh, the little darling!" said one. "He's as white as a sheet, and his heart is beating as though he were a hare worried by dogs. Aegle, my sister, what should we do with him?"

"My dear Naere," Aegle replied, "we ought to open up his breast, take out his heart, and put a sponge in its place."

"Not at all," said Melibea. "That would make him pay too dearly for his curiosity and for the pleasure he has obtained by taking us unawares. It is sufficient, this time, to inflict a lighter punishment. Should we give him a good thrashing?"

Immediately, while surrounding the monk, the sisters pulled his robe over his head, and beat him with the sheaves of thorns which they still had in their hands.

Blood had begun to flow when Naere gave the signal to desist.

"Enough!" she said. "This is my admirer! I saw right away that he looked at me tenderly, and I want to satisfy his desires by giving myself to him without further delay."

She smiled: a single long black tooth, which projected from her mouth, tickled his nose. She whispered: "Come to me, my Adonis!"

Then, suddenly enraged, she cried: "Damn it! His senses have gone numb. His coldness is an affront to my beauty. He scorns me—avenge me, my friends! Mnaïs, Aegle, Melibea, avenge your sister!"

Thus roused, they all lifted their thorny scourges again, and chastised the unhappy Fra Mino so severely that his entire body was soon very sore. They rested occasionally to cough and spit, but quickly resumed the business of plying their switches. They did not stop until they were exhausted.

"I hope," said Naere, then, "that next time he will not insult me in that unmerited fashion which still makes me blush. We will let him live. But if he betrays the secret of our games and pleasures, we will strike him dead. Au revoir, little beauty!"

So saying, the old woman crouched down over the monk and inundated him with foul liquid. Each of her sisters in turn did likewise, and then they returned, one by one, into the tomb of Saint Satyr, entering by means of a tiny crack in the lid. Their victim was left lying in a puddle which stank unbearably.

When the last one had disappeared the cock crew. Fra Mino was finally able to get up off the ground. Worn out by fatigue and pain, numb with cold, shivering with fever, half-suffocated by the vapours of the poisonous liquid, he adjusted his clothing and hauled himself off, reaching his cell just as dawn broke.

From that night on, Fra Mino could find no peace. The memory of what he had seen in Saint Michael's chapel, above Saint Satyr's tomb, troubled him during services and private prayers alike. He trembled when he accompanied the brethren into the church. When he was required by the Rule to kiss the pavement of the chancel his terrified lips discovered traces of the nymphs and he whispered: "My Saviour, do you not hear me say to you that which you once said to your Father: *Lead us not into temptation?*" For a while he had thought of sending to the Archbishop an account of what he had seen, but on due reflection he convinced himself that it would be better to meditate upon these extraordinary events at his leisure, and not make them public until he had made a more exact study of them. It transpired, moreover, that the Archbishop, allied with the Guelphs of Pisa against the Ghibellines of Florence, was presently engaged in waging war so fervently that he had hardly time to unbuckle his armour. That is why, without speaking to anyone else, Fra Mino set out to do some thorough research regarding the tomb of Saint Satyr and the chapel in which it was contained. Well-versed in the study of books though he was, he leafed through many, both ancient and modern, without shedding the least light on the problem. The treatises on Magic which he consulted served only to redouble his uncertainty.

One morning, when he had worked all night—as had become his habit—he sought to lift his spirits by taking a walk in the country. He took an uphill path which, winding between vines married to elm-trees, led to a wood of myrtles and olives, once held sacred by the Romans. With his feet in the damp grass, and his brow refreshed by the dew which dripped from the wayfaring-trees, Fra Mino had been wandering in the forest for some time when he came upon a spring over which tamarisks gently dangled their light foliage and feathery clusters of pink berries. Lower down, in a pool among the willows, motionless herons could be seen. Little birds sang among the branches of the myrtles. The moist scent of mint rose up from the ground, and the grass was spangled with those flowers of which Our Lord said: *"Solomon in all his glory was not arrayed like one of these."* Fra Mino sat down on a mossy stone and, praising that God who had made the sky and the dew, meditated upon the hidden mysteries of Nature.

Because the memory of what he had seen in the chapel never left him, he lowered his head into his hands, asking himself for the thousandth time what the dream signified. "For such a vision," he told himself, "must have a meaning; it might even have several, which it is important to discover, if not by sudden inspiration then by the precise application of the methods of scholarship. And I suppose that in this particular case the poets I have studied at Bologna, like the satirist Horace and Statius, ought to be of considerable help to me, given that so much truth is buried in their fables."

Having considered such notions for some time, and others more subtle still, he looked up, and found that he was not alone. Leaning against the cavernous trunk of an ancient ilex, an old man was gazing up through the foliage at the sky, and smiling. Blunt horns projected from his hoary brow. A white beard hung down from his flat-snouted face, on either side of which the uncommonly fleshy folds of his neck could be seen. Shaggy hair covered his chest. From his thighs to his cloven feet he was covered by a thick fleece. He held up to his lips a reed pipe, from which he extracted a faint tune. Then he sang, in voice hardly distinguishable from the music:

She fled, laughing,
Chewing the golden grapes.

But I went after her, and overtook her easily,
And my teeth crushed
The grape within her mouth.

Having seen and heard these things, Fra Mino made the sign of the cross. But the ancient creature was not at all troubled by this, and he fixed the monk with an innocent stare. Amid the deep lines of his face, his clear blue eyes sparkled like the water of a spring beside the bark of oak trees.

"Whether you are man or beast," cried Mino, "I command you in the name of the Saviour to tell me who you are."

"My son," replied the ancient, "I am Saint Satyr! Lower your voice, lest you frighten the birds."

Fra Mino went on, in a more moderate tone: "I must presume, Old One, that since the sign of the cross has no humbling effect upon you, you are not a demon or some impure spirit escaped fom Hell. But if, as you say, you are truly a man, or rather the soul of a man sanctified by a life of good works and by the favour of Our Lord, I wish that you would explain to me the wondrous fact that you have goat's horns and shaggy legs which terminate in black cloven hooves."

In response to this question the ancient lifted his arms towards the sky, and said: "My son, the nature of men, animals, plants and stones is the secret of the immortal gods, and I am as ignorant as you are regarding the origin of these horns which deck my forehead, upon which the nymphs once used to hang garlands of flowers. I know not what these folds of flesh are which droop from my neck, nor why I have the feet of an impudent goat. I can only tell you, my son, that there were once women in these woods who had horned brows and hairy shanks like mine, though their bosoms were round and white and their bellies and their loins gleamed in the sunlight.

187

The sun was young then, and loved to dapple them with its golden rays as they sheltered beneath the foliage. They were so beautiful, my son! Alas, they vanished from the woods in the end. The others of my kind perished with them, and I am all alone nowadays—the last of my race. I am very old."

"Old one, help me to understand the age which gave birth to you: your ancestry and your fatherland."

"My son, I was born of the Earth long before Saturn was dethroned by Jupiter, and my eyes were witness to the florid novelty of the world. The human race had not yet been brought forth from the clay. Alone with me, the dancing satyresses made the ground reverberate with the rhythm of their twin hooves. They were taller, and stronger, and more beautiful than nymphs or women; and their ample loins received in abundance the seed of the first-born of the Earth.

"While Jupiter reigned the nymphs began to inhabit the fountains, the woods and the mountains. Fauns, mingling with the nymphs, formed nimble choirs deep in the woods. Meanwhile, I lived happily, consuming at my leisure the wild grapes and the lips of the laughing she-fauns. I was accustomed to sleeping peaceably in the thick grass. I played my reed pipes to celebrate the succession of Saturn by Jupiter, for it was ever my wont to praise the gods who are masters of the world.

"Alas, I have grown old, for I am no god, and the centuries have bleached the hairs upon my head and upon my breast, and have put out the fire of my loins. The years were heavy upon me ere great Pan died, even more so when Jupiter met the fate which he had visited upon Saturn, and was dethroned by the Galilean. I languished as my life dragged on, until at last I met my own death, and was placed in my tomb. Truly, I am now but a shadow of my former self. If I exist at all, it is only

188

because nothing is ever really lost, and it is permitted to no one to die completely. Death is known to be no more perfect than life. My child, the beings which are lost in the ocean of things are like the waves that you can see rising and falling in the Adriatic. They have neither a beginning nor an end, they are born and they die imperceptibly. As imperceptibly as the waves, my soul drains away. A faint memory of the satyresses of the Golden Age still brightens my eyes, and from my lips the ancient hymns still silently take flight."

Having said all this, he fell silent.

Fra Mino looked at the old one, and knew that he was nothing but a phantom. "It is not entirely incredible," he said, "that you might have a cloven hoof and yet not be a demon. The creatures to which God allocated no part in Adam's heritage can no more be damned than they can be saved. I cannot believe that the centaur Charon, who was wiser than any man, suffers eternal punishment in the jaws of Leviathan. A traveller who entered Limbo said that he had seen him seated on the grass, conversing with Ripheus, the most righteous of the Trojans. Although others declare that Paradise itself has been opened to Ripheus of Troy, it is permissible to entertain doubts regarding the matter. Nevertheless, Old One, you lied when you told me that you were a saint—you who are not even a man."

The goat-foot replied: "My son, when I was young, I was no more given to lying than the ewes whose milk I sucked or the goats with which I sported, glorying in my strength and my beauty. In those days, no one lied, and the fleeces of sheep had not yet found out how to be remade in deceptive colours; I have not changed my nature in the intervening years. See—I am naked, as I was in Saturn's Golden Age. My spirit is no more veiled than my body. I am no liar. And why should you find it

189

so extraordinary, my son, that I have become a saint appointed by the Galilean? I am not descended from that mother which some call Eve and others Pyrrha—who deserves veneration under either name—but Saint Michael is no more born of woman than I; I know him, and we have sometimes conversed together. He tells me about the time when he was a cowherd on Mount Gargan..."

Fra Mino interrupted the satyr, saying: "I cannot allow Saint Michael to be described as a cowherd simply because he once kept watch over the cattle of a man named Gargan, like the mountain. But explain to me, Ancient One, how you came to be canonised."

"Only listen," the goat-foot replied, "and your curiosity will be satisfied.

"When men came from the East to the placid Arno valley, bringing the news that the Galilean had dethroned Jupiter, they felled the oaks where the peasants were wont to hang up little clay goddesses and votive tablets; they set up crosses over the sacred springs, and forbade the shepherds to carry their offerings of wine, milk and cakes to the grottos of the nymphs. The followers of Pan—the fauns and other sylvan spirits—were righteously offended. In their anger, they attacked the advocates of the new god. At night, when the apostles were asleep on their beds of dry leaves, nymphs came to pull their beards, and young fauns slipped into their stables to pull hairs out of their asses' tails. I tried vainly to dampen their ingenuous malice, and exhorted them to accept the new order. 'My children,' I would say to them, 'the era of playful ease and carefree laughter is at an end.' But they were reckless, and would not listen. They brought themselves to unhappiness.

"As for myself, having seen the end of Saturn's reign I found it both natural and appropriate that Jupiter

190

should perish in his turn. I was resigned to the fall of the great gods. I did not resist the emissaries of the Galilean. Rather, I served them in small ways. Knowing more than they did about the forest paths, I gathered apples and berries which I left on beds of leaves at the threshold of their grotto. I also left offerings of plovers' eggs. And when they were building a cabin I carried wood and stones for them upon my back. In return, they anointed my forehead with water, desirous of helping me to make my peace with Jesus Christ.

"I lived with them and like them. Those who loved them, loved me. Just as they were honoured, I was honoured in my turn, and my sanctity was apparently equal to theirs.

"I have told you, my son, that I was already very old even then. The sun hardly warmed my numb limbs. I was no better than an old hollow tree which could no longer put forth a crown of fresh leaves, deserted by the songbirds. Each new autumn increased my decrepitude. One winter morning I was found stretched out, motionless, beside the road.

"The bishop, in the presence of the other priests and their entire congregation, held a funeral mass for me. Then I was placed in a huge tomb of white marble, which was thrice marked with the sign of the cross and which bore on the front-facing wall the name of SAINT SATYR, surrounded by a garland of roses.

"In those days, my son, tombs were built by the roadsides. Mine was situated two miles from the city, on the road to Florence. A young plane-tree grew up over it, and covered it with a shadow dappled with sunlight, full of murmurous birdsong, freshness and joy. Not far away, a fountain poured its waters upon a bed of water-cress; boys and girls came to bathe together, laughing all the while. It was an enchanting place, and a holy one.

191

Young mothers brought their babies there and made them touch the monument, in order that all their limbs might grow strong and straight. It was universally believed that the newly-born brought to my sepulchre would one day surpass their fellows in vigour and courage. For that reason the flower of the noble Tuscan race was brought to me. The peasants also brought me their asses, in the hope of making them fecund. My memory was revered. Every year, at the beginning of spring, the bishop would come with his clergy to pray over my remains, and I watched from afar, as the procession of cross and candle-bearers crossed the meadows and valleys beneath its scarlet canopy, singing psalms. That was the way it was, my son, in the times of good King Bérenger.

"Meanwhile, the life of the satyrs and satyresses, the fauns and the nymphs, dragged on misguidedly and wretchedly. For them, there were no more altars of meadow-grass, no more garlands of flowers, no more offerings of milk, wheat and honey. Occasionally, but not often, some furtive goat-herd would lay a little cheese on the threshold of a sacred grotto, whose entrance was being enveloped by brambles and thorns; but only rabbits and squirrels came to eat these poor offerings. The nymphs, inhabitants of forests and other gloomy places, had been driven from their haunts by the apostles who came from the East; and to make sure that they could not return to them the priests of the Galilean God poured holy water on the trees and the stones, pronounced magical incantations of a kind in which they were well-versed, and set up crosses where the forest paths met. The Galilean understood far better than Saturn or Jupiter the virtue of formulas and signs. And so the poor rustic divinities could no longer take shelter in their sacred groves; the company of shaggy goat-foots, who once had stirred the maternal earth with their rhythmic feet, was now no more than a host of pale, mute shadows trailing the hillsides like the morning mist which is dissipated by the sun.

"Buffeted as though by a furious wind by the wrath of Heaven, those spectres were whirled about all day long in the dust of the highways. Night was a little less hostile to them, for night did not entirely belong to the Galilean god; the demons had their share of its dominion. When the shadow of night descended from the hills, the followers of Pan came to cower beside the tombs which bordered the roads, and there, under the gentle empire of the infernal powers, they would enjoy a brief repose. They preferred my tomb to the others, because it was that of a venerable ancestor. Eventually they all gathered together under the part of the cornice which was always dry and free of moss because it faced south. The folk of the air flew to it faithfully every night, like doves to a dovecôte. They found space there easily enough, having become very tiny, as light as the chaff blown away by the winnowing-fan. As for myself, I would sometimes emerge from my silent burial-chamber and sit down in their midst, under cover of the marble tiles, and sing to them, in a feeble, whispering voice, of the days of Saturn and Jupiter; reminding them of long-lost happiness. With Diana looking down on them they would come together to reproduce their ancient gambols, and tardy travellers would think that they had seen the mists of the moonlit meadows imitate the clinging bodies of lovers. Indeed, they were little more than light mist themselves. The cold made them very ill.

"One night, when the snow had covered the countryside, the nymphs Aegle, Naere, Mnaïs and Melibea glided through cracks in the marble into the narrow and gloomy chamber I inhabit. Their companions came crowding after them, and the fauns, bounding in pursuit of them, soon came to join them. My abode became theirs. We rarely left it, save to go into the woods on fine nights. Even then they would make haste to return before cock-crow; for you must understand, my son, that of all the horned race, I alone have leave to appear on earth during the daylight hours. It is a privilege granted me by virtue of my sainthood.

"My sepulchre was more revered than ever by the country folk and every day the young mothers presented their nurslings to me, lifting up their naked bodies. When the Franciscan brothers established themselves in the country and built a monastery on the hillside they asked the archbishop if he would permit them to remove my tomb to the church and keep it there. This favour having been granted to them, I was transferred with much ceremony to the chapel of Saint Michael, where I have remained ever since. My rustic family was carried here with me. It was a great honour, but I must admit that I missed the broad highway where every daybreak I could watch the peasant women carrying baskets of grapes, figs and aubergines upon their heads. Time has hardly soothed my regrets at all, and I wish that I were still beneath the plane-tree on the sacred path.

"Such is my life," concluded the old satyr. "It flows on happily, gently and unobtrusively through all the ages of the Earth. If a little sadness is mingled with its joy, that must be the will of the gods. Oh my son, let us praise the gods, the masters of the worlds!"

Fra Mino was pensive for a while, and then said: "I now understand the meaning of what I have seen, in the course of an evil night, in the chapel of Saint Michael. But there is still one point about which I am unclear. Tell me, Old One, why the nymphs who dwell with you and who give themselves to the fauns changed themselves into disgusting old women when they came towards me."

"Alas, my son," replied Saint Satyr, "time spares neither men nor gods. The latter are immortal only in the imagination of ephemeral mankind. In reality, they feel the effects of age, and tend to decline irreparably as the centuries go by. Nymphs grow old as women do. As every rose withers to a husk; so every nymph withers into a witch. When you watched the frolics of my little family you could see how, even now, the memory of their youth still embellishes nymphs and satyrs when they make love, and how their briefly reanimated ardour can renew their charms—but the ruination of centuries reappears immediately afterwards, alas. Unfortunately, the race of nymphs is ancient and decrepit."

Fra Mino was not yet done with questions: "Old One, if it is true that you have achieved beatitude by mysterious means, and if it is true, despite the absurdity of it, that you are a saint, why do you remain in the tomb with these phantoms which do not know how to praise God, and whose indecency pollutes the house of the Lord. Answer me that, Old One!"

But the goat-footed saint, without responding, vanished into thin air.

Seated on the mossy stone beside the spring, Fra Mino meditated upon the discourse which he had just heard, and found in it—albeit mingled with certain deep obscurities—a marvellous enlightenment.

"This Saint Satyr," he thought, "is comparable to the Sybil who, even in a temple of the false gods, prophesied the coming of the saviour of the world. The mire of ancient superstitions still clings to his cloven hooves, but his forehead is raised towards the light, and his lips proclaim the truth."

As the shadow of the beeches extended across the

195

grass of the hillside the monk got up from his stone and went down the narrow path which led to the convent of the Franciscan brothers. But he dared not look at the water-lilies which lay asleep upon the pools, because they reminded him of the nymphs. He re-entered his cell at the very moment when the bells began to sound the *Ave Maria*. The cell was small, with whitened walls; its only furniture was a bed, a stool and a tall writing-desk. On the wall, a mendicant friar had once painted, in the manner of Giotto, the Marys at the foot of the Cross. Below this painting was a wooden bookshelf as black and lustrous as the beams of a wine-press; some of the books were sacred, others secular, for Fra Mino studied the ancient poets in order that he might praise the handiwork of God in all the works of men, blessing Virgil the Mantuan for having prophesied the birth of the Saviour in declaring to the nations of the world: *Jam redit et Virgo.**

On the window-sill a long-stemmed lily projected from a vase of unglazed earthenware. Fra Mino loved to trace the name of the holy Virgin inscribed in the golden dust of the flower's corolla. The window was set high in the wall, and was not large, but through it one could see the sky above the purple hills.

Having enclosed himself in the peaceful tomb to which he had committed his life and his desires, Mino stationed himself at the narrow desk with the two surmounting shelves, where he was accustomed to devote himself to his studies. There, dipping his reed-pen into the inkwell fastened to the side of the bank of pigeon-holes which held his sheets of parchment, brushes, pigments and powdered gold, he prayed in the name of the Lord that the flies would not pester him, and he

* Now the Virgin also returns.

began to write an account of all that he had seen and heard in the chapel of Saint Michael during that misfortunate night, and what had transpired on that very day beside the spring in the wood. To begin with, he wrote these lines upon the parchment:

Here is recorded that which Fra Mino, of the order of Lesser Friars, has seen and heard, which he relates for the instruction of the faithful. In praise of Jesus Christ and the glory of His blessed and humble follower, St. Francis. Amen.

Then he set down in writing, omitting nothing, that which he had observed concerning the nymphs which became witches, and the old man with horns whose voice murmured in the woods as though it were the last sigh of the flute of antiquity and a prelude to the sacred harp. While he wrote, the birds sang. Night came slowly to efface the lovely colours of the day. The monk lit his lamp and continued to write. As he reported the marvels with which he had become acquainted he explained their literal and spiritual meanings, according to the rules of scholarship. And, as though he were building a wall to fortify a town, he supported his arguments with texts taken from the Scriptures. From the singular revelations which he had received he deduced these conclusions:

Firstly, that Jesus Christ is Lord of all creatures, and is the God of satyrs and fauns as well as men; that is why Saint Jerome saw in the desert centaurs who confessed their faith in Jesus Christ.

Secondly, that God communicated to the pagans certain glimmerings of truth, to the end that they might be saved; thus the sybils, such as the Cumaean, the Egyptian and the Delphic, brought about the first appearance amid the Gentile shadows of the images of the Crib, the Rods, the Reed Sceptre, the Crown of Thorns and the Cross—for which reason Saint Augustine had admitted the Erythrean sybil into the City of God.

Fra Mino gave thanks to God for having been shown these things. A great joy flooded his heart at the thought that Virgil was among the elect. And he wrote with gladness at the bottom of the last page:

Here ends the Apocalypse of Friar Mino, humble follower of Jesus Christ. I have seen the holy aureole upon the horned head of the Satyr, signifying that Jesus Christ has brought forth from Limbo the sages and poets of antiquity.

The night was already well advanced when, having completed his task, Fra Mino stretched himself out on his bed to take a little rest. Just as he was dropping off to sleep an old woman came in through the window, borne by a moonbeam. He recognised her as the most horrible of the witches whom he had seen in the chapel of Saint Michael.

"My pretty," she said to him, "what have you been doing today? We warned you, my gentle sisters and I, on no account to reveal our secrets, and that if you betrayed us, we would kill you—no matter how grievously it would wound me, on account of the tender affection which I have for you."

She took him in her arms, called him her heavenly Adonis and her little white donkey, and covered him with ardent kisses. And when he tried disgustedly to throw her off she said: "Child, you treat me with disdain because my eyes are bloodshot, my nostrils corroded by the acrid and putrid fluid which they distil, and my gums garnished by a single tooth, which is black and unnaturally long. It is true that this is the state into which your Naere has fallen. But if you love me, I will become again, through you and for you, that which I was in the Golden Age of Saturn, when I was in the full flower of my youth, and the world itself was young and flourishing. It is love, my young god, which makes the beauty of things. It only requires a little courage to make me beautiful. Get up, Mino, and display your virility!"

At these words and their accompanying gestures, Fra Mino, utterly possessed by horror and dread, fainted dead away and slid from his bed on to the stone floor of his cell. As he fell, he thought he saw, between his half-closed eyelids, a perfectly-formed nymph, whose naked body flowed over him like spilled milk.

Mino woke in broad daylight, bruised from top to toe by his fall. The sheets of parchment which he had covered in ink during the night were scattered about the desk. He read them through, folded them up, secured them with sealing-wax and tucked them inside his robe. Heedless of the threats which the witches had made twice over, he went forth to carry his revelations to the Archbishop, the battlements of whose palace loomed up in the town centre.

He found the Archbishop in the Great Hall, surrounded by men-at-arms, putting on his spurs; the pope had declared war upon the Ghibellines of Florence.

The Archbishop asked the monk to tell him the reason for his visit, and when he had been informed of it, he invited him to read out his account on the spot. Fra Mino did as he was askeed.

The Archbishop listened to the discourse until the very end. He had no particular enlightenment on the subject of apparitions, but he was animated by an ardent zeal to protect the interests of the Faith. Without delaying a single day, and without allowing the war to distract him from his purpose, he summoned twelve illustrious theologians and experts in canon law to hold an inquiry into the matter, and urged them to bring in their verdict.

After mature consideration, and not without subjecting Fra Mino to many interrogations, the scholars decided that it would be advisable to open the tomb of Saint Satyr in the chapel of Saint Michael, and subject it to a series of rites of exorcism. On the points of doctrine raised by Fra Mino they declined to issue a formal statement, although they were inclined to take the view that the Franciscan's arguments were temerous, frivolous and unprecedented.

In conformity with the advice of the theologians, and by order of the Archbishop, the tomb of Saint Satyr was opened. It contained nothing but a few ashes, over which the priests sprinkled holy water. There arose in consequence a white vapour, from which there escaped a feeble groaning sound.

On the night which followed this pious ceremony, Fra Mino dreamed that the witches, hovering over his bed, were tearing the heart out of him. He got up early in the morning, tormented by sharp pains and a raging thirst. He dragged himself as far as the well in the cloister, where the doves came to drink, but no sooner had he sipped up the few drops of water which filled a hollow in the well-head than he felt his heart swell up like a sponge, and—murmuring "My God!"—he choked to death.

****

18.

DON JUAN DECLAIMS
by James Elroy Flecker

I am Don Juan, curst from age to age
By priestly tract and sentimental stage:
Branded a villain or believed a fool,
Battered by hatred, seared by ridicule,
Noble on earth, all but a king in Hell,
I am Don Juan with a tale to tell.
    Hot leapt the dawn from deep Plutonian fires
And ran like blood among the twinkling spires.
The market quickened: carts came rattling down:
Good human music roared about the town,
'And come,' they cried, 'and buy the best of Spain's
Great fireskinned fruits with cold and streaming veins!'
Others, 'The man who'd make a lordly dish,
Would buy my speckled or my silver fish.'
And some, 'I stitch you raiment to the rule!'
And some,'I sell you attar of Stamboul!'
'And I have lapis for your love to wear,
Pearls for her neck and amber for her hair.'
Death has its gleam. They swing before me still,
The shapes and sounds and colours of Seville!

    For there I learnt to love the plot, the fight,
The masker's cloak, the ladder set for flight,
The stern pursuit, the rapier's glint of death,
The scent of starlit roses, beauty's breath,
The music and the passion and the prize,
Aragon lips and Andalusian eyes.
This day a democrat I scoured the town;

Courting, the next, I brought a princess down:
Now in some lady's panelled chamber hid
Achieved what love approves and laws forbid,
Now walked and whistled round the sleepy farms
And clasped a Dulcinea in my arms.
   I was the true, the grand idealist:
My light could pierce the pretty golden mist
That hides from common souls the starrier climes:
I loved as small men do ten-thousand times:
Rose to the blue triumphant, curved my bow,
Set high the mark and brought an angel low,
And laced with that brave body and shining soul
Learnt how to live, then learnt to love the whole.
And I first broke that jungle dark and dense,
Which hides the silver house of Commonsense,
And dissipated that disastrous lie
Which makes a god of stuffless Unity,
And drave the dark behind me, and revealed
A Pagan sunrise on a Christian field.
   My legend tells how once, by passion moved,
I slew the father of a girl I loved,
Then summoned – like an old and hardened sinner –
The brand-new statue of the dead to dinner.
My ribald guests, with Spanish wine aflame,
Were most delighted when the statue came,
Bowed to the party, made a little speech,
And bore me off beyond their human reach.
Well, priests must flourish and the truth must pale:
A very pious, entertaining tale.

   But this believe. I struck a ringing blow
At sour Authority's ancestral show,
And stirred the sawdust understuffing all
The sceptred or the surpliced ritual.
I willed my happiness, kept bright and brave

My thoughts and deeds this side the accursed grave:
Life was a ten-course banquet after all,
And neatly rounded by my funeral.
'Pale guest, why strip the roses from your brow?
We hope to feast till morning.' 'Who knocks now?'
'Twelve of the clock, Don Juan.' In came he,
That shining, tall and cold Authority,
Whost marble lips smile down on lips that pray,
And took my hand, and I was led away.

19.

OCCULT MEMORIES
by Villiers de l'Isle Adam

"Et il n'y a pas, dans toute la
contrée, de chateau plus chargé
de gloire et d'années que mon
mélancolique manoir héréditaire."
—EDGAR POE*

I am descended, he told me—I, the last of the Gaels—
from a Celtic family as durable as our rocks. I belong to
that race of mariners, the illustrious flower of Armorica,
the stock of exotic warriors, whose dazzling feats are
numbered among the jewels in History's crown.

One of those forebears, wearied even in his youth by
the sight and the tiresome social intercourse of his
neighbours, became a permanent exile from his native
land, his heart replete with scornful disregard. This was
the time of the Asian expeditions; he took himself off to
fight by the side of the Bailiff of Suffren†, and soon
distinguished himself in the Indies, by means of the

*Translator's note: This sentence seems to be misquoted—probably
quite consciously—from Baudelaire's translation of "Berenice". The
equivalent line in the original is: "Yet there are no towers in the land
more time-honoured than my gloomy, grey, hereditary halls." "Occult
Memories" is developed from an earlier prose-poem, "El Desdichado",
which carried the same epigraph, although its style is closer to that of
another of Poe's prose-poems, "Eleonora" (which begins "I am come of
a race noted for vigour of fancy and ardour of passion...")

† Translator's note: The reference is to the French admiral Pierre
André Suffren de Saint-Tropez, who fought the British in the Indian
Ocean during the American Civil War.

mysterious feats of arms which he accomplished single-handedly in the interior of the Dead Cities.

These ruined cities are set beneath white and desolate skies, in the heart of dreadful forests. Creepers, grasses and desiccated branches are strewn about, blocking the paths which were once crowded avenues, from which the noise of chariots, weapons and songs has long since vanished.

No breath of wind, no birdsong, no tinkling fountain disturbs the horrid calm of these regions. The Bengalis themselves shun the ancient ebonies which grow here, though they make such trees their own in other places. Among the litter which is heaped in the clearings, immense and monstrous flowers sprout and grow very tall, in whose sinister blooms—which are as azure-streaked, flame-tinted and cinnabar-veined as the radiant feathers of a host of extinct peacocks—the spirits of the sun subtly burn. An atmosphere warmed by the aroma of mortality weighs down upon the silent debris: it is like a vapour of funerary incense; a blue, intoxicating, tortuous, odorous sweat.

The reckless vulture which pauses over that land during its pilgrimage from the plateau of Kabul and contemplates it from the top of some black date-palm, will suddenly clutch at the lianas, urgently writhing in the agony of death.

Here and there lie broken arches, shapeless statues, and blocks of stone whose inscriptions are more eroded than those of Sardis, Palmyra or Khorsabad. On some, which once were part of the ornamental facades of the city-gates, lost in the clouds, the eye can still decipher and reconstruct the scarcely-legible sanskrit motto of the free people of those olden days:

"....AND GOD SHALL NOT PREVAIL!"

The silence is undisturbed, save for the slithering of

snakes which glide between the fallen shafts of the columns, or coil up, hissing, beneath the reddish mosses.

Occasionally, in the stormy twilight, the far-off cry of the dziggetai, mournfully alternating with claps of thunder, disturbs the solitude.

Extended beneath the ruins are subterranean passages whose entrances are lost. There, the first kings of these alien and lately masterless lands, whose names are now unknown, have slept for untold centuries. Those kings, doubtless in accordance with some sacred rites of their religion, were entombed in those vaults with their treasures.

No lamp lights the tombs.

None of them can remember the echoing footsteps of a captive of the cares of Life and Desire ever having come to disturb their slumber.

Only the torch of a Brahmin—some haggard ghost bound for Nirvana, some mute spirit, mere witness of the universal process of becoming—sometimes flickers unexpectedly, at certain times of penitence or divinely-inspired vision, at the head of a broken stairway, projecting the light of its smoky flame step by step into the depths of the caverns.

Then the relics, played upon by the glimmering light, sparkle with a kind of miraculous opulence: the chains of precious metal interlaced with the bones seem to be streaked by sudden lightning; the regal ashes, dusted with gems, scintillate like the dust of a road reddened by the last ray of sunset, before the descent of night.

The Maharajahs have set their best warriors to guard the edges of the sacred forests, especially the approaches to the clearings where the outskirts of the ruins can be seen. Also prohibited are the banks, the streams and the broken bridges of the rivers which flow through them. A silent militia, which consists of merciless and incorruptible sepoys, who have the hearts of hyenas, ceaselessly patrol every part of those deadly borderlands.

Night after night, the hero of my tale avoided their cunning traps and ambushes and escaped their constant vigilance. By suddenly sounding a horn in the darkness, from various different places, he would draw them aside with false alarms; then, he would spring forth into the starlight from the midst of the tall flowers, rapidly eviscerating their horses. The soldiers were terrified by this unexpected apparition, which seemed to them to be some malevolent demon. Endowed with the strength of a tiger, the Adventurer would proceed to overwhelm them, one by one. With a single bound he would swiftly seize each one, leaving him half-choked until, in due course, he could return and complete the massacre at his leisure.

The Exile became, in this fashion, the scourge, the terror and the exterminator of those cruel guardians whose faces were the colour of the earth. To cut a long story short, they were left behind, nailed to great trees, their own yataghans buried in their hearts.

Committed thereafter to the realm of ancient desolation, he roamed the alleyways, crossroads and streets of those ancient cities until at last, in spite of the odours, he reached the entrance of those unparalleled tombs where the remains of the Hindu kings lay at rest.

The doors being defended only by huge statues of jasper—monstrous idols with pearls or emeralds for eyes, whose forms were the creation of some forgotten theogonic imagination—he gained access easily enough, although every step he took as he descended caused the long wings of those gods to stir.

There, feeling his way through the gloomy depths with groping hands, subduing the suffocating vertigo of the dark ages whose spirits flew about his head and brushed his brow with their trailing webs, he quietly gathered together a thousand marvels. The likes of Cortez and Pizarro, who seized the treasures of the caciques and kings of Mexico and Peru, were no more intrepid than he.

With the satchels of stones in the bottom of his boat, he went silently back upriver, avoiding the dangerous moonlight. Hunched over his oars he guided his craft through the reeds, paying no heed to the plaintive cries of the children who lamented the nearness of crocodiles.

In a few hours he reached by this means a distant cavern known only to himself, in whose depths he unshipped his booty.

News of his exploit spread, and the legend of it is still recited by fakirs at the festivals of the nabobs, to the loud accompaniment of sitars. These verminous performers describe that ancestor of mine—not without an ancient frisson of hateful jealousy or respectful dread—as the Despoiler of Tombs.

There came a time, however, when the intrepid boatman allowed himself to be seduced by the insidious and honeyed persuasions of the one friend with whom he had ever joined forces, for a particularly perilous expedition—from which the other man, by a prodigious stroke of luck, escaped with his life! I refer to the notorious and aptly-named Colonel Sombre.

Thanks to this devious Irishman, the great Adventurer walked into an ambush. Blinded by his own blood, struck by bullets, encircled by twenty scimitars, he was caught off guard; he eventually perished after undergoing frightful tortures.

The Himalayan nomads, intoxicated by his death and capering madly in their triumphal dance, rushed to the cave. Once they had recovered the treasures they set out to return them to the accursed country. Their leaders piously threw the riches back into the depths of the funereal pits where the aforementioned shades of those kings of the night of the world lay at rest. And the ancient jewels shine there still, as if their eternally luminous gaze was forever fixed upon mankind.

I, alas—I, the Gael—have inherited only the heady brilliance and the hopeful ambition of that sublime soldier of fortune. Here I dwell, in the West, in this ancient fortified town, enchained by my own melancholy. Indifferent to the political affairs of my century and my fatherland, and to the ephemeral trespasses of those who are their representatives, I stay up late on those evenings when autumn solemnly tints the rusty treetops of the surrounding forests as though with flame. Amid the splendours of the dew, I walk alone through the arches of the dark alleys, as my grandfather walked through the crypts of the sparkling registry of the dead. In addition, I instinctively avoid, though I do not know why, the baleful rays of the moon and the maleficent approaches of my fellow men. Yes, I avoid them when I walk thus, in the company of my dreams....for I feel, then, that I carry in my soul a reflection of the sterile riches of countless forgotten kings.

****

20.

THE TESTAMENT OF A VIVISECTOR
by John Davidson

Appraise me! – you, Christian of any stock:
Suave Catholic, whose haunting art avails,
Though fires are damped and sophistry undone;
Evangelist, with starved and barren brain,
Preying on evil consciences; or you,
Courageous Anglican, the well-beloved,
Enfeoffed with freehold in the City of God,
And happy here upon commuted tithes –
Your vested interests snug and ancient lights;
Or you, Agnostic, fearing yes and no,
Poltroon upon conviction; you, nor you,
Vendor of poem or philosopheme,
Patriot, gossip, warrior, chapman, all
In profits dabbling and affairs of men –
Not one of you with impulse or intent
To think my thought, how can you judge my life?
Who knows the savour of forbidden fruit,
The zest of inquisition when the world
Delivers whole, unchallenged and exempt;
Who never begs that truth should benefit,
Or be at least innoxious, but frequents
The labyrinthine fires of solitude
Wherein the thinker, parched and charred, outlives
Millenniums in a moment; who reveres
Himself, and with superb despite
Maltreats the loving-kindnesses of men,
Divine ideas and abstractions fond –
He, he alone may measure and endure

My headstrong passion and austerity.
'To love and understand?' The prattlement
Of amorists, begetters, family folk
Inevitably mean, and gall-less hacks
Of wealth who ape imagined Providence!
Chief end of man, the ultimate design
Of intellect, is knowledge undefiled
With use or usufruct. Matter, unknown,
Unknowing, crawled and groped through grade on grade
Of faculty, till Thought came forth at last
With power to sift the elements. Chief end
Of Matter – of the Earth aware in us,
As of that Greater Matter orbed and lit
Throughout Eternal Night – is evermore
Self-Knowledge.

Thought achieved, the unconscious will,
Which Matter is, empowered it and enslaved
With endless lust of life triumphantly,
That knowledge might endure; and tarred it on –
This Thought, or lustful thinker, man – to know
Under a penalty without reprieve,
Of character and title manifold
Discomfort, pain, affliction, agony.

Inclement skies, antagonism in love,
Engrossing hunger, from the willing earth
Won easy knowledge apt for instant use.
Luxury, fashion, tribal vanity,
Desire of power, disease, the fear of death
Extorted many a secret, quaintly masked,
Embarrassed and provocative, or pent
Inscrutably in substance signetless;
But chiefly Death inspired the slavish Thought
With terror-stricken zeal to penetrate

211

The only mystery, Matter, mutable,
Eternal, infinite in being, power,
And semblance.

Matter's drudge, the restless Thought
Knit up with flesh of men, that builds and weaves,
Bakes, brews, and fights, and heals; that *would* express
The very seed of gold, and tamely sought
Elixir – (paragon of vanities,
And Matter's masterpiece in high chicane:
That, not content with offspring, men must scheme
To propagate their own peculiar woe!) –
This helpless Thought, solacing unbeknown
The passion for self-knowledge, crown and flower
Of that unconscious will which Matter is –
(Always the stolid will, Matter supreme!) –
I say, this anguished Thought, this mind of man,
Organ of Matter's consciousness, rebelled,
And with a wanton populace of gods,
A drift of elves, and rout of forms obscene,
Slandered Material truth; more traitorous still,
Perverted and obscured the clear Unknown
With the Immaterial, imagined God
Alone, spirit, and a hereafter – pitched
Sublimely in the empyrean Heaven,
In the abyss profoundly hollowed Hell.
'Salvation or Damnation,' Thought aspired,
'So I escape from Matter's galling yoke!'
Thus the tormented common-mind of man,
A mode of Matter warring with itself.

But at all times a more reliant Thought,
A strength of brain, a remnant less than man
And greater – in the jargon of the herd,
'Hateful to God and to God's enemies' –

212

Fulfilled the bent of Matter willingly,
And sought out Knowledge for its very sake:
It might be shrewdly as a livelihood,
Or to delight or help mankind, or make
A name, at first; but in the end to know –
Merely to know was the consuming fire
Of these strong minds, delivered and elect.
In the high sphere of knowledge which I haunt,
When I began to hew the living flesh,
I seemed to seek – I seemed; for who can tell
The drift of aims utility distorts? –
The mitigation of disease. Not long
A bias of humanity deflects
Advancement in the true Materialist!
My Thought that shared the contumacy men
Display, effeminate in things Material,
Began to turn to Matter lustfully,
With masculine intent...You start and stare!
How shall I cut and thrust conviction through
And through you!...Now, I know. This impress asks
A sheet unsoiled. Oh, for a sudden end
Of palimpsests! Expunge the o'erscored script
That blurs the mind with poetry and prose
Of every age; and yield it gladly up
For me to carve with knowledge, and to seal
With Matter's signet. Listen now, and think.

Daily I passed a common, chapped and seamed
By weeks of headlong heat. A rotten hack,
Compunctious hideful of rheumatic joints
Larded with dung and clay, gaunt spectacle
Of ringbone, spavin, canker, shambled about,
And grazed the faded, sparse, disrelished tufts
That the sun's tongue of flame had left half-licked:
Family physician, coster, cat's-meat-man –

These, the indifferent fates who ruled his life.
The last had turned him loose to dissipate
A day or two of grace. But when he came –
The raw-faced knacker with his knuckly fists –
I ransomed Dobbin, pitying his case,
He seemed so cheerful maugre destiny.

Enfranchised in my meadow, all his hours
Were golden, till the end with autumn came,
Even while my impulse sundered husk and shell
Of habit and utility. Two days
He lay a-dying, and could not die. Endowed
With strength, affection, blood, nerve, hearing, sight;
Laden with lust of life for the behoof
Of Matter; gelded, bitted, scourged, starved, dying –
Where could the meaning of the riddle lie?
Submissively, like a somnambulist
Who solves his problem in a dream, I found
The atonement of it, and became its lord –
Lord of the riddle of the Universe,
Aware at full of Matter's stolid will
In me accomplishing its useless aim.
The whip's-man felt no keener ecstasy
When a fair harlot at the cart's-tail shrieked,
And rags of flesh with blood-soaked tawdry lace
Girdled her shuddering loins. No hallowed awe
That ever rapt a pale inquisitor,
Beholding pangs of stubborn heresy
A-sweat upon the rack, surpassed the fierce
Exalted anguish of my thought. I fixed
The creature, impotent and moribund,
With gag and fetter; sheared his filthy mane;
Cut a foot's length, tissue and tendon, 'twixt
His poll and festering withers, and hammered out
Three arches of his spine. In ropy bulk,

Stripped to my forceps, marrow, Matter's pith
Itself! A twitch, a needle's faint appeal
Recalled the gelding's life, supplied each stop
And register of sense with vibrant power,
And made this faithful, dying, loathsome drudge,
One diapason of intensest pain,
Sublime and terrible in martyrdom.

I study pain, measure it and invent –
I and my compeers; for I hold again
That every passionate Materialist,
Who rends the living subject, soon is purged
Of vulgar tenderness in diligent
Delighted tormentry of bird and beast;
And, conscious or unconscious of his aim,
Fulfils the will of Matter, cutting out
A path to knowledge, undefiled with use
Or usufruct, by Matter's own resource,
Pain, alkahest of all intelligence.
I study pain – pain only: I broach and tap
The agony of Matter, and work its will,
Detecting useless items – I and those
Who tortured fourscore solipeds to carve
A scale of feeling on the spinal cord;
Quilted with nails, and mangled flights of fowl,
Litters and nests of vermin happily
Throughout a year, discerning in the end
That anguished breath and breath of healthy ease
Differ in function by a jot, perhaps;
Or Pisan doctors whom the Florentine
Furnished with criminals from a gentler doom
Withdrawn to undergo anatomy,
And masters who, before the world grew tame,
Enjoyed the handling in their honoured troughs
Of countless men and women alive and well.

215

'Have I no pain?' – I live alone: my wife
Forsook me, and my daughters. In the night,
From silted fountains sprung, insurgent tears
Arouse me, a marauder in the past
Against my will – one of the nightly gang
Impressed by sleep to serve Insomnia,
The queen of waking dreams. Caught in her snare,
The man-trap Memory, towards the recreant hour
When life is at the ebb, I rise and think
To end it now; but always stay my hand,
Because we cannot put an end to that
In which we live and move and have our being,
Nor anywhere escape it: air is Matter;
The interstellar spaces, Matter cold
And thin, the darksome vehicle of light.
To the Materialist there is no Unknown;
All, all is Matter. Pain? I am one ache –
But never when I work; there Matter wins!
And I believe that they who delve the soil,
Who reap the grain, who dig and smelt the ore,
The girl who plucks a rose, the sweetest voice
That thrills the air with sound, give Matter pain:
Think you the sun is happy in his flames,
Or that the cooling earth no anguish feels,
Nor quails from her contraction? Rather say,
The systems, constellations, galaxies
That strew the ethereal waste are whirling there
In agony unutterable. Pain?
It may be Matter in itself is pain,
Sweetened in sexual love that so mankind,
The medium of Matter's consciousness,
May never cease to know – the stolid bent
Of Matter, the infinite vanity
Of the Universe, being evermore

216

Self-knowledge.

21.

CROWD SCENE
by Octave Mirbeau

It was Christmas Eve. Although seasonal verses and prints insist that on that day the sky must be leaden, that the houses and gardens must be covered in snow, and that poor men must shiver with cold, on this occasion the sun was warm and bright. The gentle sunlight brought a golden glow to houses and faces alike, and caressed the backs of the little old men who sat on the benches on the promenade, staring out to sea. The streets of the little town of C— were full of light, and there were a great many people strolling lazily this way and that in family groups, dressed absurdly in their Sunday best. The workshops were silent, the shops resplendent; the air was filled with the scent of oranges and varnished wood. The shop windows were sumptuously decorated, setting out the usual seasonal and perennial temptations amid all the pomp and splendour that their cunning dressers could contrive: luxuriant garlands of flowers, costume jewellery, rare delicacies of every kind.

It was not a particularly happy scene, for pleasure is never to be found in crowds, especially holiday crowds. There was something serious and reserved, almost austere, to be glimpsed in the guarded expressions of the faces which stopped and stared at the lace curtains and silken drapes, the sparkling jewel-boxes, the great edifices of candied fruits, and the little sucking-pigs— fat, pink, smooth, like clergymen, each one softly couched with a rose in its snout upon a bed made of greenery and multicoloured jelly, precisely mounted and ornamented.

The members of the crowd, though they went arm in arm with one another, were following their own trains of thought, each according to the dictates of his or her personality....

A very elegant and very pretty woman stepped down from her carriage in front of a confectioner's shop. She was not a permanent resident of the town but was very well known there; she came to C— every winter for the sake of her health, which required a milder climate and a more tranquil existence than Paris, with its dirt and tumult, could provide. She was rich, but lived unostentatiously in a villa with impeccably-kept gardens; she was generous too, and the poor knew that they would never be turned away from her door in their hour of need. She was well-liked—or perhaps one should rather say well-respected—on account of the money which she spent in the town, but the local people found her habits puzzling and alien. She imported into that exceedingly bourgeois little town a delicate scent of liberty, a charming and original individualism, and a determination to live according to her own desires and not the expectations of others—all of which was bound to disturb the local people, enmeshed as they were in the squalor of ancient prejudices and narrow traditions...and besides all that, she was married to a Jew.

The woman entered the shop, which was already full to overflowing. The establishment was widely famed for the imaginative and bizarre window-displays wrought by its proprietor: scenery depicted in sugar, sentimental anecdotes in bonbons, graphic military motifs in candied fruit. These never failed to catch the attention of curious passers-by, who would often come to see them as they might go to see a performance at a theatre, or a panorama; there was always a crowd gathered before the window, constantly renewed throughout the day. That part of the pavement was always half-blocked, despite the efforts of a patrolling policeman to keep it clear, and it was difficult to get past.

Having noticed a little velvet bag with a gold frame which had been left on the cushions of the carriage—perhaps forgotten by the woman—a beggar suddenly moved forward to grab it, taking advantage of the general confusion. He was a woeful and emaciated creature with jaundiced skin, dressed entirely in rags. He was thwarted in his purpose because the coachman, who happened to turn around at that precise moment, let out a loud cry:

"Thief! Stop, thief!"

The people who had paused, entranced, before the window also turned round when they heard the cry. All of a sudden their faces became contorted, their eyes gleaming with an astonished, almost horrible wildness.

"What? What is it?" the crowd roared.

The wrathful coachman, mouth agape, repeated: "Thief! Stop the thief!"

Someone waving a fist shouted: "Which thief!"

"Where's the thief?" cried another, eyes widening with hatred and fear.

Every man in the crowd struck a defensive pose, and they yelled with a united and fraternal voice: "Which is the thief?"

"There! There! That's the one!" cried the coachman, pointing. He touched the emaciated face of the beggar with the end of his whip.

The man he had pointed out was immediately surrounded by a circle of faces. Forty fists were raised above him; twenty mouths vomited abuse into his face: "He's a thief! He has stolen...!"

"What? What? What has he stolen?"

"The commissaire of police! Here's the commissaire of police!"

It was indeed the commissaire of police, who had been strolling in the street with his family. Seeing the assembled mob, with fists held aloft and faces contorted, he had thrust himself through the crowd.

"What have we here?"

"He's a thief! He has stolen....!"

"Who has stolen...?"

"The thief, of course!"

"Where is he?"

"There! There he is!"

"What has he stolen?"

The crowd did not know, and fell silent. The coachman, assuming his most dignified pose, condescended to explain. "He tried to steal madame's handbag!"

Using the end of his whip again, he pointed to the little bag which, as though intimidated by so much noise, was cowering half-hidden in a corner of the carriage....

"Aha!" said the magistrate. "This is very serious...indeed, it is abominable! Take hold of him, someone! Grab the thief!...Take him to the cells!..."

"To the cells! Yes, yes! To jail with him!"

The crowd applauded loudly, transported by vengeful joy.

At that moment, the elegant woman came out of the shop. She stopped on the threshold, astonished and alarmed by the agitation. She demanded to know the reason for it. The crowd cheered her. A few hats, raised high in triumph, were made to dance on the tops of raised walking-sticks.

"We caught him! He's been caught!"

"Who has been caught?" asked the woman.

"The thief! The thief!"

"What thief?"

"The thief, of course...that thief!"

The commissaire came forward solemnly, his hat in his hand.

"Yes madame," he said, with an exaggerated bow. "He has been caught! Fortunately, for the good name of the town."

The woman, even more astonished, repeated: "Who has been caught?"

"The thief!"

"What thief?"

"The thief who has stolen your bag...or, at least, that was certainly his intention!"

"Yes! Yes!" put in the crowd.

"It's a beggar...a ragamuffin!"

"Yes! Yes!"

"He's in a pretty pickle now!"

"Bravo!...Bravo!"

The woman caught sight of the little bag which she had left behind in her carriage; then looked at the beggar with the emaciated face, whose shoulder was gripped by the brutal hand of an agent of the police.

"To the cells with him!" commanded the commissaire.

"Yes! Yes! Off to jail! Thump him!..."

"Pull out his hair!..."

"Skin him alive!..."

"Smack him in the mouth!..."

"I beg your pardon, monsieur le commissaire," said the woman, "but it really isn't serious...in fact it's nothing. Seeing that I still have my bag, I don't require you to take the poor man away to prison."

The shouts of the crowd melted into murmurs. Ohs! and ahs! could be heard on every side as its members agreed with one another.

"But that is impossible, madame," explained the

commissaire. "An example must be made...for the sake of the town's good name."

"The good name of the town is not in question, monsieur," she told him. "I have suffered no injury; I shall make no complaint. I demand that you release that man."

The commissaire was obdurate: "But, madame, the law! The town...respect....my duty as a magistrate, and as a local man..."

"Release that man!"

The grumblings of the crowd increased. The faces were at first astonished, then furious, then hateful. The expressions of hatred were directed towards the woman, but she refused to see them. Some evil-sounding words were spoken—injurious and insulting—but she took no notice of them. Having become impatient, she declared in an imperious voice: "I want you to release that man. I insist that you do so! Have I made myself clear, this time?"

The crowd exploded. All the anger and indignation which had earlier been directed at the beggar was now turned upon the woman. Obscene insults and vile threats were hurled at her. For several seconds she was forced to suffer the horrible and violent enmity of every person in the frantic crowd. A child grabbed at the reins of the horses, launching a mouthful of abuse.

"Tramp!"

"Trollop!"

"Get out of here!"

"Death to the Jews!"

"You are savages!" cried the woman. Then she became still, maintaining her composure in spite of the jeers. She waited for the beggar to be set free.

The beggar's face was bloodied. Part of his beard had been torn out. His bald head was bare, his miserable hat having rolled away down the street.

He scuttled off, his legs all a-tremble.

Only then did the woman, who was also quivering, condescend to climb back into her carriage. She too set off, followed by a chorus of booing from the crowd—that mob from whose claws and fangs the deft fingers of a woman had snatched away a little morsel of human flesh.

****

22.

BERENICE
by Edgar Allan Poe

Dicebant mihi sodales, si sepulchrum amicæ visitarem, curas meas aliquantulum fore levatas. - EBN ZAIAT.

Misery is manifold. The wretchedness of earth is multiform. Overreaching the wide horizon as the rainbow, its hues are as various as the hues of that arch; as distinct too, yet as intimately blended. Overreaching the wide horizon as the rainbow! How is it that from beauty I have derived a type of unloveliness? from the covenant of peace a simile of sorrow? But, as in ethics, evil is a consequence of good, so, in fact, out of joy is sorrow born. Either the memory of past bliss is the anguish of to-day, or the agonies which *are*, have their origin in the ecstasies which *might have been*.

My baptismal name is Egæus; that of my family I will not mention. Yet there are no towers in the land more time-honoured than my gloomy, gray, hereditary halls. Our line has been called a race of visionaries; and in many striking particulars – in the character of the family mansion, in the frescoes of the chief saloon, in the tapestries of the dormitories, in the chiselling of some buttresses in the armory, but more especially in the gallery of antique paintings, in the fashion of the library chamber, and, lastly, in the very peculiar nature of the library's contents – there is more than sufficient evidence to warrant the belief.

The recollections of my earliest years are connected

with that chamber, and with its volumes; of which latter I will say no more. Here died my mother. Herein was I born. But it is mere idleness to say that I had not lived before, that the soul has no previous existence. You deny it? Let us not argue the matter. Convinced myself, I seek not to convince. There is, however, a remembrance of aerial forms, of spiritual and meaning eyes, of sounds, musical yet sad; a remembrance which will not be excluded; a memory like a shadow, vague, variable, indefinite, unsteady; and like a shadow, too, in the impossibility of my getting rid of it while the sunlight of my reason shall exist.

In that chamber was I born. Thus awaking from the long night of what seemed, but was not, nonentity, at once into the very regions of fairy-land, into a palace of imagination, into the wild dominions of monastic thought and erudition, it is not singular that I gazed around me with a startled and ardent eye, that I loitered away my boyhood in books, and dissipated my youth in revery; but it is singular that as years rolled away, and the noon of manhood found me still in the mansion of my fathers, it is wonderful what a stagnation there fell upon the springs of my life – wonderful how total an inversion took place in the character of my commonest thought. The realities of the world affected me as visions, and as visions only, while the wild ideas of the land of dreams became, in turn, not the material of my every-day existence, but in very deed that existence utterly and solely in itself.

....

Berenice and I were cousins, and we grew up together in my paternal halls. Yet differently we grew: I, ill of health, buried in gloom, she, agile, graceful, and overflowing with energy; hers the ramble on the hillside, mine, the studies of the cloister; I, living within my own heart and addicted, body and soul, to the most intense and painful meditation, she, roaming carelessly through life, with no thought of the shadows in her path, or the silent flight of the raven-winged hours. Berenice! I call upon her name – Berenice! and from the gray ruins of memory a thousand tumultuous recollections are startled at the sound! Ah, vividly is her image before me now, as in the early days of her light-heartedness and joy! O gorgeous yet fantastic beauty! O sylph amid the shrubberies of Arnheim! O naiad among its fountains! And then – then all is mystery and terror, and a tale which should not be told. Disease, a fatal disease, fell like the simoon upon her frame; and even while I gazed upon her the spirit of change swept over her, pervading her mind, her habits, and her character, and, in a manner the most subtle and terrible, disturbing even the identity of her person! Alas! the destroyer came and went! and the victim – where is she? I knew her not – or knew her no longer as Berenice!

Among the numerous train of maladies superinduced by that fatal and primary one which effected a revolution of so horrible a kind in the moral and physical being of my cousin may be mentioned, as the most distressing and obstinate in its nature, a species of epilepsy not unfrequently terminating in trance itself – trance very nearly resembling positive dissolution, and from which her manner of recovery was, in most instances, startlingly abrupt. In the meantime, my own disease – for I have been told that I should call it by no other appellation – my own disease, then, grew rapidly upon me, and assumed finally a monomaniac character of a novel and extraordinary form, hourly and momently gaining vigour, and at length obtaining over me the most incomprehensible ascendency. This monomania, if I must so term it, consisted in a morbid irritability of those properties of the mind in metaphysical science termed the "attentive." It is more than probable that I am not understood; but I fear, indeed, that it is in no manner possible to convey to the mind of the merely general reader an adequate idea of that nervous intensity of interest with which, in my case, the powers of meditation (not to speak technically) busied and buried themselves, in the contemplation of even the most ordinary objects of the universe.

To muse for long unwearied hours, with my attention riveted to some frivolous device on the margin or in the typography of a book; to become absorbed, for the better part of a summer's day, in a quaint shadow falling aslant upon the tapestry or upon the floor; to lose myself, for an entire night, in watching the steady flame of a lamp or the embers of a fire; to dream away whole days over the perfume of a flower; to repeat, monotonously, some common word, until the sound, by dint of frequent repetition, ceased to convey any idea whatever to the mind; to lose all sense of motion or physical existence, by means of absolute bodily quiescence long and obstinately persevered in, – such were a few of the most common and least pernicious vagaries induced by a condition of the mental faculties, not, indeed, altogether unparalleled, but certainly bidding defiance to anything like analysis or explanation.

Yet let me not be misapprehended. The undue, earnest, and morbid attention thus excited by objects, in their own nature frivolous, must not be confounded in character with that ruminating propensity common to all mankind, and more especially indulged in by persons of ardent imagination. It was not even, as might be at first supposed, an extreme condition, or exaggeration of such propensity, but primarily and essentially distinct

228

and different. In the one instance, the dreamer, or enthusiast, being interested by an object usually not frivolous, imperceptibly loses sight of this object in a wilderness of deductions and suggestions issuing therefrom, until, at the conclusion of a day-dream often replete with luxury, he finds the *incitamentum*, or first cause of his musings, entirely vanished and forgotten. In my case, the primary object was invariably frivolous, although assuming, through the medium of my distempered vision, a refracted and unreal importance. Few deductions, if any, were made; and those few pertinaciously returning in upon the original object as a centre. The meditations were never pleasurable; and at the termination of the revery the first cause, so far from being out of sight, had attained that supernaturally exaggerated interest which was the prevailing feature of the disease. In a word, the powers of mind more particularly exercised were, with me, as I have said before, the attentive, and are, with the day-dreamer, the speculative.

My books, at this epoch, if they did not actually serve to irritate the disorder, partook, it will be perceived, largely, in their imaginative and inconsequential nature, of the characteristic qualities of the disorder itself. I well remember, among others, the treatise of the noble Italian, Cœlius Secundus Curio, *De Amplitudine Beati Regni Dei;* St. Austin's great work, *The City of God;* and Tertullian's *De Carne Christi,* in which the paradoxical sentence, *"Mortuus est Dei filius; credibile est quia ineptum est; et sepultus resurrexit; certum est quia impossibile est,"* occupied my undivided time, for many weeks of laborious and fruitless investigation.

Thus it will appear that, shaken from its balance only by trivial things, my reason bore resemblance to that ocean-crag spoken of by Ptolemy Hephestion, which, steadily resisting the attacks of human violence, and the fiercer fury of the waters and the winds, trembled only to the touch of the flower called asphodel. And although, to a careless thinker, it might appear a matter beyond doubt, that the alteration produced by her unhappy malady, in the moral condition of Berenice, would afford me many objects for the exercise of that intense and abnormal meditation whose nature I have been at some trouble in explaining, yet such was not in any degree the case. In the lucid intervals of my infirmity, her calamity, indeed, gave me pain, and, taking deeply to heart that total wreck of her fair and gentle life, I did not fail to ponder, frequently and bitterly, upon the wonder-working means by which so strange a revolution had been so suddenly brought to pass. But these reflections partook not of the idiosyncrasy of my disease, and were such as would have occurred, under similar circumstances, to the ordinary mass of mankind. True to its own character, my disorder revelled in the less important but more startling changes wrought in the physical frame of Berenice – in the singular and most appalling distortion of her personal identity.

During the brightest days of her unparalleled beauty, most surely I had never loved her. In the strange anomaly of my existence, feelings with me had never been of the heart, and my passions always were of the mind. Through the gray of the early morning, among the trellised shadows of the forest at noonday, and in the silence of my library at night she had flitted by my eyes, and I had seen her, not as the living and breathing Berenice, but as the Berenice of a dream; not as a being of the earth, earthy, but as the abstraction of such a being; not as a thing to admire, but to analyze; not as an object of love, but as the theme of the most abstruse although desultory speculation. And now – now I shuddered in her presence and grew pale at her approach; yet, bitterly lamenting her fallen and desolate condition, I called to mind that she had loved me long, and in an evil moment I spoke to her of marriage.

And at length the period of our nuptials was approaching, when, upon an afternoon in the winter of the year, one of those unseasonably warm, calm, and misty days which are the nurse of the beautiful Halcyon,[1] I sat (and sat, as I thought alone), in the inner apartment of the library. But, uplifting my eyes, I saw that Berenice stood before me.

Was it my own excited imagination, or the misty influence of the atmosphere, or the uncertain twilight of the chamber, or the gray draperies which fell around her figure that caused in it so vacillating and indistinct an outline? I could not tell. She spoke no word; and I – not for worlds could I have uttered a syllable! An icy chill ran through my frame; a sense of insufferable anxiety oppressed me; a consuming curiosity pervaded my soul; and, sinking back upon the chair, I remained for some time breathless and motionless, with my eyes riveted upon her person. Alas! its emaciation was excessive, and not one vestige of the former being lurked in any single line of the contour. My burning glances at length fell upon the face.

The forehead was high and very pale, and singularly placid; and the once jetty hair fell partially over it, and overshadowed the hollow temples with innumerable ringlets, now of a vivid yellow, and jarring discordantly, in their fantastic character, with the reigning melancholy of the countenance. The eyes were lifeless, and lustreless, and seemingly pupilless, and I shrank involuntarily

[1] For as Jove, during the winter season, gives twice seven days of warmth, men have called this clement and temperate time the nurse of the beautiful Halcyon.–Simonides

231

from their glassy stare to the contemplation of the thin and shrunken lips. They parted; and in a smile of peculiar meaning the teeth of the changed Berenice disclosed themselves slowly to my view. Would to God that I had never beheld them, or that, having done so, I had died!

....

The shutting of a door disturbed me, and, looking up, I found that my cousin had departed from the chamber. But from the disordered chamber of my brain had not, alas! departed, and would not be driven away, the white and ghastly spectrum of the teeth. Not a speck on their surface, not a shade on their enamel, not an indenture in their edges but what that brief period of her smile had sufficed to brand in upon my memory. I saw them now even more unequivocally than I beheld them then. The teeth! the teeth! they were here, and there, and everywhere, and visibly and palpably before me; long, narrow, and excessively white, with the pale lips writhing about them, as in the very moment of their first terrible development. Then came the full fury of my monomania, and I struggled in vain against its strange and irresistible influence. In the multiplied objects of the external world I had no thoughts but for the teeth. For these I longed with a frenzied desire. All other matters and all different interests became absorbed in their single contemplation. They, they alone were present to the mental eye, and they, in their sole individuality, became the essence of my mental life. I held them in every light. I turned them in every attitude. I surveyed their characteristics. I dwelt upon their peculiarities. I pondered upon their conformation. I mused upon the alteration in their nature. I shuddered as I assigned to them, in imagination, a sensitive and sentient power, and, even when unassisted by the lips, a capability of moral expression. Of Mademoiselle Salle it has been well said: *"Que tous ses pas étaient des sentiments,"* and of Berenice I more seriously believed *que tous ses dents étaient des idées. Des idées!* ah, here was the idiotic thought that destroyed me! *Des idées!* ah, therefore it was that I coveted them so madly! I felt that their possession could alone ever restore me to peace, in giving me back to reason.

And the evening closed in upon me thus, and then the darkness came and tarried and went, and the day again dawned, and the mists of a second night were now gathering around, and still I sat motionless in that solitary room, and still I sat buried in meditation, and still the phantasma of the teeth maintained its terrible ascendency, as, with the most vivid and hideous distinctness, it floated about amid the changing lights and shadows of the chamber. At length there broke in upon my dreams a cry as of horror and dismay, and thereunto, after a pause, succeeded the sound of troubled voices, intermingled with many low moanings of sorrow or of pain. I arose from my seat, and throwing open one of the doors of the library, saw standing out in the antechamber a servant maiden, all in tears, who told me that Berenice was – no more! She had been seized with epilepsy in the early morning, and now, at the closing in of the night, the grave was ready for its tenant, and all the preparations for the burial were completed.

....

I found myself sitting in the library, and again sitting there alone. It seemed to me that I had newly awakened from a confused and exciting dream. I knew that it was not midnight, and I was well aware that, since the setting of the sun, Berenice had been interred. But of that dreary period which intervened I had no positive, at

233

least no definite, comprehension. Yet its memory was replete with horror – horror more horrible from being vague, and terror more terrible from ambiguity. It was a fearful page in the record of my existence, written all over with dim, and hideous, and unintelligible recollections. I strived to decipher them, but in vain; while ever and anon, like the spirit of a departed sound, the shrill and piercing shriek of a female voice seemed to be ringing in my ears. I had done a deed; what was it? I asked myself the question aloud, and the whispering echoes of the chamber answered me, "What was it?"

On the table beside me burned a lamp, and near it lay a little box. It was of no remarkable character, and I had seen it frequently before, for it was the property of the family physician; but how came it there, upon my table, and why did I shudder in regarding it? These things were in no manner to be accounted for, and my eyes at length dropped to the open pages of a book, and to a sentence underscored therein. The words were the singular but simple ones of the poet Ebn Zaiat: - *"Dicebant mihi sodales si sepulchrum amicæ visitarem, curas meas aliquantulum fore levatas."* Why, then, as I perused them, did the hairs of my head erect themselves on end, and the blood of my body become congealed within my veins?

There came a light tap at the library door, and, pale as the tenant of a tomb, a menial entered upon tiptoe. His looks were wild with terror, and he spoke to me in a voice tremulous, husky, and very low. What said he? Some broken sentences I heard. He told of a wild cry disturbing the silence of the night, of the gathering together of the household, of a search in the direction of the sound; and then his tones grew thrillingly distinct as he whispered to me of a violated grave, of a disfigured body enshrouded, yet still breathing, still palpitating, still alive!

He pointed to my garments; they were muddy and clotted with gore. I spoke not, and he took me gently by the hand: it was indented with the impress of human nails. He directed my attention to some object against the wall. I looked at it for some minutes: it was a spade. With a shriek I bounded to the table, and grasped the box that lay upon it. But I could not force it open; and in my tremor it slipped from my hands and fell heavily, and burst into pieces; and from it, with a rattling sound, there rolled out some instruments of dental surgery, intermingled with thirty-two small, white, and ivory-looking substances that were scattered to and fro about the floor.

23.

THE CORD
by Charles Baudelaire

"There are perhaps as many illusions," my friend said to me, "as there are relationships between men, or between men and things. And when an illusion is dispelled—which is to say, when we perceive an entity as it really is in the outside world—we cannot help but experience a strange combination of sensations in which regret for the phantom which has vanished is mingled with pleasant surprise at the novelty of the reality which now confronts us.

"If there is one phenomenon which can be reckoned trite, obvious and invariable, concerning whose nature it is impossible to be deceived, it is motherly love. It is as difficult to imagine a mother devoid of maternal feelings as it is to imagine a flame which puts forth no heat; is it not, then, perfectly legitimate to attribute to the impulse of motherly love all the words and actions of a mother in respect of her child? And yet...let me tell you this brief story, of how I was completely misled by this entirely natural illusion.

"My vocation as a painter leads me to pay close attention to the faces and the features of all those I encounter in my daily routine—you know what enjoyment we obtain from the exercise of a faculty which makes our existence more vivid and significant than that of other men. In the quiet suburb where I live, where the buildings are separated by grassy wastelands, I frequently had occasion to observe a child, who stood out from his fellows by virtue of his eager and mischievous face, which I found most appealing. He began to pose for me, and I cast him in various roles—as a little vagabond, as an angel, as the mythical Eros. I gave him a gypsy's fiddle to carry, or Cupid's torch, or dressed him in the crown of thorns and the nails of the crucifixion. I obtained such a lively pleasure from his company that in the end I asked his parents—who were poor folk—to let him come to live with me, promising that he would be well clothed, amply supplied with money, and given no household duties save for cleaning my brushes and running errands.

"The child, once he was tidied up, became very charming, and life in my household must have seemed like paradise compared to conditions in the miserable hovel in which his parents lived. Still, I must admit that the little fellow astounded me at times, when he was gripped by fits of depression unusual in one so young. He quickly developed an immoderate taste for sweets and liquors—so much so that one day when I discovered that, in spite of numerous warnings I had given him, he had been stealing such things, I threatened to send him back to his parents. Afterwards, I had to go out on business, and I was away from home for some time.

"Imagine my horror and astonishment when, on returning home, the first thing which met my eyes was my little friend—my mischievous companion—hanging from the top of that wardrobe!

"His feet were almost touching the floor; a chair, which he had obviously thrust away with his foot, was overturned beside him; his head was awkwardly twisted to one side. At first his swollen features and his wide-open, fearfully-staring eyes made me think that he was still alive, but he was not.

"Getting him down was more difficult than you might think. *Rigor mortis* had already set in, and I was poss-

237

essed by an inexplicable horror at the thought of letting him fall to the floor. I had to support his entire weight with one arm while I cut the cord with my other hand. But even when that was accomplished there was more to be done; the little monster had used a kind of thin twine which had cut deep into his flesh. I was forced to get a small pair of scissors, and force the points between the two cushions of swollen flesh, in order to free his neck.

"I have neglected to mention that I had called loudly for help, but my neighbours were reluctant to lend their aid, all of them holding faithfully to the principle that a wise man never involves himself—Heaven knows why not!—in the matter of a hanging. In the end, a doctor arrived, and confirmed that the child had been dead for several hours. When, much later, we had to undress him in order that he could be prepared for burial, his corpse was so rigidly set that we despaired of bending his limbs; we had to rip and cut the garments in order to remove them.

"The official to whom I had, in the fullness of time, to report the accident looked sideways at me and said: 'There's something fishy about this!' He was presumably impelled by innate desire and professional duty to attempt to strike fear into the innocent and the guilty alike.

"There still remained one supremely important duty for me to perform, the mere thought of which caused me terrible anguish: I had to inform the boy's parents. My feet at first refused to carry me to their door, but in the end I plucked up the courage to do what I had to. To my amazement, though, the mother seemed quite unmoved; there was no hint of a tear in the corner of her eye. This strange reaction I put down to the effect of the horror she must feel, remembering the common saying that the most terrible sorrows are suffered silently.

"As for the father, he contented himself with observing, in a manner half-brutal and half-thoughtful: 'All things considered, it's probably for the best; he was bound to come to a bad end!'

"In the meantime, the corpse was laid out on my couch. I went home, and was making the final preparations for the burial, assisted by a servant, when the mother came into my studio. She said that she wanted to see the body of her son. I could not, in all decency, deny her the opportunity to drink her fill of grief or refuse her that ultimately sombre consolation.

"Afterwards, she begged me to show her the place where her little one had hanged himself. 'Oh no, madame,' I replied, 'that would do you no good at all'...and as, involuntarily, my eyes were drawn towards the fatal wardrobe, I perceived—my disgust mingled with horror and anger—that the nail was still there, driven into the wood above the door, with a long piece of cord still trailing from it.

"I moved instantly to remove these last evidences of the unfortunate incident, but as I was about to hurl them through the open window the poor woman seized my arm and appealed to me with irresistible fervour: 'Oh, sir, let me have that! I beg you! I beseech you!' It seemed to me—and I did not doubt it—that her despair must have become so frantic that she had been overwhelmed with tenderness towards that which had served as the instrument of her son's death, and that she wished to keep it like some horrible but cherished relic...and so she took possession of the nail and the twine.

"At last it was all over. It only remained for me to get on with my work, more assiduously than before, in the hope that I might thus drive out by degrees the memory

239

of the little corpse which still haunted me...the phantom whose fixed stare sapped my strength....

"But the next day I received a batch of letters. Some were from other tenants of the building, others from neighbouring houses—one from the first flooor, another from the second, another from the third, and so on. Some were in a semi-humorous style, as though their writers sought to disguise by superficial badinage the earnestness of their request; others combined gross effrontery with appalling spelling; but all had the same purpose in view—namely, to obtain from me a piece of the fatal and glorious cord. Among the signatories there were, I must admit, more women than men—but not all, believe me, belonged to the lowest and most vulgar class of person. I can show you the letters.

"All of a sudden, the truth dawned on me. I understood then why the mother had been so very eager to snatch the twine from me, and what kind of commerce would provide the means of her consolation."

****

24.

WITCH IN-GRAIN
by R. Murray Gilchrist

Of late Michal had been much engrossed in the reading of the black-letter books that Philosopher Bale brought from France. As you know I am no Latinist – though one while she was earnest in her desire to instruct me; but the open air had ever greater charms for me than had the dry precincts of a library. So I grudged the time she spent apart, and throughout the spring I would have been all day at her side, talking such foolery as lovers use. But ever she must steal away and hide herself amongst dead volumes.

Yestereven I crossed the Roods, and entered the garden, to find the girl sitting under a yew-tree. Her face was haggard and her eyes sunken: for the time it seemed as if many years had passed over her head, but somehow the change had only added to her beauty. And I marvelled greatly, but ere I could speak a huge bird, whose plumage was as the brightest gold, fluttered out of her lap from under the silken apron; and looking on her uncovered bosom I saw that his beak had pierced her tender flesh. I cried aloud, and would have caught the thing, but it rose slowly, laughing like a man, and, beating upwards, passed out of sight in the quincunx. Then Michal drew long breaths, and her youth came back in some measure. But she frowned, and said, 'What is it, sweetheart? Why hast awakened me? I dreamed that I fed the Dragon of the Hesperidean Garden.' Meanwhile, her gaze set on the place whither the bird had flown.

'Thou hast chosen a filthy mammet,' I said. 'Tell me

how came it hither?'

She rose without reply, and kissed her hands to the gaudy wings, which were nearing through the trees. Then, lifting up a great tome that had lain at her feet, she turned towards the house. But ere she had reached the end of the maze she stopped, and smiled with strange subtlety.

'How camest *thou* hither, O satyr?' she cried. 'Even when the Dragon slept, and the fruit hung naked to my touch....The gates fell to.'

Perplexed and sore adread, I followed to the hall; and found in the herb garden the men struggling with an ancient woman – a foul crone, brown and puckered as a rotten costard. At sight of Michal she thrust out her hands, crying, 'Save me, mistress!' The girl cowered, and ran up the perron and indoors. But for me, I questioned Simon, who stood well out of reach of the wretch's nails, as to the wherefore of this hurly-burly.

His underlings bound the runnion with cords, and haled her to the closet in the banqueting gallery. Then, her beldering being stilled, Simon entreated me to compel Michal to prick her arm. So I went down to the library, and found my sweetheart sitting by the window, tranced with seeing that goblin fowl go tumbling on the lawn.

My heart was full of terror and anguish. 'Dearest Michal,' I prayed, 'for the sake of our passion let me command. Here is a knife.' I took a poniard from Sir Roger's stand of arms. 'Come with me now; I will tell you all.'

Her gaze still shed her heart upon the popinjay; and when I took her hand and drew her from the room, she strove hard to escape. In the gallery I pressed her fingers round the haft, and knowing that the witch was bound, flung open the door so that they faced each other. But

Mother Benmusk's eyes glared like fire, so that Michal was withered up, and sank swooning into my arms. And a chuckle of disdain leaped from the hag's ragged lips. Simon and the others came hurrying, and when Michal had found her life, we begged her to cut into one of those knotted arms. Yet she would none of it, but turned her face and signed no – no – she would not. And as we strove to prevail with her, word came that one of the Bishop's horses had cast a shoe in the village, and that his lordship craved the hospitality of Ford, until the smith had mended the mishap. Nigh at the heels of his message came the divine, and having heard and pondered our tale, he would fain speak with her.

I took her to the withdrawing-room, where at the sight of him she burst into such a loud fit of laughter that the old man rose in fear and went away.

'Surely it is an obsession,' he cried; 'nought can be done until the witch takes back her spells!'

So I bade the servants carry Benmusk to the mere, and cast her in the muddy part thereof where her head would lie above water. That was fifteen hours ago, but methinks I still hear her screams clanging through the stagnant air. Never was the hag so fierce and full of strength! All along the garden I saw a track of uprooted flowers. Amongst the sedges the turmoil grew and grew till every heron fled. They threw her in, and the whole mere seethed as if the floor of it were hell. For full an hour she cursed us fearsomely: then, finding that every time she neared the land the men thrust her back again, her spirit waxed abject, and she fell to whimpering. Two hours before twelve she cried that she would tell all she knew. So we landed her, and she was loosened of her bonds and she mumbled in my ear: 'I swear by Satan that I am innocent of this harm! I ha'none but pawtry secrets. Go at midnight to the lows and watch Baldus's tomb. There thou shalt find all.'

The beldam tottered away, her bemired petticoats clapping her legs; and I bade them let her rest in peace until I had certainly proved her guilt. With this I returned to the house; but, finding that Michal had retired for the night, I sat by the fire, waiting for the time to pass. A clock struck the half before eleven, and I set out for King Baldus's grave, whither, had not such a great matter been at stake, I dared not have ventured after dark. I stole from the garden and through the first copse. The moon lay against a brazen curtain; little snail-like clouds were crawling underneath, and the horns of them pricked her face.

As I neared the lane to the waste, a most unholy dawn broke behind the fringe of pines, looping the boles with strings of grey-golden light. Surely a figure moved there? I ran. A curious motley and a noisy swarmed forth at me.

Another moment, and I was in the midst of a host of weasels and hares and such-like creatures, all flying from the precincts of the tomb. I quaked with dread, and the hair of my flesh stood upright. But I thrust on, and parted the thorn boughs, and looked up at the mound.

On the summit thereof sat Michal, triumphing, invested with flames. And the Shape approached, and wrapped her in his blackness.

25.

AUTUMNAL LAMENT
by Stéphane Mallarmé

Ever since Maria left me to go to another star – which one? Orion? Altair? You, verdant Venus? – I have cherished solitude. What long days I have spent alone with my cat. By alone I mean without any material being, for my cat is a mystical companion: a spirit. I may say, therefore, that I have spent long days alone with my cat, and alone, also, with one of the later authors of the Latin Decadence – for since the white creature is no more I have become strangely and singularly fond of everything which was implied by the word: Fall. Thus, my favourite season of the year is the last languid days of summer, the immediate predecessors of the autumn, and when I go for a walk during the day, it is at the hour when the sun rests on the horizon before vanishing, when cuprous yellow rays of light colour the grey walls and cuprous red the window panes. Similarly, the literature from which my spirit demands sensual pleasure will be the tortuous poetry of Rome's last days, provided that it has not the least breath of the rejuvenating advent of the Barbarians, and that it does not stammer the infantile Latin of early Christian prose.

I was, consequently, reading one of these beloved poems (whose cosmetic masks enchant me more powerfully than the incarnation of youth) and plunging my hand into the fur of the purified animal, when a barrel organ began to play its lazy and melancholy tune beneath my window. It was playing in the wide avenue of poplars, whose leaves seemed dull to me even in the spring, ever since Maria passed along it for the last time, by candle-light. The instrument brought forth sadness – yes, truly; the piano sparkles, the violin lights up its stripped fibres, but the barrel organ, in the dusk of memory, awoke in me a hopeless dream. While it murmured its merrily vulgar tune, which brought gaiety to the heart of the suburbs – an old-fashioned, banal tune – how did it come about that its refrain echoed in my soul and made me weep as though it were a romantic ballad? I savoured it slowly, but I did not throw a coin from the window for fear of upsetting myself, and of becoming aware that the instrument was not singing by itself.

26.

DUKE VIRGIL
by Richard Garnett

The citizens of Mantua were weary of revolutions.
They had acknowledged the suzerainty of the Emperor
Frederick and shaken it off. They had had a Podestà of
their own and had shaken him off. They had expelled a
Papal Legate, incurring excommunication thereby. They
had tried dictators, consuls, prætors, councils of ten, and
other numbers odd and even, and ere the middle of the
thirteenth century were luxuriating in the enjoyment of
perfect anarchy.

An assembly met daily in quest of a remedy, but its
members were forbidden to propose anything old, and
were unable to invent anything new.

"Why not consult Manto, the alchemist's daughter,
our prophetess, our Sibyl?" the young Benedetto asked
at last.

"Why not?" repeated Eustachio, an elderly man.

"Why not, indeed?" interrogated Leonardo, a man of
mature years.

All the speakers were noble. Benedetto was Manto's
lover; Eustachio her father's friend; Leonardo his creditor.
Their advice prevailed, and the three were chosen as a
deputation to wait on the prophetess. Before proceeding
formally on their embassy the three envoys managed to
obtain private interviews, the two elders with Manto's
father, the youth with Manto herself. The creditor
promised that if he became Duke by the alchemist's
influence with his daughter he would forgive the debt;
the friend went further, and vowed that he would pay it.

The old man promised his good word to both, but when he went to confer with his daughter he found her closeted with Benedetto, and returned without disburdening himself of his errand. The youth had just risen from his knees, pleading with her, and drawing glowing pictures of their felicity when he should be Duke and she Duchess.

She answered, "Benedetto, in all Mantua there is not one man fit to rule another. To name any living person would be to set a tyrant over my native city. I will repair to the shades and seek a ruler among the dead."

"And why should not Mantua have a tyrant?" demanded Benedetto. "The freedom of the mechanic is the bondage of the noble, who values no liberty save that of making the base-born do his bidding. 'Tis hell to a man of spirit to be contradicted by his tailor. If I could see my heart's desire on the knaves, little would I reck submitting to the sway of the Emperor."

"I know that well, Benedetto," said Manto, "and hence will take good heed not to counsel Mantua to choose thee. No, the Duke I will give her shall be one without passions to gratify or injuries to avenge, and shall already be crowned with a crown to make the ducal cap as nothing in his eyes, if eyes he had."

Benedetto departed in hot displeasure, and the alchemist came forward to announce that the commissioners waited.

"My projection," he whispered, "only wants one more piece of gold to insure success, and Eustachio proffers thirty. Oh, give him Mantua in exchange for boundless riches!"

"And they call thee a philosopher and me a visionary!" said Manto, patting his cheek.

The envoys' commission having been unfolded, she took not a moment to reply, "Be your Duke Virgil."

The deputation respectfully represented that although Virgil was no doubt Mantua's greatest citizen, he laboured under the disqualification of having been dead more than twelve hundred years. Nothing further, however, could be extorted from the prophetess, and the ambassadors were obliged to withdraw.

The interpretation of Manto's oracle naturally provoked much diversity of opinion in the council.

"Obviously," said a poet, "the prophetess would have us confer the ducal dignity upon the contemporary bard who doth most nearly accede to the vestiges of the divine Maro; and he, as I judge, is even now in the midst of you."

"Virgil the poet," said a priest, who had long laboured under the suspicion of occult practices, "was a fool to Virgil the enchanter. The wise woman evidently demands one competent to put the devil into a hole – an operation which I have striven to perform all my life."

"Canst thou balance our city upon an egg?" inquired Eustachio.

"Better upon an egg than upon a quack!" retorted the priest.

But such was not the opinion of Eustachio himself, who privately conferred with Leonardo. Eustachio had a character, but no parts; Leonardo had parts, but no character.

"I see not why these fools should deride the oracle of the prophetess," he said. "She would doubtless impress upon us that a dead master is in divers respects preferable to a living one."

"Surely," said Eustachio, "provided always that the servant is a man of exemplary character, and that he presumes not upon his lord's withdrawal to another sphere, trusting thereby to commit malpractices with impunity, but doth, on the contrary, deport himself as ever in his great taskmaster's eye."

"Eustachio," said Leonardo, with admiration, "it is the misery of Mantua that she hath no citizen who can act half as well as thou canst talk. I would fain have further discourse with thee."

The two statesmen laid their heads together, and ere long the mob were crying, "A Virgil! A Virgil!"

The councillors reassembled and passed resolutions.

"But who shall be Regent?" inquired some one when Virgil had been elected unanimously.

"Who but we?" asked Eustachio and Leonardo. "Are we not the heads of the Virgilian party?"

Thus had the enthusiastic Manto, purest of idealists, installed in authority the two most unprincipled politicians in the republic; and she had lost her lover besides, for Benedetto fled the city, vowing vengeance.

Anyhow, the dead poet was enthroned Duke of Mantua; Eustachio and Leonardo became Regents, with the style of Consuls, and it was provided that in doubtful cases reference should be made to the Sortes Virgilianæ. And truly, if we may believe the chronicles, the arrangement worked for a time surprisingly well. The Mantuans, in an irrational way, had done what it behoves all communities to do rationally if they can. They had sought for a good and worthy citizen to rule them; it was their misfortune that such a one could only be found among the dead. They felt prouder of themselves for being governed by a great man – one in comparison with whom kings and pontiffs were the creatures of a day. They would not, if they could help it, disgrace themselves by disgracing their hero; they would not have it said that Mantua, which had not been too weak to bear him, had been too weak to endure his government. The very hucksters and usurers among them felt dimly that there was such a thing as an Ideal.

A glimmering perception dawned upon mailed, steel-fisted barons that there was a such a thing as an Idea, and they felt uneasily apprehensive, like beasts of prey who have for the first time sniffed gunpowder. The railleries and mockeries of Mantua's neighbours, moreover, stimulated Mantua's citizens to persevere in their course, and deterred them from doing aught to approve themselves fools. Were not Verona, Cremona, Lodi, Pavia, Crema, cities that could never enthrone the Virgil they had never produced, watching with undissembled expectation to see them trip? The hollow-hearted Eustachio and the rapacious Leonardo, their virtual rulers, might indeed be little sensible to this enthusiasm, but they could not disregard the general drift of public opinion, which said clearly: "Mantua is trying a great experiment. Woe to you if you bring it to nought by your selfish quarrels!"

The best proof that there was something in Manto's idea was that after a while the Emperor Frederick took alarm, and signified to the Mantuans that they must cease their mumming and fooling and acknowledge him as their sovereign, failing which he would besiege their city.

II

Mantua was girt by a zone of fire and steel. Her villas and homesteads flamed or smoked; her orchards flared heavenward in a torrent of sparks or stood black sapless trunks charred to their inmost pith; the promise of her harvests lay as grey ashes over the land. But her ramparts, though breached in places, were yet manned by her sons, and their assailants recoiled pierced by the shafts or stunned by the catapults of the defence. Kaiser Frederick sat in his tent, giving secret audience to one who had stolen in disguise over from the city in the grey of the morning. By the Emperor's side stood a tall

251

martial figure, wearing a visor which he never removed.

"Your Majesty," Leonardo was saying, for it was he, "this madness will soon pass away. The people will weary of sacrificing themselves for a dead heathen."

"And Liberty?" asked the Emperor, "is not that a name dear to those misguided creatures?"

"So dear, please your Majesty, that if they have but the name they will perfectly dispense with the thing. I do not advise that your imperial yoke should be too palpably adjusted to their stiff necks. Leave them in appearance the choice of their magistrate, but insure its falling upon one of approved fidelity, certain to execute obsequiously all your Majesty's mandates; such a one in short, as your faithful vassal Leonardo. It would only be necessary to decapitate that dangerous revolutionist, Eustachio."

"And the citizens are really ready for this?"

"All the respectable citizens. All of whom your Majesty need take account. All men of standing and substance."

"I rejoice to hear it," said the Emperor, "and do the more readily credit thee inasmuch as a most virtuous and honourable citizen hath already been beforehand with thee, assuring me of the same thing, and affirming that but one traitor, whose name, methinks, sounded like thine, stands between me and the subjugation of Mantua."

And, withdrawing a curtain, he disclosed the figure of Eustachio.

"I thought he was asleep," muttered Eustachio.

"That noodle to have been beforehand with me!" murmured Leonardo.

"What perplexes me," continued Frederick, after enjoying the confusion of the pair for a few moments, "is that our masked friend here will have it that he is the man for the Dukedom, and offers to open the gates to me

252

by a method of his own."

"By fair fighting, an' please my liege," observed the visored personage, "not by these dastardly treacheries."

"How inhuman!" sighed Eustachio.

"How old-fashioned!" sneered Leonardo.

"The truth is," continued Frederick, "he gravely doubts whether either of you possesses the influence which you allege, and has devised a method of putting this to the proof, which I trust will commend itself to you."

Leonardo and Eustachio expressed their readiness to submit their credit with their fellow-citizens to any reasonable trial.

"He proposes, then," pursued the Emperor, "that ye, disarmed and bound, should be placed at the head of the storming column, and in that situation should, as questionless ye would, exert your entire moral influence with your fellow-citizens to dissuade them from shooting you. If the column, thus shielded, enters the city without resistance, ye will both have earned the Dukedom, and the question who shall have it may be decided by single combat between yourselves. But should the people, rather than submit to our clemency, impiously slay their elected magistrates, it will be apparent that the methods of our martial friend are the only ones corresponding to the exigency of the case. Is the storming column ready?"

"All but the first file, please your Majesty," responded the man in the visor.

"Let it be equipped," returned Frederick, and in half-an-hour Eustachio and Leonardo, their hands tied behind them, were stumbling up the breach, impelled by pikes in the rear, and confronting the catapults, *chevaux de frise*, hidden pitfalls, Greek fire, and boiling water provided by their own direction, and certified to them the preceding evening as all that could be desired. They had, however, the full use of their voices, and this they

253

turned to the best account. Never had Leonardo been so cogent, or Eustachio so pathetic. The Mantuans, already disorganised by the unaccountable disappearance of the Executive, were entirely irresolute what to do. As they hesitated the visored chief incited his followers. All seemed lost, when a tall female figure appeared among the defenders. It was Manto.

"Fools and cowards!" she exclaimed, "must ye learn your duty from a woman?"

And, seizing a catapult, she discharged a stone which laid the masked warrior stunned and senseless on the ground. The next instant Eustachio and Leonardo fell dead, pierced by showers of arrows. The Mantuans sallied forth. The dismayed Imperialists fled to their camp. The bodies of the fallen magistrates and of the unconscious chieftain in the mask were brought into the city. Manto herself undid the fallen man's visor, and uttered a fearful shriek as she recognised Benedetto.

"What shall be done with him, mistress?" they asked.

Manto long stood silent, torn by conflicting emotions. At length she said, in a strange, unnatural voice:

"Put him into the Square Tower."

"And now, mistress, what further? How to choose the new consuls?"

"Ask me no more," she said. "I shall never prophesy again. Virtue has gone away from me."

The leaders departed, to intrigue for the vacant posts, and devise tortures for Benedetto. Manto sat on the rampart, still and silent as its stones. Anon she rose, and roved about as if distraught, reciting verses from Virgil.

Night had fallen. Benedetto lay wakeful in his cell. A female figure stood before him bearing a lamp. It was Manto.

"Benedetto," she said, "I am a wretch, faithless to my

country and to my master. I did but even now open his sacred volume at hazard, and on what did my eye first fall?

Trojaque nunc stares, Priamique arx alta maneres.

But I can no other. I am a woman. May Mantua never entrust her fortunes to the likes of me again! Come with me, I will release thee."

She unlocked his chains; she guided him through the secret passage under the moat; they stood at the exit, in the open air.

"Fly," she said, "and never again draw sword against thy mother. I will return to my house, and do that to myself which it behoved me to have done ere I released thee."

"Manto," exclaimed Benedetto, "a truce to this folly! Forsake thy dead Duke, and that cheat of Liberty more crazy and fantastic still. Wed a living Duke in me!"

"Never!" exclaimed Manto. "I love thee more than any man living on earth, and I would not espouse thee if the earth held no other."

"Thou canst not help thyself," he rejoined; "thou hast revealed to me the secret of this passage. I hasten to the camp. I return in an hour with an army, and wilt thou, wilt thou not, to-morrow's sun shall behold thee the partner of my throne!"

Manto wore a poniard. She struck Benedetto to the heart, and he fell dead. She drew the corpse back into the passage, and hurried to her home. Opening her master's volume again, she read:

Tædet coeli convexa tueri.

A few minutes afterwards her father entered the chamber to tell her he had at last found the philosopher's stone, but, perceiving his daughter hanging by her girdle, he forbore to intrude upon her, and returned to his laboratory.

It was time. A sentinel of the besiegers had marked Benedetto's fall, and the disappearance of the body into the earth. A pool of blood revealed the entrance to the passage. Ere sunrise Mantua was full of Frederick's soldiers, full also of burning houses, rifled sanctuaries, violated damsels, children playing with their dead mothers' breasts, especially full of citizens protesting that they had ever longed for the restoration of the Emperor, and that this was the happiest day of their lives. Frederick waited till everybody was killed, then entered the city and proclaimed an amnesty. Virgil's bust was broken, and his writings burned with Manto's body. The flames glowed on the dead face, which gleamed as it were with pleasure. The old alchemist had been slain among his crucibles; *his* scrolls were preserved with jealous care.

But Manto found another father. She sat at Virgil's feet in Elysium; and as he stroked the fair head, now golden with perpetual youth, listened to his mild reproofs and his cheerful oracles. By her side stood a bowl filled with the untasted waters of Lethe.

"Woe," said Virgil – but his manner contradicted his speech – "woe to the idealist and enthusiast! Woe to them who live in the world to come! Woe to them who live only for a hope whose fulfilment they will not behold on earth! Drink not, therefore, of that cup, dear child, lest Duke Virgil's day should come, and thou shouldst not know it. For come it will, and all the sooner for thy tragedy and thy comedy."

27.

THE SHUTTER
by Pierre Louÿs

"This is my secret," she said to me at last. "You are so anxious to hear it, dear heart, that I will tell you this evening why I have never wished to marry.

"Your question is more loving than the silence of others, in which I so often detect a hurtful reticence. One cannot ignore the fact that my family is wealthy, and when a rich young girl will not get married it is usually assumed to be out of vanity, or ambition, or ugliness, or doubtful morality: suppositions regarding my life which people are quite free to make, provided that they are charitable enough not to adopt all four at the same time.

"Believe me, I have not refused my suitors because of any faults of theirs. It is the idea of having a husband, or any lover, whether legalised or not—which I have avoided, with a kind of terror which has only begun to subside since I reached the relative safety of my fortieth year. Don't jump to any conclusions; my story is not that of an unhappy love affair. Indeed, I have never loved at all; I grew old too quickly, in the space of a single evening, when I was only seventeen...

"Listen—it isn't a long story.

"After all, perhaps you will scarcely understand why such a banal occurrence, so commonplace, has stripped my life of all subsequent pleasures. It was the kind of thing one reads about in the daily papers; you can find such items on page three of any one of them, and I am not even one of the characters in the story which I have to tell. If my solitary existence has been disturbed by it for so long, it's only because I saw it happen with my own eyes, not more than a few feet away from me. To you it is merely an anecdote, and you will feel nothing of what I have felt."

Mlle. N— rested her forehead upon her hand and began her tale, with her gaze fixed on the ground, never once lifting her eyes towards me:

"Twenty-five years ago, my mother and I were living in an old house in the shadow of Saint-Sulpice. It was an ordinary house, with no courtyard or outbuildings; all the windows looked out on the street, but the street was as quiet as a forest path.

"One night, in midsummer, I was unable to sleep because of the stifling heat in my room. I dared not open my window for fear of waking my mother. After an hour of insomnia I got up, put on my slippers, and went downstairs in my nightgown to the drawing-room on the ground floor.

"Here...but you must understand the situation of the room. The house had once been separated from the street by a garden, but that land had been sold, the town council having appropriated part of it in order to widen the road. One window of the room opened, in consequence, upon a shadowed corner of a dark and mysterious covert, beyond the reach of the light of the street-lamps.

"On entering the room, I saw that this window had not been closed, although the outer shutters had been drawn to. Enervated by the heat, feeling that I was nearly suffocating, I climbed up on the ledge, parted the oblique laths of the blind with the tips of my fingers, and breathed in, filling myself from top to toe with the delicious freshness of the night air.

"That remains the last instant of unalloyed pleasure I ever experienced.

"I was there for no more than a minute before a couple emerged on to the other side of the street.

"The man drew the young girl into a shadowy corner of the covert. The man was a workman of sorts—one of those who work for three weeks and then take six months off, because their good looks permit them to hold honest labour in contempt. The female I recognised at once. She was a fifteen-year-old girl to whom my mother had been very kind, and who was employed in a house which I had visited more than once. She wore a black skirt which was too short and a grey jacket; she had no corset, but scarcely needed one. Her blonde hair was caught up in a short plait, fastened by a pin at the top of her head.

"Her companion, who held her by both shoulders, spoke to her brusquely.

" 'This'll do? D'you want it?'

"She replied weakly: 'Let me go...let me go...'

"The tone of her voice implied that she had repeated the phrase two hundred times since leaving the restaurant.

"The man continued: 'Look here, kid, you said yes to me, and yes it is. No two ways about it. What's said's said, okay? Here's okay—what's wrong with you?'

" 'No...not here...not here....'

" 'Well, where then? You haven't a brass farthing, and neither have I; I can't pay for a room. If you want to go out to the old fortifications you'd better start walking—it'll take us an hour.'

"She made a dismissive gesture. The man was becoming exasperated.

" 'Titine, give it to me straight. D'you fancy me or not? Because, if you don't, there are others who....'

"The poor child burst into tears. She sobbed so

259

violently, pressed against the blind on which I was leaning, that I could feel every tumultuous beat of her poor young heart.

" 'Yes, I really love you,' she said. 'But not like *that*, not like that...I don't know how to say it, but that isn't love...I love you because you're gentle, because you don't take to me like the others, because I'm so glad when I see you coming. I love you, and I want to put my arms around you—oh, as much of that as you want, every night, all the time! But, since you told me about the other things, no—don't you understand? I don't want to...especially with you...it seems to me that it would be wrong.'

"The man shrugged his shoulders, and fell to cursing.

" 'Damned crazy bitch....'

"He went on and on; I won't repeat it.

"Then, he took a knife out from beneath his coat...a cleaver...a butcher's cleaver...something like a short sword, and drove it into the shutter, level with my breast, and said in a low, violent voice: 'Now, there's just the two of us. If you mess me about, I'll cut you.'

"The girl stiffened. It was becoming a terrible scene....

"The street was absolutely deserted, and the silence was as deep and unbroken as the profound silence of the countryside. None of the usual city sounds could be heard. What time was it? Perhaps two o'clock in the morning. The whole neighbourhood was asleep, except for that couple and the terrified spectator: me.

"I was so close that I could have touched them had I only extended my fingers to do it. The girl resisted with an energy which nearly gave her strength enough to prevail. She was bent over, head down, knees pressed together. She wheezed like a panting animal. When her arms were seized she closed her child-like legs, and when her skirt was grabbed she lashed out with her hands....It was a protracted struggle, lasting longer than you would have believed possible—but as in the Greek ballad in which Charon eventually casts down the shepherd, she was in the end overcome.

"Then she beat the air with her hands, one of which fastened on something that was stuck in the shutter.... She did not know what it was, poor child; she was no longer aware that it was a knife—and so, armed by chance, she struck back one more time against the one who was wounding her, irreparably, in body and in soul.

"Alas! Human flesh is nothing but clay: soft, fragile clay which yields to the first blow...The blade went into his throat, and flashed out the other side....

"A spurt of blood....Here, you see, at either side of the neck, there are two main arteries, from which blood gushes under the pressure of the heart....

"Warm blood deluged the shutter, passing through the fissures to splash my waist.

"The man, choking upon the blade, his eyes bulging out from their sockets, opened his mouth in horror, but could not utter so much as a sigh. As he fell forward on to his face, though, the girl—the murderess, recoiling and hopping about like a little blackbird—could not help but shatter the silence of the street with a series of cries....three cries of horror....

"Ah! those howls for the dead! I have never heard anything quite so appalling.

"What followed afterwards...is of no importance to you, I suppose. My mother, suddenly awakened and fearing for my safety when she found my bed empty, came searching for me, calling my name throughout the house until she found me at last, standing by the window, red and sticky with blood which she thought at

261

first was mine....it was not for that part of the drama that I have told you the story.

"What remained deep in my memory was sufficient. I was seventeen. In the space of half an hour, I who knew nothing of real life, found it suddenly laid bare before me: all the secrets of life, love and death. I knew what it was that novels called *desire*, and what it was for a man to be *in love*, and what it was, too, for a man to die.

"The world does not know or care why I have chosen to live alone, but at least you will share my secret from now on, my dear."

****

28.

THE DOER OF GOOD
by Oscar Wilde

It was night-time and He was alone.

And He saw afar-off the walls of a round city and went towards the city.

And when He came near be heard within the city the tread of the feet of joy, and the laughter of the mouth of gladness and the loud noise of many lutes. And He knocked at the gate and certain of the gate-keepers opened to him.

And He beheld a house that was of marble and had fair pillars of marble before it. The pillars were hung with garlands, and within and without there were torches of cedar. And he entered the house.

And when He had passed through the hall of chalcedony and the hall of jasper, and reached the long hall of feasting, He saw lying on a couch of sea-purple one whose hair was crowned with red roses and whose lips were red with wine.

And He went behind him and touched him on the shoulder and said to him, "Why do you live like this?"

And the young man turned round and recognised Him, and made answer and said, "But I was a leper once, and you healed me. How else should I live?"

And He passed out of the house and went again into the street.

And after a little while He saw one whose face and raiment were painted and whose feet were shod with pearls. And behind her came, slowly as a hunter, a young man who wore a cloak of two colours. Now the face of the woman was as the fair face of an idol, and the eyes of the young man were bright with lust.

And He followed swiftly and touched the hand of the young man and said to him, "Why do you look at this woman and in such wise?"

And the young man turned round and recognised Him and said, "But I was blind once, and you gave me sight. At what else should I look?"

And He ran forward and touched the painted raiment of the woman and said to her, "Is there no other way in which to walk save the way of sin?"

And the woman turned round and recognised Him, and laughed and said, "But you forgave my sins, and the way is a pleasant way."

And He passed out of the city.

And when He had passed out of the city He saw seated by the roadside a young man who was weeping.

And He went towards him and touched the long locks of his hair and said to him, "Why are you weeping?"

And the young man looked up and recognised Him and made answer, "But I was dead once and you raised me from the dead. What else should I do but weep?"

29.

THE VANQUISHED SHADOW
by Catulle Mendès

Everyone in the world knew that a treasure was hidden in a certain room, which was the only one in an ancient château whose walls were still standing and whose ceiling had not collapsed. It was a treasure of inestimable value, consisting of pearls and precious stones, concealed under a flagstone or behind some pillar. Anyone who came to possess it would not only become richer than emperors and kings; he would also attain boundless happiness and limitless fame, for every one of the precious stones and the pearls was a magical object of irresistible power.

There was certainly no shortage of people determined to lay hands on that treasure. The people who lived in the neighbouring town and those who lived in the surrounding countryside no longer devoted themselves to their business affairs or their work. They forgot to open their shops and they let the fields lie fallow; their one and only thought was to discover the hiding-place in that ancient room.

Indeed, people came from all the countries of the world to the ruins of the château; some on foot, others in stage-coaches or mounted on horses harnessed with gold. They all came: beggars and rich men, villains and gentlemen, poor women and princesses, all drawn by the prospect of an incomparable windfall. No one, however, was successful in this enterprise.

Why should this be? Was the room sealed by a door so tightly shut or so solid that none had the power to open or penetrate it? By no means; it had no door at all, and the entrance was as large as the hallway of a palace. In that case, was one met upon the threshold by basilisks or dragons spitting fumes and flames? Certainly not; no being or thing menaced the visitors, who could enter at will.

The only thing which prevented anyone from putting a hand upon the treasure was the fact that the room, whatever the hour or the season, was filled with an obscurity so black and so thick that the best eyes in the world could see nothing at all within it. There is no way to describe the intensity of the darkness which reigned there: the densest of other shadows, when compared to that one, appeared to have the transparency of dawn. The bright sun could hurl into that shadow its most luminous rays, but no light could ever insinuate itself, despite the vastness of the entrance, into the mysterious interior of the room. It was as though it were defended by a door of black diamond: impalpable, invisible, but utterly resistant to daylight.

Some of those who accepted the hazards implicit in entering the gloomy place subsequently said that it seemed that the pupils of their eyes had been plastered over by bitumen or pitch. Many who entered never did come out again, possibly having died of hunger before finding the opening.

By what means could one contrive to find, in that unparalleled darkness, a hidden treasure? One scarcely needs to say that all the imaginable methods of illuminating the room had been tried and tried again. The people of the town had brought their lamps and torches, the peasants their sheaves of straw or corn, thoroughly dried-out and set vividly alight. The moment that such devices were brought to the opening, their flames were extinguished like sighs in a storm, even though no perceptible wind came out of the room. Bombs and shells had been hurled into it, and all manner of explosive devices; they would explode with an exceedingly loud noise, but without the least spark of light!

Emperors and princes, avid to possess the riches and the magical objects buried in the shadow, summoned their wise men, and said to them: "You will receive a share of the treasure if you manage to bring daylight to that room." The wise men did their utmost, inventing new combinations of oils and gases, which could burn even at the bottom of the sea. They rediscovered the secret of Greek Fire. They constructed an optical instrument whose barrel, containing a thousand lenses, could focus at a single point all the luminosity of the brightest noon.

All of this produced not the slightest effect; nothing was capable of bringing the slightest relief to that invincible darkness.

At that time there were in the land two poor children, a boy of sixteen years old and a girl of fifteen. They were handsome children, but they went about half-naked and in rags. They wandered about the roads, begging when there was anyone else about, collecting flowers when no one passed by—and they were better pleased to find a faded wild rose than to receive a newly-minted five centime piece.

You might have asked all the swallows who nested under the eaves, where the home of the children was, but they could not have told you, never having seen them enter or leave any house while they twittered with their heads outside their nests; the bare-foot urchins had neither home nor family. But in their turn, the swallows could remember very distinctly how they had brushed the children with their wings, morning, noon and night, out in the fields, or beside the streams, or in the golden greenery of the woods—everywhere, in fact, where there were buttercups which shone, dragonflies which hovered, sedge-warblers which sang.

These vagabonds rejoiced in the mere fact of being alive. It was their pleasure to wander in deserted places, sunlit and flowery; the more they were by themselves, the more they felt part of everything. They had no troubles at all, save only to find in one village or another a little bread which they might eat, some distance from the road, in the depths of some thicket, biting into the same crust until their teeth met in the middle.

All meals are exquisite to those who have a kiss for dessert, and if they had not the wherewithal to buy bread, they contented themselves with blackberries, or crab-apples, which they disputed with the hedge-sparrows.

When they lay down to sleep without a roof over their heads they felt no sense of deprivation; what roof, be it a hovel or a palace, could be better than the crowns of the trees, or the stars which studded the sky like sequins? And they had little to complain about because they were in rags, because—thanks to the holes in those tattered garments—they had no need to undress so that their bodies might come together.

It is true, of course, that it is not always spring or summer; that there are dull days in autumn and freezing nights in winter. December is the cruellest month; the snow is a cloak which does not prevent one from catching cold. Hunger comes upon one whether or not there are berries on the brambles or apples on the trees to appease it; it is painful to have to go to sleep on an empty stomach, on hard ground, under leafless branches. But how can they suffer, those who love and are loved? I ask you, frankly, if it is possible to be cold when one is enveloped by the flames of the heart, and whether one regrets having nothing to chew upon when one can put one's lips to an adored mouth?

Now it happened that while they were climbing a hill one warm afternoon, these two were overtaken by a great thunderstorm. There was a torrential downpour, interrupted by flashes of lightning and rolls of thunder. They took shelter under a tree, but they were given hardly any respite; the rain soon began to come through the canopy. They resolved to let it wet them—they were, after all, at liberty to shake their rags as the birds shook their feathers—but then they espied, closeby, a large opening among the remains of a collapsed wall, heaped about with stones. They quickly entered—into the room where the eternal shadow reigned!

At first they were a little alarmed by the darkness all around them. They alone, in all the land, did not know the story of the treasure hidden within the impenetrable shadow, being more attentive to the songs of fieldfares than the chattering of wayfarers. But they were not afraid, because they were able to take one another by the hand.

They sat down on the flagstones within the chamber, huddling close together. They entwined their arms about one another, tenderly and happily.

"I love you!" said she.

"I love you," said he.

And then, because they had spoken that word—that sacred Word, which made the daylight and the heavens, that divine Word!—all the immensity of the room became suddenly more luminous than a plain of golden sand beneath the bright July sun!

Hearing their cries of astonishment, men and women flocked to the place in great numbers—for there were always people prowling nearby, in the hope that some accident of fate might liberate the treasure.

A great tumult grew up among that greedy crowd when its members beheld, through a crack in the wall, the scintillation and the radiance flamboyantly produced by glorious heaps of pearls and gemstones. With madly flaring eyes and grinding teeth, elbowing one another out of the way, falling over themselves in their urgency, they threw themselves forward.

They found within those walls such an abundance of wealth and so many magical objects that there was enough for everybody; many of those who were there that day became richer than emperors and more powerful than magicians.

The poor children who, in saying "I love you!" had dispersed the invincible shadows, were the only ones who did not think to demand a share of the treasure. They had another, gentler treasure which was sufficient for their needs.

The storm having passed over, they resumed their journey across the countryside. A man passed by, and they asked him for five centimes.

"No!" said the man.

They did not complain. They smiled. They amused themselves by watching the sodden forest dry out beneath the re-emerged sun. The raindrops which dripped from the leaves were like jewels, and there were trembling pearls at the tip of every blade of grass.

****

30.

THE OUTCAST SPIRIT
by Lady Dilke

A girl was born of the desire that her father, the son of a great man, had unto a beggar-maid. But, when the great man heard that his son had taken the beggar to wife, he cast him out from his doors, bidding him to live as befitted one that had his liking in those of low estate.

Then, the man's soul was heavy and the beggar reproached him, for she had thought to wed her rags with wealth and ease, and her words stung the man like adders' tongues, seeing that he had lost all for her sake, and their days were very sorrowful. So it was, that when a child was born to them, there was no joy in the man's heart, and the milk of the woman's breasts was bitter.

The gold and silver which the man had brought with him from his father's house were soon spent. Hunger sat with them at meat, nor, when eventide befell, was there any bed for them to lie on. In his sore need the man bethought him of his younger brother, and he went to him and craved a gift at his hands, but his younger brother, being in fear of his father, refused him. Nor was there any help of any other man. And the reviling of the beggar was as a sharp sword, and her curses were like stones.

And things were so, that, as the child grew, she saw the evil things of the world and the hard things thereof, yet was she undefiled: only she became very silent, and her lips were as those of one that is dumb. At the last, it came to pass that the father knew himself to be sick unto death, and seeing the girl, his daughter, to be excellently fair and even as a light shining in the darkness, he sent

271

her to his own people, that they might take her unto them for their name's sake. But they would not, and one refused her, saying, "There are kitchen wenches enough and to spare already within our walls."

When he heard these things, the father was more grieved, but the beggar laughed, for she had it in her mind how she would make money of her daughter.

Not many days after, seeing that the man could not move, but lay as one that was dead, the beggar spoke aloud of the bargain she had made and counted the pieces of money before his face, and the girl, sitting there, watched her the while with a great terror in her eyes. And, in her rejoicing, the woman arose, and coming near to the place where he, who had been son to the great man, now lay low, she chinked the money in her hands, crying, "This, truly, is more than ever I thought to have gotten by thee!"

But, as she spoke these words, he, who lay there before her, raised himself, as by a great effort, and caught her by the hair, drawing her down backwards upon his knees, and all the money which she had in her hands was scattered on the floor. When he now had her at his mercy, the man so twisted the kerchief that was about her neck that in a short space she died, making no moan. Having done this, he turned, and seeing the girl, his daughter, watching him, he pointed to the door, crying "Go! This is the house of Death."

Then the girl fled out into the streets, and he who had bargained for her coming there shortly after, found her not. And, when this one saw the pieces of money that the beggar had received of him, scattered on the floor, and, looking to the bed, beheld the body of the man fallen forward upon that of the woman his wife, he was afraid. So he went his way, and the people of the house entered in and took up the money, and sending for a priest, they

272

paid therewith for the burial of those two; – the son of the great man and the beggar his wife. But, no one took any thought for the girl.

Now, when she had gone forth in her fear, the girl would fain have taken refuge with her mother's kinsfolk, and for that night only they gave her shelter, but on the morrow, seeing that her ways were strange to them, they hardened their hearts and drave her from their doors, saying, "Go hence, we are poorer than thou!" Then, these words were in her ears, even as the echo of her father's voice crying "Go!" And, again she went forth and walked in the streets and ways. But, as the second night drew on, she was much troubled, for she knew not where she was, nor whether there were any of whom she might ask a lodging.

And as she came out from a narrow lane leading down a steep place on the outskirts of the city, she heard, beneath her feet, the sound of rushing waters, and knew that she was standing on the bridge where a great river from the snow mountains passed on its way to the sea. The waters called to her, and she followed them until she came to a causeway not far from the shore, and on each side it was defended against the drifting sands by a low wall. The night was very still, and in the darkness she heard voices singing and, as the waves rolled in, the voices rose higher, and this was what they sang in her ears:

"Three men stood on the quarter-deck,
One had a red ring round his neck,
And two the salt seas could not drown
For the sin that was sinned in their father's town.

Three women met in the garden patch,
One had lifted the hangman's latch,

Two, they carried the nameless thing
The witch fiend's daughter had bade them bring.

When six shall meet on the whirlpool's brink,
The souls of seven shall with them sink,
And the folk of hell shall frighted flee
Before the face of that company."

When the girl heard these words she was afraid, and
would have gone further, but coming to an opening in
the wall she espied some stairs, and at the foot of the
stairs was light, as of a fire. So, being very cold, she went
down them, and there, by a stage at the water's edge to
which many boats were moored, she found a great
company of boatmen, and by the stage there was a fire,
and those boatmen whose voices she had heard singing
in the darkness were sitting round it. Going up to them,
the girl then asked of them that she might warm her
hands at their fire, for it was winter and the cold was
very bitter. Then they said, "Draw near," and she drew
near. But, when she stood in the light of the fire and they
saw her, one knew her for the daughter of that beggar
who had wedded with the son of the great man, and he
derided her, saying, "Where be thy serving-men, thy
runners and thy women? Lo! this is but poor state for the
lord thy father's daughter!" And, when the girl answered
him not, he swore that she should sing to him, saying,
"Come, let us hear thy voice!" and taking her by the
shoulders, would have forced her to sit down with him.

At this moment, on a sudden, there were lights on the
stair, and the priest, who had come from the burying of
her dead, stepped down to the stage that he might be put
across the bay. Seeing the girl standing there, he called
her to him and sharply questioned her with many
questions, but she could give no account of herself, nor

of how she had come to that place. At this the priest was angered, and he bade her forthwith confess how it had come to pass that she had left the dead, saying that it should go ill with her if she concealed aught from him. Then the girl, who had eaten nothing since that hour, remembering all the terror of it, became as one distraught, and stretching forth her hands before her, "Go!" she cried, and fell down at his feet as one dead.

At this the priest, thinking much evil of her, for he had heard of the money that had been found on the floor and that the death of the beggar had seemed strange to all men, was sore perplexed, asking himself what he should do.

Had it not been for shame of those that stood by, he would have left her, but, having spoken as one that was in authority over her, this misliked him. And he thought, "Should I take her to a religious house, they would not willingly receive her, seeing that she hath no dowry!" but, at the last, he said to the boatmen, "Take up the girl and put her in the boat, and steer the boat for the water-gate of the palace that is on the other side." And they did so.

Now when they had come to the stairs of the palace, the priest bade them that were with him to take the girl and carry her into the hall where the great man, her father's father, sat at meat. And when they were come there, the priest stayed his steps on the threshold, and so standing he spoke with a loud voice and said, "Lo! my Lord, thy son whom thou hadst cast out, is dead, and the beggar whom he had taken to wife is dead also, and this, his child, have I brought unto thee that thou mayest give order concerning her."

And the great man answered the priest never a word, but he called his servants, and bid them that they should give him to eat.

As for the girl, whether it were for pity or for shame, he desired the women that were there in the hall to take her and carry her to a far chamber. And when she was come to herself, they put black garments upon her, and they gave her counsel that by no means should she show herself, in that palace, where she might offend the eyes of her father's father or of any of her kindred.

So, the girl lived her life alone, and no man cared for her. By day, she sat solitary, and when the evening drew on and the night was at hand she walked in a fair garden that was beneath her windows, and in the garden was a terrace, raised between two rows of cypress, upon the wall over above the sea, and at times, looking thence, beyond the purple shadows of the twilight, she could see the eternal snows on distant mountains flushing scarlet against the sunset sky.

It came to pass that one night, when she was walking in that garden, the girl met Death, and he seemed to her not terrible, but only very sad, and she went near to him and said, "I, too, am sad, and my heart is heavy; let me be of thy company!" And, she put her hand in his.

Then, Death held up her fingers to the light and said, "There should be many days 'twixt me and thee," and he refused her. And, as she turned from him, she heard from below the voices of men singing in a boat close under the wall whereon the terrace was raised, and these were the words which came to her ears:

"And two the salt seas would not drown
For the sin that was sinned in their father's town."

Then, she knew that the song which they sang was even the same as that she had heard in the darkness on the night when the priest, who had buried her dead, had met her by the water's edge, and had brought her to the

276

palace of her father's father.

Seeing now, that she had no place on earth and that Death would not willingly have her of his company, the girl sought for herself the means whereby she might part from life. And, before many days had gone by, they that entered her chamber in the morning found her on her bed, and when they spoke she answered not, neither did she stir when they laid hands upon her. Then one of the women took a mirror and held it before her mouth, and, seeing that the silver remained without stain, they said, "She is dead." So, they went and told the old man, her father's father, and he said, "It is well." And, having sewn her decently in a white shroud, they laid lilies on her and shining daisies from the garden in which she had walked, and they carried her forth and buried her.

Now, the girl had thought that her spirit, in the hour of her parting, should escape and should wander, free from fear, in the palace that had been her father's habitation. But it was otherwise. For, even as she passed, the spirits of the house came about her, and they were a vast company, crying, "Who art thou? How camest thou hither?" So, they drave her before them, and, as she fled from room to room of that palace, they gathered to an innumerable host. Then she went forth into the garden and stayed her flight at the terrace walk where she had met Death, but even there she was pursued by that terrible company.

At this, the spirit knew that for those who have no place in life, neither is there any place in death, and shuddering, passed out upon the night.

31.

TO EACH HIS CHIMERA
by Charles Baudelaire

Beneath a great grey sky, on a vast and trackless arid plain where no grass grew, nor any thistle, nor any stinging nettle, I came across a company of men who walked with bowed heads. Each one carried upon his back a huge chimera, as heavy as a sack of flour or coal, or the pack of a Roman infantryman. But the monstrous beasts did not lie like dead weights upon their victims; each one enveloped and oppressed her carrier, clinging with taut and powerful muscles, clawing at his breast with her two enormous talons, and her fabulous head sat atop the man's brow like one of the horned helmets by means of which the warriors of old hoped to strike terror into the hearts of their enemies.

I questioned one of these men, asking him why the company went forth in such a fashion. He replied that neither he nor any of the others had any answer to offer, but that it was obvious that they had somewhere to go because they were urged onwards by a compulsive desire to march.

One curious thing I observed: not one of the travellers gave any indication of being annoyed by the ferocious creature dangling about his neck; it was as if each of them considered it to be a part of himself. Although their faces were solemn and weary, not one of them gave evidence of despair; beneath the melancholy dome of the sky, their feet plodding through the dust of an earth as desolate as the heavens, they continued on their way with the resigned expressions of men condemned to hope unendingly. Thus the company passed me by, ultimately to fade into the haze which blurred the horizon where the curvature of the earth reveals itself to the curiosity of the human eye.

For a little while I tried stubbornly to unravel this mystery, but an irresistible Indifference soon settled upon me, overwhelming and weighing me down no less heavily than those men had been weighed down by their crushing Chimeras.

****

32.

THE VISIT
by Ernest Dowson

As though I were still struggling through the meshes of some riotous dream, I heard his knock upon the door. As in a dream, I bade him enter, but with his entry, I awoke. Yet when he entered it seemed to me that I was dreaming, for there was nothing strange in that supreme and sorrowful smile which shone through the mask which I knew. And just as though I had not always been afraid of him I said: "Welcome."

And he said very simply, "I am here."

Dreaming I had thought myself, but the reproachful sorrow of his smile showed me that I was awake. Then dared I open my eyes and I saw my old body on the bed, and the room in which I had grown so tired, and in the middle of the room the pan of charcoal which still smouldered. And dimly I remembered my great weariness and the lost whiteness of Lalage and last year's snows; and these things had been agonies.

Darkly, as in a dream, I wondered why they gave me no more hurt, as I looked at my old body on the bed; why, they were like old maid's fancies (as I look at my grey body on the bed of my agonies) — like silly toys of children that fond mothers lay up in lavender (as I looked at the twisted limbs of my old body), for these things had been agonies.

But all my wonder was gone when I looked again into the eyes of my guest, and I said:

"I have wanted you all my life."

Then said Death (and what reproachful tenderness

was shadowed in his obscure smile):
    "You had only to call."

33.

BEATRICE
by Marcel Schwob

Only a few moments of life remain to me; I feel it and
I know it. I have tried to procure a quiet death, knowing
that the sound of my own cries would inflict upon me the
agony of further torture. The increasingly powerful
phantom which is the sound of my voice is something I
dread far more than the perfumed water into which I
have plunged myself. That water is now as cloudy as a
block of opal; it is gradually taking on the pinkish tint of
my flowing blood, and when the liquid aurora has
attained its full redness, I will begin my descent into
oblivion. I have not sliced the artery of my right hand,
which spits out these lines upon writing-paper white as
ivory; three gushing fountains will suffice to empty the
well of my heart, which is not so profound that it will
long resist the draining process. I have already wept into
that chamber all the blood that was in my tears.

I can sob no more, because a frightful terror grips me
by the throat when I hear my sobs. I pray that God draws
consciousness out of me before the sound of my
approaching death-rattle assaults my ears.

My fingers are becoming feeble; it is time to record
what has happened to me. I must collect my thoughts
while I still can, and make haste to offer my mute
confession. I cannot any longer bear to let the earthly air
carry my voice.

Between myself and Beatrice a tender friendship had
long existed. When she was very small she used to come

to my father's house. She was a serious child, with deep-set eyes which were strangely speckled with yellow. Her figure was lightly angular, her features rather pronounced, and her skin as white as marble; she was a piece of statuary which no apprentice had ever touched, on which the master-sculptor himself had engraved the strong writing of his chisel. The flowing lines of her features were cleanly and sharply cut, never softened by trepidation. When any emotion coloured her face, it was as though a figure of alabaster were being illuminated from within by a rosy lamp.

She was meticulously graceful, and the suppleness of her gestures was somehow enduring, for her operations were so precise that they remained fixed in one's sight. When she curled the locks of her hair down over her forehead, the perfect symmetry of the movements were very different from the rapid flight of the arms of most young girls, which resemble a fluttering of scarcely-lifted wings. Her movements seemed instead to be the condescending acts of an unmovable goddess.

To me, always plunged into antiquarian contemplation by my devoted study of all things Greek, Beatrice was a marble statue from an earlier era than the humanised art of Phidias: a figure sculpted by the Olympia master, following immutable rules of superior harmony.

For many years, Beatrice and I shared the delights of reading the immortal poets of Greece, and treasured our studies of the philosophers of Classical Era. We would weep to think of the lost poems of Xenophanes and Empedocles which no human eye of today would ever see. Plato, in particular, charmed us with the infinite grace of his eloquence, but we were rather repelled by the ideas which the divine sage developed regarding the soul. A few lines written in his youth, which revealed to me the true tenor of his thought, plunged me into unhappiness.

This was the terrible couplet upon which my eyes happened to fall that day, recorded in a book compiled by a grammarian of the Decadence:

While I kissed Agathon, my soul rose up to my lips: it desired, the poor unfortunate, to pass between them.

As soon as I fully understood the meaning of these words of the divine Plato, I experienced an explosive enlightenment. I realised that the soul was in no way different from life itself: it is the animating breath which possesses the body. I also understood that in love, it is the souls of the lovers which are striving to change places at the moment when they are moved to kiss one another upon the mouth. The soul of the female lover wishes to dwell in the beautiful body of the one which she loves, and the soul of the male lover ardently desires to dissolve itself in the substance of his mistress. Alas, that exchange is never attained. The souls climb up to the lovers' lips; they meet one another; they mingle with one another...but they cannot migrate.

I could not help but wonder whether there could be any pleasure more heavenly than such a loving exchange of souls. Could any rapture surpass that of lending to one another the vestments of flesh which were so warmly caressed, so passionately desired? What an astonishing abnegation, what a supreme abandonment it would be to donate one's body to the soul of another, to the animating breath of another! Surely it would be better than any mere conjunction; better than any ephemeral possession; better than the useless and deceptive mingling of the breath which is a kiss. It would be the supreme gift of the lover and his mistress; the perfect exchange of which lovers so vainly dream; the unattainable goal of so many embraces and devouring gestures.

Now, I loved Beatrice and she loved me. We would often say so to one another, while we were reading the melancholy pages of the poet Longus, whose couplets of prose fall with such a monotonous cadence. But were we not just as ignorant of the love of our souls as Daphnis and Chloe were ignorant of the love of their bodies? And yet, had not those lines written by the divine Plato revealed to us the eternal secret by means of which our loving souls could possess one another perfectly? Once we had been visited by that enlightenment, Beatrice and I could no longer believe that in the kind of union we had already achieved we were truly abandoning ourselves to one another.

But it was at this point that we encountered an indefinable horror, that this true kiss of life would never succeed in marrying us indissolubly. *It was necessary instead that one of us should make a sacrificial offering to the other.* We knew that the voyage of our souls was not to be a reciprocal migration. We both knew it, secretly—but we dared not declare our fear openly to one another. I had a heinous weakness which is inherent in the egoism of a man's soul, and could not bear to speak, leaving Beatrice lost in her own uncertainty.

The sculptured beauty of my loved one had already begun to wane. The rosy lamp had ceased to illuminate from within her face of alabaster. The doctors called her illness anaemia, but I knew that it was a sickness of her anxious soul, which had retreated within her body. She turned away from my anxious gaze with a sad smile.

Her limbs became emaciated. Her features soon became so pale and drawn that her eyes seemed to shine with a sombre fire. Brief blushes appeared and vanished about her cheeks and her lips, like the last flickerings of a flame which was soon to be extinguished.

I knew, in the end, that Beatrice must belong to me entirely within a few days—and, in spite of my infinite sadness, a mysterious joy extended itself within me.

On the last night of her life, Beatrice lay on the white sheets of her bed, having the appearance of a statue of virginal wax. She turned her body slowly towards mine, and said: "At the moment when I die, I wish that you would kiss me on the mouth and that my last breath should pass into you."

I believe that I had never really noticed before how warm and vibrant her voice was; when she spoke these words it seemed that a tepid fluid washed over me.

Almost at once, her pleading eyes sought mine, and I understood that the moment had arrived. I placed my lips upon hers, in order to drink her soul.

Oh horror! Infernal and demonic horror! *It was not the soul of Beatrice which passed into me; it was the voice!* The cry which I let out made me stagger and swoon—for that cry ought to have escaped the lips of the dead woman, and it was *my* throat which shot it out.

My voice had become warm and vibrant, and when I spoke it seemed that a tepid fluid washed over me.

I had killed Beatrice, and I had killed my own voice; the voice of Beatrice dwelt in me now: a voice tepid with the moment of death, which terrified me.

But none of the servants appeared to perceive it! They were hurrying around the dead woman to perform their various functions.

The following night was still and heavy. The candles in their brackets burned straight and very high, their flames nearly licking the ponderous wall-hangings. The god of Terror had extended his hand over me. Every one of my sobs caused me to die a thousand deaths: each one

286

was exactly the same as the sobs which Beatrice had emitted when, before falling unconscious, she had lamented her dying. And while I wept, kneeling beside the bed with my head resting on the bedclothes, it was *her* tears which seemed to well up in me, *her* impassioned voice which seemed to float in the air, bewailing her miserable death.

Should I not have anticipated this? The voice, after all, is eternal: the word does not perish. It is the perpetual migration of human thoughts, the vehicle of souls. On leaves of paper, words lie dead and desiccated, like pressed flowers, but the voice which speaks them aloud makes them live again, assuring their eternal life—for the voice is nothing more than the movement of molecules of air under the impulsion of the soul, *and the soul of Beatrice was in me.* I could not comprehend and feel her soul, save as a *voice.*

Now that the moment of our deliverance is at hand, my terror has subsided...but it is beginning to renew itself! I sense its coming—the arrival of that inexpressible horror which we call the *death-rattle*....and *my* death-rattle, which is warm and vibrant, more tepid than the water in my bath, *is the death-rattle of Beatrice!*

****

34.

NARCISSUS
by James Elroy Flecker

O thou with whom I dallied
Through all the hours of noon –
Sweet water-boy, more pallid
Than any watery moon;
Above thy body turning
White lily-buds were strewn:
Alas, the silver morning,
Alas, the golden noon!

Alas, the clouds of sorrow,
The waters of despair!
I sought thee on the morrow,
And never found thee there.
Since first I saw thee splendid,
Since last I called thee fair,
My happy ways have ended
By waters of despair.

The pool that was thy dwelling
I hardly knew again,
So black it was, and swelling
With bitter wind and rain.
Amid the reeds I lingered
Between desire and pain
Till evening, rosy-fingered,
Beckoned to night again.

Yet once when sudden quiet
Had visited the skies,
And stilled the stormy riot,
I looked upon thine eyes.
I saw they wept and trembled
With glittering mysteries,
But yellow clouds assembled
Redarkening the skies.

O listless thou art lying
In waters cool and sweet,
While I, dumb brother, dying,
Faint in the desert heat.
Though thou dost love another,
Still let my lips entreat:
Men call me fair, O brother,
And women honey-sweet.

35.

A HEROIC DEATH
by Charles Baudelaire

Fancioulle was a most admirable clown, whose standing was such that he was almost to be reckoned a friend of the Prince. Unfortunately, those whose vocation is to play the buffoon often have a fatal attraction towards serious things. Strange as it may seem that ideas such as Patriotism and Liberty should exert their authoritarian influence upon the mind of a player, Fancioulle was eventually led to involve himself in a conspiracy of noble malcontents.

Everywere in the world there are good and sensible men who can be depended upon to denounce those acrimoniously-disposed individuals who seek to depose princes and—without bothering to consult it—restructure society. The noblemen in question were arrested, together with Fancioulle, and condemned to death.

I would be quite prepared to believe that the Prince was almost sorry to find his favourite comedian among the rebels; he was neither better nor worse than others of his kind, although an excessive sensitivity did dispose him to act, in many cases, more cruelly and more despotically than some of those in similar positions. Passionately devoted to the fine arts, and a great connoisseur besides, he was insatiable in his pursuit of sensual delights. Equally indifferent to men and morality, a true artist in his own right, he reckoned no enemy more dreadful than Ennui. The ingenious lengths to which he would go in order to evade or vanquish that earthly emperor would certainly have earned him—in the opinion of a scrupulous historian—the title of "monster", had it been permissible in the land which he ruled, to write anything at all which was not devoted entirely to the production of pleasure, or to that astonishment which is one of the most delicate forms of pleasure.

The greatest disappointment of the Prince was that he had never found a theatre great enough to display his genius. An unpremeditative Providence had given him powers of vision far more grandiose than his estates. (There are many such would-be Neros whose ambitions are stifled by limitations of practicality which confine them too narrowly, whose names and great ambitions are destined to remain unknown to future generations.)

Soon after the arrest of the would-be rebels, the rumour suddenly spread abroad that the sovereign had decided to pardon those who had conspired against him. The inspiration of this rumour was the announcement that a great dramatic event was to be staged, in which Fancioulle would play one of his greatest and most popular roles—which, it was said, the condemned noblemen would be permitted to watch. This was an obvious indication—or so, at least, those with superficial minds adjudged—that the Prince against whom these men had offended was for once inclined to be merciful. Of a man so naturally and calculatedly eccentric, anything seemed possible—even virtue or mercy!—always provided that he might hope to find therein some unexpected pleasure.

To those like myself, however, who had a more penetrating insight into the abyss of that strange, sick soul, it seemed infinitely more probable that the Prince wished to judge the quality of the acting ability of a man condemned to death. He surely wished to make full use of his opportunity to carry out a psychological experiment of considerable interest, to investigate the extent to which the usual faculties of the player would be altered or modified by the extraordinary circumstances in which he found himself. Perhaps the Prince also had in mind some vague or half-formed disposition towards clemency, but that is a matter which has never been clarified.

Eventually, the great day arrived. The little court displayed as much pomp as it could contrive—and it is difficult to imagine, unless one has actually seen it, how much the privileged class of a tiny nation with limited resources can achieve by way of splendour for the sake of a truly solemn occasion. The solemnity of this particular occasion was greatly enhanced, not only by the unparalleled luxury of the display but also by the element of mystery and the moral implications inherent in it.

Master Fancioulle always displayed his particular excellence in those parts which are either silent or little burdened with words—parts which are often of special significance in those fairy tale dramas whose aim is to represent in symbolic terms the great mystery of life—and it was such a role that he was to perform. He made his entrance lightly and with perfect ease, and thus immediately contrived to secure, in the minds of the watching noblemen, an impression of gentleness and forgiveness.

When one says of an actor, "Here is a great comedian," one tacitly implies that within the character the performer may still be discerned—that his art, his effort, and his intention are perceptible. If such an actor were to contrive to be, in relation to the character which he is supposed to represent, what the finest Classical statues—miraculously animated, made to walk and to see—would be in relation to the confused general idea of beauty, one would undoubtedly deem it extraordinary, and perhaps unprecedented. But that night, Fancioulle's performance was so perfect that it was impossible to see the character as anything other than alive, possible and real.

The clown entered, departed, laughed, wept, was convulsed. About his head there was a halo of immortality—a halo invisible to everyone but myself alone—in which were combined as though in some magical amalgam, both the radiance of the Artist and the glory of the Martyr. Fancioulle imported, by virtue of some inexplicable special grace, the divine and the supernatural into his buffooneries—even to the most extravagant of them. My pen trembles in my hand, and my eyes brim with tears born of an everpresent emotion, as I try to describe for you that unforgettable evening. Fancioulle proved to me, in an indubitable and irrefutable manner, that the intoxication of Artistry is more fitted than any other possibility of human experience to the task of drawing a veil across the face of the terrifying abyss. I understood that true genius can compose a comedy on the very brink of the grave with a joyousness which forbids it to see the waiting tomb, lost as it is in a paradise which excludes any idea of death and destruction.

The entire audience, as blasé and frivolous its members were inclined to be, soon fell under the all-powerful spell of the actor. All thought of death, of suffering, of punishment, was banished. Everyone there gave himself up, without hesitation, to the myriad delights afforded to them by the sight of a theatrical masterpiece. Spontaneous outbursts of pleasure and admiration continually raised the roof, and the very walls resonated with the thunderous sound.

The Prince, uplifted by the intoxication of the occasion,

joined in the applause of his courtiers. Even so, it was evident to a discerning eye that his emotions were not unmixed. Did he feel that his despotic power was somehow being successfully challenged? Did he feel that his power to strike terror into the heart and a chill into the soul was somehow called into question? Some such suspicion—perhaps not wholly justified but not entirely without justification either—was born in my mind as I studied the face of the Prince, whose usual pallor seemed to be taking on a further degree of whiteness, as if fresh snow were falling on snow already settled. His lips became more and more tightly compressed and his eyes flared up with an inner fire, seemingly ignited by envy or rancour—but all the while he ostentatiously applauded the talents of his old friend, that strange buffoon who clowned so beautifully even in the face of death. Then, momentarily, I saw his Highness lean towards a page-boy who was stationed behind him, and whisper into his ear. The mischievous face of the handsome child lit up with a smile, and he promptly left the box in order to carry out some urgent mission.

A few minutes later a long, shrill hiss split the auditorium, interrupting Fancioulle at a critical moment. It was as though it tore through ear and heart alike. In the corner of the arena whence this unexpected insult had come, a child darted back into the corridor, stifling the sound of his laughter.

Fancioulle shuddered, having suddenly awakened from his trance; he closed his eyes, but reopened them almost at once, extraordinarily wide; he opened his mouth as if to take a deep, convulsive breath, staggered backwards, then forwards—and fell to the boards, stone dead.

Had that hiss, swift as a striking dagger, cheated the hangman?

Could the Prince have foreseen the homicidal effect of his petty trick? (Reason suggests that it is doubtful.)

Did he regret the loss of his beloved, inimitable Fancioulle? (One might as well have the generosity to suppose so.)

The guilty noblemen had enjoyed the performance of a comedy for the last time. That same night, their lives were made forfeit.

Since that occasion, many justly celebrated mime-artists from all over the world have played before that nameless court; but not one has ever been able to reproduce the marvellous ability of Fancioulle, or achieve the same favour as he.

****

36.

AN ORIGINAL REVENGE
by W. C. Morrow

On a certain day I received a letter from a private soldier, named Gratmar, attached to the garrison of San Francisco. I had known him but slightly, the acquaintance having come about through his interest in some stories which I had published, and which he had a way of calling 'psychological studies.' He was a dreamy, romantic, fine-grained lad, proud as a tiger-lily and sensitive as a bluebell. What mad caprice led him to join the army I never knew; but I did know that there he was wretchedly out of place, and I foresaw that his rude and repellant environment would make of him in time a deserter, or a suicide, or a murderer. The letter at first seemed a wild outpouring of despair, for it informed me that before it should reach me its author would be dead by his own hand. But when I had read farther I understood its spirit, and realised how coolly formed a scheme it disclosed, and how terrible its purport was intended to be. The worst of the contents was the information that a certain officer (whom he named) had driven him to the deed, and that *he was committing suicide for the sole purpose of gaining thereby the power to revenge himself upon his enemy!* I learned afterward that the officer had received a similar letter.

This was so puzzling that I sat down to reflect upon the young man's peculiarities. He had always seemed somewhat uncanny, and had I proved more sympathetic, he doubtless would have gone farther and told me of certain problems which he professed to have solved concerning the life beyond this. One thing that he had said came back vividly: 'If I could only overcome that purely gross and animal love of life that makes us all shun death, I would kill myself, for I know how far more powerful I could be in spirit than in flesh.'

The manner of the suicide was startling, and that was what might have been expected from this odd character. Evidently scorning the flummery of funerals, he had gone into a little canyon near the military reservation and blown himself into a million fragments with dynamite, so that all of him that was ever found was some minute particles of flesh and bone.

I kept the letter a secret, for I desired to observe the officer without rousing his suspicion of my purpose; it would be an admirable test of a dead man's power and deliberate intention to haunt the living, for so I interpreted the letter. The officer thus to be punished was an oldish man, short, apoplectic, overbearing, and irascible. Generally he was kind to most of the men in a way; but he was gross and mean, and that explained sufficiently his harsh treatment of young Gratmar, whom he could not understand, and his efforts to break that flighty young man's spirit.

Not very long after the suicide certain modifications in the officer's conduct became apparent to my watchful oversight. His choler, though none the less sporadic, developed a quality which had some of the characteristics of senility; and yet he was still in his prime, and passed for a sound man. He was a bachelor, and had lived always alone; but presently he began to shirk solitude at night and court it in daylight. His brother officers chaffed him, and thereupon he would laugh in a rather forced and silly fashion, quite different from the ordinary way with him, and would sometimes, on these occasions, blush so violently that his face would become almost purple. His soldierly alertness and sternness relaxed surprisingly at some times, and at others were exaggerated into unnecessary acerbity, his conduct in this regard suggesting that of a drunken man who knows that he is drunk, and who now and then makes a brave effort to appear sober. All these things, and more, indicating some mental strain, or some dreadful apprehension, or perhaps something worse than either, were observed partly by me and partly by an intelligent officer whose watch upon the man had been secured by me.

To be more particular, the afflicted man was observed often to start suddenly and in alarm, look quickly round, and make some unintelligent monosyllabic answer, seemingly to an inaudible question that no visible person had asked. He acquired the reputation, too, of having taken lately to nightmares, for in the middle of the night he would shriek in the most dreadful fashion, alarming his room-mates prodigiously. After these attacks he would sit up in bed, his ruddy face devoid of colour, his eyes glassy and shining, his breathing broken with gasps, and his body wet with a cold perspiration.

Knowledge of these developments and transformations spread throughout the garrison; but the few (mostly women) who dared to express sympathy or suggest a tonic encountered so violent rebuffs that they blessed Heaven for escaping alive from his word-volleys. Even the garrison surgeon, who had a kindly manner, and the commanding general, who was constructed on dignified and impressive lines, received little thanks for their solicitude. Clearly the doughty old officer, who had fought like a bulldog in two wars and a hundred battles, was suffering deeply from some undiscoverable malady.

The next extraordinary thing which he did was to

visit one evening (not so clandestinely as to escape my watch) a spirit medium – extraordinary, because he always had scoffed at the idea of spirit communications. I saw him as he was leaving the medium's rooms. His face was purple, his eyes were bulging and terrified, and he tottered in his walk. A policeman, seeing his distress, advanced to assist him; whereupon the soldier hoarsely begged, –

'Call a hack.'

Into it he fell, and asked to be driven to his quarters. I hastily ascended to the medium's rooms, and found her lying unconscious on the floor. Soon, with my aid, she recalled her wits, but her conscious state was even more alarming than the other. At first she regarded me with terror, and cried, –

'It is horrible for you to hound him so!'

I assured her that I was hounding no one.

'Oh, I thought you were the spir – I mean – I – oh, but it was standing exactly where you are!' she exclaimed.

'I suppose so,' I agreed, 'but you can see that I am not the young man's spirit. However, I am familiar with this whole case, madam, and if I can be of any service in the matter I should be glad if you would inform me. I am aware that our friend is persecuted by a spirit, which visits him frequently, and I am positive that through you it has informed him that the end is not far away, and that our elderly friend's death will assume some terrible form. Is there anything that I can do to avert the tragedy?'

The woman stared at me in a horrified silence. 'How did you know these things?' she gasped.

'That is immaterial. When will the tragedy occur? Can I prevent it?'

'Yes, yes!' she exclaimed. 'It will happen this very night! But no earthly power can prevent it!'

She came close to me and looked at me with an expression of the most acute terror.

'Merciful God! what will become of me? He is to be murdered, you understand – murdered in cold blood by a spirit – and he knows it and *I know it!* If he is spared long enough he will tell them at the garrison, and they will all think that I had something to do with it! Oh, this is terrible, terrible, and yet I dare not say a word in advance – nobody there would believe in what the spirits say, and they will think that I had a hand in the murder!' The woman's agony was pitiful.

'Be assured that he will say nothing about it,' I said; 'and if you keep your tongue from wagging you need fear nothing.'

With this and a few other hurried words of comfort, I soothed her and hastened away.

For I had interesting work on hand: it is not often that one may be in at such a murder as that! I ran to a livery stable, secured a swift horse, mounted him, and spurred furiously for the reservation. The hack, with its generous start, had gone far on its way, but my horse was nimble, and his legs felt the pricking of my eagerness. A few miles of this furious pursuit brought me within sight of the hack just as it was crossing a dark ravine near the reservation. As I came nearer I imagined that the hack swayed somewhat, and that a fleeing shadow escaped from it into the tree-banked further wall of the ravine. I certainly was not in error with regard to the swaying, for it had roused the dull notice of the driver. I saw him turn, with an air of alarm in his action, and then pull up with a heavy swing upon the reins. At this moment I dashed up and halted.

'Anything the matter?' I asked.

'I don't know,' he answered, getting down. 'I felt the carriage sway, and I see that the door's wide open. Guess my load thought he'd sobered up enough to get out and walk, without troubling me or his pocket-book.'

Meanwhile I too had alighted; then struck a match, and by its light we discovered, through the open door, the 'load' huddled confusedly on the floor of the hack, face upward, his chin compressed upon his breast by his leaning against the further door, and looking altogether vulgar, misshapen, and miserably unlike a soldier. He neither moved nor spoke when we called. We hastily clambered within and lifted him upon the seat, but his head rolled about with an awful looseness and freedom, and another match disclosed a ghastly dead face and wide eyes that stared horribly at nothing.

'You had better drive the body to headquarters,' I said.

Instead of following, I cantered back to town, housed my horse, and went straightway to bed; and this will prove to be the first information that I was the 'mysterious man on a horse,' whom the coroner could never find.

About a year afterwards I received the following letter (which is observed to be in fair English) from Stockholm, Sweden:

'DEAR SIR, – For some years I have been reading your remarkable psychological studies with great interest, and I take the liberty to suggest a theme for your able pen. I have just found in a library here a newspaper, dated about a year ago, in which is an account of the mysterious death of a military officer in a hack.'

Then followed the particulars, as I have already detailed them, and the very theme of post-mortem revenge which I have adopted in this setting out of facts. Some persons may regard the coincidence between my

301

correspondent's suggestion and my private and exclusive knowledge as being a very remarkable thing; but there are likely even more wonderful things in the world, and at none of them do I longer marvel. More extraordinary still is his suggestion that in the dynamite explosion a dog or a quarter of beef might as well have been employed as a suicide-minded man; that, in short, the man may not have killed himself at all, but might have employed a presumption of such an occurrence to render more effective a physical persecution ending in murder by the living man who had posed as a spirit. The letter even suggested an arrangement with a spirit medium, and I regard that also as a queer thing.

The declared purpose of this letter was to suggest material for another of my 'psychological studies'; but I submit that the whole affair is of too grave a character for treatment in the levity of fiction. And if the facts and coincidences should prove less puzzling to others than to me, a praiseworthy service might be done to humanity by the presentation of whatever solution a better understanding than mine might evolve.

The only remaining disclosure which I am prepared now to make is that my correspondent signed himself 'Ramtarg,' – an odd-sounding name, but for all I know it may be respectable in Sweden. And yet there is something about the name that haunts me unceasingly, much as does some strange dream which we know we have dreamt and yet which it is impossible to remember.

37.

A POSTHUMOUS PROTEST
by Jean Lorrain

Suspended above the bed, the head with painted lips,
Calmly and palely yields its thickened blood
To the care of a brightly-burnished copper bowl
Filled up to the rim with lilies and hyacinths.

The pupils of the eye are drowned in deep sea-green,
The red-blonde tresses, like a halo of flavescent gold,
Enfold the harsh purplish gouts of blood which spatter
The martyred neck, choked with muffled accusations.

The one who painted them, while drunk with wild hope,
When the fire in his hearth had died away to ashes,
Languorously kissed that rouged mouth,

Hung the head on the wall, dressed in mourning,
And made of his human sentiment a dismal flattery:
An artist in love with the plaster which he brought to life.

****

"And what is that head which you have up there? Is it
made of plaster or of painted wax? The expression of
horror is very well-done—it displays a nicely-perverted
taste, the chopped-off head above a copper bowl brimming with lilies-of-the-valley and hyacinths! It is surely
an Old Master...perhaps a depiction of St. Cecilia...is it
very old?" So saying, de Romer lifted himself up on tiptoe, elevating his myopic eye from the tapestry he had

been inspecting, his curiosity prodigiously excited by the painted plaster head hanging on the wall of my studio.

I confessed that the Old Master which he admired so frankly was actually a copy made from a cast taken from an original in the Louvre—from the famous *Unknown Woman* of Donatello, in fact—which I had decapitated in accordance with a whim. I had been possessed by a fancy which had led me to represent her head as the head of a martyr, covered in blood; the disengagement of the bust had been my own idea, and I had commissioned the moulder to add on the clots of blood. I felt slightly embarrassed, as if I were a child caught in some petty fault, when I explained that the barbaric colouring of the plaster—the greyish-green of the dead eyes, the faded pinkness of the lips, the touches of gold in the hair and the lurid crimson of the blood-clots—were my own paintwork: the result of an idle day wasted in maladroit fumbling.

"This is not so very maladroit," mumbled de Romer, reaching out to touch the plaster moulding which had taken him in, feeling the clots of blood. "Not so maladroit at all. On the contrary, although the execution is naive you have captured some essential truth of sentiment and sensation...guided, I suppose, by intuition, for I take it for granted that you have never actually seen the head of a guillotined woman!"

"Certainly not!" I replied, stammering slightly with embarrassment.

Then de Romer turned to face me, having suddenly become very serious, and captured my gaze with his own penetrating eyes. "So the perversion and the audacity is all your own, then? You have taken to mutilating masterpieces now!"

Stunned by the aggression in his tone, I shook my

304

head.

He was not to be fobbed off so easily. "You are guilty of a crime against Donatello—a crime against his artistry, a profanation. You have decapitated his dream, and martyred his creation. That unknown woman whose head you have taken off and remade has a life of her own, if not in reality then at least in the mind of the artist— a life infinitely superior to your miserable human existence. Since she was first evoked by those visionary eyes which were extinguished long ago she has crossed the centuries, outlasting revolutions; even in the tedium of our dismal museums she continues to haunt us—we moderns who have all but lost the gifts of vision and faith—with her beautiful smile and her imperishable beauty."

"Do you really believe that?" I murmured, moved in spite of myself by the passionate seriousness of his tone.

"For myself, I believe nothing," said de Romer, "except that you are an executioner. What kind of Satanic impulse can have taken hold of you, to make you mutilate that bust? Your fancy must have been diabolical in origin, have no doubt of it. Not that you have lost any sleep over it, I suppose? Oh, you are a great criminal, quite unconscious of your crime—and that is the most dangerous kind. Have you slept in this room—or, if you have not actually slept, have you worked late into the evening, alone here by night? And you have never had nightmares, or experienced any disturbance? Oh well, you evidently have a good constitution. I am sure that I could not have given such a good account of myself."

I did not know what he meant, and tried to draw him out further, but he would not be drawn.

"I have nothing more to say to you," he said, putting an end to the conversation, "except that the mutilation of a masterpiece is a veritable act of murder, and that it

305

can be a dangerous game to play." And without further ado he shook me by the hand and took himself off.

I concluded that de Romer was a little touched—that he had been unbalanced by the power of his own imagination. His common sense had foundered in a sea of occult ideas and obsessions, which had been whipped up into a storm by reading Eliphas Levi, and by close encounters with the terrified mysticism of Huysmans and the charlatanry of the Rosicrucian lodges. I had too much good sense to give any credit to such crackpot notions as those put into his head by the moulding which he had found in my house. If everyone thought like that, the studios of sculptors would be populated by visionaries and the Academy of Fine Arts would be a branch-office of the School of Charcot—whereas all the sculptors of my acquaintance were happy souls with full beards, clear complexions and sturdy constitutions, far more interested in actual sensations than mere illusions. The kind of scare-stories contained in de Romer's daydreams would not prevent me, of all people, from sleeping peacefully.

A few days later, there was an evening when I had occasion to work late. I was beside the hearth, in the silence and solitude of my workroom; all the servants had gone to bed and I was the only person in the household still awake. I suddenly stopped writing, instinctively raising my head, beset by a troubling sensation that I was no longer alone, and that someone I could not see was in the room with me. I looked around, anxiously scanning the length of the four walls. There was no one to be seen, save for the vague inhabitants of an old tapestry, living their silent life of knotted woollen threads and eclipsed silks, and the heavy drapes hanging down in front of hermetically sealed windows. Here and there amid the shadows, illuminated by the intermittent

306

glow of the firelight, there was the glimmer of a gilded picture-frame or the briefly-flaring scintillation of some trinket lodged in a display-case, but there was nothing else.

The sleeping house was located in a secluded quarter of a suburb blanketed by snow, and the silence was profound—still more profound since my pen had ceased to scratch upon the paper which lay before me. My breathing became ragged and hoarse as the conviction grew in me that *there was someone there*, if not in the room itself then just outside the door. I had the horrible feeling that the door was about to open, pushed by some creature or thing unknown, whose uncanny footfalls made no noise at all but whose presence was palpable.

Feeling that any revelation would be better than the anguish of doubt, I prepared to rise from my place and go to the door—but the intention was punctured and I fell back helplessly into my armchair.

The room had once had a second door, but it had been sealed up and hidden away behind a curtain of green Turkish silk embroidered with silver; now I perceived, protruding from behind that curtain, clearly outlined against the blue of the carpet, a bare foot.

The foot was alive. The extended toes were surmounted by pearly nails, the heel was pink and rounded, and the texture of the pale skin was so uniform that one might have mistaken it for a precious *objet d'art*—a piece of alabaster or jade placed on the carpet, but it was a real foot. Oh, the exquisite curve of that arch, the perfection of its flesh! The green silk curtain cut it off just above the ankle, but the ankle was so delicate that the foot could only have been a woman's.

I got up, and was propelled in spite of myself towards the lovely apparition—but when I reached the curtain, the foot was no longer there.

Have you ever noticed the almost-imperceptible perfume of ether which emerges from fresh snow? Snow has an effect on me which is similar to the effect of ether: it unbalances and disturbs me. There are people who become a little crazy when it snows, and it had been snowing for three days when I had my vision. I attributed my experience to the effect of the snow.

I remained anxious for several days lest the apparition should return, but as time went by my anxieties were quieted, and I soon resumed my habit of working late into the night. A few weeks went by before my experience was repeated.

I had stayed up late to correct some notes, and had become absorbed by the task when I suddenly started up in my armchair, abruptly seized by the same horrible certainty that something strange was nearby, lurking somewhere between the tapestry and the wall. My eyes went instinctively to the curtain of green Turkish silk.

This time there were two bare feet, delicate and feminine, extended upon the carpet. Their toes were clenched as though they were excited by febrile impatience. Above their ankles the green silk hung modestly down, but it bulged here and there, filled out with the impression of a pair of hips and two breasts. The figure of a woman was outlined there: the figure of a woman standing behind the curtain.

I rose up as I had before, in the grip of some horrid enchantment. Some power far stronger than my own will drew me, and with eyes dilated by terror and my hands held out before me I moved towards the outlined figure. I had the impression of a young girl—lissom, lithe, *cold*—but it had already vanished. My impatient hands clutched empty space, my fingernails barely grazing the embroidered silk as it collapsed.

No snow had fallen that night.

Fatigued by conflict, I began to harbour suspicions regarding my curtain of pale green silks and silver arabesques. I had bought it in Tunis, in one of those bazaars which they have out there, and I had always suspected that there was something peculiar about it. The matter of its origin began to cause me some disquiet, and I began to look for hidden meanings in its embroidered designs depicting birds and flowers.

I had the curtain taken away; the balance of the room suffered, but when it had gone I soon recovered my composure and was able to resume the normal course of my affairs, including my nocturnal labours, as if nothng had happened.

But it was all to no avail.

When some little time had gone by there came an evening when I became sleepy after dinner, and fell asleep in my armchair with my feet resting on the edge of the fireplace, bathing in the soft warmth of the friendly hearth. I woke up abruptly in darkness, shivering with cold and faint of heart, to find that the fire was out.

The whole room was plunged in darkness—a darkness so profound that it seemed to weigh upon me like a cloak, pressing my shoulders down upon the armchair in which I had awakened. It was opposite the place where the decorated plaster moulded in the form of the *Unknown Woman* hung on the wall, and I saw—oh horror!—that the cut-off head shone strangely in the gloom. The fixed eyes were illuminated by a halo of light which bathed her, surrounding her golden hair with a radiant aureole. From those staring eyes—her terrible eyes, whose dead pupils I had myself outlined in ultramarine—darted two rays of light, directed at the sealed door, now laid bare by the curtain which I had removed.

There, in the embrasure of that sealed door, appeared a female body: the naked corpse, blue with cold, of a decapitated woman; a cadaver resting against the wooden door. Between the two shoulders there was a great red gaping wound, from which trickles of blood were still leaking.

And as the plaster head hanging on the wall looked upon the body, the cadaver drew itself up and away from the accursed door....and on the sombre carpet the two feet twisted and writhed, as though contorted by some atrocious agony.

At that precise moment, the head turned upon me that frightful stare from beyond the grave, and I rolled over, collapsing upon the carpet, grovelling before those tortured feet.

****

38.

THE CONQUEROR WORM
by Edgar Allan Poe

Lo! 'tis a gala night
    Within the lonesome latter years!
An angel throng, bewinged, bedight
    In veils, and drowned in tears,
Sit in a theatre, to see
    A play of hopes and fears,
While the orchestra breathes fitfully
    The music of the spheres.

Mimes, in the form of God on high,
    Mutter and mumble low,
And hither and thither fly –
    Mere puppets they, who come and fro,
At bidding of vast formless things
    That shift the scenery to and fro,
Flapping from out their Condor wings
    Invisible Woe!

That motley drama – oh, be sure
    It shall not be forgot!
With its Phantom chased for evermore,
    By a crowd that seize it not,
Through a circle that returneth in
    To the self-same spot,
And much of Madness, and more of Sin,
    And Horror the soul of the plot.

But see, amid the mimic rout
	A crawling shape intrude!
A blood-red thing that writhes from out
	The scenic solitude!
It writhes! – it writhes! – with mortal pangs
	The mimes become its food ,
And the angels sob at vermin fangs
	In human gore imbued.

Out – out are the lights – out all!
	And, over each quivering form,
The curtain, a funeral pall,
	Comes down with the rush of a storm,
And the angels, all pallid and wan,
	Uprising, unveiling, affirm
That the play is the tragedy "Man,"
	And its hero the Conqueror Worm.

39.

THE TEMPTATIONS:
Eros, Plutus, and Fame
by Charles Baudelaire

Two magnificent Demons, and a Demoness no less extraordinary than they, ascended by night that mysterious stairway by which Hell is granted access to the frailty of the sleeping man, in order to hold secret communion with him. They came to stand before me in all their glory, as though they were posing on a stage. A sulphurous splendour emanated from all three of these beings, who had somehow contrived to draw themselves out of the black heart of the night. Their manner was so proud, and so full of authority, that at first I took them for three of the true Gods.

The face of the first Demon might have belonged to one of either sex; the contours of his body were as soft as those of the ancient Dionysus. His beautiful languid eyes, whose colour was shadowy and indeterminate, were like violets still burdened with the heavy tears of a recent storm; his slightly-parted lips were like warm censers which exhaled the sweet scents of a perfumery; and every time he breathed out, blowflies were illuminated where they flew by the heat of his exhalation.

Around his purple tunic, like a sash, there was entwined an iridescent serpent, which raised its head and languorously turned towards him eyes like glowing embers. From this living girdle dangled flasks full of sinister liquors, alternating with gleaming knives and surgical instruments. In the right hand he held yet another flask, which contained a luminous red liquid; it bore the bizarre inscription: *Drink of this my blood, the ultimate stimulant.* In the left hand he carried a violin, which doubtless served to sing his pleasures and his pains, and to pour out the contagion of his madness on the nights of the Sabbat. About his delicate ankles trailed the links of a broken golden chain, and when this hindrance caused him to look down at the ground he studied his toenails—which were polished like finely-cut gems—admiringly.

This Demon watched me with eyes which were brimming with inconsolable grief and insidious intoxication, and said to me in a musical voice: *If thou wilt, if thou wilt, I would appoint thee an overlord of souls, and thou shalt be a greater master of living clay than any sculptor could ever be of his own material; thou shalt understand the pleasure, perpetually renewed, of emerging from thyself to forget thyself in others, and of drawing other souls to merge with thine own.*

I answered him thus: "Many thanks! I doubt that I would obtain by such means any merchandise more valuable than my own miserable self. Although I am haunted by my memories I have no desire to forget anything; and even if I did not know thee for what thou art, ancient monster, that mysterious cutlery of thine, those enigmatic flasks, and the chain which binds thy feet are symbols which clearly demonstrate the inconvenience of thy friendship. Keep thy gifts."

The second Demon had not the same tragic-yet-smiling attitude as the first, nor his pleasantly insinuating manner, nor his delicate and sweetly-scented beauty. This one was a giant, with a coarse face devoid of eyes, and a heavy paunch overhanging his hips; the whole of his skin was gilded and covered, after the fashion of the tattooist's art, by moving pictures which illustrated the countless miseries of the world. There were starveling men who hung themselves willingly from nails; there were deformed and ugly dwarfs, whose beseeching eyes pleaded more eloquently for alms than their outstretched hands; there were careworn mothers who carried puny clutching infants at their pendulous breasts....and there were plenty more of a similar kind.

This gross Demon pounded his fist upon his immense belly, which resonated like a beaten gong—a sound which eventually faded away into a wordless moaning, as of a multitude of human voices. And he laughed, carelessly displaying his broken teeth—an imbecilic laugh like those one hears everywhere from men who have dined too well.

This one said to me: *I can offer thee that which will obtain everything, which hath infinite value, which replaceth anything whatever!* And he tapped his monstrous belly, to bring forth a sonorous echo which complemented his obscene speech.

I turned away in disgust, and I answered him thus: "I do not require, for my own edification, the misery of anyone else; nor do I desire to have such a sad wealth of misfortunes embroidered upon my skin, as though I were a tapestry."

As for the Demoness, I would be lying if I did not admit that at first sight I found her strangely charming. I can only explain that charm by comparing it to the glamour of those very beautiful women who seem ageless once they are no longer young, and whose beauty has something of the magic which haunts ruins. Her attitude was at once imperious and ungainly, and her eyes, though shadowed beneath, exerted a forceful fascination. I was particularly struck by her mysterious voice, which reminded me of the most delectable *contralti*, although it had a certain hoarseness suggestive of a throat laved by too much brandy.

Wouldst thou know my power? said the false goddess, in her charming and paradoxical voice. *Listen, then!*

She put to her mouth a gigantic trumpet, decorated after the fashion of a mirliton with the titles of all the world's newspapers, and with this instrument she sounded my name, so that it reverberated in the air like the sound of a hundred thousand thunderclaps, and sent echoes back at me even from the furthest of the planets.

"Devil!" I cried, yielding a little to temptation. *"There* is something worth having!" But when I examined the seductive harlot more attentively, I had the vague impression that I had seen her hobnobbing with certain artless fellows with whom I was acquainted; and her raucous brazenness recalled to my ears an impression I could not quite grasp, of some other prostituted instrument.

And so I answered her as I had answered the others, with as much disdain as I could muster: "Go away! I am not about to marry the mistress of those whose names I would not deign to speak."

I had every right to be proud of so courageous a renunciation. Unfortunately, however, I awoke—and all my resolve drained away.

"In truth," I said to myself, "I must have been sleeping very heavily, to have entertained such scruples. If only such tempters could come to me while I am awake, I would not be so very delicate!" And I invoked them in a loud voice, begging their pardon, offering to lower myself as far as might be necessary to win their favours.

Alas, I had undoubtedly offended them too deeply, for they have never come again.

****

40.

A WINE OF WIZARDRY
by George Sterling

"When mountains were stained as with wine
By the dawning of Time, and as wine
Were the seas."
                    — AMBROSE BIERCE.

Without, the battlements of sunset shine,
'Mid domes the sea-winds rear and overwhelm.
Into a crystal cup the dusky wine
I pour, and, musing at so rich a shrine,
I watch the star that haunts its ruddy gloom.
Now Fancy, empress of a purpled realm,
Awakes with brow caressed by poppy-bloom,
And wings in sudden dalliance her flight
To strands where opals of the shattered light
Gleam in the wind-strewn foam, and maidens flee
A little past the striving billows' reach,
Or seek the russet mosses of the sea,
And wrinkled shells that lure along the beach,
And please the heart of Fancy; yet she turns,
Tho trembling, to a grotto rosy-sparred,
Where wattled monsters redly gape, that guard
A cowled magician peering on the damned
Through vials in which a splendid poison burns,
Sifting Satanic gules athwart his brow.
So Fancy will not gaze with him, and now
She wanders to an iceberg oriflammed
With rayed, auroral guidons of the North —
Where arctic elves have hidden wintry gems
And treasuries of frozen anadems,

Alight with timid sapphires of the snow.
But she would dream of warmer gems, and so
Ere long her eyes in fastnesses look forth
O'er blue profounds mysterious whence glow
The coals of Tartarus on the moonless air,
As Titans plan to storm Olympus' throne,
'Mid pulse of dungeoned forges down the stunned,
Undominated firmament, and glare
Of Cyclopean furnaces unsunned.

Then hastens she in refuge to a lone,
Immortal garden of the eastern hours,
Where Dawn upon a pansy's breast has laid
A single tear, and whence the wind has flown
And left a silence. Far on shadowy tow'rs
Droop blazoned banners, and the woodland shade,
With leafy flames and dyes autumnal hung,
Makes beautiful the twilight of the year.
For this the fays will dance, for elfin cheer,
Within a dell where some mad girl has flung
A bracelet that the painted lizards fear –
Red pyres of muffled light! Yet Fancy spurns
The revel, and to eastward hazard turns,
And glaring beacons of the Soldan's shores,
When in a Syrian treasure-house she pours,
From caskets rich and amethystine urns,
Dull fires of dusty jewels that have bound
The brows of naked Ashtaroth around.
Or hushed, at fall of some disastrous night,
When sunset, like a crimson throat to Hell,
Is cavernous, she marks the seaward flight
Of homing dragons dark upon the West;
Till, drawn by tales the winds of ocean tell,
And mute amid the splendors of her quest,
To some red city of the Djinns she flees

318

And, lost in palaces of silence, sees
Within a porphyry crypt the murderous light
Of garnet-crusted lamps whereunder sit
Perturbéd men that tremble at a sound,
And ponder words on ghastly vellum writ,
In vipers' blood, to whispers from the night –
Infernal rubrics, sung to Satan's might,
Or chaunted to the Dragon in his gyre.
But she would blot from memory the sight,
And seeks a stainéd twilight of the South,
When crafty gnomes with scarlet eyes conspire
To quench Aldebaran's affronting fire,
Low sparkling just beyond their cavern's mouth,
Above a wicked queen's unhallowed tomb.
There lichens brown, incredulous of fame,
Whisper to veinéd flowers her body shame,
'Mid stillness of all pageantries of bloom.
Within, lurk orbs that graven monsters clasp;
Red-embered rubies smolder in the gloom,
Betrayed by lamps that nurse a sullen flame,
And livid roots writhe in the marble's grasp,
As moaning airs invoke the conquered rust
Of lordly helms made equal in the dust.
Without, where baleful cypresses make rich
The bleeding sun's phantasmagoric gules,
Are fungus-tapers of the twilight witch
(Seen by the bat above unfathomed pools)
And tiger-lilies known to silent ghouls,
Whose king has digged a somber carcanet
And necklaces with fevered opals set.
But Fancy, well affrighted at his gaze,
Flies to a violet headland of the West,
About whose base the sun-lashed billows blaze,
Ending in precious foam their fatal quest,
As far below the deep-hued ocean molds,

With waters' toil and polished pebbles' fret,
The tiny twilight in the jacinth set,
The wintry orb the moonstone-crystal holds.
Snapt coral twigs and winy agates wet,
Translucencies of jasper, and the folds
Of banded onyx, and vermilion breast
Of cinnabar. Anear on orange sands,
With prows of bronze the sea-stained galleys rest,
And swarthy mariners from alien strands
Stare at the red horizon, for their eyes
Behold a beacon burn on evening skies,
As fed with sanguine oils at touch of night.
Forth from that pharos-flame a radiance flies,
To spill in vinous gleams on ruddy decks;
And overside, when leap the startled waves
And crimson bubbles rise from battle-wrecks,
Unresting hydras wrought of bloody light
Dip to the ocean's phosphorescent caves.

So Fancy's carvel seeks an isle afar,
Led by the Scorpion's rubescent star,
Until in templed zones she smiles to see
Black incense glow, and scarlet-bellied snakes
Sway to the tawny flutes of sorcery.
There priestesses in purple robes hold each
A sultry garnet to the sea-linkt sun,
Or, just before the colored morning shakes
A splendor on the ruby-sanded beach,
Cry unto Betelgeuse a mystic word.
But Fancy, amorous of evening, takes
Her flight to groves whence lustrous rivers run,
Thro hyacincth, a minister wall to gird,
Where, in the hushed cathedral's jeweled gloom,
Ere Faith return, and azure censers fume,
She kneels, in solemn quietude, to mark

The suppliant day from gorgeous oriels float
And altar-lamps immure the deathless spark;
Till, all her dreams made rich with fervent hues,
She goes to watch, beside a lurid moat,
The kingdoms of the afterglow suffuse
A sentinel mountain stationed toward the night –
Whose broken tombs betray their ghastly trust,
Till bloodshot gems stare up like eyes of lust.
And now she knows, at agate portals bright,
How Circe and her poisons have a home,
Carved in one ruby that a Titan lost,
Where icy philters brim with scarlet foam,
'Mid hiss of oils in burnished caldrons tost,
While thickly from her prey his life-tide drips,
In turbid dyes that tinage her torture-dome,
As craftily she gleans her deadly dews,
With gyving spells not Pluto's queen can use,
Or listens to her victim's moan, and sips
Her darkest wine, and smiles with wicked lips.
Nor comes a god with any power to break
The red alembics whence her gleaming broths
Obscenely fume, as asp or adder froths,
To lethal mists whose writhing vapors make
Dim augury, till shapes of men that were
Point, weeping, at tremendous dooms to be,
When pillared pomps and thrones supreme shall stir,
Unstable as the foam-dreams of the sea.

But Fancy still is fugitive, and turns
To caverns where a demon altar burns,
And Satan, yawning on his brazen seat,
Fondles a screaming thing his fiends have flayed,
Ere Lilith come his indolence to greet,
Who leads from Hell his whitest queens, arrayed
In chains so heated at their master's fire

That one new-damned had thought their bright attire
Indeed were coral, till the dazzling dance
So terribly that brilliance shall enhance.
But Fancy is unsatisfied, and soon
She seeks the silence of a vaster night,
Where powers of wizardry, with faltering sight
(Whenas the hours creep farthest from the noon)
Seek by the glow-worm's lantern cold and dull
A crimson spider hidden in a skull,
Or search for mottled vines with berries white,
Where waters mutter to the gibbous moon.
There, clothed in cerements of malignant light,
A sick enchantress scans the dark to curse,
Beside a caldron vext with harlots' blood,
The stars of that red Sign which spells her doom.

Then Fancy cleaves the palmy skies adverse
To sunset barriers. By the Ganges' flood,
She sees, in her dim temple, Siva loom
And, visioned with a monstrous ruby, glare
On distant twilight where the burning-ghaut
Is lit with glowering pyres that seem the eyes
Of her abhorrent dragon-worms that bear
The pestilence, by Death in darkness wrought.
So Fancy's wings forsake the Asian skies,
And now her heart is curious of halls
In which dead Merlin's prowling ape has split
A vial squat whose scarlet venom crawls
To ciphers bright and terrible, that tell
The sins of demons and the encharneled guilt
That breathes a phantom at whose cry the owl,
Malignly mute above the midnight well,
Is dolorous, and Hecate lifts her cowl
To mutter swift a minatory rune;
And, ere the tomb-thrown echoings have ceased,

The blue-eyed vampire, sated at her feast,
Smiles bloodily against the leprous moon.

But evening now is come, and Fancy folds
Her splendid plumes, nor any longer holds
Adventurous quest o'er stainéd lands and seas –
Fled to a star above the sunset lees,
O'er onyx waters stilled by gorgeous oils
That toward the twilight reach emblazoned coils.
And I, albeit Merlin-sage has said,
"A vyper lurketh in ye wine-cuppe redde,"
Gaze pensively upon the way she went,
Drink at her font, and smile as one content.

NOTES ON THE CONTRIBUTORS

CHARLES BAUDELAIRE (1821-1867) was the father-figure of the French Decadent Movement, and was the first person to whom the label of Decadent was ever applied (by Théophile Gautier). His collection *Les Fleurs du Mal* (1857) and the prose poems initially intended to be issued as *Le spleen de Paris* (1869) are central documents in the tradition of literary Decadence, and his investigation of *Les paradis artificiels* (1860) is an important exploration of drug-induced altered states of consciousness. His translation into French of the works of Edgar Allan Poe made them available as a key resource to all those later French writers who dabbled in Decadent fantasy. According to Des Esseintes, Baudelaire was the first explorer to reach and reveal those "regions of the soul where the monstrous vegetation of the sick mind flourishes" and to transplant said monstrous vegetations into "the dismal forcing-house of ennui, where they could be brought by careful artifice to aesthetic perfection."

JOHN DAVIDSON (1857-1909) was the elder statesman of the Rhymers' Club, which met at the Cheshire Cheese in Fleet Street in the early 1890s, all of whose members were infected with an interest in Decadence by the enthusiasm of Arthur Symons (1865-1945). Davidson's particular philosophy of Decadence was heavily influenced by the ideas of Nietzsche, which were popularised in England by the Rhymers' fellow-traveller Havelock Ellis (1859-1939). In the series of "Testaments" (of which "The Testament of a Vivisector" was the first), which he wrote in the last decade of his life, he flirted with a kind of calculated satanism, and eventually threw himself off a cliff near Penzance.

LADY DILKE (1840-1904) was born Emilia Frances Strong. Her first marriage was to the literary clergyman Mark Pattison, who was twenty-seven years her senior, but she and her husband lived such separate lives as to encourage speculation that they may have been the models for Casaubon and Dorothea in George Eliot's *Middlemarch*. After Pattison's death in 1884 she married the M. P. Charles Wentworth Dilke, who would probably have succeeded Gladstone as Liberal leader had his career not been ruined by the spectacular scandal which ensued when he was cited as co-respondent in a messy divorce case. It was shortly after this that Lady Dilke— who was by vocation a historian of French art—published two volumes of stylistically ornate and relentlessly downbeat prose-poems, *The Shrine of Death* (1886) and *The Shrine of Love* (1891); "The Outcast Spirit" is from the latter volume.

ERNEST DOWSON (1867-1900) was a member of the Rhymers' Club and a friend of Aubrey Beardsley and Oscar Wilde. He fell in love with a twelve-year-old girl in 1891, and was converted to Catholicism—apparently, like Huysmans, more on aesthetic grounds than anything else. He was educated in France and lived much of his life there; he was well acquainted with contemporary French literature, translating a good deal of work by Verlaine. Both his parents contracted tuberculosis and both committed suicide in 1895, the year before he published his first book of poetry. He always expected to die of the same disease, and duly did.

JAMES ELROY FLECKER (1884-1915) was born too late to participate in the short-lived English Decadent Movement, but he was the principal inheritor of its stillborn tradition. He developed a love of the Orient, which was carefully refined during a stint in the consular service; his affection and experience are reflected in his most famous works, *The Golden Journey to Samarkand* (1913) and the posthumously-published *Hassan* (1922). Discretion led him to remove some of the more explicitly homoerotic verses from the former work before its publication, but with the precedent of the "somewhat surprising chapter" of John Davidson's *Earl Lavender,* before him (see *The Dedalus Book of Decadence*) he was content to include an enthusiastic but entirely gratuitous flagellation scene in his eccentric novel *The King of Alsander* (1913). Like Dowson, he died young thanks to the effects of tuberculosis.

ANATOLE FRANCE was the pseudonym of Jacques-Anatole-François Thibault (1944-1922). He was perhaps the leading man of letters in France in the 1890s and was awarded the Nobel Prize for Literature in 1921. His work is many-faceted and his strong commitment to socialism prevented his ever embracing the Decadent philosophy, but he is allied with the Decadents by virtue of his vitriolic anti-clericalism, which eventually developed into a liberal species of satanism. His exotic novel of the Orient *Thaïs* (1890) champions Epicurean values against the asceticism and illiberality of the Church, as do the stories in *Le Puits de Sainte Clare* (1895), which include "Saint Satyr" and his satanist fantasy novella "Le Tragedie Humaine". His full-length satanist fantasy *La Révolte des anges* (1914) is a masterpiece.

RICHARD GARNETT (1835-1906) worked for the greater part of his life in the British Museum Library, serving as Supervisor of the Reading Room and as Keeper of Printed Books. Most of his writings were scholarly, but he produced one extraordinary book of exotic stories,*The Twilight of the Gods*, which is one of the landmarks of British fantasy fiction. It was first issued in 1888 but was enlarged from sixteen stories to twenty-eight in the second edition of 1903. Many are parables which champion liberal humanist values against the excesses of stern moralists, and beneath the superficial flirtatiousness of their stylistic ornamentation their subject matter is mischievously and extravagantly opposed to Victorian ideas and ideals. They are similar in spirit to the morally-subversive fantasies of Vernon Lee and Oscar Wilde.

R. MURRAY GILCHRIST (1868-1917) quickly put his brief flirtation with Decadent style and substance behind him, and subsequently devoted himself to narrative realism, with the result that he is utterly forgotten except for those aficionados of horror fiction who still remember and admire his little book of stylised baroque fantasies, *The Stone Dragon and Other Tragic Romances* (1894), from which the two tales in this collection are taken.

REMY DE GOURMONT (1858-1915) was a prolific writer more celebrated for his critical writings than his fiction; along with Paul Bourget he was one of the principal champions and explicators of the Decadent Movement and the Symbolist Movement which developed out of it. His novels are unremarkable, save for the extended Epicurean conte philosophique *Une Nuite au Luxembourg* (1906) but his short fiction, consisting mainly of delicate erotic fantasies and strangely lyrical *contes cruels* is very much underrated. His most extended erotic fantasy is *Le Fantôme* (1891), reprinted in *Le Pélerin du silence* (1896); others are to be found in *Proses*

327

moroses (1894); *Couleurs* (1908); and *Histoires Magiques* (1894), from which "Péhor" is taken.

JORIS-KARL HUYSMANS (1848-1907) combined the early part of his writing career with a minor post in the Sûreté—the French equivalent of Scotland Yard—before becoming briefly entranced with satanism en route to reinvestment in the Catholic faith. *À Rebours* (1884), as the introduction to this volume elaborately testifies, was the foundation-stone of the Decadent Movement and is indispensable in defining literary Decadence and establishing its boundaries; it is a unique and unparalleled work.

THE COMTE DE LAUTRÉAMONT was the fanciful pseudonym (borrowed from a character of Eugene Sue's) adopted by the mysterious and short-lived Isidore Ducasse (1846-1870), who came to Paris from Montevideo in order to obtain an education, but instead spent his time producing a series of remarkable prose poems, in which the Byronic anti-hero Maldoror pours extravagant scorn upon his fellow human beings and their conventional morality. The most fabulously delirious and gloatingly Sadistic of these passages had an even greater influence on the surrealists than they had had on the writers of the Decadent Movement, but they are key forerunners of literary Decadence and were recognised as such by Remy de Gourmont. Maldoror is far more assertive than Des Esseintes, but is instantly recognisable as his kindred spirit.

VERNON LEE was the pseudonym of Violet Paget (1856-1935), who was born in France and lived most of her life in voluntary exile. She was the half-sister of the poet Eugene Lee-Hamilton (1845-1907), who spent most of his life as a chronic invalid but eventually recovered his health by mysterious means (only to be accused by some of his friends of having been a hypochondriac all along). Violet also became a habitual sufferer of nervous breakdowns, and her life was further complicated by her ill-concealed lesbianism. Her clever, morally-subversive fiction makes extensive use of the figure of the femme fatale, which is featured in the intense "Amour Dure" and "Dionea" (both in *Hauntings*, 1890), and in the bitterly sentimental Yellow Book fantasy "Prince Alberic and the Snake Lady" (1896; reprinted in *Pope Jacynth and Other Fantastic Tales*, 1904). "The Virgin of the Seven Daggers", written in 1889, was belatedly reprinted in *For Maurice: Five Unlikely Stories* (1927).

JEAN LORRAIN was the pseudonym of Paul Duval (1856-1906), who was one of the central figures of the French Decadent Movement and a friend of Oscar Wilde's. He is almost forgotten today, being more famous for once having fought a duel with Marcel Proust than for anything he wrote. (Actually, "fought" is an overstatement—pistols were chosen as weapons, and both men fired into the air, allowing honour to be satisfied without risk of injury. The duel was occasioned by a poisonous review which Lorrain wrote, possibly motivated by a probably incorrect belief that Proust was one of the lovers of the Comte de Montesquiou, whom he loathed intensely despite his fondness for dropping his name into his stories.) Lorrain's most interesting stories, from the collections *Sonyeuse* (1891) and *Buveurs d'âmes* (1893), are hallucinatory extravaganzas belonging to a group which he described as having been "designed by ether"—which he took for medicinal purposes (he also tried other exotic quack cures, like drinking fresh animal blood in the abattoir) in the hope of curing the tuberculosis which ultimately killed him. His novel *Monsieur de Phocas* (1901) is an extended study of the Decadent personality, and might be regarded as a retrospective summation of all that the Movement stood for.

PIERRE LOUŸS (1870-1925) was one of the two writers who helped Oscar Wilde polish the final draft of *Salomé*. He was too young to participate in the Decadent Movement proper but he carried forward one of its main strands in developing a series of gorgeously exotic Classical fantasies which embody a considerable fascination with lesbianism. These include a series of ornately ironic prose poems issued between 1893 and 1896, which were subsequently collected as *Le Crépuscule des nymphs* (1925); a series of poems ostensibly by a contemporary of Sappho, *Les Chansons de Bilitis* (1894); and the magnificent extended erotic fantasy *Aphrodite* (1896), set in Alexandria during the reign of Cleopatra's elder sister Berenike. His Rabelaisian fantasy *Les Aventures du roi Pausole* (1901), set in the imaginary realm of Tryphême, is much more satirical in tone, as are most of the short stories in *Sanguines* (1903), from which "The Shutter" is taken.

STÉPHANE MALLARMÉ (1842-1898) was heavily influenced by Baudelaire but ultimately developed into a much more cerebral poet, whose incomplete quest for a philosophical synthesis kept him from wholeheartedly embracing the Decadent philosophy. He was, however, one of the writers on whom Des Esseintes lavished unstinting praise—praise which helped enormously to make his reputation—and he became a vital stylistic influence on the Decadents and the central figure of the Symbolist Movement which emerged out of the Decadent Movement. His poems and prose poems are unusually dense and cryptic, but it was Mallarmé's prose poetry rather than Baudelaire's which inspired Des Esseintes to declare that the prose poem was: "the dry juice, the osmazome of literature, the essential oil of art".

CATULLE MENDÈS (1841-1909) was a prolific writer of fiction, poetry and non-fiction whose literary reputation was already established before Decadence became fashionable, but who took to it with some enthusiasm. His lifestyle was reputedly more Decadent than his writings, but such novels as *Zo'har* (1886), *La Première maîtresse* (1887) and *Méphistophéla* (1890) were typical products of the Movement. His short fiction mostly manifests a slick cynicism, but he would occasionally produce calculatedly overstated parables like the example here included (from *Lesbia*, 1887) satirising moralistic fairy tales.

OCTAVE MIRBEAU (1848-1917) was a radical journalist whose fierce political commitment to the philosophy of anarchism kept him apart from the Decadent Movement, though his bitter misanthropism made him a prolific producer of *contes cruels*, and hence links his concerns with those of certain Decadents. His unique novel *Le Jardin de supplices* (1899), known in English as *Torture Garden* combines a vitriolic satire on human perversity with an extended fantasy in which a Des Esseintean fascination with exotic flowers is harnessed to a Sadistic display of tortures, to great dramatic effect. There is nothing in his shorter fiction to match it, but he did have a certain flair for brief and brutal naturalistic stories displaying his contempt for the hypocrisies of provincial Frenchmen; "Crowd Scene" is typical of his work in this vein.

WILLIAM CHAMBERS MORROW (1854-1923) was one of a small group of American writers—all resident in or near San Francisco—who were the closest thing to a Decadent Movement that America produced. The other influential figures in the movement were Ambrose Bierce and Emma Frances Dawson, and they were the main inspiration of George Sterling and—via Sterling—Clark Ashton Smith, who were later to develop the exoticism of the Decadent philosophy to its logical extreme. The best of Morrow's bizarre *contes cruels* were collected in *The Ape, the Idiot and Other People* (1897), from which "An Original Revenge" is taken.

EDGAR ALLAN POE (1809-1849) has to be reckoned the grandfather of Decadence if Baudelaire is to be reckoned its father. Poe has always been rated far more highly in France than in his native land—which may well have much to do with the fact that Baudelaire was his translator—and his constant interest in morbid states of mind, often attributed to the enfeebling effects of hereditary degeneracy, echoes throughout the range of French Decadent prose. His lush poetry, too, is more in tune with the rhythms and themes of French verse than with later American poetry. Because he was a drunk who married his cousin while she was still a child, and who once mysteriously disappeared for a fortnight before returning in a state of delirium, only to die within days, he could also function reasonably well as a role-model for would-be Decadents. Des Esseintes considered him the "wise and wonderful" counterpart to Baudelaire, who concentrated on the psychological study of terror and moral agony while Baudelaire celebrated emotional turmoil on its own terms. According to Des Esseintes, Poe was the man who rescued death from the abuses to which it had been subjected by generations of dramatists and gave it a "new look" and a "sharper edge" by introducing into it "an algebraic and superhuman element".

ARTHUR RIMBAUD (1854-1891) was a child prodigy who ran away from school to live with Paul Verlaine. The two of them attempted to put into practice what Rimbaud had already preached, living beyond the limits of good and evil and attempting to accomplish a "rational disordering of the senses" in their life and their art. Rimbaud forgave Verlaine for shooting him (though the law would not), but could not forgive the elder poet's subsequent relapse into maudlin Catholicism. Disgusted with everything, Rimbaud set off for the Orient in search of adventure, but ultimately found only disease and disability; he returned home to die and discovered that Verlaine had published almost all the work he left behind when he went (advertising it as "posthumous"). "Une saison en enfer" was written in the summer of 1873, and was probably the last thing he ever wrote. He plumbed depths of sarcastic self-hatred unreached by other writers, and his conversion of Verlaine to the philosophy of Decadence provided the Movement of the 1880s with an appropriately rotten core around which to organise itself.

MARCEL SCHWOB (1867-1905) helped Pierre Louÿs to polish the final draft of Wilde's *Salomé*. His father had been at school with Flaubert, was a friend of Gautier and Banville, and once collaborated with Jules Verne; his uncle, Leon Cahun, was a historical novelist. He is the dedicatee of Wilde's "The Sphinx" and Alfred Jarry's *Ubu roi* (Jarry thought enough of him to don mourning dress for his funeral, having earlier caused something of a scandal by appearing at Mallarmé's funeral wearing a pair of yellow shoes which he borrowed from Rachilde). *Coeur double* (1891)—from which both the stories here reprinted are taken—is a collection of Poesque horror stories; it was followed by a more varied collection, *Le Roi au masque d'or* (1892) which includes many *contes cruels* based on episodes of French history, and by the collection of prose poems *Mimes* (1893). His *Le Livre de Monelle* (1894) is a classic exercise in self-pity inspired by the death of his mistress, and his *Vies imaginaires* (1896) is a collection of ironically fanciful biographies of persons about whom historians knew next to nothing. *The King in the Golden Mask and Other Stories* (Carcanet 1982) is an excellent sampler of his work for English readers.

COUNT STANISLAUS ERIC STENBOCK (1859-1895) became a legend in his own lifetime by virtue of his eccentric lifestyle; his acquaintances loved to tell tales about his habit of sleeping in a silk-lined coffin and his penchant for entertaining his pet toads and snakes at the dinner table. He was a drunkard, a drug addict, the founder of the Idiot's Club and a practitioner of a species of ceremonial magic whose rituals he devised for himself. If only his preciously homoerotic literary fantasies had been in the same league as his lifestyle fantasies he might have been a great Decadent writer, but they were not (the same is true of Aleister Crowley, who presumably took a certain inspiration from Stenbock's example). Arthur Symons was very rude about him, but Symons never really did have the stomach to appreciate—or be—a real Decadent. "Viol d'Amor" comes from Stenbock's only collection of prose tales, *Studies of Death* (1894), which was recently reprinted by Garland in tandem with the poetry collection *The Shadow of Death* (1893).

334

GEORGE STERLING (1869-1926) was a protegé of Ambrose Bierce, and his poetry is very strongly influenced by Bierce's aesthetic theories. With the examples of Poe and the English "graveyard poet" Edward Young as his starting-points, Sterling developed a species of "stellar poetry" which placed morbid meditations on death and destiny within a peculiar cosmic perspective, syncretically mixing together modern astronomical ideas about the size and composition of the universe and all manner of eclectically-chosen mythological notions. First developed in the collection *The Testimony of the Suns* (1903), this unique world-view was brought to perfection in "A Wine of Wizardry" (1907), which provoked a fierce controversy when Bierce persuaded the editor of *Cosmopolitan* to publish it; unfortunately, the scandal was soon forgotten and Sterling was condemned to an obscurity from which he has never been redeemed. He killed himself by drinking cyanide, but his literary cause was taken up and carried to further extremes by his own protegé, Clark Ashton Smith, who produced numerous poems in the same cosmic vein and was for a brief while able to publish prose of a closely-related kind in the pages of the pulp magazine *Weird Tales*.

ALGERNON CHARLES SWINBURNE (1837-1909) was a prolific poet who, like many other Englishmen, found his constitution inadequate to sustain a Decadent lifestyle, and was forced as a result of his attempts to do so to make a career of being an invalid. His fluently fervent verses were of interest to the Decadents primarily because of his lifelong interest in sado-masochistic imagery, which is exhibited to its best effect in some of the poems contained in the first volume of *Poems and Ballads* (1866).

VILLIERS DE L'ISLE ADAM (1840-1889) was—
unlike Lautréamont—an authentic Count, and thus
thought it unnecessary to display his title in his by-line,
even when he fell on hard times. He failed miserably to
redeem his ill-fortune despite many attempts to marry
money; the fierce misogyny resulting from this experience
motivated him to produce *L'Eve future* (1886), in which
a disillusioned nobleman asks Thomas Alva Edison to
build him an all-electric woman far more worthy of a
man's love than the perfidious products of nature. His
tremendous admiration for Poe is demonstrated in his
short novel *Claire Lenoir* (1867), the first of a series of
tales which he initially dubbed *histoires moroses* but
eventually rechristened in the title of his collection
Contes cruels (1883), which gave its name to the entire
sub-genre. His work was praised by Des Esseintes for its
"unorthodox observations" and its "pungent irony". Also
allied to the concerns of the Decadent Movement is his
visionary drama *Axël* (1890).

OSCAR WILDE (1854-1900) was born in Ireland,
debauched in London and crucified in Reading Gaol; the
Marquess of Queensberry being a more accomplished
executioner than Pontius Pilate, it took him a lot longer
than three days to re-emerge into the light of day; he was
exiled thereafter to France, but found it impossible to
further exercise his genius, and died of a broken heart.
Although he was aided and abetted in some small
measure by Richard Garnett, Vernon Lee and Laurence
Housman, it was he who conspicuously brought to
rebellious fruition the covert moral unease which British
fantastic fiction had contrived to preserve throughout
the long years when these islands were tyrannised by
that appalling species of sanctimonious puritanism which
was symbolised and enacted by its unhappy and

unfortunate queen. *The Picture of Dorian Gray* (1891), though conventionally regarded as a horror story, is actually an allegory revealing and regretting the folly of trying to live one's life as a work of art; it unwittingly prefigures the eventual fall of its creator, damned by forces of repression which he had finally driven to vengeful outrage. *The House of Pomegranates*, issued in the same year, follows up Wilde's earlier collection of unorthodoxly-moralistic children's stories, *The Happy Prince and Other Tales* (1888) with four longer and more sophisticated parables, each of which combines consummate stylistic elegance with considerable depth of feeling. All four are bitter parables in which human folly, vanity and infidelity cause considerable misery— as of course they still do.

Titles in the Decadence from Dedalus Series include:

The Child of Pleasure - Gabriele D'Annunzio £7.99
Triumph of Death - Gabriele D'Annunzio £6.99
L'Innocente (the Victim) - Gabriele D'Annunzio £7.99
Senso (and other stories) - Camillo Boito £6.99
Angels of Perversity - Remy de Gourmont £6.99
La-Bas - J.K. Huysmans £6.99
The Green Face - Gustav Meyrink £7.99
Torture Garden - Octave Mirbeau £6.99
The Diary of a Chambermaid - Octave Mirbeau £7.99
Le Calvaire - Octave Mirbeau £7.99
The Dedalus Book of Decadence -
  editor Brian Stableford £7.99
The Second Dedalus Book of Decadence -
  editor Brian Stableford £8.99

forthcoming:

The Dedalus Book of Russian Decadence -
  editor Natalia Rubenstein
The Dedalus Book of Chinese Decadence -
  editor Richard Ings

All these titles can be obtained from your local bookshop
or newsagent, or directly from Dedalus by writing to :
**Cash sales, Dedalus Ltd, Langford Lodge,
St Judith's Lane, Sawtry, Cambs, PE17 5XE.**
Please enclose a cheque to the value of the books ordered
+75p pp for the first book, 50p for the second and subsequent
books up to a maximum of £2.

En Route - *J.K.Huysmans*

En Route continues the story of Durtal from *La-Bas*, a modern anti-hero; solitary, agonised and alienated. Robbed of religion and plunged into decadence by the pressure of modern life, Durtal discovers a new road to Rome .

Art, architecture and music light his way back to God . For Durtal, God's death is a temporary demise, and by the end of the novel, he is morally mended and spiritually healed.

First published in 1895, *En Route* earned the hostility of the Catholic Church and was condemned for obscenity.

£6.95   ISBN 0 946626 56 1   B. Format Paperback

The Cathedral - *J.K.Huysmans*

The Cathedral is the most ambitious and controversial of Huysmans' novels . Durtal's conversion from satanism (*La-Bas*) to Roman Catholicism incensed French catholics who tried to get the novel banned. The symbolists defended *The Cathedral* as a major step forward in the development of the novel.

All the various facets of Huysmans' writing -aestheticism, decadence, spirituality, art and architecture -come together in *The Cathedral* to produce his masterpiece.

"A wonderful picture of the inner meaning of Gothic architecture" - *Daily Telegraph*

" a most astonishing piece of fiction." - *The Bookman*

£6.95 ISBN 0 946626 49 9 B.Format Paperback

The Angels of Perversity - *Remy de Gourmont*

Remy de Gourmont (1858 -1915) was one of the leading French literary critics of the fin de siècle period as well as a major novelist and short story writer. *Angels of Perversity* offers an eclectic selection from his three major volumes of short stories .

They are key examples of early Symbolist prose shaped and inspired by the French Decadent consciousness and must rank among the best short stories of the 1890s.

The tone of his stories is unique, with an unusual mixture of decadence and eroticism, balanced by an ironic and sentimental view of the world .

Dedalus is in the forefront of bringing about a reappraisal of the work of Remy de Gourmont, and has featured his work in *The Dedalus Book of Decadence* and *The Second Dedalus Book of Decadence.*

£6.99 ISBN 0 946626 81 2 B.Format Paperback

Torture Garden - *Octave Mirbeau*

" This decadent classic flays civilized society down to its hypocritical bones and is *le dernier cri* in kinky exoticism."
                                                                - Time Out

" A decadent masterpiece." - *The Times*

" Octave Mirbeau's long suppressed 1898 classic is ably translated in this edition which conveys all the off-centre force and vitality of the original" - *City Limits*

£6.99 ISBN 0 946626 68 5 B.Format Paperback

Also by Octave Mirbeau :
The Diary of a Chambermaid £7.99 ISBN 0 946626 82 0
Le Calvaire   £7.99 ISBN 0 946626 99 5

The Green Face - *Gustav Meyrink*

The Green Face is Meyrink's second novel, and was published in Germany in 1916 to critical and commercial acclaim. Its setting is Amsterdam, which is used in the novel as a symbol of European decadence, and is ultimately destroyed.

The hero, Fortunatus Hauberrisser, like Athanasius Pernath in the Golem, is a seeker after spiritual truth. He is surrounded by a galaxy of grotesque characters who either guide him in his quest, or hinder him as they attempt to lead him astray.

The novel's combination of the occult, the mystical, the grotesque with Meyrink's vision of a Europe on the brink of catastrophe makes it one of the masterpieces of European decadence.

£7.99 ISBN 0 946626 92 8 B. Format

Senso (and other stories) - *Camillo Boito*

The combination of decadence, the macabre and the demonic with depraved female heroines made Boito's stories an immediate and popular success in fin de siècle Italy. Today Boito is seen as one of the major Italian authors of his period and the master of the novella form. Outside Italy he is totally unknown except for the Visconti film, which brilliantly captured the atmosphere and ambience of his novella Senso.

This selection contains his most celebrated novelle, including A Corpse, the bizarre tale of rivalry between an artist and a student of anatomy for the beautiful body of Carlotta, the artist's dead mistress.

£6.99 ISBN 0 946626 83 9 B. Format